MAR 18

BEYOND SCANDAL AND DESIRE

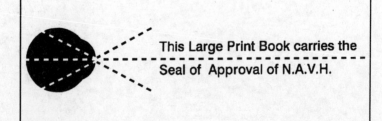

This Large Print Book carries the
Seal of Approval of N.A.V.H.

A SINS FOR ALL SEASONS NOVEL

BEYOND SCANDAL AND DESIRE

LORRAINE HEATH

THORNDIKE PRESS

A part of Gale, a Cengage Company

Farmington Hills, Mich • San Francisco • New York • Waterville, Maine
Meriden, Conn • Mason, Ohio • Chicago

Copyright © 2018 by Jan Nowasky
Thorndike Press, a part of Gale, a Cengage Company.

ALL RIGHTS RESERVED
This is a work of fiction. Names, characters, places, and incidents are either the product of the author's imagination or are used fictitiously. Any resemblance to actual events, locales, organizations, or persons, living or dead, is entirely coincidental.
Thorndike Press® Large Print Romance.
The text of this Large Print edition is unabridged.
Other aspects of the book may vary from the original edition.
Set in 16 pt. Plantin.

**LIBRARY OF CONGRESS CIP DATA ON FILE.
CATALOGUING IN PUBLICATION FOR THIS BOOK
IS AVAILABLE FROM THE LIBRARY OF CONGRESS**

ISBN-13: 978-1-4328-4857-6 (hardcover)

Published in 2018 by arrangement with Avon Books, an imprint of HarperCollins Publishers

Printed in the United States of America
1 2 3 4 5 6 7 22 21 20 19 18

*In loving memory of
Patti Wade Hickerson.
You lived life to the fullest, my dear
friend. Thank you for all the smiles,
laughter, hugs, and fond memories. My
life was enriched by your friendship.*

PROLOGUE

London
1840

He was scared. More scared than he'd ever been in all of his twenty-four years.

For sixteen hours, drowning in more scotch than was wise, he'd prayed for the torment to end while his love screamed. Odd, then, that when the silence finally arrived, it filled him with such unheralded terror. His gaze never leaving the door that opened into her bedchamber, he sat as still as death in the straight-backed chair in the dimly lit hallway. Unable to make his limbs move, he merely waited, barely breathing, listening intently, praying now that he would hear no cries, that the babe would be stillborn.

But the howls of outrage at being forced into a cruel world eventually came, strong and robust, and he cursed heaven and hell for the unfairness of it.

The heavy oak door opened. A young maid — damn, what was her name? He didn't remember; he didn't care — gave a quick curtsy. "It's a boy, Your Grace."

Swearing harshly, he squeezed his eyes shut. The gender shouldn't have mattered, and yet the pronouncement hit him like a solid blow to the chest.

After setting aside his glass, he slowly, laboriously shoved himself to his feet and, on legs that did not seem to belong to him, staggered into the room that smelled of sweat, blood and fear. The child had ceased its bellowing. Wrapped in a swaddling blanket bearing the ducal crest, it was now cradled in the arms of another maid.

She smiled hopefully at him. "He's a fine one, Your Grace."

He took no pride, no comfort in her words. Cautiously he approached. He saw the thatch of thick black hair, the same shade as his, the pinched face. It was difficult to believe something so tiny could be the cause of so much pain, grief and despair.

"Would you care to hold him, sir?"

Knowing he would be lost if he did, he shook his head. "Leave us now. All of you. Get out."

She placed the bundle into the bassinet before scurrying after the midwife and other maid, closing the door in their wake, leaving him to face what must be done in this room that still seemed to echo his love's agony.

Quietly, hesitantly, he wandered over to the four-poster where she lay, her face averted, her gaze on the windows and the inky midnight blackness beyond them. It seemed appropriate for the child to arrive in the dead of night, in this residence where his own father had kept his mistress. They were both long gone, but the dwelling still had its uses, assured no memories of this night would haunt his beloved estates or London residence.

The woman on the bed was another matter entirely. Having endured what she had, how could she not be haunted? He'd never known her to be so pale, so lifeless, all joy and dreams sucked from her. Taking her hand, he wasn't surprised to find it as cold as ice. "Have you seen him?"

Her head barely moved in a shake. "He's a bastard. You know what you must do," she rasped, then turned imploring, tear-filled eyes toward him. "For me. We must be rid of him. You know we must." She released a sob, bit down on her knuckles and began to cry in earnest.

Sitting on the edge of the mattress, he

enfolded her into his arms and rocked her gently. This child should have never come into existence. He knew its presence would plague her unmercifully. "Shh, my love, don't fret. I shall see to it."

"I'm sorry, I'm so incredibly sorry."

"You are not to blame. If I'd taken greater care . . ." His voice trailed off, the incriminations clogging his throat. He hadn't taken the precautions necessary to protect her. Now he would do everything necessary to save her from scandal.

He held her until she quieted, until she fell into a fitful sleep. Then he took the babe from the bassinet in which it had been placed. It. It. He would not think of it as a child, but as a creature. It looked up at him with huge blue eyes. Carrying his burden, he strode from the room without looking back.

The journey in his coach was the longest of his life. It seemed wrong to set the child down, so he held it, all the while sensing its gaze upon him, knowing he would feel that unblinking stare until the day he died.

At last the coach came to a stop outside a ramshackle dwelling on the outskirts of London. The thickening fog swirling silently over the stoop made it seem all the more ominous. Hesitating, he shook his head.

Now was not the time to turn cowardly. With the babe clasped against his chest, he disembarked and made his mind go blank so he couldn't consider the ramifications of what he was doing.

He knocked briskly on the door. The youth of the woman who opened it shocked him. She was not at all what he'd expected, but then he could very well have the wrong residence. "I'm in search of the Widow Trewlove."

"You have found her." Her dark eyes dipped to the burden he carried, her face impassive as though she, too, could not acknowledge what was about to transpire. "Will you be paying by the month, or am I to take in your bastard completely?"

Her voice held no accusation, no condemnation. He almost imagined he heard a bit of sympathy, of kindness, in it.

"Completely."

"Fifteen pounds."

He knew the amount. He'd read her advert carefully a hundred times during the passing months while he awaited the arrival. Widows taking in children born out of wedlock was a common enough practice. One of his friends farmed out all his illegitimate whelps. With a single payment one never had to think of them again. Or at least that was the theory. He doubted he'd ever forget this one.

Mrs. Trewlove took the child and cradled it in her arms as though it were something precious. Meeting his gaze, she held out her hand. He dropped the heavy pouch into her waiting palm, his stomach queasy as she closed her fingers around the blood money.

"I'm paying ten times what you ask. I don't want it to suffer."

"Never you fret. I'll take proper care of your by-blow." Turning, she went inside and closed the door quietly behind her.

Spinning on his heel, he hurried back to the coach, leaped inside and pounded the ceiling. As the conveyance took off at a fast clip, he let the tears fall and acknowledged himself for the monster he was.

He could only hope his actions tonight would help to restore his love's sanity, would return her to him as she'd once been.

Although he doubted that he, himself, would ever again be able to look at his reflection in a mirror.

CHAPTER 1

London
1871
Mick Trewlove was intimately familiar with Cremorne Gardens, but as a rule he limited his visits to the later hours when loose women could be had cheaply, cutthroats abounded, decadence flourished, men well into their cups were willing to spill secrets, and those who had once slighted him could be paid back in full.

But wandering along the path this early into the night — as twilight was beginning to settle in and full darkness was but a whispered promise of seduction — made his skin itch and his well-tailored clothing feel far too tight. Decent folk meandered about enjoying the evening's innocent entertainments, some taking pleasure in doing little more than leisurely strolling through the gardens that the Thames kept lush and green. He couldn't imagine having so few cares, of being so relaxed that his laughter would easily fill the air. Although in all fairness, he wasn't known for laughing — at least not with joy. His harsh bark tended to make people wary, especially when it was directed at them. With good reason. It was usually a signal that he was on the verge of claiming his retribution.

"Why are we following that couple?"

He'd always known the young beauty on his arm was no fool, but he'd hoped finally satisfying her curiosity about the gardens would have distracted her from his purpose. "I know not of what you speak."

"Liar." With one arm entwined around his, she slapped him with her free hand. He hadn't given any thought to the fact that, in escorting her publicly, she might undermine his hard-earned reputation for being the unforgiving sort. Although he doubted any of his acquaintances were here at this early hour. "An assortment of people have passed in front of us, and you've not even given them a withering glance. When someone gets in our way, you stiffen and hurry around them as though they're an obstruction to your goals. You've totally ignored the jugglers and tumblers no matter how hard they strive to catch your attention. I've deduced your reason for bringing me here

14

was not as a gift for my birthday — as you claimed — but because you decided you would be less noticeable with a woman on your arm."

"You're but a girl, pet."

"I'm ten and seven. Old enough to marry."

"You're not marrying."

"Someday I will."

"There's not a bloke alive to whom I'd grant approval to take you to wife."

"It's not your decision to make."

"With no father about, as your eldest brother, it damn well is."

The little brat slapped at his upper arm again. "You're trying to distract me so I won't pester you with my questions. I won't fall for it."

The couple ahead stopped to listen to a small orchestra playing a soft yet somber tune. Stilling as well, he glanced down in order to see his sister's triumphant expression as he groused, "You're too smart by half."

With the praise, she squeezed his arm and smiled brightly. "Tell me everything about them."

"Shh. Keep your voice low." He didn't need someone easing by them to hear his words, to know he did indeed have a keen interest in the couple.

"I will," she whispered. "Who are they?"

"He's the Earl of Kipwick, son to the Duke of Hedley — a title he will one day hold."

"Something about him seems familiar. Can't we move to the other side of them so I can see him more clearly?"

"No. Not yet anyway." He had no desire for her to examine the earl too closely, to figure out precisely why he had a keen interest in this particular lord.

"Do I know him?"

"I doubt it. He doesn't exactly frequent your circles."

"Does he frequent yours?"

"He will . . . eventually."

"And the woman on his arm? Tell me what you know of her."

Because she'd only recently come to his attention, he didn't yet possess a great deal of information about her, but that would change in time. If his plan went accordingly, she'd eagerly fill in the particulars. "She's Lady Aslyn Hastings, daughter to the Earl of Eames. Although she's been the Duke of Hedley's ward since her parents died when she was a girl."

Sorrow washed over his sister's face. She was far too sensitive for the world in which she lived. "Then she's an orphan, like you."

She was nothing like him. No one was like him.

"Do you know how her parents died?" Fancy asked, sadness woven through the curiosity in her voice, perhaps because she'd never known her own father, had always referred to herself as a half orphan, a much kinder term than the one attributed to him.

"Not yet." But eventually he would know every small detail about her: her likes, her dislikes, her dreams, her fears, her hopes, her worries.

"She's rather pretty. I always think when someone is comely she — or he for that matter — is immune to misfortune."

"No one is immune to misfortune."

The couple began strolling off, obviously having grown bored with the musicale. Fancy didn't hesitate when Mick started walking again, quickening his pace to keep them within sight as they entered an area where the crowds thickened and more entertainers sought to earn their keep, presenting small performances, hoping a coin or two would be tossed their way.

"So why are we following them?" Fancy asked.

"I'm seeking an opportunity to make the earl's acquaintance."

"To what purpose?"

"I intend to take from him everything he holds dear — including the lady at his side."

With her arm snugly entwined around the Earl of Kipwick's, Lady Aslyn Hastings couldn't shake off the ominous sensation she was being watched. But then, if she were honest, she always felt under scrutiny. Perhaps it was because of her overly protective guardians or all the dire warnings about the dangers lurking about in the world that the Duchess of Hedley continually cast her way. Or the fact the duchess never left the residence and encouraged Aslyn to follow her example by staying within Hedley Hall. Except Aslyn longed for more: the independence afforded those who weren't expected to make a suitable match, the carefree moments enjoyed by those not shackled by duty, the excitement offered within the shadows of the night.

Those very shadows were falling rapidly and deepening now. The occasional streetlamp was being lit, but the dim light was little match for the darkness easing in around her. She was hoping to convince Kip to stay within the gardens long past the time proper folk did. She wanted to catch a glimpse of the naughty undertakings that had been alluded to in the newspaper articles and gossip rags she read when no one was keeping a watchful eye over her. They hadn't gone into great detail — only enough to titillate the imagination.

Fortunately — or unfortunately depending on one's perspective — Aslyn had always possessed a rather active and creative imagination. She assumed the music that filled the air after ten o'clock was not something found among her music sheets nor would her fingertips be allowed to coax it forth from ivory keys. The gowns worn by the ladies who strolled with the gents would reveal a good deal more than the hint of a bosom. The women would certainly be snuggled against their escort's side — not walking along as she was with her hand merely resting on her escort's arm as lightly as a butterfly might settle upon a rose petal. There would be nothing proper, nothing decent in the other ladies' actions. But there her imagination ground to a halt, because she couldn't quite envision what the indecent activities might entail. Might a gentleman press his lips to her bared shoulder? Might he nuzzle her neck?

And what would that feel like?

For all of Kip's interest in her, he'd never been untoward, never even tried to steal a kiss. He respected her, honored her, fought his baser instincts to ensure she came to the marriage bed untouched. Which the duchess assured her was how it should be between a man and a woman — if a man truly cared for her. Only the most morally inept would seek to take advantage of a lady, would seek to seduce her outside the bonds of marriage. Aslyn didn't want to admit what it said about her own morals that she was rather hoping tonight Kip might ask for permission to place his lips against hers, to remove his glove and touch her cheek, to whisper sweet, passionate words in her ear.

She was all of twenty and had never been kissed. Not that she knew any not-yet-betrothed maiden who had been. Ladies in her position were to guard their virtue and be above reproach at all times. Still, there were moments when being morally upright chafed. One could flirt innocently but was never to engage in any questionable action. Buttons were to remain buttoned, lacings laced and skirt hems hiding ankles.

She wasn't about to place herself in a compromising position, but she did often wonder if Kip found all the rules as bothersome as she did, if he yearned to do more than simply stroll along beside her. Guilt pricked her conscience because she should be grateful he was such a considerate, upstanding beau so she never had to ward off any unwelcome advances.

"I hear the siren call of a soprano," Kip said suddenly, placing his hand over hers where it rested on his arm and squeezing ever so slightly. "Shall we head in that direction?"

"If you like."

He glanced down on her. While the shadows were moving in so his hat cast shade over his face, she could still make out his handsome features. He'd inherited his father's brilliant blue eyes, thick black hair and the distinctive cleft in his chin. It had fascinated her as a child, and she'd often poked her finger into it, especially when she caught him sleeping. It had become more pronounced as he'd aged and left no doubt he was indeed his father's heir. Not that anyone would doubt it really. The duke and duchess were devoted to each other, so much so that, at times, it was as though no one existed beyond them.

"Are you not enjoying yourself?" he asked. "Is there something else you'd rather see?"

Not anything she could voice aloud without gaining a disapproving glare from him, so she kept her thoughts to herself as she was wont to do and smiled up at him. "I am indeed having a jolly good time. It's just that it's a bit tamer than I was expecting." It had taken her weeks of cajoling to get him to bring her, and she knew it unlikely he would escort her here again. The duchess had been vehemently opposed to the outing, fearing it would place her ward in some sort of danger. Kip had spent a good deal of dinner the evening before convincing his mother that he'd keep Aslyn safe. She didn't know if she'd ever cared for him more than she had at that moment when he'd fought to give her something she wanted: an evening at Cremorne. While she *was* enjoying it, she couldn't help feeling something was missing. "Have you ever been to the gardens when it's not quite so cultured?"

"A gentleman does not speak of activities that are not suitable for a young lady's ears to hear."

But he had no such concerns regarding an old lady's ears? She could hardly wait until she was deemed ancient enough to be privy to such knowledge presently denied her. "So you have."

Rolling his eyes, he sighed with exasperation. "I may —"

Unexpectedly he was lurching forward, arms windmilling, striving to catch his balance as his hat went flying. To stop herself from tumbling after him, she'd quickly released her hold on him. Hearing a feminine gasp, she glanced over her shoulder to see a young woman wearing a horrified expression, her eyes open wide, her hands pressed to her gaping mouth.

"Dear sir, my sincerest apologies. I was so caught up in observing my surroundings that I wasn't watching where I was going. Pray tell me I did no damage to you."

Reaching down, Kip snatched up his hat and flicked his fingers over it to remove any dirt. She'd expected him to immediately plant it on top of his dark head. Instead, he stilled, perhaps finally getting a clear look at the young woman before him. She was a girl, really, younger than Aslyn, but her eyes, a strange golden hue that reminded her of a cat's, spoke volumes, hinting at a life that was not without challenges. In spite of her lovely lilac frock and beribboned bonnet, she gave the impression she'd not always been accustomed to such comforts.

"No harm done, Missssss . . ." He dragged out the word as though a part of it was absent and he was seeking the lost piece.

"Miss Fancy Trewlove."

"Fancy? Unusual name."

"My mum chose it, hoping I would grow up to marry a fancy man, live in a fancy house and have fancy things. So far, her hopes have been dashed, but I am not one to give up on dreams so easily. And you, sir. May I inquire regarding your name?"

"Lord Kipwick."

"Oh, my word." Paling, she curtsied deeply, elegantly. "My lord, please forgive my utter and despicable clumsiness."

"Easily forgiven when no harm was done. My companion and I were equally engrossed in the festivities this evening. Lady Aslyn Hastings, allow me to introduce Miss Trewlove."

"It's indeed a pleasure," Aslyn said, fighting to hide her surprise that Kip would go to such lengths to introduce her to a commoner.

"My lady." The girl curtsied again. It was a proper curtsy. Aslyn would wager she'd had lessons. Her mother was depending on more than her name to give her that fancy life. "I hope I didn't ruin your outing. My brother is always telling me I must slow down, but there is so much to see I fear missing out on something wonderful and get quite lost in the frivolities." She turned slightly. "Don't I, Mick?"

"You do indeed."

The deep voice sent a shimmer of awareness through Aslyn, and she found herself

24

staring at the man who approached, as quietly as fog rolling in, through the encroaching darkness as though he were at once swallowed by it and master of it. She knew without a doubt he was the sort who prowled these environs after the good folk were safely tucked away in their beds. He was well-dressed, his clothing of the finest cloth and the shiniest of buttons. She suspected he had a personal tailor because his black coat rested comfortably over his broad shoulders. His midnight locks were unfashionably long, curling along his collar. His thick beard was evenly trimmed, and she was rather certain he gave it great care. But it was his dark eyes that held her ensnared. There was a somberness, a solemnity, to them. His gaze landed on her like a physical presence.

"Mick, allow me to introduce you to Lord Kipwick and Lady Aslyn."

"I believe, Fancy," he said in a raspy voice that indicated he might have spent a good deal of his life shouting, "that in proper circles I am to be introduced to them."

"Of course. I suppose I should have paid more attention during etiquette lessons, but the teacher would drone on and on incessantly. I fear I grew quickly bored and wasted your coin while at it."

"We don't have to be so formal," Kip said quickly, uncharacteristically doing away with customs he generally followed as though they were the dictate of a divine being. "Based on the conversation with Miss Trewlove thus far, I assume you're Mick Trewlove."

Aslyn fought to hide her shock that Kip would know of this man, this creature of the night, this commoner. Even more stunned that he appeared to be encouraging a discourse with someone beneath him. Kip, like most in the aristocracy, tended to lord his position over those who weren't quite up to snuff.

The gentleman, in a grand gesture, swept his hat from his head. "I am indeed. Pleased to make your acquaintance, my lord, my lady."

"I've heard of you, Mr. Trewlove."

Aslyn wondered how he knew of the gentleman, what things Mick Trewlove might have done that had brought him to Kip's attention. Nothing good, she suspected.

"Nothing good, I suspect."

She nearly gasped as he gave voice to her exact thoughts. She did hope they weren't reflected in her face, that the man wasn't aware that while he had piqued her curiosity, she didn't quite trust him. Or perhaps it was that she didn't trust herself, because if she were honest, he intrigued every inch of her being. She'd never before met anyone with such majestic bearing as though he ruled over everything upon which he gazed. He had a commanding presence that was both unsettling and thrilling.

"On the contrary. I hear you have a nose for helping men make fortunes."

He lifted a shoulder, ducked his head in a way that would appear humble in most men, but she sensed he didn't have a modest bone in that marvelously tall, broad-shouldered body of his. There was an uncivilized aspect to him that had her most feminine parts quivering — shamefully. She'd never had such a blatant physical reaction to a man. She wanted to run her fingers over his beard to see if it felt as soft and luxurious as it looked, even as she had a strong urge to dash off and protect herself as the duchess had warned her far too many times was the appropriate response when confronted by a dangerous man. Instinctually, she knew he was dangerous, very dangerous indeed, in ways she'd never even considered a man might be perilous.

"Sometimes our endeavors meet with financial success," he said. "Few men boast about the times when they don't."

"Please, let's not get into business," Miss Trewlove lamented. "The fireworks will be filling the sky soon. I've heard they're marvelous, and this will be my first time to see them. I don't want to miss out on a single burst. My lord, you wouldn't happen to know the best place for viewing them, would you?"

"Indeed, I would."

With gloved hands clasped before her, Miss Trewlove hopped up to him as though she were a rambunctious puppy who had just divined who held a treat. "Would you be so kind as to show me?"

"I'd be delighted to have that honor. If you've never seen them before, you must view them from the best advantage."

And *he* would go with them, this man who merely watched, watched her as though striving to uncover every facet of her. She wasn't quite certain she wanted him near. Something told her that she would be safer if he remained behind. She didn't fear that he would strike her or harm her in any way. Yet she couldn't quite shake off the sense that this man was laying claim to her. It was a ridiculous notion. She didn't know him. He was a commoner. After tonight, they would never again cross paths, and all her curiosity about him would fade away.

"Aslyn?"

Jerking her head to the side, breaking free of whatever spell Mick Trewlove had cast over her, she looked at Kip, surprised to see his hand extended toward her.

"Shall we?" he asked.

"Yes, of course." She forced herself to move up and place her hand on his arm when she would have preferred to stand there like a silly goose and study Mick Trewlove. She'd never known a man who gave away none of his thoughts or emotions. He didn't seem bothered by his sister's forwardness, but then it wasn't like a paramour dallying with another man. Although most certainly the girl had been flirting, no doubt testing the waters in order to determine if Kip might turn out to be the fancy man her mother wanted for her. But he was spoken for. Not formally announced, yet all of London — all of Great Britain for that matter — knew to whom he belonged, whom he would eventually marry, who would become his countess.

She was aware of Miss Trewlove and her brother following behind them. Once again, she had the strange sensation of being watched. She wanted to look back, to see if his eyes were upon her. Instead she marched forward, wondering what she might have done if he had offered her his arm before Kip had. She rather feared she might have taken it. Something about him called to her, drew her in. She didn't understand this attraction, wasn't certain she wanted to.

CHAPTER 2

Mick was torn between being furious with Fancy for taking matters into her own hands and applauding her ingenuity. For gaining him the introduction he'd desired, she'd be insufferable for at least a sennight. But as he followed the couple leading the way toward the fireworks, he couldn't seem to hold on to his irritation with his sister, nor take his gaze away from the woman. She wasn't exactly what he'd been expecting. Ladies of the nobility tended to be haughty, unapproachable. They looked at him as though he were muck to be scraped off the bottom of their shoe.

But Lady Aslyn didn't seem to fit so easily into that mold. Her eyes, the blue of a summer sky, had reflected curiosity, perhaps something even more provocative: temptation. He intrigued her. From the moment she'd become aware of his existence, she'd not taken her gaze from him, but had studied him with her fine brow delicately furrowed as though he were a puzzle to be sorted out. He'd wager half his fortune she'd been striving to place him, to wonder from whence she knew him. She was unlikely to make the connection — not until his plans were completed. Then she would know the truth of him, the truth of those she considered family, those whom she loved. Both truths were likely to bring her to tears, fill her with shame and mortification. And certainly kill any desire for him that might have been sparked within her breast.

If he were any other man, he might experience a measure of remorse, but he'd learned early on there was no capital found in regrets.

"I've never spoken to nobility before," Fancy said quietly. "They seem rather pleasant."

"Stay away from them after tonight." He'd been reckless to bring her, to let her get even a glimpse of his quarry.

"Why?"

"Because he has designs on you." That, too, had been obvious from the start. There had been greed, desire, lust in the earl's eyes, and it had taken every bit of control Mick possessed not to introduce his fist to that little dent in his lordship's chin.

"You implied he was interested in the lady."

"She is the sort he marries. You are the sort he beds."

Her eyes widened, her cheeks reddened. "And the lady on *his* arm? Is she the sort you wed?"

"Never in a million years."

She stopped walking, causing him to do the same. "Yet you're going to strive to take her away from him. What has he done to earn your wrath?"

He'd been born, protected, loved. Although in truth, he wasn't the one with whom Mick found fault, but he was the means to achieving satisfaction. Not that he was willing to explain any of his reasons to his sister. She'd find fault with him. Generally he didn't care what people thought about him, but from the moment she was born, she'd been the only pure thing to ever love him. He'd do whatever necessary to ensure nothing ever tainted that purity. "For tonight, simply enjoy the fireworks."

"But I'm part of your scheme now."

"Not after tonight."

"I gained you an introduction. I can do more —"

"You were correct earlier, Fancy. You were

merely to serve as part of my disguise. What is going to transpire beyond tonight is not for a lady of your sensibilities." Not for anyone with a shred of kindness or civility, but his education in the streets had ensured he grew up to possess neither of those irritating and limiting qualities. If they lingered about at all, he was unable to locate even a remnant of their existence within his character, his soul, his heart.

"I despise the way you discount me so easily with so little care."

"I'm not discounting you, I'm protecting you."

She opened her mouth, no doubt to protest more, reminding him of a dog he'd once owned that never released his hold on a bone once he had it clamped between his jaws. "We can leave now if you prefer," he said curtly before she could give voice to more objections.

Her face fell, no doubt because she'd realized to argue with him was a losing battle. Men with far more worldly experience could not stand up to him, so how could a mere slip of a girl? "I want to see the fireworks."

He was impressed she managed not to sound too churlish or petulant. "Then let this go."

She quickly stuck her tongue out at him before marching forward. Her short legs were no deterrent for his longer ones, and he easily caught up with her. Odd that she didn't realize her childish actions proved his point: she was not made for the world in which he survived.

Kipwick and Lady Aslyn were waiting in an open area that would give them a clear view of the sky. The lady moved to greet Fancy as though they were long lost friends, which left the earl and Mick standing behind them. He should have used the opportunity to study his foe, but he couldn't seem to drag his gaze from Lady Aslyn's profile as she smiled and spoke with his sister.

Her features were not perfect. The end of her nose tipped up ever so slightly as though she'd spent her youth with it pressed up against a shop window, longing for something she'd spied on a shelf. A distant light glinted off her eyelashes, which were unusually long, and he suspected when she slept, they fanned out over her cheeks. Her eyes tilted up slightly as though the corners near her temples were shoved into place by her overly high cheekbones. Yet each imperfection wove into the fabric of her face to give her the appearance of perfection.

Her alabaster skin was flawless, not a freckle in sight, and he doubted she'd ever allowed the sun to touch her face. Nor a man for that matter. Beneath her frilly hat, a few blond tendrils, curling and loose, had broken free of their pins. He suspected they were the most rebellious part of her. Her posture, the way she held herself stiffly, the lack of animation in her movements spoke of a woman who understood she was continually on display and must constantly portray control and a proper bearing.

He was quite looking forward to the challenge of destroying that control.

"Have we met before?" Kipwick asked quietly.

Mick slid his gaze over to the man, who was perhaps an inch shorter than he and much more slender. But then his lordship had never had to haul rubbish out of the city in order to earn a few shillings so his family didn't go hungry. "No."

The earl's thick dark eyebrows drew together, causing a deep crease to form between them. "You look familiar. I could swear our paths have crossed at some point."

"I don't move about in your circles, my lord. And I doubt very much you move about in mine."

Kipwick blanched, averted his gaze. Mick

36

wasn't surprised. He'd learned enough about the earl during the past few months to have a relatively good idea of the circles he preferred. Before summer drew to a close, they would be his downfall.

"Although it's quite possible you saw me in passing at the Cerberus Club. It seems to be a crossroads for the various stations in life, a place where the upper and lower classes don't mind mingling because their common interests override all else."

"Hardly likely I've seen you there, as I haven't garnered a membership."

Mick was well aware Kipwick had been making inquiries about the club, knew he'd never been. The establishment was merely a lure, the first step in guiding the earl toward his downfall. "Membership isn't required. Merely a hefty purse."

He was acutely aware of the earl coming to sharp attention. Disappointment washed through him. He'd anticipated a bit of a challenge, had hoped Kipwick would at least resist being led to slaughter. Nothing in Mick's life had ever come easy. He didn't want revenge handed to him on a silver platter without his having worked for it.

"To be honest," Kipwick said hesitantly, "I wasn't certain the place truly existed. No one of my acquaintance has ever admitted to spending time at the gaming hell."

"I'm not surprised. Most of the aristocrats who frequent the place have been barred from the more respectable clubs. Admitting to frequenting Cerberus hardly improves one's reputation."

"You think I've been barred?"

The cutting edge to his voice indicated he'd been insulted. Perhaps this wouldn't be so easy after all. "No, my lord. I was trying to offer a suggestion for where we might have possibly crossed paths. You strike me as a man with a keen intellect who would have success at the tables, and a bit of an adventurer who might be in search of various types of entertainment. I suspect you bore easily."

"You deduced all that from a chance meeting?" No, he'd deduced it all from months of research, but he needed to squelch the earl's suspicions.

"Quite right. Simply because I enjoy the more daring environs doesn't mean all men do." Especially ones who were spoiled and pampered, who'd lived in privilege, a privilege Mick should have enjoyed, at least partially. A proper school, proper house, proper food, proper clothing. He didn't mind making his way as a man, but as a boy he shouldn't have had to do the things he'd done to survive. However, he didn't allow the seething fury to rise to the surface, to inhabit his stance or his voice. "My apologies for believing we had something in common."

"I didn't take offense. I'm merely curious about your knowledge."

And apparently not very trusting. He wondered at that. "You come from a storied family. I've read accounts in the papers."

"You pay attention to all families?"

"I pay attention and remember everything. I'm a businessman. I never know where an idea or opportunity for a new venture might appear. I'm also very skilled at quickly judging a fellow's worth, so I don't take on an investor I ought not."

"Now, I must be the one to apologize. I have on occasion had men strive to take advantage of my position. It makes one wary."

"It is always good to approach strangers with caution."

Kipwick scoffed. "These were friends. Or so I thought. I must admit to being curious about the Cerberus Club. But as I understand it, its location is a closely guarded secret."

Mick shrugged negligently. "Meet me at the entrance to these gardens tomorrow night at ten and I'll take you there."

The earl's mouth shifted up into a smile. "I may just do that."

He would do it. His debt had caused him to lose his membership in one gentlemen's club, and he was on the cusp of losing it in another. The earl had a penchant for gambling when he ought not, for raising the stakes when the odds were not in his favor. Apparently he was an atrocious cardplayer, unable to divine when fortune had turned against him.

An explosion rent the stillness of the night and only then did Mick notice the red and green blossoms filling the sky. He heard Fancy's startled gasp. She no doubt didn't remember he'd shown her a fireworks display when she was four. Sitting on his shoulders, she'd cheered with glee then, her enthusiasm knocking aside his hat. Now she clapped with a bit more decorum but her elation wreathed her face.

What surprised him was how delighted Lady Aslyn appeared. He'd had to shift his stance slightly and inconspicuously in order to still view her profile. With the colored flares dancing over her features and the brightness of her smile, she was beautiful in a way he'd overlooked before. Childlike in her joy. He was suddenly struck by how young she appeared, not much older than Fancy. Innocent. He suspected she'd never sinned in her life.

If he were a decent man, he'd cast aside his plans. But having clawed his way out of the sewer into which he'd been tossed, Mick Trewlove was neither decent nor one to give up simply because he'd misjudged certain elements of his scheme. He was known for being a stubborn bastard. That stubborn streak had gained him wealth and a reputation for being ruthless when it came to acquiring whatever he desired.

Presently he desired an acknowledgment of his place in the world. Without it, he was merely a thug. With it, he would become one of the most powerful men in Great Britain. Doors once slammed in his face would open wide. Those who had previously shunned him would embrace him.

He'd been scheming for far too long to cast it all aside now. He'd climbed as far as he could up the social ladder. To reach the higher rungs, others had to fall — far and spectacularly, like fireworks burning out on their way down. He would be paid what he was owed. And God's mercy on anyone who stood in his way.

Aslyn could sense Mick Trewlove's gaze on

41

her. Odd thing about that: it made her tingle all over as though he were touching her with his hands rather than his eyes. She couldn't recall ever being so aware of a man. It was thrilling, frightening, confusing. It made her long to snuggle against him and jump out of her skin at the same time. It made it almost impossible to concentrate on the beauty of the magnificent fireworks bursting overhead.

And it made her feel guilty. Guilty because her reaction to Kip whenever he was near paled in comparison. She told herself it was because she was familiar with her childhood friend, had known him for most of her life, lived within his parents' residence, frequently enjoyed meals with him, danced with him at balls, and had such a close relationship with him that her guardians didn't require she travel about with a chaperone when in his company, because they knew he would not take advantage.

She suspected the sternest of chaperones would be no deterrent to Mick Trewlove if he wanted to take advantage of her in order to engage in some sort of mischievous behavior. He was no doubt quite skilled at slipping an untoward touch by the matronly as well as stealing kisses from willing lasses. She was unnerved by her horrifying realization she wouldn't mind being one of those lasses. Only for a moment or two.

Blast it all! When had she become obsessed with kissing, with the yearning to experience the press of a man's lips upon her own, to know the secrets of passion that had thus far eluded her?

She was a lady, and ladies behaved in proper ways. They did not allow themselves to be caught in compromising positions — indeed, they did not *get* themselves into compromising positions. They did not create scandals nor were they to be the object of a scandal created by someone else. They most certainly did not contemplate removing a glove and running bared fingers through a gentleman's beard. The duchess would be appalled to learn all her dire warnings about how easily a gentleman could slip off the leash of propriety were being nudged into the corner of her ward's mind where they could merely prick ineffectually at her conscience.

Or not so ineffectually. She should not be having these thoughts about Mick Trewlove. If she were to have them at all, they should revolve around Kip. She should yearn for him to break free of Society's tether and kiss her. It was unconscionable to be so aware of the stranger standing behind her.

Since her coming out, she'd been introduced to many young, eligible men but none had sparked her interest. Only Kip had ever held her attention — until now. And that was rather disconcerting.

"The fireworks are spectacular," Miss Trewlove whispered on a sigh as though she feared if she spoke too loudly she would disturb others' enjoyment of the fantastical display. "Do you watch them often?"

"This is my first time to visit the gardens."

"Your brother seems as difficult to manage as mine."

Aslyn furrowed her brow. "My brother?"

Miss Trewlove glanced back over her shoulder, gave her head a small jerk.

"Kipwick?" Surprised by the girl's assumption, Aslyn laughed softly. "He's not my brother."

Miss Trewlove blinked repeatedly. "But you have no chaperone."

Her tone was one of disbelief, echoing the possibility of scandal.

"I'm a ward of his parents. He's practically a brother." Even as she said it, it seemed wrong to refer to her future husband in those terms, to even consider him in a neutral sort of way. "I mean, he's more than that, of course. But he wouldn't take advantage."

"Mick tells me all men will take advantage."

"Kip wouldn't."

"How fortunate you are. My brothers would never let me step out with a man to whom I wasn't related. Although if Mick has his way, I'll never be allowed to step out with a man at all."

"How many brothers have you?" she asked.

"Four. And a sister, who is older and granted far more freedom than I. It's quite exasperating."

Discreetly, Aslyn pointed over her shoulder. "Is he the eldest?"

Miss Trewlove nodded, rolled her eyes. "And the bossiest."

Yes, she could well imagine that. She was accustomed to being around confident men, but none of them exuded self-assurance to such a degree that it seemed to overwhelm every other aspect of a person. Mick Trewlove did. She could practically see it coming from him in waves that had the power to encompass everything around him — including herself. She wanted to experience that power, be drawn into it, captured by it, seduced within it. All these untamed thoughts were remarkable, brought a self-awareness she'd never before experienced.

For the first time in her life, she recognized a woman had needs — *she* had needs — that went beyond polite dances and courteous strolls through a garden. She wanted hands touching where they shouldn't, lips gliding where they ought not. She wanted her self-control shattered, her morals in danger —

Suddenly she became aware of people around her cheering, clapping, wandering off, and she realized the fireworks had come to an end. There was an odd fragrance of smoke and something more drifting on the air. Whatever powered the explosions, she supposed. She inhaled deeply, wondering if exploding passion possessed a unique scent.

"Well, we'd best be off," Kip said. "I promised Mother to have you home before ten."

"Surely not all the entertainments are drawing to a close now."

"The ones you're allowed to enjoy are."

She might have argued if the Trewloves weren't still standing nearby, but a proper lady did not create a scene in public. Besides, remaining in Mick Trewlove's company was causing riots within her imagination and body. She was likely to embarrass herself if she wasn't careful. "It was lovely to meet you, Miss Trewlove."

The girl smiled. "It was an honor to share the fireworks with you." She bowed her head slightly, gave a quick curtsy. "My lord."

"Miss Trewlove."

Aslyn turned to Miss Trewlove's brother and fought not to imagine all the various explosions, from small to large, that he might create within a woman. "Mr. Trewlove."

Taking her hand, he brought it to his lips, his eyes never leaving hers. Through her glove, she could feel the warmth and strength of his fingers, the heat of his mouth seeping through the kidskin. "Lady Aslyn, thank you for your kindness to my sister."

She could do little more than nod and withdraw her hand. Whatever was wrong with her? During her Seasons, numerous men had held her gloved hand, even kissed it, but none had caused her throat to knot up. She was vaguely aware of Kip taking her arm and leading her away.

Not looking back over her shoulder for one final glance at Mick Trewlove was a challenge. She didn't know why the knowledge she would never again see him left her with a sense of loss.

As his carriage rattled through the street, Mick stared out the window and tried to concentrate on his encounter with Kipwick and how best to take advantage of their upcoming meeting, but his mind kept drifting to Lady Aslyn — and his plans for her. They required a bit more finesse. She wasn't likely to arrange a rendezvous with a scoundrel. Ensuring their paths crossed so he could lure her into his arms was going to be a bit tricky. The affairs she attended were not ones to which he was invited. At least not presently, but in the near future —

"I suspect you don't want Mum to know about your true purpose in escorting me to the gardens tonight," Fancy said, and the tone in her voice alerted him that he was going to pay dearly for her silence. He might view her as an innocent child, but she'd always been too cunning by half. When he'd come home, battered and bruised, it might have been his sister Gillie who patched him up, but it had been Fancy who'd squatted on her haunches before him and watched with keen interest, declaring when all was said and done that she was in need of sweets to keep her mouth busy so it didn't tell their mum what she'd seen.

She was most fortunate that he loved her as much as he did. "What's the price?" he grumbled. Most men took a step back when he used that tone. She merely smiled.

48

"A bookshop."

He furrowed his brow. "You want to go shopping for a book?"

"No. I want to own a bookshop."

His laughter echoed through the conveyance. "Don't be daft. You'll be married within the year."

"Earlier you claimed I'd never marry."

"Yes, well, I misspoke. The truth is, Fancy, that seeing you well married is my goal — everyone's goal, to be honest."

"Tonight's efforts were a part of that goal?"

Crucial to it. "Don't worry your pretty little head about it."

"Until my marriage comes to pass, I could have a shop."

"Fancy —"

"You're putting up all those buildings. Why not give me a shop? You helped Gillie acquire her tavern."

"It's different with Gillie."

"Why? Because you don't think any man will have her?"

"Because I don't think she'd have any man. She's too independent by half, always has been."

"I'd like to be independent, as well."

"You will be. You'll just be married and independent." He glanced out the window.

49

"We're home. Let's leave it there."

As the vehicle came to a smooth halt outside the rundown residence in one of London's most notorious rookeries, Mick deeply regretted that his mum refused to accept his offer to be moved to a more luxurious dwelling. He suspected her refusal was twofold: she didn't think she was deserving of anything nicer than the squalor that surrounded her and her irrational fear that whoever moved in after her would do a bit of gardening and discover the dark secrets buried behind the residence.

Mick had been eight when he'd uncovered them. He hadn't been trying to plant a new bush or shrub but had been searching for buried treasure. What he'd found was the truth about his past.

Before his footman could reach the door, he shoved it open and leaped out. Turning back, he handed his sister down. She'd only recently returned from boarding school to live here. He'd offered to provide her with an apartment or a town house in a fancier area, but she didn't like the notion of their mum living alone. It was his hope that in time, Fancy would convince Ettie Trewlove that it was in everyone's best interest to leave all her sins behind.

He didn't bother knocking, but simply

opened the door, allowing Fancy to precede him into the warmth of the dwelling. Although it was impossible to tell from the outside, the inside was quite welcoming. Mick and his brothers had seen to it, gutting most of the residence and rebuilding it to ensure their mum had the comforts to which they thought she was entitled.

The landlord hadn't objected. Indeed, when Mick had confronted him, he'd been only too glad to hand over all his properties in the area for a very modest sum. Eventually Mick would raze everything and build anew. But doing that would uncover all the skeletal remains, so he bided his time.

Smiling at them, his mum shoved herself up from the plush orange and yellow brocade chair by the low fire. She never complained of being cold now that Mick had coal delivered every day. He wanted to hire a maid of all work to see to her needs, but again, her fears wouldn't allow that. He couldn't stand watching the tears well in her eyes — which they did anytime he suggested some change to how she lived.

She shuffled toward the small kitchen area. "I'll put the kettle on." Always she was offering tea.

"None for me," he said gently. "I won't be staying."

She glanced at him over her shoulder. "Why must you rush off? You've not been around much lately."

"I've been busy."

"Surely you can spare a few minutes."

"He can," Fancy said, hanging up her shawl before taking over the task of preparing the tea. "While I see to this, convince him that I should have a bookshop."

Whenever the females of this family ganged up on him, he knew his only defeats.

His mum returned to her chair and sat, placing her feet on the small, embroidered stool. "She's always loved books. I might have done better by all of you had I known how to read better, but it was always a struggle to make sense of the letters."

Taking the wing-backed chair opposite her, he stretched out his legs. "You did well enough by us."

"You've had to work so hard."

"I take pleasure in the work."

"I'd like to know that sort of pleasure," Fancy called out. "The satisfaction of accomplishment."

"I paid for you to attend a posh school for a reason — to give you the refinement you needed to marry well."

"Why can't I marry and have a shop?"

"She has a point," his mum said.

"She'll be a lady of quality, too busy to muck about in a shop."

"How is she going to meet a gent of quality?"

"I'm working on that."

The woman who had raised Mick studied him intently. Most of her black hair had turned gray, and she swore to knowing which strands each son was responsible for turning. Mick feared most were a result of his actions.

"I'm worried about Gillie," she said softly, changing the topic to one that periodically concerned her.

"She can take care of herself." His other sister was nothing if she wasn't self-reliant. As a child, she'd always hung on to his shirt-tail. Perhaps he should have been more protective, but at the time, they'd all been striving to survive.

"But managing a tavern . . ." Her voice trailed off as though she couldn't quite decide what to make of that.

Gillie more than managed it; she owned it. Mick had seen to that. Neither of his sisters was going to be under any man's thumb as their mum had been. He was going to make damned sure of that, no matter the cost. "I'll stop by and see her tonight."

Relief washed over her wrinkled features.

"Thank you."

"With that, I should be off." He rose.

"Oh, no you don't." Fancy approached, holding a tray. "I've only just finished preparing your tea."

Slipping a finger beneath her chin, he tilted up her face and winked at her. "Why settle for tea when Gil will give me whiskey?"

Walking over to his mum, he bent low and pressed a kiss to her forehead. "Don't worry overly much. I have everything well in hand. Ask Fancy to describe the fireworks to you."

She patted his cheek. "You've been a blessing from the beginning."

"As have you." Heading for the door, he slipped his hand inside his jacket pocket and rubbed his fingers over the faded and fraying threads that formed the Hedley crest, all that remained of the blanket in which he'd been swaddled when the duke had handed him over to her.

CHAPTER 3

Wallowing in the warmth beneath the mound of coverings, Aslyn raised her hands over her head and stretched, determined to shake off her irritation with Kip. It wasn't fair. Not fifteen minutes after he'd delivered her home last night, he had pressed a kiss to her forehead before making his excuses and heading out — most certainly to indulge in an assortment of vices. Gambling, drinking, possibly whoring. While everyone expected them to wed, he'd not announced his intentions, so she supposed she couldn't get distressed about his dalliances.

In return, he couldn't be distraught that Mick Trewlove had made a place for himself in the corner of her mind. Never before had she been so curious about a man. How had he gained his wealth? Was he a man of leisure? If she removed his gloves, would she discover his hands were rough and scarred from years of labor? She hadn't asked Kip any questions about the man because she'd been taken aback by her interest in him. Kip would have no doubt found it untoward.

Proper ladies didn't make inquiries about improper men. Instinctually she knew Mick Trewlove was improper — in spite of his obvious kind regard toward his sister. He had studied Aslyn far too intently and intensely. No man had ever looked at her as though he were contemplating kissing her from her head to her toes.

Flinging back the covers, she scrambled out of bed, rushed over to the nightstand and splashed cold water on her face. What was it about the man that had such wicked thoughts bursting forth as though they were perfectly normal? Never before had she experienced the sort of musings that caused her to grow so warm. She didn't understand why she couldn't exorcise him from her mind. Nor was there anyone with whom she could discuss these wayward thoughts.

She couldn't make inquiries of the duchess because then she might have to explain about talking with commoners, strangers at that, and inviting them to watch the fireworks with them. Kip and she had agreed they'd not mention the brother and sister who had crossed their paths the night before. If the duchess thought Aslyn was carrying on conversations with people not listed in *Debrett's,* whose lineage could not be traced back generations, she'd no doubt restrict her ward's outings even further, and they were few and far between as it was, with barely any liberty at all.

She splashed more water on her face, then grabbed the towel to dry it. When the door opened, she gave a start as though caught doing something she shouldn't.

"I didn't realize you were already awake, m'lady. You didn't ring for me."

Nan tended to slip in and draw back the curtains, allowing the sunlight to gently awaken her mistress. "I've only just arisen."

Closing the door, the servant looked rather guilty doing it. Then she approached cautiously. "I have something for you, m'lady," she whispered, as though the walls had ears. "A gentleman knocked on the servants' entrance near the crack of dawn. He told the lad who answered he needed to speak with Lady Aslyn's maid. So I was fetched. He gave me this, said it was for you and I was to tell no one about it."

In her palm rested a small leather box. Aslyn couldn't quite bring herself to reach for it. "What did he look like?"

"Like the sort who should come in

through the front door. Finely tailored clothing. Boots polished to a shine. Well groomed. Dark hair. A full beard. It was too dark for me to get a good look at his eyes, and his hat shadowed them anyway. He held himself with confidence, but I had the fleeting thought if I were someone up to no good I'd never want to run across him in a darkened alley."

Even though she'd already deduced who he was, she asked, "He didn't give his name?"

"No, m'lady. I asked for it, but he merely smiled — and it was a rather wolfish one at that if I'm to be honest, set my heart to fluttering it did — and went on his merry way. I don't think he wanted it known."

Aslyn was surprised to find her fingers trembling slightly when she took the box. Although she kept no secrets from her maid, she still turned away and walked over to the sitting area to give herself a modicum of privacy. When she opened the box, she was greeted with a folded bit of foolscap. Lifting it out, she gasped at what lay beneath: the most beautiful cameo she'd ever seen. The background was a pale blue that matched the shade of her eyes almost perfectly. She unfolded the note and read the words scrawled with a masculine hand: *In apprecia-*

tion for your kindness to my sister.

No name, no initials, no verification as to the identity of the person who'd written it, but then she didn't need verification. The hints abounded. She wondered how he'd acquired a gift so quickly. Was it something he'd had on hand for someone else? A treasured family heirloom? Had he located a jeweler who would open his shop in the wee hours?

Her curiosity regarding Mick Trewlove only increased with the arrival of his gift. She had no idea how to locate him, to rebuff the inappropriate gesture — or how to send him an appropriate letter expressing her appreciation should she decide to keep it. He'd taken the choice out of her hands. She didn't know whether to be irritated or grateful.

She slipped the note back into the box and closed it. Clutching it close to her breast, she strolled over to her vanity. "You're to say nothing of this, Nan."

"I never would, miss. Think the gent would find me in my sleep and strangle me."

Opening a small drawer, Aslyn carefully placed the gift inside. "I don't think he'd do any such thing, but I don't want to cause the duchess any distress. She certainly wouldn't approve of any gifts being delivered to me by a gentleman who hasn't made his intentions clear." Not that making his intentions clear would get him anywhere. Her guardians would never allow her to be associated with a commoner, much less marry one. Although she absolutely wasn't considering marrying him. Her life had been planned out, and she'd been groomed to one day take on the mantle of duchess. Kip was her destiny. He had been since she was a young girl. Even her parents had agreed he was the one she'd marry. They'd named the Duke and Duchess of Hedley as her guardians to ensure their desires for her came to fruition.

An hour later, Aslyn entered the breakfast dining room to find the duke still at the table, enjoying his creamed eggs, ham and other assorted offerings while reading his newspaper. The duchess took her first meal of the day in her bed, encouraged Aslyn to do the same, but she found it too quiet and lonely.

The duke stood. "Ah, what lovely company I have joining me this morning." He'd said the same thing the first time she'd snuck out of the nursery at the age of nine and insisted on having breakfast at the big table. He'd indulged her that day, and every one since, creating a little ritual between them that she would miss when she moved into her own residence.

Walking over to him, she lifted up on her toes and bussed a kiss over his freshly shaven cheek. "I wouldn't miss out on starting my day with my favorite gent."

"Did you enjoy your visit to the pleasure gardens last night?"

"I did. The music, the entertainments, the fireworks — they were all amazing. I'm hoping to convince Kip to take me again in the very near future."

Spinning around, she headed to the sideboard and prepared her plate, choosing the creamed eggs, but opting for bacon rather than ham, some banana slices and strawberries. As she approached the table, a footman pulled out the chair for her. She settled into place and waited as the servant settled the napkin over her lap. Waited a moment longer as he poured her tea. She added three lumps of sugar and stirred her tea, distantly aware of the duke finally retaking his seat.

"What did you enjoy most?" Hedley asked.

Meeting Mick Trewlove. "The fireworks, I should think."

"I've heard they're quite the thing."

"You should take the duchess to see them."

A sadness washed over his features. The duchess seldom left the residence, never attended balls or soirees. Aslyn suspected they might have never left the country estate if it were not for the fact a lady of her position should have Seasons, even if her path to the altar was set. She needed to begin establishing her place in Society so she could be a proper wife and see to her duties. "I shall speak with her about it," he said quietly.

Yet Aslyn knew as well as he did the discussion wouldn't bear fruit. She wondered if Kip would be as patient with her idiosyncrasies as the duke was with his wife's. She knew the couple loved each other deeply. It wasn't unusual to find them sitting in the garden in the evenings holding hands. Aslyn suspected there was nothing for which the duchess could ask that the duke would not give her.

"What are your plans for the day?" he asked.

"A few morning calls. I have a fitting at the dressmaker's at half two. I'm hoping my gown will be finished in time for the Collinsworth ball next week."

"The duchess and I shall pass on that one, I think. Collinsworth has become a bit intolerable since he gained his heir." Always he made an excuse for their never going out, as if after all this time justifications were still needed.

"Aren't all men intolerable once they gain their firstborn son?" she asked teasingly.

"We men do have an odd sense regarding what should count as an accomplishment."

Sometimes she wondered why the duke and duchess hadn't acquired a spare or any other children, but it was the sort of subject about which a lady of quality did not make inquiries. Kip, only twenty-eight, had come relatively early in their marriage, the duchess young enough to bear more children. Perhaps she'd suffered some sort of injury during the birthing — another subject forbidden to discuss. When it came to the body and all its mysteries, it seemed she would be relegated to uncovering the truths herself, through personal experiences rather than knowledge shared by someone who possessed all the answers.

"Is Kip joining us for dinner this evening?" the duke asked.

"Yes, I believe so." He leased a town house not too far away. Three years ago, at the age of twenty-five, he'd announced he was old enough to have his own residence, that a young man sowing his oats shouldn't reside under his parents' roof. Another bit of unfairness that sometimes irked. Although she dearly loved the duke and duchess, she did occasionally find it an inconvenience not to have her own place, but then young ladies of her station didn't move out of their parents' or guardians' residence until they were wed and could move into their husband's. She wondered if Miss Trewlove lived with her parents or if, as a commoner, she was free to live wherever she wished. Certainly her brother appeared to have the means to give her anything her heart desired.

Aslyn considered asking the duke if he'd ever heard of Mick Trewlove, but that might lead to a conversation more awkward than discussing bedding and birthing. Besides, she'd be breaking her promise to Kip to keep last night's encounter between them. With a sigh, having eaten very little, she shoved aside her plate. "Well, I suppose I should see about getting dressed for my outing."

The duke's brow furrowed. "You've hardly touched your breakfast."

Because her stomach knotted anytime she thought of Mick Trewlove.

"Are you unwell?" he asked.

Offering him a soft smile, she shook her head. "Just not very hungry this morning. I'll make up for it this evening."

"See that you do. I don't want you wasting away."

She laughed lightly. "If it hasn't happened by now, it's not going to happen." She'd always been far too slender, no matter how much she ate. The duchess, as well as a few other ladies who had known her mother, had long ago informed her that she'd taken after her mother in height and build. While she found comfort and a bit of melancholy joy in knowing she resembled her mother, she did sometimes fear she didn't give a man enough to hold on to — that perhaps Kip's lack of overtures stemmed from not being physically drawn to her, no matter how much he loved her.

"I'll see you at dinner." Shoving back her chair, she stood.

"Two footmen, two maids."

Sighing, she forced herself to smile. "Always." They were so overprotective. She supposed she couldn't blame them. They'd become responsible for her when her parents had died in a railway accident. Frightened, confused and grieving, she'd had it confirmed that life was precarious, never to be taken for granted. The duchess had reinforced that lesson with her constant worries.

Two hours later, she found herself being

escorted into a solicitor's office, a detour on her way to the dressmaker's that she had decided at the last minute before leaving the residence was necessary.

"Lady Aslyn."

"Mr. Beckwith," she said with a soft smile as the gentleman rose from his leather chair behind his desk. She didn't think she'd ever seen anyone with kinder eyes. After her father's passing, he'd handled the earl's business affairs, seen his estate settled and read his will. Although only seven at the time, she still remembered the gentleness with which he'd promised her that everything would turn out well in the end. He'd given her a rag doll and told her to squeeze it tight whenever grief overtook her. All these years later, she still had moments when she hugged the frayed doll.

"Please, have a seat," he said. "Shall I send for tea?"

"No, thank you. I shan't be here long."

He waited until she was settled in the plush chair before taking his seat and clasping his hands on the oak desk. "How might I be of service?"

"I was wondering if you know a gentleman who goes by the name of Mick Trewlove."

He studied her for a moment, and she

fought not to squirm. The spectacles that rested on the bridge of his slender nose enlarged his blue eyes and made it seem that he could peer directly into someone's soul. "I am familiar with him," he finally said very quietly and flatly, giving nothing away regarding what his opinion of the man might be.

"He struck me as the sort of man who — if he found himself in need of a solicitor — would come to you, as he would no doubt be willing to pay for the best London had to offer."

"You flatter me."

She knew he dearly wanted to ask how she had become acquainted with Mick Trewlove, but if Mr. Beckwith was known for anything at all, it was for being discreet and respecting others' privacy. "Would he happen to be a client of yours?"

He tilted his head slightly. "I am not at liberty to disclose who my clients are."

The discreetness that had brought her to him was a deterrent to her gaining what she wanted. "I don't suppose you would happen to know where his office or home is located."

Clearing his throat, he leaned back. "If he were a client, it would be inappropriate for me to share any information I have regarding him. Just as I would not share any particulars regarding you."

"If I were to leave a box on the corner of your desk, do you think it might magically make its way to him?"

"If I don't know where he is, I am certain I could find someone who does."

"Then I shall leave it in your care." She removed the small leather box from her reticule and carefully set it on the edge of his desk.

"Is there a message that should accompany it?"

"No, I think the message will be quite clear when he receives it." She rose. Mr. Beckwith shoved himself to his feet. "I appreciate you not asking questions."

"My role in life is to be of service — not to judge."

"I knew I could count on your discretion. Thank you, Mr. Beckwith. I hope you have a good day."

"Lady Aslyn, every day I am alive is a good day."

Strolling from the office, she wondered if Mick Trewlove was having a good day, as well.

She'd bloody well returned his gift. Charles Beckwith had arrived at Mick's office without an appointment and delivered it himself, along with an admonishment in his gaze: Lady Aslyn was not to be bothered by the likes of Mick Trewlove.

He had thought the earl would be a challenge, but he'd never expected it of the lady. When he set his sights on a woman, he generally enjoyed her before the night was done. He'd known an aristocratic woman would take a bit more cajoling and enticing. He'd thought dangling trinkets before her, especially when they were procured in the middle of the night from a jeweler who owed him, was the key.

He'd been wrong.

Standing at the office window on the top floor of his hotel, gazing out on the small patch of London that belonged to him, he watched as the workers carted lumber, hammered planks into place, stacked bricks, attached roofs, inserted glass. The shops would bring more business to the area, more customers to his hotel. The lodgings he planned to build beyond would bring in rents from those who worked in the shops, those he would hire to keep the area clean, those who would see to the various tasks that most people didn't even consider.

In his youth, he'd worked as a dustbin boy and then a dustman, selling the soot and dirt he collected to brick-makers — until he'd been able to afford his own brick and mortar business. London was expanding quickly. There was good money to be had in bricks. Once he had the bricks, he began building. His life had been one small step leading to another, until he was able to permanently wash off the dust. But it wasn't enough.

He wanted to be acknowledged as the better son, to prove his worth was more than that of the legitimate spawn. He wanted his father to know he had vastly misjudged his bastard's potential, to regret he had ever sentenced him to death.

CHAPTER 4

"Father, what do you know of Mick Trewlove?" Kip asked, and Aslyn very nearly choked on her glazed pheasant. They'd agreed not to mention him, and here he was mentioning him.

Oddly, the duke concentrated on slicing his poultry as though it required precision. "I'm not familiar with the man."

"He's razed all the buildings in a rundown area of London and is now replacing the structures. He's already built a massive hotel and from what I can gather has plans for a series of shops. I thought we might consider investing with him —"

"Let's not talk business during dinner."

"Oh, let's," Aslyn blurted, wanting to hear more about the enigmatic Mr. Trewlove, although she knew it was improper to show any interest in another man. But her interest was mere curiosity, not anything untoward. "Well, not business necessarily, but of

71

the new shops. Ladies always have an interest in new shops. What sort exactly?"

"I'm not sure," Kip said. "He's rather tightlipped about his plans."

"You've spoken with him, then." *When, where? What had he said?*

"No, but some gents at the club have. He made them a fortune in another venture."

"It's crass to discuss money," the duchess said from her place at her husband's side. She appeared so small and frail next to the robust duke. She wore a pale pink gown that went well with her salt and pepper hair. "Besides, do we even know the gentleman's family?"

"I doubt it. There's some question as to his" — Kip cleared his throat — "legitimacy."

The duchess appeared absolutely scandalized. "Then you should not be associating with him, much less discussing him at the dining table with two ladies present."

Mick Trewlove was born in sin? Little wonder he had the devil's look about him. She'd welcomed him holding her hand, kissing it, when in truth he shouldn't have been allowed near enough to breathe the same air as she.

"It's not as though I'm planning to invite him to dinner," Kip said. "But he has

72

become a man of wealth —"

"We do not associate with the immoral."

"But is it not his mother to whom that designation should apply?" Aslyn asked. "Surely a child cannot be held accountable for his parents' sins."

"A child born out of wedlock is tainted." The duchess became more agitated. "You must not associate with this man, Kip. I forbid it."

"But —" the earl began.

"You heard your mother," the duke said, cutting off any objections his son might have put forth. "There will be no further discussion regarding this man or this matter."

"However, you may pray for his soul for it is certainly in need of redemption," the duchess said. "Aslyn, how was your visit with the dressmaker?"

The abrupt change in topic had her head spinning. She glanced over at Kip, who was signaling for more wine — an indication he wasn't going to pursue his preferred avenue of conversation. They would not be discussing the more interesting Mick Trewlove. Rather she would have to entertain them with talk of silk and satin. "My new gown is coming along. I'll return in a few days for my final fitting."

"It would be more convenient to have the

seamstress come here."

Which was how the duchess handled it when she wanted new clothing. But Aslyn couldn't live her life without moving beyond these walls. "It was a lovely day. I welcomed the excuse to go out." And she'd needed to speak with Mr. Beckwith. She wondered if he'd made the delivery she'd requested.

The conversation turned toward the balls and affairs she and Kip would attend. Never was a ball hosted here. She wondered if the duchess missed them. Or did a time come when they no longer held any appeal, when they were attended out of duty rather than enjoyment?

Finally dinner came to an end.

"Worsted, Lady Aslyn and I shall have tea in the parlor," the duchess announced to the butler. The duke stood and pulled out her chair. Aslyn rose and Kip came to his feet.

"Kip and I shall have our port in the library," Hedley said, "then we'll meet you ladies in the parlor."

"Actually I won't be staying," Kip said. "I have an appointment."

"This time of night?" his mother asked.

Kip blushed. "It's barely nine. Most bachelors my age have appointments this time of night."

"I was hoping for a game of cribbage," Aslyn said. It wasn't fair that he could go off and do what he wanted, and she was left here with very little in the way of entertainment.

"You know how much I enjoy playing against you, but I've already made these plans, and there are those who are counting on me to make an appearance. Perhaps you can trounce me another time."

She did usually win. "I'll walk you to the door, then, shall I?"

He bowed slightly and smiled. "I would enjoy that."

She doubted it as she was going to give him a piece of her mind.

"I'll join you in the library," the duchess said to the duke, and Aslyn watched them walk off, arm in arm, before turning her attention back to Kip, who was coming around the table to join her.

"Don't scowl," he said, offering his arm. "I got you out of drinking tea."

She wound her arm around his. "Are you headed to Cremorne?"

"As a matter of fact, I am." He escorted her from the dining room and along the hallway.

"I should like to go with you."

"I'm staying late tonight."

"With Mr. Trewlove? And before you deny it, I overheard you making arrangements last night."

"Little scamp."

Which wasn't exactly a denial that she had the right of it. "Your parents won't be pleased to discover you're spending time in his company."

"Which is the reason you won't mention it to them."

"If you take me with you."

Coming to a stop in the foyer, he faced her, his features set in a determined mask. "We're going to be engaged in activities inappropriate for women."

"I could stand in the shadows. No one would notice me."

He tucked a finger beneath her chin. "They would definitely notice you. Going with me tonight is absolutely out of the question."

"Will you take me to the gardens again sometime? Very soon?"

"Not in the too near future," he said with an exaggerated scowl, which she knew indicated he didn't mean it. "I wouldn't want you to get spoiled."

But if he loved her, shouldn't he want to spoil her? The unkind musing raced unbidden through her mind. She'd never before had a harsh thought toward him, but then she'd never before had anyone to compare him against, had never had any interest whatsoever in anyone other than him. She tried to convince herself that she still didn't, but the little falsehood mocked her.

Trewlove. It was a name that sent ice skittering down his spine, even after all these years.

Gerard Lennox, Duke of Hedley, had received from the man a half-dozen letters seeking an audience with him. The words had been terse and to the point: *I am your bastard. I want you to publicly acknowledge me.*

He'd ignored them all, except for the first, as he had no intention of ever acknowledging the bastard. He'd given the Widow Trewlove extra coins so the child might have a fair start in life. Other than that, Hedley would take no responsibility for him.

"Darling?"

He glanced up at his wife, who sat in the plush chair opposite him, sipping her brandy while the fire roared, comfortably warming her, yet causing him to sweat. "Yes, my sweet?"

"You seem miles away."

Years away. Thirty-one to be exact. He'd

been young, frightened and so afraid of losing the only woman he'd ever loved. Reckless in his actions, actions that haunted him every hour of every day. He'd been stupid, careless, not nearly as cautious as he should have been. All of his focus had been on doing what was best for his love. In spite of everything, that night had cost them both, and he'd lost her.

There were moments when he still searched for her, hoped to find her again.

"What were your thoughts?" his wife asked.

"I was just thinking that Kip is of an age where he needs more responsibilities. At twenty-eight he plays far too much."

"Marriage will change all that. It did for you."

Ah, yes, it had changed him, not necessarily for the better. Sipping his port, he stared at the fire. If he only knew then what he knew now. Hindsight was a curse.

"I always thought Kip and Aslyn would settle on each other," Bella said. "But if he doesn't ask her this Season . . . she's all of twenty. He will see her on the shelf."

"Don't fret. I'll have a word with him."

She nodded. "He is a good lad. He will make a good husband." She smiled softly, whimsically. "You've set a fine example."

He had been a good husband, but he wasn't altogether certain he'd been the best of men. And *the bastard* was likely to make him pay for his error in judgment.

The Earl of Kipwick was a reckless gambler. Mick knew it within fifteen minutes of sitting him down at a table within the Cerberus Club. They'd met at the entrance to Cremorne Gardens and ridden together in the earl's carriage, not a word spoken, as though his new friend was distracted by the possibilities of the night's adventures.

Before long, he was going to be distracted by the lightness of his purse.

The club was dark, loud, filled with smoke. Commoner and nobility alike frequented this place, played against each other. The tables made disparate men equals.

Aiden Trewlove had strict rules governing behavior at his club. Cheating wasn't tolerated. He'd been known to break fingers, had taken great pleasure in snapping a duke's once. Titles were left at the door. They had no place in the world Aiden had created within the confines of these walls. Mick often wondered what would happen if Aiden's father or one of his legitimate sons walked through the door. He suspected a good many fingers might be broken.

Odd how little care those who had brought problems to Ettie Trewlove's door had taken to hide their identities. But then what weight would her words carry when compared against those spoken by someone of means, influence and power? They'd all thought themselves safe against a desperate widow in need of coins in order to survive, willing to do whatever necessary to ensure her continued existence.

His father, at least, would soon learn he'd been wrong to believe himself protected from his sins.

"Does your sister come here?" Kipwick asked, lifting his cards from the table to study them.

Mick felt a jolt of protectiveness shoot through him. A few women were gambling — not a one of them noble or even giving the appearance they had a farthing to spare, but then their currency usually involved a hiking of the skirts. "No."

Kipwick lifted his gaze to Mick's, no doubt taken aback by his curt response. "I assume she is well."

"She is."

The earl grinned. "You don't like me asking after her."

" 'E's protective of 'is sisters 'e is," the

bricklayer to his right offered.

"Sisters?"

" 'E's got two of 'em. One's the daintiest thing ye've ever seen. The other not so much. Tall as a lamppost."

"I'd hate for Gillie to stop serving you gin, Billy," Mick said, his low voice directed the bricklayer's way.

"Didn't mean nuffin' by it. She's a fine woman, she is, your sister. Just not to me tastes."

"Button your lip while you're ahead."

The man gave a brusque nod and studied his cards as though his life depended on them adding up to twenty-one.

"She sounds fascinating," Kipwick said. "She wasn't with you last night?"

"She was otherwise occupied." While he hadn't liked the inquiries regarding his sisters, he was well aware it would make his own less suspicious. He signaled to a nearby lad to fill Kipwick's glass. "The woman on your arm — I assume you have an interest in her."

Kipwick downed the swill. The glass was immediately refilled. The earl seemed to have an equal interest in drinking and wagering. "We're expected to marry."

Odd phrasing that. Before Mick could contemplate further, Kipwick smiled wistfully. "I've adored her since we were children."

So there was an investment there. Always more satisfying to take from a man when he'd given part of himself into that which was being taken.

"Our parents were close. From the moment she was born, they saw us as a match. Ancient families, political allies and all that."

Ancient families who fought to keep their bloodlines pure by ridding themselves of the impure who littered their dynasties. Mick had no plans to be gotten rid of so easily. Satisfaction was to be found in rising from the ashes.

Kipwick lost the hand with relaxed aplomb. He even laughed about it, as though money meant nothing to him. Easy to do when a man had never done without, had never been forced to scrape the bottom of the barrel for sustenance, had never felt hunger gnawing at his belly, the frigid winds taking up residence in his bones, or the ache of muscles pushed beyond their limits.

The earl signaled for more whiskey, then met Mick's gaze. "I have an interest in investing with you."

"I'm not currently in need of investors." He took satisfaction in his words, in the disappointment washing over Kipwick's face before he downed his whiskey in one long swallow and gestured for another pour. After the lad filled the glass, the earl simply claimed the bottle and banged it on the table, obviously determined to finish off the contents himself.

"You must have some sort of business opportunity on the horizon. You're not known for being idle."

"Gathering information about me?"

"Merely reading the newspapers and gossip rags." Kipwick's brow furrowed. "Although I had no luck finding anything about you in the Society pages."

"Society frowns on my presence."

"Wealth can make them overlook a great many ills. Wealth as well as the right friends, of course. Someone who could introduce you around. Say, if he were a partner."

"I'll keep that in mind." The earl seemed rather displeased that Mick didn't jump on the offer. *But it will be a cold day in hell before I take any action that will put coins in your pockets.*

Although he could certainly see why Kipwick seemed desperate for money. He had no luck at all at the games, losing far more hands than he won. His glass was continually refilled with whiskey and tossed back. A man who didn't keep a clear head when gambling garnered no sympathy from Mick when the gent found himself with an empty purse. By the time the earl discovered himself in that position, his reasoning ability had deserted him, and he was certain the next hand would reverse his fortunes.

With the earl's signature on a sheet of foolscap, the owner of the club loaned Kipwick five hundred pounds, which he promptly lost. Mick doubted it would be the first marker Aiden collected. If the earl had been able to keep his head from lolling about, Aiden might have loaned him more, but Aiden Trewlove did possess a small amount of scruples.

Mick gathered up the earl. "Come along, let's get you home."

"I've yet to win back my losses."

"Another night, perhaps."

Kipwick might have been on the verge of nodding. Instead when his head went back, his eyes slammed closed, and he promptly crashed to the floor. Mick knelt beside him, checked for a pulse. Still alive.

"He's a drunkard," Aiden said from just over Mick's shoulder.

"Apparently."

"What are you going to do with him?"

"Tonight I'll see him to his residence." But one night in the future, he wouldn't be

84

so accommodating and the earl could remain wherever he fell.

Mick stood to the side while a couple of Aiden's men trundled Kipwick inside the waiting carriage.

"Christ, you two look alike," Aiden whispered beside him. "I don't understand how he can't see the resemblance."

"The nobility never truly looks into the faces of those they consider beneath them. Besides, the beard helps. And he's not looking for a resemblance. You are."

"Like you and Kipwick, Finn and I have the same father and different mothers but we favor each other not in the least. But the two of you —"

"We favor our father. That will serve me well when the time comes."

"How long before that happens?"

"Not long." He held up two fingers. "I'll take the marker."

Aiden slipped it between the extended fingers. Mick tucked it into a pocket, patted it lovingly. "Now that he knows where the place is, he's bound to come here without me in the future. Keep a watch over him and send word when he does. His vices will lead to his downfall."

"And the girl?"

"I'll be the path to her downfall."

Leaving his brother where he stood, Mick climbed into the carriage and settled himself on the squabs opposite Kipwick. No lantern burned inside the conveyance. Just as well. He didn't want to have to take note of the similarities between them, didn't want to be forced to acknowledge he was related to this man, this gent who had been raised within their father's shadow.

The resentment boiled anew and he tamped it down. He didn't want to contemplate that if his father had farmed him out to another woman, he might not be here now; he might be rotting in the soil instead.

His father. He needed another word for the man who'd sired him. *Devil's spawn* perhaps.

The carriage came to a halt in front of a rather modest town house. Mick had been surprised the first time he'd seen it. Kipwick and Lady Aslyn would live here, he supposed. Eventually. When they married. If they married.

He leaped out of the carriage, then reached back in to drag out his half brother. Another word that didn't quite fit the meaning. He had brothers — none of whom carried the same blood as he did, but he'd die for each of them without remorse, regret or hesitation. This one, though, this one to whom he actually had a familial bond —

He handed him over to the waiting foot-man. "Take care with him."

He wanted to bite his tongue at the words. What did it matter to him if the earl was handled gently or roughly?

"Give you a ride somewhere, sir?" the coachman asked.

"No, thanks. I'll walk." He was familiar with the neighborhood, had been strolling through it quite a bit of late.

Not even an hour later, he was standing outside Hedley Hall. His thoughts should have been turned toward the duke. Instead, he focused on the one room with a light shining in the window on the upper floor, and he wondered if that chamber belonged to Lady Aslyn. More, he wondered what she might be doing. Reading, embroidering, penning a love letter to Kipwick. The latter didn't sit well with him. Did she know her precious earl was prone to abusing spirits, to signing away portions of his inheritance for a few more minutes at the gaming tables?

He wondered if in ruining her, he might actually be saving her.

His laughter echoing around him, he turned on his heel and began striding down the lane. Mick Trewlove had never saved a soul in his life. He certainly wasn't going to start with her.

CHAPTER 5

Three afternoons later, two footmen and two maids followed Aslyn as she made her way toward the milliner's after finishing with her final dress fitting. It was an unseasonably warm day, the sun shining brightly. The street was teeming with carriages and riders. The footpaths were bustling with people taking advantage of the nicer weather to do their shopping. Much easier to handle packages when one wasn't carrying an open umbrella — even if she had the footmen to haul her packages for her. Perhaps after seeing to a new bonnet, she would visit the cobbler —

A smartly dressed lad, the top of whose head barely reached above her waist, bumped into her. He hopped back, doffed his hat and gave her a beguiling grin. "Beggin' yer pardon, miss."

Then he was racing off in the direction in which he'd been heading. He couldn't have been more than eight or nine. It wasn't unusual to see young children running about unaccompanied, just not ones so well decked out. She felt a measure of jealousy that he might have succeeded in escaping the attention of his nanny. When she was a girl, she'd certainly contemplated running away from her governess on more than one occasion. To know that freedom, to have a few moments where not every skip, jump or hop was criticized, when she didn't have to keep her shoulders back, her spine straight —

"Ow! Oh! Let me go, ye bloody toff!"

Hearing the cries of distress, she stopped and turned, her heart kicking against her ribs at the sight of Mick Trewlove holding on to the boy's collar and dragging the flailing-armed youth behind him. He didn't stop until he reached her.

"Lady Aslyn." With his free hand, he swept his hat from his head, while the lad continued to squirm at his side.

She couldn't help but stare. In the sunlight she could see his eyes more clearly than she had the other night. They were a deep rich blue, like sapphires, not the dark she'd originally thought. The darkness of his hair and beard made them stand out all the more. She swallowed in an attempt to moisten her suddenly dry mouth. "Mr. Trewlove."

He gave the boy a hard shake. "Hand it over."

"Dunno what yer talkin' about, guv."

Mick Trewlove's glare was hard, threatening in a manner intended to send grown men scrambling for their lives. Yes, she could see why Nan did not want to cross paths with him in a darkened alley. It was intimidating enough running into him here on the open street in broad daylight.

"Caw, blimey," the lad grumbled as he reached into his jacket pocket, brought out a short string of pearls and dropped them into Mick Trewlove's waiting palm.

With a gasp, Aslyn slapped her hand over her gloved wrist where only a few minutes earlier a pearl bracelet had been encircling it. "You little thief."

The pickpocket kicked Mick Trewlove in the shin, causing him to grunt and release his hold. The criminal dashed off. The two footmen started after him.

"Let him go!" Trewlove shouted with such authority that both servants ground to a halt as though the order had come from God. "He's quick, and I suspect he knows these streets and warrens like the back of his hand. Besides, we've reclaimed what was stolen."

We had nothing to do with it. He had done it all.

His gaze landed back on her. "If you'll give me your wrist . . ."

She had the unsettling thought she might be willing to give him every part of her person. Dear God, her cheeks felt as though the sun had dipped down to land on them. If she were to look in a mirror, she'd no doubt find them as red as an apple. Still, she did as he requested, extending her arm, hoping he wouldn't notice any flush on her face.

Quickly he removed his gloves, no doubt because of the delicate nature of the under-taking. His hands were bronzed, his fingers well-manicured. The only marring was a few small, faint scars here and there, and she wondered if he'd obtained them in his youth. She imagined he'd been quite the rapscallion, getting into one scrape after another.

Dipping his head, he concentrated on securing her bracelet to her wrist as though he were in no hurry to complete the task. Although she wore gloves, she was still incredibly aware of his fingers brushing near her pulse, the way it seemed to speed up with his nearness. It was such a mesmer-izing, intimate service, his practically dress-ing her. Air suddenly became too hot to take into her lungs, a slight dizziness assailed her. Surely she was not on the verge of swooning.

Why did this man have such an effect on her? Why did everyone else seem so small in comparison?

People were walking by, slowing their step, staring, but she was barely aware of them, considered them more as an intrusion than anything, refused to allow them to distract her from noticing everything about Mick Trewlove that she could.

His fingers, so long and thick compared to hers, should have been clumsy and awkward as he slid one end of the tiny clasp into the other, and yet there was nothing at all inelegant in his motions. Finally his large hands fell away, and she watched with no small measure of fascination and regret as he tugged on his black leather gloves. She could have looked at his bare hands all day. They were a laborer's hands. She should have been put off by their nearness to her, yet she'd been drawn to them as though they'd lived the leisurely life experienced by a gentleman.

Kip's hands were slender, smooth, unblemished. The veins didn't jut up like unruly mountain ranges, rough in their appearance, yet also majestic. They didn't reflect strength, competence, courage. She couldn't imagine Mick Trewlove's hands shying away from any task. From the simplest to the most complex, from the easiest to the most difficult, they wouldn't hesitate to do what needed to be done. One of the reasons for the existence of the faint scars she'd noticed marring them; yet they did nothing to distract from the beauty of his hands. If anything, they added character, hinted at tales best told near a warm fire in the late hours of the night.

Never before had she given so much thought to hands, never before had any so fascinated her.

"Thank you." She sounded breathless, embarrassingly so, as though unnerved by him, by his presence, when in truth she'd never felt safer in her life. "How did you know what he'd done?"

"I witnessed his bumping into you. I doubted it was innocent or an accident."

"But he was attired in such fine clothing. A child of the aristocracy."

"A kidsman will find a way to dress the children he manages so they blend in with their surroundings. Makes them more effective at picking pockets if they're not suspected of being thieves."

"How do you know such things?"

"The streets upon which I grew up" — he glanced around — "were not so posh."

His words piqued her curiosity. Where had he grown up? How was it that he now gave the appearance of being a gentleman? What had his life been like? How had he garnered success? It had to have been a slow process to get to the point of having the means to tear down structures and rebuild them. But something else nagged at her. She blamed her next question on the duchess and her varied suspicions regarding the good intentions of people. She trusted very few. "Quite the coincidence, you being here to rescue my bracelet."

"More fortuitous, I should think, that I happened to be in the area shopping for a parasol for my sister. Once the lad disappeared and you noticed the absence of your jewelry, you'd have never seen it again."

There was the slightest chastisement in his voice, as though he fought not to be offended that she was questioning his sudden presence. She felt rather ungrateful that she had. "Quite right. I would have mourned losing a bracelet that had once belonged to my mother. Is your sister about?"

"No, the gift is to be a surprise. For her birthday."

"You're a rather thoughtful brother."

"Hardly. I'm seeking peace. She's mentioned at least a dozen times during the past week that she is in want of one."

"M'lady, perhaps we should continue on with our errands," Nan suggested quietly, her diplomatic way of informing Aslyn she'd been talking too long on the street with a gentleman to whom she was not related. At least she thought that was her purpose. She couldn't be completely certain, as she'd never before spent so much time in the company of a man other than the duke or Kip. No suitors had ever called upon her, because they'd thought it would be a waste of their time, that she was spoken for, or would be in short order.

"Yes, we must be off." She held up her hand, the sunlight catching and glinting off the pearls. "Thank you again for the rescue." She lowered her voice, barely able to hear the words she uttered. "And the other."

"Yet you returned it."

So Mr. Beckwith had seen after the matter. She wasn't surprised. Even if Mick Trewlove wasn't a client, Mr. Beckwith was a man of considerable resource. "It would be inappropriate for me to accept a gift such as that from a gentleman I barely know."

"I delivered it in such a manner that no one of any consequence need know of its arrival."

"I would have known."

"Do you never do anything you ought not, Lady Aslyn?"

Right that moment, she was thinking a good many things about the wonderful shape of his mouth that she ought not. "Again, thank you for rescuing my bracelet. I shall pay more attention to my surroundings when I take my daily stroll through the park at four — to ensure no one else takes advantage of my naïveté."

He lifted a thick, dark eyebrow. "Hyde Park, I presume."

Wondering at her boldness, she could merely nod. Had she truly just arranged an assignation? She couldn't deny that the man intrigued her, that she'd like to know more about him. Perhaps because he was forbidden and never before had she been so daring as to risk seeking out that which was forbidden — not even a biscuit from the tin when the cook wasn't looking. She'd always been so deuced good. Where was the harm in a little naughtiness that wouldn't go beyond a walk?

He tipped his hat. "I shall keep that in mind should I ever find time for a stroll through the park. Good day, Lady Aslyn."

"Good day, Mr. Trewlove."

She watched him walk away. He cut a fine figure, his strides long, but unhurried. He had such broad shoulders. She suspected he could heft and cart around any burdens, regardless of their weight.

"He's the sort the duchess has warned you about, m'lady," Nan said quietly near her shoulder.

Yes, she very much suspected he was. Strange how at that precise moment — weary of being so innocent, so protected, and in fear of her own shadow — she couldn't seem to make herself care.

Business was thriving at the Mermaid and Unicorn tonight, but then Mick had yet to see an evening when it wasn't. The excellent fare was delivered by confident girls wearing saucy smiles who knew if any gent dared pat them on the rump, the proprietor would have him banned from ever coming back. In spite of the raucousness, the men behaved. No one wanted to be on Gillie's bad side — especially her brothers, two of whom, Aiden and Finn, were presently sitting at the table with him, taking long, slow draws of their beer while Mick preferred the whiskey served in his sister's establishment.

"Did I earn the extra shillin', guv?"

Mick looked over at the urchin with the hopeful eyes who had planted his clasped, soiled hands on the table. He wasn't decked out in such finery now, but neither was he wearing rags. "You didn't have to kick my shin so hard."

The lad scowled. " 'Course I did. 'Ad to make me escape look real. The bird wouldna believed it otherwise."

"The lady."

"She was a fancy one, she was. Bet ye gotta be all clean afore ye can even kiss 'er."

"What do you know about kissing girls?"

"Everythink. I kiss 'em all the time."

He doubted it. The scrawny lad couldn't be more than eight. Reaching two fingers into his waistcoat pocket, he withdrew a coin and tossed it toward the boy, who caught it with a wide grin.

"Caw! Blimey! A crown! Thanks, guv. Ye need some-think else nicked —" He jabbed his thumb against his skinny chest. "— ye just let me know." Then he was racing off, no doubt in search of bulging pockets.

"What was that about?" Aiden asked.

Mick shook his head. "Just a little task

with which I needed some assistance." It hadn't been coincidence he'd crossed paths with Lady Aslyn. Ever since she'd left her residence earlier that afternoon, he'd been following her, waiting for the most opportune moment to approach her. He'd known she was going out because he paid a footman to deliver a message whenever he learned of the lady's plans for the day. In any household, there was always a servant more loyal to coin than to his employer.

She'd spent so much time at the dressmaker's he'd begun to wonder if she'd moved into the shop. When she'd finally emerged and he'd overheard her tell the servants she was heading to the milliner's, he knew the time had come to take advantage. It had gone much better than he'd imagined, even if he had ended up purchasing a parasol for Fancy because guilt had pricked his conscience for baldly lying to the lady's face. He didn't understand that reaction on his part. A good deal of his climbing out of the gutter had involved lies and half-truths. He was accustomed to telling them with a straight face and moving on, but this afternoon he'd spent coins on a bit of frippery. Not that Fancy hadn't been pleased with the gift.

"I don't like you using my boys for your

nefarious deeds," Gillie said as she set another glass of whiskey in front of him and tankards in front of Aiden and Finn.

"He's not *your* boy."

"He works for me. He's mine."

Like their mum, she had a soft heart. Unlike their mum, who was short of stature, Gillie was nearly as tall as Mick. Her hair was cropped short like a man's. Her loose shirt and boots were reminiscent of a laborer's attire. Her brown skirt was plain, hung off her hips as though there were no petticoats beneath it. Probably weren't. While Fancy loved all the trappings of ladies' attire, Gillie abhorred them. If he'd purchased her a parasol, she'd have conked him over the head with it for spending coin on something for which she had no use.

From the moment Ettie Trewlove had taken Gillie in, she'd dressed her as a boy. Mick had assumed it was because the Widow Trewlove had lad's clothing to pass down and didn't have the pennies to spare for frocks. He'd thought she cut Gillie's hair whenever she trimmed the boys' because she didn't have the time to brush and braid long tresses, and the shorter style was less likely to attract lice. It was only when he'd inadvertently caught her wrapping linen around Gillie's chest when she was twelve that he realized she'd made her appear to be a boy in order to protect her from unwanted advances — or worse.

He suspected if Gillie ever grew out her hair and put on a proper dress, her features might appear more comely and she might draw a man's attention. Although if a fellow stared at her for too long, he was likely to earn a black eye. Gillie was as quick with her fist as she was with a kindness.

"It was a harmless prank," he told her. "He never left my sight. He was never in any danger."

"Nicking a bracelet from a lady clad in silk could get him hanged."

He fought not to grimace. The next time, he'd explain to the little urchin to keep his mouth shut regarding the specifics of his task if he wanted to earn extra coins.

Gillie yanked out a chair and dropped unceremoniously into it in a manner he doubted Lady Aslyn had ever used to take a seat. She would slowly, elegantly alight —

"Why are you stirring things up, Mick?" she asked pointedly, always too forthright. He reconsidered his earlier assessment. Even if she grew out her hair and put on a pretty frock, no man was going to court her when she was always so damned irritatingly blunt, looking a man straight in the eye while carrying on her inquisition, demanding he answer truthfully or suffer the consequences. "Our lives aren't half bad."

"We were sentenced to death, and we did nothing to deserve it except be born on the wrong side of the blanket."

"Not all the widows murdered the children handed over to them."

"A good many did." Over a thousand graves had been discovered in one woman's garden.

"Don't you ever wonder about where you came from, Gillie?" Finn asked.

She shook her head. "No. Unlike you lot, I don't know who fathered me, or anything at all about the immoral woman who lay on her back for him, but Ettie Trewlove is my mum. That's all I need to know."

None of them knew anything about the women who'd given birth to them, although Aiden's and Finn's sire had delivered them to Ettie Trewlove's door within weeks of each other so everyone assumed the man had possessed two mistresses.

"Don't you want to know if the woman who brought you into the world was his lover or just someone he took for the night?" Finn asked. "I wonder about my mum, if she meant anything at all to him."

"If she had, do you think he'd have gotten

103

rid of you?" Gillie asked. "Don't be daft, lads. The women who gave birth to us were mistresses or prostitutes or, heaven forbid, some poor servant girl who got cornered in the linen pantry. Keeping us would have ruined their lives, made them as unwanted as we were. Look ahead, lads, not back. Nothing to be seen in the rear but heartache."

But Mick couldn't help but wonder if sometimes heartache was needed in order to move forward.

CHAPTER 6

Everyone who wanted to be seen was in Hyde Park. Generally Mick preferred to do his business in the shadows, but he recognized there were times when a man needed to step into the sunlight in order to be effective and gain what he wanted. This afternoon was one of those times.

Sitting astride his gelding gave him a clearer view, and it didn't take him long to spy Lady Aslyn. He'd expected to find her amid a gaggle of females. Instead she appeared to be alone, except for the entourage of servants who had been accompanying her the day before. Not wanting to appear overly eager, he hadn't joined her at the park yesterday. Seduction required subtlety and patience. Especially when the lady was supposedly enamored of another.

He didn't cut a direct path to her, but instead meandered about, tipping his hat whenever any lord with whom he might have done business acknowledged him. The occurrences were few, but that would change once his place within high Society was recognized. Once his place was established, Fancy's would be, as well. Ever since he'd learned at the age of fourteen that his mum was with child, he'd put all his efforts into protecting her and the babe. It was only then he'd fully understood the price Ettie Trewlove was paying to the landlord every Black Monday when she didn't have enough coins for her weekly rent. If he'd been older or bigger or stronger, perhaps he could have protected her from the lecherous proprietor sooner, with his fists.

He damned well protected her now — and the daughter to whom she'd given birth out of wedlock, in shame and in sin. When it came to children, the law required nothing of the man and everything of the woman. Ettie Trewlove had little to give except for her heart, but it was enough, enough for her own daughter and the five unwanted children she'd taken under her wing. He owed his mum a price he could never repay, so he would make a proper place in the world for her daughter, her blood, even if it cost him his soul to do it.

He knew the moment Lady Aslyn spotted him. She stopped walking, tipped up her parasol slightly along with her chin and smiled softly as though she'd been kept indoors all day because of the rain — and the sun had suddenly made an appearance.

Drawing his horse to a halt, he dismounted with ease, removed his hat and waited for a more public acknowledgment from her.

"Mr. Trewlove."

"Lady Aslyn, what a pleasure it is to find you in the park this afternoon."

"And you, sir. I thought I might have seen you yesterday."

What a bold chit she was. He'd not expected the subtle reprimand. "I had business that kept me away." He cast a furtive glance at the servants hovering nearby, all appearing to be ready to pounce if he made an untoward movement. He resettled his gaze on the lady. "But you occupied my thoughts."

A lovely blush rose up her neck to encompass her face and make her cheeks more pronounced. He had the fleeting thought that he was looking forward to discovering if the flush began at her toes. And he would discover it. Before the month was done, he intended to have her in his bed. She would be to him whatever the woman who had given birth to him had been to his father —

and he'd throw the similarities into the duke's face. Looking at her youth and innocence now, he refused to feel remorseful about the role she would play in his gaining satisfaction. He'd given the duke the opportunity to publicly recognize him, and the damned man had ignored each missive save one.

"Might we stroll together for a while?" he asked.

Her blush deepened, but she looked slightly uncomfortable as though uncertain where to go from here. She gave a barely perceptible nod. "I suppose there's no harm in walking together for a few minutes."

Guilt nagged at him. Was he a blackguard for using a girl who seemed far too innocent to be out alone among the wolves? He didn't bother to offer his arm, because he wasn't certain she'd take it, and he never took any action unless he was certain of the outcome. In a distant corner of his mind, an irritating thought nagged at him that he also hadn't offered his arm because he'd be distracted by her touch. She had small hands, no doubt fragile and delicate. There'd never been anything gentle in his life. Everything he'd experienced had been hard, harsh and challenging. Even his bedding rituals had a rough, wild element to them. The women he took were strong, fierce, gave as good as they got. He couldn't imagine Lady Aslyn on all fours acting the mare to his stallion.

Damnation. She wasn't touching him, but simply gazing on her distracted him from his purpose. He walked with his hands clasped tightly behind his back, the reins held firmly as the gelding followed, providing an effectual barrier between the lady and her footmen who traipsed along behind. While he walked to her left, the two maids had taken up positions to her right, but they were keeping a respectful distance, allowing them a bit of privacy as long as they spoke quietly.

"Did you find a parasol for your sister?" Lady Aslyn asked, as she glanced askance at him.

"I did. A white lacy thing. She seemed to fancy it."

"White goes with anything."

Only then did he notice her pink parasol, resting against her right shoulder, was the same shade as her frock. She no doubt possessed a hundred of the blasted things, one for every outfit. She lived in a world where coins were taken for granted. While he was now in a position to be generous with his, he never forgot the price paid for each one.

Silence eased in around them. He supposed she was waiting for him to continue their discussion of ladies' paraphernalia. Flirtation involved speaking of inconsequential things. If he had any hope at all of seducing her, he needed to move quickly before the duke or the earl realized his intentions.

"How many languages do you speak?" she asked, catching him off guard with the change in topic. Was she trying to discern where he'd been educated? The rookeries had been his classroom, poverty and vulnerability his harsh tutors. He'd learned their lessons well. They'd never again threaten to break him.

"The Queen's English." He could speak a few words of other languages, enough to communicate with laborers when needed, but mentioning them might put her in the mood to test him, and he wasn't going to show himself lacking in any regard. Although he'd never seen the advantage to boasting. Better to keep one's talents close to the vest. "You?"

"Five," she said blithely. "English, of course. French. Handkerchief, fan and parasol."

He stared at the impish smile she gave him. It transformed her face into rare beauty, something that went beyond the surface. He had no desire to be intrigued or mesmerized by her teasing — no one dared tease him — yet she seemed completely unaware of the danger he presented. "I beg your pardon? Handkerchief, fan, parasol?"

"Any lady of good breeding knows them. Did you not teach them to your sister when you gifted her with the parasol?"

"I am not a lady of good breeding."

Her smile deepened, causing a strange sensation in his chest, something he'd experienced once when a large wooden crate had toppled onto him. It had been terribly unpleasant, then. It wasn't so much so now, and yet he still found it difficult to breathe. "No, I suppose you're not. Do you see that couple walking over there, the lady in the purple gown, the gent with the gray cravat? Her parasol rests against her left shoulder. She is displeased with him. He's said something that upset her."

"Perhaps it keeps the sun out of her eyes better on that side."

She laughed lightly. "My dear sir, carrying a parasol has little to do with the sun."

Dear sir? He was not her dear anything. He knew that, knew she didn't understand the consequences of words spoken. Still the endearment left a strange longing that he

111

did not wish to examine. He was thirty-one, reaching the time in his life when it would be natural to take a wife, to have someone who called him dear. He'd never really contemplated that before, didn't know why he was doing so now. She was not to be a permanent part of his life. She served a purpose, and when that purpose waned, he would release her. He wondered why he suddenly feared he might do so with regrets.

"Do you see the woman in blue who has folded up her parasol and is touching the handle to her lips?"

"The one who has wasted her coins by purchasing something designed to protect from the sun and is using it most ineffectually?"

"Depends on your definition of effectual, I suppose. She is signaling to the gent walking beside her that she would like to kiss him."

"You're bloody well putting me on, aren't you?"

Her eyes widened at his sharp tone, or perhaps his profanity, but he hated little more than he hated being made a fool of. She shook her head. "No. Women aren't allowed to speak their minds, to declare what they want, so they have to do it through bits of frippery."

Her voice was edged with a hardness he'd have not expected of her. He didn't know why it pleased him to realize she had a bit of a temper, one that she no doubt controlled because of societal expectations. "And what is it you want to declare?"

She blinked slowly, stared at him. Suddenly laughed. "At this precise moment, I don't know."

"You never have to watch your words with me." Which wasn't fair, as he'd always be watchful of what he revealed to her. "My sisters always speak their minds."

"And do what they want, I suppose. The sister who accompanied you the other night no doubt was allowed to stay at Cremorne Gardens after the riffraff arrived."

"No, I strive to protect her from the less savory elements of London."

"My apologies." She sighed. "Sometimes I yearn to rebel against proper behavior."

"Why don't you?"

"Scandal would serve me no good. Lord Kipwick would be dismayed and disappointed in me."

He found it difficult to believe anyone would ever be disappointed in her, that she had it within her to bring about censure — on her own at least. With his assistance, she was going to find herself engulfed in improper behavior. She would disappoint. She would bring about censure. She would despise him. Regret began to well, and he shoved it aside. It could overwhelm him later, but not now, not while his plans were still in their infancy, before they'd come to fruition.

"Why is he not here?" he asked, working to keep his voice neutral, when in truth there was a small corner of his soul that was angry on her behalf, because unlike the myriad of other ladies, she was not being escorted by her swain.

"The park bores him no end."

"But surely you do not. I would suffer through any dull activity to be at the side of a woman who interests me." And she interested him, far more than she should have, far more than he wanted her to.

That blush again, accompanied by a fluttering of her eyelashes that he suspected had nothing at all to do with flirtation, but rather his words had taken her unawares, as she'd not considered the message a man's absence might be communicating. While he'd given it a great deal of thought. If she didn't mean as much to Kipwick as the gossip sheets hinted, then she was no longer a crucial part of his plan. For some unfathomable reason, he was more disappointed on her behalf than on his.

"It seems a lady would be most fortunate to have your attentions, then." She averted her gaze, released a taut laugh. "It seems our couple with the closed parasol has secreted away."

"Have you ever been secreted away?"

She snapped her gaze back to him. "Of course not. A lady in my position does not engage in such inappropriate behavior, but must act in a manner that ensures she stay above rumormongering."

"Is there not some part of you, some deep, dark part of you, that longs for scandal?"

He watched in fascination as the delicate muscles at her ivory throat worked while she swallowed. "Absolutely not." There was little force behind the words. "I have delayed your enjoyment of the park long enough, I think."

She was dismissing him. He should have taken offense. Instead he viewed it as a victory. He was getting to her, making her doubt Kipwick's devotion. He wondered why he took no satisfaction in the knowledge.

"Indeed." He bowed his head slightly. "I have a meeting with my solicitor regarding some new property I wish to obtain. He charges me double when I'm tardy."

"Then I shan't keep you."

"One question before I go — what does it signal when a lady rests her parasol on her right shoulder?" As she had done throughout their entire stroll.

"That she welcomes the gentleman speaking to her."

"Quite innocent, then."

"I suppose it depends upon what she welcomes him speaking to her about."

He chuckled low. "I suppose it does at that." He gave an elegant bow. "It has been my pleasure to spend a few minutes with you, Lady Aslyn. I do hope our paths will cross again."

"I'm not certain that would be wise."

"Sometimes a man gains more by being unwise." Before she could respond, he mounted his horse, tipped his hat to her and took off at a gentle canter.

She was not as he'd expected. He did want to cross paths with her again, and it had little do with reprisal. The thought making him uncomfortable, he shifted in the saddle and spurred his horse on. If he were a smart man, he'd cast aside this part of his plan. But then he'd already admitted to finding profit in not always being wise.

"I heard you were seen strolling through

Hyde Park with Trewlove yesterday afternoon."

Aslyn stared up at her waltzing partner's somber face. She'd never known Kip to look so serious. She'd arrived at the Collinsworth ball, maid in tow, respectfully late, expecting him to arrive even later. Instead he'd already been there. As soon as she'd greeted the host and hostess, he swept her onto the dance floor.

The inquisition began without his even asking how she'd fared since he'd last seen her. "It wasn't arranged." Exactly. "Our paths simply crossed, and he was gentlemanly enough to spare me a few moments."

"He's a bastard, Aslyn."

Her mouth dropped open at the harsh word, delivered cuttingly, in a manner she knew he'd never say it to Mick Trewlove's face. His voice held disapproval, disappointment, but also a measure of something she thought might be jealousy. "You indicated the other night during dinner his illegitimacy was only rumor."

"Now I know it to be fact."

With the knowledge, she should have thought less of Mick Trewlove, been horrified at the way she'd stared at his hands as he assisted her with her bracelet, been mortified by the gladness she'd felt as he escorted her in the park. Yet she seemed incapable of viewing him any differently. "Have you ceased your associations with him?"

Kip appeared decidedly uncomfortable, glancing around quickly as though fearful someone might overhear their conversation, while all along his terse expression was going to be cause for much gossip and speculation. "It will do your reputation no good to be seen speaking with him."

"So if he approaches, what am I to do? Give him a cut?"

"Simply don't acknowledge him. If you do not speak to him first, he cannot speak to you."

"Did he strike you as someone who follows Society's rules?"

"You cannot encourage him or give any indication that you overlook the circumstances of his birth."

"That's hardly fair. He's done nothing to deserve my censure."

"He was born on the wrong side of the blanket."

"How is that his fault?"

He released an exasperated sigh. "My parents would not be at all pleased to know you'd spoken with him. They made that perfectly clear the other night."

"You were the one who brought him up during dinner after we both agreed we wouldn't mention the encounter."

His cheeks flamed red. "I didn't mention the encounter, only the man. You are the one who is going to cause problems if you continue to associate with him."

"I'm not *associating* with him. We merely spoke when our paths crossed in the park." And near the shops. Not that she was going to mention that. It would only heighten his upset, which she was finding distressing enough, as he'd never been cross with her before.

"How did he know you'd be in the park?"

Having never seen him so blistering mad, she was feeling rather put upon. "How do you think? I sent him a missive and told him to meet me there."

The anger that flashed in his eyes gave her pause, made her realize it might be best not to taunt him. But communicating with her fan left a great deal to be desired, and at the moment, she had a need to speak what was on her mind. She had the fleeting thought that Mick Trewlove would applaud her, and inappropriately, she took a measure of pleasure in that. "Honestly, Kip, you can't think I encouraged him in any way." Although she had, just a tad, when she'd

119

mentioned the hour she usually strolled through the park. She did hope the heat rushing into her cheeks was not giving her away. She'd longed to do something she shouldn't, to take a chance, a risk, and then Mick Trewlove had come along, dark, dangerous and tempting. Even though she'd never go beyond a stroll with him, she'd been flattered to know she appealed to someone other than Kip.

"It's frightfully warm in here," he said curtly. "Shall we take a turn about the gardens, allow the fresh air to cool our tempers?"

"This heated discussion seems to warrant it."

With her hand on his arm, he escorted her out through the open doors onto the terrace and down the steps into the gardens. Lighted torches lining the paths revealed other couples walking about. She wondered how many ladies were holding folded fans to their lips, signaling they wanted a kiss. Would Kip accommodate her should she make use of her fan? She wished she possessed more courage, wasn't hesitant to find out. Not that she was particularly in the mood for a kiss at the moment. They'd never before been out of sorts with each other, had never had a row. She didn't much like it now, although in a strange way it made her feel very much alive, as though she'd gone through life in a trance, simply existing from one moment to the next.

"My meeting him was merely coincidence," she admitted, wondering why she felt she had to be the first to offer an olive branch. "If you must know, he even asked after you, wondered why you weren't in the park."

"I was told you strolled with him for a considerable distance."

"Nothing untoward happened." She hated apologizing for something not her fault. "Have you people spying on me?"

"That's the thing, Aslyn. Among our set everything is noticed and commented on. A couple of fellows mentioned it at the club, and not in a kind way. He's not the sort with whom you should be seen consorting."

"I wasn't *consorting*. How many times must I say it? Besides, you seem to like him well enough."

"A man is allowed to associate with whomever he wants. A woman cannot."

"It was an innocent walk."

"I simply find it odd that within the space of a few days, you've twice crossed paths with the man."

He wouldn't be at all pleased to discover

there was a third time — or a gift. "He was probably always about before. We just never noticed him because we'd never been introduced to him."

"He doesn't strike me as a man not noticed."

"Are you jealous?" The hope-filled words popped out before she could stop them.

"I simply don't want him to take advantage of you."

"We were in a park where an abundance of people were strolling about, and my servants were in attendance. I don't see how that could happen."

"If it were his intent, he would find a way."

"You speak so poorly of him, and yet I thought you wanted to go into business with him."

"I don't trust him. At least where you're concerned." He laughed harshly. "Good God, perhaps I am jealous. Have I reason to be?"

"No." At least she didn't think so. A man like Mick Trewlove would never be accepted by the Duke and Duchess of Hedley. She wasn't even certain he would have been welcomed by her parents. Kip was the sort a woman of her station married. It helped that he'd been her friend for so long. The fact that he didn't create the strange stirrings within her that Mick Trewlove did was no doubt a good thing. A lady should at all times be calm, collected and in control of all her thoughts, putting errant ones to rest quickly. "I care for you deeply, Kip."

"And I you."

"Then why have you never kissed me?" She despised the surfacing doubts regarding his desire for her, hers for him. She was beginning to wish they'd never gone to Cremorne. Everything seemed to have changed that night: the way she viewed him, herself, their future.

"Out of respect. A man doesn't dally with a woman he intends to marry."

Her heart gave a little kick as she stopped walking and faced him. "That's the first time you've made your intentions regarding me clear."

"It's always been implied. I thought you knew that."

"Yes, but a lady likes to have the clarity. I've been extremely loyal, welcomed no other advances or interest. And I'm not getting any younger."

"Neither am I, actually. My father pointed that out to me recently." His deep sigh filled the night. "Shall we make it official, then?"

Stunned, she watched as he went down on one knee and took her hand. "I adore you, Lady Aslyn Hastings. Will you honor me by becoming my wife?"

The words ebbed and flowed around her, at once ghost-like, yet solid. She wasn't quite certain what she'd expected of a proposal. A declaration of undying love perhaps. Her heart pounding with an erratic rhythm. Birds taking flight. The sun replacing the moon. Stars shooting across the sky. She'd waited eons for this moment. It seemed it should be more profound, causing her knees to tremble and her lungs to cease functioning. Instead her body gave no reaction at all, as though his proposal had yet to penetrate.

"Aslyn?" he prompted. "I'd welcome a quick response as there's a pebble digging into my knee most painfully."

His words brought her back to the reality of the moment. Wasn't a simple proposal more profound? Didn't it speak to a more honest relationship that didn't require fancy words or decorative phrases?

"Oh, yes! I'm sorry." Covering her mouth with her hands, she laughed, striving to not become hysterical at what should have been an incredibly romantic moment. "Yes, yes, of course, I'll marry you."

"Marvelous." He rose, dipped his head. She closed her eyes, waited —

"Oh, my word! Kipwick, did we just see you down on bended knee?" a lady called out.

Her eyes flew open as Lady Lavinia and her escort, the Duke of Thornley, neared. Blast it all! She didn't mind that they'd seen the proposal, but couldn't the lady have held her tongue until after she'd been kissed?

"You did say yes, didn't you, Lady Aslyn?" Lady Lavinia asked.

"Naturally."

"I daresay it's about time you two got on with things, and at my family's ball, no less. You will allow me to make the announcement once we return to the salon, won't you? I won't take no for an answer."

Raising a brow, Kip looked at her. "I see no harm in that. We're moving forward, after all."

She felt her face grow warm. This was truly happening. The fanfare was about to begin, and once the announcement was made, there would be no turning back, no changing of minds for either of them. "Shouldn't we wait until we've told your parents?"

Grinning, he tweaked her nose. "They know, silly girl. My father is your guardian, and I had to get his blessing first."

"Oh, yes, of course." When had that happened? Shouldn't she have been consulted? No, it had always been assumed —

"Congratulations, old chap," Thornley said, holding out his hand. "Even if it did cost me five hundred pounds."

He was no doubt referring to the stupid wager made at White's regarding when Kip would ask for her hand. She felt distant, separated from herself as she watched her betrothed shake the duke's hand. Now that the moment was actually here, it didn't feel real.

"My luck is much better than yours," Kip said. "I shall soon have the lovely Lady Aslyn as my wife."

"Let's go announce it, then," Lady Lavinia said, "as I can hardly wait to make a splash."

As she wound her arm around Aslyn's and began leading her back to the house, Aslyn couldn't help but think that this moment wasn't about Lady Lavinia at all — and yet the girl was going to make it so.

"I'm so excited for you," Lady Lavinia said. "Kipwick is quite the catch. I know a few ladies who are going to be disappointed. Even though we all expected him to marry you, some were foolish enough to hold out hope."

She wondered if any gentlemen had held

126

out hope for her, if Mick Trewlove's recent attentiveness had been more than kindness. What did it matter? She'd been traveling this path for most of her life. It was reassuring to see the destination on the horizon — at long last. Still, it seemed she should have been experiencing a measure of excitement rather than simple relief.

"Oh my dear, we could not be happier," the duchess said as she enveloped Aslyn in a warm hug.

The duke and duchess had been waiting for them when they returned from the ball. She'd barely handed her wrap over to a footman before Kip declared that he'd proposed and she'd accepted. It was an announcement she'd been expecting for a long time, and yet it seemed odd having it associated with her.

"This calls for a drink," the duke said, and she found herself whisked into the parlor where a decanter of brandy and four snifters were waiting on a low table.

They'd known the proposal was coming tonight. She shouldn't have been surprised, as Kip had told her he'd spoken with the duke, and yet she couldn't help but feel as though everything was moving far too quickly.

"Your parents would be delighted," the duchess said while the duke poured the brandy.

"I'm sure they would." Although she wasn't sure at all. Her memories of them were faint and distant, and recently she'd found herself mourning their absence as much as she'd mourned the loss of her parents. She took the snifter the duke offered her.

He lifted his. "If you love each other half as much as Bella and I love each other, then you'll be richer than most. To a long, happy and fruitful marriage."

She felt her cheeks warming with the reference to *fruitful.* Children. They would have lots of children.

"Hear, hear!" Kip said, before tossing back a good portion of his drink, while she rather wished he'd claimed to love her more than his parents loved each other. She was horrid to want some reassurance regarding the strength of his feelings for her.

She took a sip, not understanding all these doubts suddenly plaguing her.

The duchess sat on the sofa and patted the cushion beside her. "Sit, tell me everything. Where did it happen?"

Aslyn eased herself down. "In the gardens."

"How romantic."

It should have been, yes, but in retrospect it hadn't, not really. "I was quite taken by surprise."

"Surely you knew my intentions," Kip said.

"Yes, but I wasn't certain when you might ask."

"Now we have a wedding to plan," the duchess said. "I suppose we should have an engagement ball. Here. At Hedley Hall."

She could see the anxiety in her guardian's face. "Perhaps a dinner. A small one. Intimate."

"I like that idea," Kip said, smiling warmly at her as though he recognized she was striving to spare his mother worry.

"Yes," the duchess said. "We'll discuss the particulars tomorrow. When would you like the wedding to take place?"

"We haven't really discussed it," Aslyn said.

"I'll leave it to you ladies to work out the details," Kip said. "I must away."

In disbelief, disappointment and ire, Aslyn stared at him. "You're leaving?"

"I must make the most of the bachelor days that remain to me."

"You can stay longer," the duke said.

"No," Aslyn said, suddenly in want of time

alone, to ponder her feelings, to what she had agreed, to wonder why there was not a livelier air of celebration. Because it had all been expected? Because there had been no anticipation? "It's quite all right. I'm actually rather exhausted from all the excitement and merry-making that took place at the ball once Lady Lavinia announced my good fortune. However, I shall walk you out." *And have a word in private.* Setting aside her snifter, she rose and took the arm he offered.

Once they were outside on the steps, with the door closed behind them, she took a deep breath, released it slowly. "Do you really wish to marry me?"

"I'd have not proposed otherwise."

She studied the face she'd loved for years, searching for the truth, for something more. "You haven't even kissed me."

"I suppose I've spent so many years keeping my desire for you tamped down and on a short leash that it's become a habit."

She hated that his words gave her such hope, that words were needed to give her any hope at all. Shouldn't love communicate in other ways? "You desire me?"

"Without a doubt." He cradled her cheek with one bare hand. When they'd arrived home, he'd removed his gloves, had yet to put them on. His skin was smooth, his palm without calluses. Warmth radiated from his fingertips, but no heat. "Aslyn, I intend to do right by you."

"Would a kiss be wrong, then?"

He grinned, glanced back over his shoulder to the windows. "I don't think anyone is watching."

But if they were, what would it matter now? They were betrothed. He could compromise her all he wanted, and the outcome for their futures would not change.

He lowered his lips to hers. Her eyes slid closed at the warmth, the gentleness, the way his mouth moved softly over hers. Slowly he drew back. "I shan't sleep tonight, thinking of you."

"You shan't sleep because you'll be up to no good."

He flashed a grin. "I have an appointment with cards. Not another lady. Know this, Aslyn, for me there is no other lady."

Her heart tightened, tears pricked her eyes. "You've always been the one for me, Kip."

"Don't set a date that's too far off." With that he tweaked her nose, before dashing down the steps.

The man certainly knew how to ruin a romantic moment, but then he'd tweaked her nose ever since she was a girl. There was a familiarity and a lovingness to it. But she feared the gesture was more appropriately directed toward a younger sister, not a wife, not a lady a man wished to bed.

They were to marry, and yet she felt like a child playing at pretend, not a woman anticipating the days — and nights — to come with relish. She'd been brought up to always feel calm and steady, but at that moment she desired only to feel *more*.

CHAPTER 7

Mick sat at the desk in his office scouring the *Times,* one of a half-dozen periodicals he devoured every morning along with his coffee. While he knew most gents caught up on the news over breakfast, he'd never gotten into the habit of enjoying a leisurely beginning to the day. He awoke, dressed and headed into his office — which was a short walk from his nearby apartment on the same floor.

Of late he'd been giving attention to the Society news, and so it was that he saw the announcement regarding Lady Aslyn Hastings's betrothal to the Earl of Kipwick. It shouldn't have come as such a shock, shouldn't have felt like a kick in the gut from a recently shod horse. He'd known of the earl's interest; had known of the lady's, as well. It worked to his benefit that they were engaged to marry. It upped the stakes, made his stealing the lady away even more of an embarrassment for the earl, and, as a result, the duke. His heir couldn't hold on to his woman. It would portend that the earl was too weak to hold on to much else.

It should have made him glad. Instead it filled him with a sense of loss, made him feel as though something had been stolen from him. Ridiculous, that. Yet the sensation was there, grinding into his thoughts, making everything else seem inconsequential.

"Tittlefitz!"

The door burst open as though his secretary had been standing with his ear pressed against the thick oak. But then the man always seemed at the ready to serve. "Yes, sir?"

"The gathering we have planned to celebrate our opening of the hotel for business . . . the grand salon . . . I want an area of it made available for dancing."

The slender young man blinked. His hair was a harsh red, his face covered in a constellation of freckles. Like Mick, he was born a bastard. Unlike Mick, he'd not been abandoned by his mother, and both had suffered because of it. The government aided the poor, but not the poor with illegitimate offspring. While there was finally an interest in reforming the *Bastardy Act* and protecting infants, Mick doubted the negative opinions or behavior regarding those born on the wrong side of the blanket were going to be changing anytime soon.

"We'll have to hire an orchestra," Tittlefitz said.

"Then hire one." He had the means to hire a dozen.

"What of the harpist who was going to perform?"

"Move her to the lobby. I don't care. Your job is to make happen what I ask, and not bother me with the details of how you manage it. If I have to think about it, then what service am I paying you so well to provide?"

"Quite right, sir. I shall see to it posthaste. Anything else, sir?"

"No, that'll be it." He shoved back his chair, stood, and strode over to the coatrack. He shrugged into his coat and grabbed his hat. "I'm going out. Don't let things fall apart while I'm gone."

"When will you be returning?"

When his mind was no longer filled with images of Aslyn saying yes to Kipwick's proposal, of looking up at him with joy wreathing her face. She was a means to his gaining the acceptance he required. He should be bloody grateful things were progressing as quickly as they were.

Only he wasn't. As he walked along the street where buildings were in various stages of being completed, he imagined she experienced the same sort of happiness when she received the earl's proposal as he did when he watched the structures arise from the rubble of what had once been a vermin-infested area of London. He'd gotten the property cheap, acres of it. This street and the next, he'd mapped out for shops. The remaining area would be town houses where only a single family would reside. The rents wouldn't be exorbitant. He doubted he'd ever break even.

The shops and his hotel were another story. They would provide employment for those who lived in this area. He was going to employ proper street sweepers who received a salary, not lads who were tossed a coin after clearing a path for the posh. His streets would be free of horse dung and rubbish. He had grand plans, plans that would create pride in the folk who lived and worked here, plans that would allow ladies to walk about without fear of ruining the hems of their skirts.

Thinking of skirts had him thinking about Aslyn again. He wanted her to attend his celebration of success. He wanted her to witness his accomplishments, to give her a chance to compare him against Kipwick. He wished every building would be finished when he opened the hotel, but there was no reason to hold off making money on it. Besides, he needed to find tenants for some of the shops, and some potential ones would be there during the festivities. Although, perhaps she would see the potential here as he did.

He realized, much to his consternation, it wasn't his need to lord his achievements over Kipwick's that had him contemplating how he might ensure she attend his affair, but a desire to share all this with her, to catch a glimpse of it through her eyes. To see if she took as much delight in it as he did.

All foolishness on his part. He couldn't lose sight of his ultimate goal or the fact that when it was achieved, Lady Aslyn would despise him.

"I need him to win tonight."

Standing in a shadowed corner beside Aiden, Mick watched as Kipwick finally strolled through the entrance of the Cerberus Club and shrugged out of his coat, handing it off to a young fellow who was tasked with seeing to each visitor's possessions. He'd expected him to be here tonight as his appearance had become a habit, and each morning Aiden sent over the earl's markers.

"That seems to be contrary to your plans," Aiden said, his tone neutral, yet Mick heard his brother's silent question: *What are you about?*

"I want him in a jovial mood."

"Not a bad idea to let him win. He's had a string of losses the past few nights. To be honest, I'm surprised he returned."

"He lost his membership in yet another club, the last of any reputation that would have him. He has nowhere else to go."

"There are plenty of places — less reputable to be sure, more dangerous certainly — for a man with an addiction to appease his demons, and your earl is addicted to wagering."

"He's not my earl."

"I saw in the newspaper that he is *hers.*"

The words struck hard and quick, a solid blow that knocked him mentally off balance. His teeth clenched of their own accord, his gut tightened, his hands balled into fists at his side, but his face reflected no emotion whatsoever. Nor did his voice when he finally found the wherewithal to speak. "The reason I need him in a jovial mood. If I keep accidentally crossing paths with her, she'll become suspicious. It's to my benefit for him to arrange the next encounter."

"You know I don't condone cheating."

"I also know you have a dealer with the skills to control which cards land in front of which gents. I want him at that table where the earl just sat down."

Aiden patted his shoulder. "Remind me to never get on your bad side." Then he strolled away to make arrangements with his talented dealer as though he hadn't a care in the world, when Mick knew his cares were plenty. He wasn't alone in that. Ettie Trewlove's brood all carried far too many burdens.

The cards were with him tonight. Kipwick had felt the turn in the tide half an hour into play, when a new dealer had relieved the other. The past few nights he'd been bleeding money, and while he wasn't presently winning as quickly as he'd lost, his abrupt change in fortune was a start toward putting matters to rights. If he wasn't careful, he was going to be unable to keep his father from learning of his ever-increasing debt. Although the debt wouldn't be with him for much longer. Aslyn's dowry would go a long way toward putting him back on a strong financial footing.

The fact that his father had recently transferred the nonentailed holdings into his keeping was also quite beneficial. When he needed to prove his solvency in order to gain a loan, he had only to point to the properties.

He cleaned out one gent — although referring to him as a gent was a stretch of the term — and watched as the large fellow scraped back his chair and wandered off. Most of the people here, commoners, were beneath him. The few aristocrats he recognized were black sheep, usually second sons, not likely to report anything of note to his father since they weren't welcomed in most parlors. He liked the Cerberus Club and all that it offered: decadence at its most primal. It was an honest place, took pride in what it was. It didn't try to fancy itself up with liveried footmen, wood-paneled walls, crystal chandeliers or quiet rooms housing books so a man could pretend what he did outside those rooms was respectable.

Here he wasn't a lord, with expectations weighing on him. Here he was just a man. And he loved it.

Glancing over as the chair that was just vacated was pulled out farther, he grinned at Mick Trewlove as he sat and went about exchanging a thousand quid for tokens. "I was beginning to wonder if you'd ever return."

Without looking at him, Trewlove carefully lined up his chips. "I've been monstrously busy preparing to open my hotel for business."

"I've heard it's quite the thing." The ante was called for. Chips were tossed into the center of the table, cards were dealt. He received a pair of jacks. The night was certainly going his way. "Perhaps you'd give me a tour."

"I'll do you one better. I'll invite you to the ball I'm hosting to celebrate the opening."

Furrowing his brow, Kipwick pretended to consider his cards when in truth he was striving to determine the ramifications of attending should word get back to his father. "Unfortunately I'm not available."

"I haven't told you the date yet." The tone was quiet, deathly so, brimming with displeasure. "Surely it's not my bastardy that's keeping you away."

Lifting his gaze, Kipwick saw a face as solid as marble, all the features more pronounced, the blue eyes as hard as flint. No movement occurred at the table, as though everyone, including the dealer, was waiting to see if an insult was on the horizon, one that would no doubt be followed by a quick jab to his chin. "No insult intended, but I don't usually attend public balls."

Trewlove tossed away two cards. Movement began. Kipwick breathed, only then realizing his lungs had been frozen.

"My apologies," Trewlove said, never taking his eyes from his stack of chips. "I thought you had an interest in investing."

"I do."

His gaze slid over to Kipwick, fairly impaled him. "My investors will be attending. Men of wealth who often hear of other opportunities for investment, sharing what they know of those prospects. I daresay I learn more by mingling informally with knowledgeable men than I learn by holding meetings with them."

Kipwick exchanged three of his cards, fighting not to smile at the third jack. "It sounds as though it could prove a fruitful evening. When is it?"

"Tuesday next."

He nodded. "I shall be there."

A round of wagering. When it got to Trewlove, he raised the stakes by a hundred quid. Kipwick's heart pounded. Before that moment, during all the hands he'd played that night, the most anyone had wagered was ten. Those tokens symbolizing so much were like a siren call. He matched the wager and raised another two hundred.

"Perhaps you'd bring Lady Aslyn," Trewlove said as he called and raised another hundred.

Everyone else folded, until it was only the two of them. "Her guardians would not approve."

"You don't have to tell them. Besides, my sister would take great delight in seeing her again. And we must have women about else with whom are we to dance? A ball hosted by a commoner is not that different from one hosted by a duke."

"Will other nobles be in attendance?"

"A select few are invited."

He shook his head, striving to determine whether to call or raise. "It will do her reputation no good."

Trewlove tapped his cards on the table. "Let's make this interesting. If I win this round, you bring Lady Aslyn. If you win" — he dramatically waved his hand over the tokens — "all my remaining chips are yours."

Kipwick's mouth went dry. With what others had added to the pot, he'd win well over a thousand quid. Three jacks were sure to beat whatever Trewlove held. There was no risk in this. Aslyn would not be associating with those beneath her. While he would leave here with bulging pockets. "I accept the terms."

"You first."

Fighting not to gloat, he turned over his three jacks. "I'd like to see you beat that."

"I'd have thought you'd have preferred for me to lose." He tossed down his cards, face up, and Kipwick found himself staring into the eyes of three kings. Odd how he felt as though they were mocking him.

Trewlove began gathering up his chips. "I shall see you and Lady Aslyn Tuesday next."

"Are you done here?"

"I am."

Sitting back, he wasn't at all happy with the suspicion taking hold. "Your entire purpose in sitting down here was to get Aslyn to your ball." He didn't bother to hide his irritation.

"Your presence will add to the affair's prestige."

He liked that *his* presence was included but still he was bothered. "I heard you took her on a stroll through the park."

" 'Took her' implies I was responsible for our being there. It was a chance encounter. Nothing untoward occurred."

"So she claimed."

"Did you not believe her?"

144

"Of course I did. She hasn't a deceptive bone in her body." He wasn't certain the same could be said of Trewlove. "She will make me an excellent wife." He felt compelled to remind the man that she was claimed.

"I've no doubt. I'll let Fancy know she'll be attending the ball. It'll please her immensely."

It was with a bit of regret that he watched Trewlove walk off with his winnings. He sighed. He should have quit while he was ahead. Studying the tokens that rested before him, he knew he should gather them up and leave as well, but with a bit of luck and a few more hands, he could regain what he'd lost. Without much care, he tossed a token onto the center of the table and waited for the cards to be dealt.

Three hands in, each one a loss, Aiden Trewlove approached, leaned in and whispered, "I know about the wager you made with my brother. If you don't pay him what is owed, you'll find these doors locked to you."

"I don't need a threat. My word is binding."

"Considering you've yet to make good on any of your markers, I wasn't certain."

145

"You need not worry. I will pay you what I owe."

"I'm in no hurry, but the interest will be steep, my lord, steeper than I suspect you imagine."

"I'm good for it."

Aiden Trewlove clapped him on the back and laughed. "Glad to hear it, as I believe we could have a most profitable friendship."

As the man walked off, Kipwick acknowledged it wasn't the sort of profits that Aiden could provide that interested him. It was the profits that being closer to Mick Trewlove could gain him that held his attention. If he played his cards right, untold fortune rested on his horizon.

CHAPTER 8

"I can't remember the last time we went to the theater," Aslyn said as the well-sprung carriage clattered through the streets, carrying her and Kip toward their destination. Since their betrothal, his visits had been rare, which had only served to cause her to question her wisdom in consenting so quickly. Not that she could have imagined herself saying no, but perhaps if she'd paused a bit longer, if she'd forced him to work a little more diligently for her agreement, he'd be paying her more attention.

Sitting across from her, even though he could now sit beside her since they had an understanding, decked out in his finery, his top hat and cane resting in his lap, he cleared his throat, glanced out the window, returned his gaze to her. "Actually we're not going to the theater."

"But you invited me. You told your parents —"

"Yes, well, because I knew they wouldn't approve of this excursion."

Her heart gave a little kick against her ribs. It wasn't terribly late, just after eight, but still his words gave her hope for some excitement. "Are we on the verge of doing something we ought not?"

"You might say that. We received an invitation to a ball celebrating the opening of Mick Trewlove's hotel. I thought you might enjoy attending."

While she did have a keen interest in the man's hotel, in seeing what he might have accomplished, she was rather confused by the change in the night's plans. "You chastised me for walking with him in the park. Surely he will be there tonight. Am I to give him the cut you suggested?"

"Absolutely not. In hindsight I may have overreacted to the park situation. He assured me nothing untoward took place."

His words irked. "I assured you. Did you not believe me?"

"Without a doubt I did," he said hastily. "Aslyn, you're missing the entire point. I know you were disappointed that I wouldn't take you to Cremorne during the improper hours, so I thought to make it up to you by bringing you with me tonight."

"You've been spending more time in his

company." Her tone wasn't accusatory but it was pointed, a statement indicating she knew the truth.

"Some, yes. My father doesn't understand that we can't continue to rely on the income from our estates to sustain us. We must expand our horizons if we want to increase our revenue. I'll meet investors tonight. And becoming closer to Trewlove will also open up opportunities. I want him to come to me the next time he needs capital."

She wasn't quite certain the man really needed anything.

"His sister's going to be there. You liked her well enough, didn't you?"

"Yes."

"And you like parties. As you said, we'll be doing something we ought not. We'll have a jolly good time at it. You can pretend it's Cremorne Gardens' in the later hours. There are bound to be some sordid sorts about."

She couldn't deny she was intrigued by the opportunity to catch a glimpse into Mick Trewlove's world. "How often have you seen Mr. Trewlove since the night at Cremorne?"

The light from the lamp allowed her to see his shrug. "A couple of times. He gained me access to a club that suits me. On occasion he's there."

"I assume this club is a gambling den."

"The very best kind. All they offer is gambling and drinks. It's rough and exciting. Nothing at all like a gentlemen's club."

"So Mr. Trewlove gambles."

He furrowed his brow. "Not very much actually. Mostly he watches. Not a man for taking risks, I suppose."

"This venture of his seems a huge risk." She'd managed to find an article about his developments. "To tear things down and build anew — it can't be cheap."

"He can afford it."

"Only as long as he has success. Unless he's succeeded in growing money on trees."

Kip laughed. "I'd purchase one of those trees from him right quick without even quibbling over the cost."

"I doubt they'd be for sale."

"I wouldn't put it past him. From what I've gathered, he'd find a way to make even more money off it."

"You admire him." She heard it in the tone of his voice.

"It is difficult not to admire someone who came from nothing and managed to rise above it. Still, my admiration goes only so far. I'd best not catch him flirting with you."

"He'll be too busy with his other guests to

give me much notice."

"I wouldn't be so sure. You look very lovely tonight. But remember you belong to me."

She wrinkled her nose. "What? Like a pair of boots?"

Grinning, he leaned toward her, took one of her hands and placed a kiss on her gloved knuckles, all the while holding her gaze. "Like something I treasure. Have you set a date?"

"No. Your mother wants the end of the Season, but I was thinking Christmas."

"Choose the date you want."

"But your mother has been so kind to me. An earlier wedding seems a small thing to give her."

"She chose the day she married. You should choose yours."

"You have no preference?"

"My preference is for you to be happy."

The words were comforting, and yet she rather wished he'd claimed to be unable to wait until Christmas. Why was it that ever since she'd said yes, she was finding fault with him and questioning whether she should have said no?

The carriage slowed, drew to a halt. Glancing out the window, she was vaguely aware of a line of carriages, while the major-

151

ity of her attention was arrested by the huge brick building. "Is that it?"

Kip leaned over, looked out. "I would say so, yes."

"It's monstrously large."

"I believe he considers it his crowning glory. It sets the stage for the area."

"It's going to be a grand area, isn't it?"

"If the rumors are to be believed."

She snapped her attention to him. "How can you look at that and not believe?"

"Too pragmatic, I suppose. I have to wait for the results."

The results would be spectacular. She had no doubt. A man who could create something like this was a man with vision, and a determination to ensuring it came to fruition.

The carriage moved up slowly, bit by bit, eventually reaching the front of the building, with its sweeping steps leading up to the glass doors. An assortment of people — some much more posh than others — were swarming toward them, disappearing inside.

A waiting footman opened the carriage door. Kip exited, then reached back and helped her to descend. The building was even more impressive when she was so near to it. She was suddenly incredibly grateful that Kip had accepted Mr. Trewlove's invitation, that she was on the verge of seeing something so grand, of being part of a night that would have repercussions for years to come. The man was starting something here tonight that would spread out to have an impact on others, like a pebble tossed into a pond creating expanding ripples that eventually touched shore. Placing her hand in the crook of Kip's elbow, she began the ascent into what would surely be paradise.

Mick Trewlove had remarkable taste. That was her initial thought when they stepped into the lobby where the plucked strings of a harp created a calming ambience. Well-heeled footmen walked about carrying silver trays holding flutes of champagne or small bites of food that could be easily eaten while standing. Gaslights burned in an array of glittering crystal chandeliers that illuminated everything. The walls were a dark wood she couldn't help but believe reflected their owner.

Their owner. Who stood near the red-carpeted, sweeping staircase with its polished dark banister and balustrade. He wore evening attire: a black swallow-tailed coat, waistcoat, trousers. A pristine white shirt with a perfectly knotted gray cravat. White gloves covered his large, roughened hands, laborer's hands. If she hadn't seen them in the flesh, she wouldn't know of the host of tales they revealed, now hidden away. Proper clothing could make the most common of men appear nearly royal — and Mick Trewlove, regardless of his birth, was anything but common.

His beard was neatly trimmed. His black hair was more styled than she'd ever seen it — and she would swear it was a tad shorter, as though he'd clipped it just for this occasion. He stood a head taller than anyone surrounding him, so it was with ease that he captured and held her gaze. She'd never seen anyone exude such confidence, such power, such self-assurance. He fairly took one's breath.

Or at least he seemed to have seized hers because her lungs were apparently incapable of drawing in air. Her chest might have been hit with one of the sledgehammers that surely had been used to raze the buildings that had once stood here. She'd forgotten the impact of his presence, the way it could unnerve while at the same time providing comfort, offering a cocoon of protection while asking for nothing in return.

The hotel was grand because *he* was grand, because he had built it in his own image, because it was a reflection of a man who had risen above the rubble of his beginnings. The circumstances of his birth should have relegated him to the gutter, but without knowing his entire story, she knew he had clawed his way out to reign over all he surveyed. How could anyone not give him the respect he'd so rightfully earned?

"He gives the impression he's holding court," Kip said. "Like a king."

More than a king. Kings would bow to him, willingly serve at his pleasure. He was lord of his domain and all that surrounded him. She couldn't help but wonder at the satisfaction a woman might feel if she stood at his side. She would wield her own power, be someone to be reckoned with in her own right because he was the sort who required a partner of strength and influence equal to his own.

Had he lived a thousand years ago or even five hundred, he would have been a conqueror, one who toppled empires, not to enslave but to free.

Then he was striding toward them, cutting a swath through the crowd as easily as she sliced off a bit of butter for her bread. When he was near enough, he took her hand in his, lifted it to his lips, placed a lingering kiss on her knuckles, the heat from his mouth seeping through the kidskin and traveling through every inch of her. *Inappropriate!* screamed through her mind and yet she couldn't seem to care.

"Lady Aslyn, I'm so glad you were able to join us."

"I welcome the opportunity to wish you well with your business venture." Did she have to sound as though she had raced into this room, with her breaths coming in short, shallow gasps? Even if she hadn't known their destination until they were on their way, her words weren't a lie. She did wish him well, wished him more success than any man had ever achieved.

Releasing his hold on her, he turned to Kip. "Lord Kipwick. I'm equally glad you saw yourself free to join us."

"I wouldn't have missed it. I daresay it'll be the talk of London on the morrow. You've outdone yourself here. It's much grander than I expected."

"I've always believed dreams should be larger than ourselves. May I show you around?"

"We couldn't impose," Aslyn said. "You have so many guests."

"It would be no imposition, and I'm certain they won't mind."

Before she could accept his offer, she heard, "Lady Aslyn. Lord Kipwick. What a lovely surprise! Mick didn't tell me he'd invited you."

Kip bowed slightly, took Miss Trewlove's hand. "It's a pleasure to see you again."

"And you, my lord. And lady." She smiled softly at Aslyn. "Isn't it luxurious? My brother comes across so rough sometimes that you wouldn't think he could create something of such beauty."

"The hotel is quite elegant," Aslyn told Miss Trewlove, although the comment was really made for Mick Trewlove. She wanted him to know how impressed she was with his efforts, but a lady in her position didn't fawn over a gentleman or his achievements.

"You should see what Tittlefitz has done with the grand salon," Miss Trewlove added.

"Tittlefitz?" Aslyn asked.

"Mick's secretary. He's decorated it with so many flowers and garlands I doubt there is a single blossom left in any flower shop. I daresay there's not a ballroom in all of London that can compare. I've been striving to talk my brothers into joining me there for a dance. But they act as though they'll turn into toads if they escort a girl onto the dance floor."

"They've not had the lessons you've had," Mick Trewlove said.

"I suspect you dance like a dream, my

lord," she said, fairly ignoring her brother's remark and giving Kip all of her attention.

He grinned. "I would not be so crass as to boast about my skills. What do you think, Aslyn?"

"I agree. You would not be so crass." Mr. Trewlove grinned, and a strange fluttering took up residence in her stomach. She really should do nothing to encourage his smiles. They were devastating to a woman's equilibrium.

Miss Trewlove's tinkling laughter circled them. "Perhaps you'll demonstrate your talents for me later, my lord."

"I would be delighted."

"And perhaps that will force my brothers into proving themselves." Glancing over her shoulder, she motioned toward someone or *someones*.

Three gentlemen quickly joined their group. Two men were slightly similar in appearance. The third was a great hulk with black hair that hung down over one side of his face in a manner that seemed deliberate as though he sought to shield it.

"Lady Aslyn, Lord Kipwick, allow me the honor of introducing Aiden" — she touched the arm of a brown-haired man — "Finn" — who was blond — "and Ben."

"Beast," the dark-haired man said in a

curt deep voice. "People call me Beast."

Yes, she could well imagine they did. None of them looked anything like Mick Trewlove. To be honest, she thought his appearance was nearer to Kip's, but perhaps it was merely because his evening attire more closely resembled the earl's than the plain jackets his brothers wore. Because they looked so disparate, she couldn't help but wonder if they were all born on the wrong side of the blanket, if their mother was of such low moral character that she had consorted with an assortment of men. She was horrified by the thought, even more so by the realization it could very well be true. Little wonder the duchess had objections to her being in the company of those with no pedigree to their name.

"I say, Your Lordship," Aiden began, "we've set up some card games in a small salon. My brothers and I were about to head in and test our luck. Care to join us?"

For some reason, his brow furrowed, a question in his eyes, Kip turned to Mick Trewlove as though seeking permission. "A few hands couldn't hurt."

"They might even help. Several investors have already made their way to the tables. Aiden can introduce you."

"Jolly good." Finally he looked at her. She

didn't miss the guilt wreathing his face. "You wouldn't mind, would you, darling, if I left you in the company of the lovely Miss Trewlove?" She was surprised by the endearment. He didn't usually use them. As a matter of fact, she couldn't recall a single time when he had, yet this one had a possessive edge to it.

He leaned in, whispered, "I'm seeking to secure our future."

She supposed he was referring to the opportunity to become acquainted with men of business. Although she did mind a tad that he was planning to go off without her, she wanted to do some exploring and doubted he'd be interested in looking at furnishings and wallpaper. "I'm sure I can entertain myself." After all, he never stayed with her for any length of time at balls, although at those affairs she knew a good many of the people in attendance, could always find a lady or two with whom to gossip. Here, as she looked around, she realized her acquaintances were few. Two to be exact, not bothering to count the brothers to whom she'd just been introduced.

"I won't be long, and when I'm done, I promise you each a dance."

She watched as he walked off, chatting and laughing with the Trewlove brothers —

except for Mick. She wasn't surprised he remained behind since he was the host and had responsibilities that required his attention. Apparently he took them very seriously, but then a man with his success would not have achieved it if he were a slacker in any regard.

"Men and their wagering," Miss Trewlove said, clearly irritated by the sudden abandonment. "My brothers will never get married if they are so quick to leave the company of women." Her eyes widened. "And speaking of marriage, I understand congratulations are in order, Lady Aslyn. How lucky you are to have made such a fine catch."

With Mr. Trewlove studying her, she suddenly felt uncomfortable under his intense scrutiny, almost felt as though he didn't approve of her betrothal. Which were ridiculous musings on her part, for why would he care? "Thank you, Miss Trewlove. I consider myself fortunate indeed."

"We don't need so much formality between us. At least not tonight. You must call me Fancy."

"You must call me Aslyn." Every time it seemed her breath was returning, a quick glance at Mick Trewlove snatched it away again. "Is your other sister about?"

"No, unfortunately, she declined my invitation," he said, and she heard the true regret in his tone.

"Because she would have to wear a proper dress," Fancy said.

"Does she not dress properly?" Aslyn asked.

"Her attire is somewhere between what a man and a gypsy might wear. It's terribly unflattering. I've told Gillie a thousand times that with a bit of effort she could be beautiful. But she won't have it."

"She has her reasons," he said.

"I suppose a beautiful tavern keeper would find naught but trouble."

"She has a tavern?" Aslyn asked.

Fancy beamed. "In Whitechapel. Mick helped her acquire it, just as he's going to assist me in gaining a bookshop."

"Fancy —" His low gravelly voice should have been frightening. Instead Aslyn was intrigued, imagined it even lower, whispered in shadows.

"The little shop on the corner across the street would be perfect. The windows on two sides would allow in light —"

"A wall of windows means you can't have a wall of books."

"So you've been thinking about it?" She was smiling so brightly Aslyn was surprised she didn't throw her arms around her brother's neck with glee.

He sighed, and in the sound she heard his defeat, wondered if it was the first one he'd ever suffered. Yet, she found no fault with it, because she knew he was going to give his sister what she craved, and she envied Fancy for having a brother who didn't let pride get in his way or dictate his actions. "We'll discuss it later."

"I do love you, you know. Oh, and there's Tittlefitz. I must have a word with him regarding the champagne. If you'll excuse me."

And she was gone, leaving Aslyn alone with the enigmatic Mick Trewlove. Well, not completely alone. Many people were wandering about, but she didn't see anyone she recognized. Although surely she and Kip weren't the only nobles here. She'd probably find some ladies she knew in the ballroom. She should make her excuses —

"You look beautiful tonight."

She was ashamed to admit she'd have selected a more revealing gown had she known this was her destination, grateful she'd worn the pearl necklace that flattered the slender column of her throat. The pearl and diamond comb nestled in her upswept hair always gave her confidence. "Do I not always?"

"You know you do."

She released a self-conscious laugh. "Actually I don't. I have a funnily shaped nose. Tips up on the end most unattractively. My cousin who inherited my father's title once told me I reminded him of a pig. Of course, he was only nine at the time, two years older than I, but still. I don't know why, but as though I needed to prove his point, I began snorting and grunting as though I were wallowing in pig slop."

"I'm certain whatever sounds you made only endeared you to him."

"Oh, I seriously doubt it. I've not seen him since my parents' funeral. We were never close. Just as well, I suppose." She glanced around. "Is your mother about?"

"No. Like Gillie, she wouldn't be comfortable in such exquisite surroundings, wouldn't feel as though she belonged — no matter how much I assure her otherwise."

"The Duchess of Hedley, my guardian, is the same. I've never known her to attend so much as an afternoon tea away from her own residence. I find it sad, and yet she seems content enough. It's a shame your mother can't see all this."

"I've given her a private tour. Would you care for one?"

■ ■ ■ ■

He was being rude to his other guests. He knew that and he didn't care. He'd set up the card room with the hope Kipwick would abandon his fiancée, leaving Mick with free rein to see to her needs, needs she probably didn't even realize she had. Any and all needs he would satisfy, willingly, eagerly. She had but to ask. She didn't even need to use her voice. Her eyes, a crook of her finger, a blush. But at the moment, she gave him none of those.

In her expression, he could see the impropriety of his request had her mind spinning. At least she hadn't declined outright, which meant she was considering it. As a footman walked past, Mick reached out and grabbed two flutes of champagne, handed her one, watched as she sipped delicately, imagined her sipping at his mouth in the same manner. He was not a novice when it came to women, but no other had caused his head to spin with so many inappropriate thoughts. Yet it wasn't lust that drove him. It was something he didn't understand, seemed unable to comprehend in any meaningful manner.

"How private?" she finally asked.

"Only as private as you're comfortable with. Why don't we start by going up the stairs so you can look out over the balcony? The view is better."

Glancing up, she nodded. He offered his arm. She laid her fingers on his forearm, and his groin tightened with her light touch. Good God, he'd probably double over if she touched him with any real purpose. He acknowledged a few people he passed: a baker, a dressmaker, a milliner, all of whom would be tenants in his shops. He'd extended invitations to several in the nobility but fewer than half a dozen, not counting Kipwick and Lady Aslyn, had made an appearance. The ones who had were young bucks with no reputation to worry over. For the others, he was good enough to invest with but not to socialize with. Always the stigma of his birth haunted him.

"This hotel suits you," she said quietly. "It's strong and bold, masculine and yet warm and welcoming. A lady would feel comfortable here."

"I hope so. I need those of the feminine persuasion to visit my tearoom."

She smiled at him. "You have a tearoom?"

"Fancy insisted. Then we have an area for the gents with billiards and spirits. My brothers were responsible for that."

166

"I think it's wonderful that you welcome their opinions."

"They're going to offer them whether or not I welcome them."

"It must be marvelous to have so many siblings. Kip and I would have each grown up alone if my parents hadn't died."

"How did they die?" he asked.

"Railway accident. Horrendous thing. Twenty-seven souls lost. I wasn't the only child of a nobleman to be orphaned that night. I've yet to take a journey by railway. Can't bring myself to do it. Even riding in a carriage makes me nervous. I'd rather walk where I am in control of my legs or ride a horse where I am in control of the reins. I suppose that makes me a bit of a coward."

"I don't find you cowardly at all." But he would like to take her on the railway. When he was younger, he'd find ways to slip onto a car without a ticket. He'd made a vow to himself that one day he'd own his own car and travel wherever he damned well pleased. That goal had come to pass, and his car came in useful as he was scouting out areas in smaller towns that he could develop. He was especially interested in building a hotel at the seaside. People had more leisure time, and they were interested in escaping London for short periods of time. A man of vision could capitalize on that.

They reached the landing, and he walked her around to the balcony that looked down on the lobby. Behind them were a series of doors.

"What are the rooms up here for?" she asked. "Sleeping?"

"Not in this section. They can be rented for meetings or leased as offices."

"Have you an office here?"

"On the top floor. I have suites where I live, offices where I work."

"That must make things convenient."

"For now." Eventually he would build a majestic manor on a large stretch of land where his wife would entertain and his children could run barefoot over cool green grass instead of dirty cobblestones. Although for the most part, he suspected they'd be wearing shoes because they would always have shoes that fit and clothes that were not handed down from an older sibling or discovered on a rubbish heap and mended to be made serviceable.

People, who held no titles but possessed full coffers, wandered by, nodded toward him. A few tossed out a comment: "Splendid!", "Well done, old chap!" But he cared little for their praise, cared only what she thought. None were dressed as fancy as she;

none were as elegant. All lacked her polish. She didn't have to scream she was above them, didn't have to do anything at all to proclaim her place in the world. She had been born into it, had worn it all her life. Yet, he suspected even if she'd been taken to Ettie Trewlove's door, she'd have still grown up to reflect her origins.

"Who are all these people?" she asked softly.

"Some will be tenants in the residences we will soon begin to build. Others will lease the shops. A few are friends, a couple I grew up with. Then there are lawyers, bankers, railway owners."

"Do you invest in railways?"

"No, but it's helpful to know where they are going to be built. A railway in the area increases the number of travelers who will be passing by the shops or who might require lodging for a night or two."

"I'm impressed. A great deal of thought goes into what you do."

"I like the challenge of it, figuring out how to maximize profits."

She was studying his face closely, too closely. He knew his best course was to look away, to distract her, but he enjoyed cataloging her features, imagining his lips trailing along the edge where cloth failed to cover skin. He wanted to discover one freckle, one tiny freckle, to know the sun had kissed her where he longed to. It was torturous being in her company, not being allowed to touch, knowing he should never possess. He should send her on her way, ensure she wasn't in his presence. Never before had he ever been so weak-willed. He was a man of strength, and yet he thought for her he'd go to his knees.

"How did you come to build your empire?" she asked.

"It's hardly an empire."

She leaned toward him slightly. "My goodness, are you blushing?"

"Absolutely not." He was horrified with the thought. If there was any color rising in his face at all, it was because her nearness caused cool air to abandon him as he pondered capturing those luscious pink lips, devouring that sultry mouth, knowing her taste —

"I think you are. You're modest."

"Hardly. Modesty does not serve a man well when he needs his accomplishments known in order to garner the trust of those with the means to help him up the ladder."

"I can't imagine you needing much help. Tell me how you came to be where you are."

Your guardian cast me aside. "I worked as

a dustbin boy, gathering up soot from houses."

"Like a chimney sweep?"

"Not exactly, although I worked for one for a while until I got too big to scurry up the chimneys." He was certain she didn't know the particulars of how residences were kept spotless. "Between occasions when one has the chimney cleaned by a sweep, something must be done with the soot and ash that collects on the hearth. It's placed in metal pails, set outside for bin boys to pick up. We'd sell it to brick-makers who use it in the making of bricks."

"I had no idea."

"Why should you need to know all that goes into keeping you comfortable?"

"I don't know, and yet it seems I should. You can't have earned much money doing that."

"No, but I began to think, why sell the soot and ash when I could use it to make my own bricks? I saved up until I could purchase a factory. I was eighteen. I earned more money selling the bricks to bricklayers and builders. From there, I decided why sell the bricks when I could use them to build homes or shops?"

Her eyes widened slightly. "The bricks in this building, they're yours?"

171

"They come from my factory. It will provide all the bricks for all the buildings in this area."

"What a remarkable achievement."

Until that moment he'd never thought of it that way. It had all been what he'd needed to do in order to get ahead in the world. She made him feel as though his clothes were too tight. Why did she have to do that? Why did she have to make him feel as though he were extraordinary? Her admiration would make the seduction easier, only he didn't want easier. He wanted to earn the privilege of having her in his bed.

Damnation! What an odd thought. What did it matter how she got there? It only mattered that she did, that she would be denied the duke's heir, and instead be saddled with the duke's bastard. That the duke would recognize his failings to see after his ward just as he'd failed his illegitimate son. That every aspect of the duke's legacy — his heir, his ward, his titles, his estates, his wealth, his position, his respect — could be brought to ruin by one man, the one he'd treated shabbily, failed to recognize.

"I've kept you from your other guests, Mr. Trewlove."

Her voice brought his wandering thoughts back to the task at hand. "Call me Mick."

"It wouldn't be appropriate."

"Do you always do what's appropriate?"

"I try. I think I should like to see the ballroom."

"I'll escort you there."

"That's not necessary."

"I insist." Once more he offered his arm. Once more, she took it. He imagined her hand on his arm when he was an old man. Was it possible that she could come to love him, that she would stay with him when she learned the truth? The notion taunted and teased, made him wonder if she could see him as *good enough* when no one else in Society would.

"Are your brothers partners in your business?" she asked.

"They have shares in it. But they have achieved success in their own rights with their own ventures."

They began descending the stairs. "They look to be near you in age."

"They are. Only a few months separate us."

"How can that be?"

"Our mum, Ettie Trewlove, did not give birth to us. She merely took us in." He shook his head. "I should not say merely. It was a burden for her, but she managed."

"Where is she now?"

"The rundown place where we grew up. I would provide her with suites here, but she has no desire to leave behind what she knows."

"I think most of us find it difficult to venture beyond what we know, what we are comfortable with. I know I'm not nearly as daring as I wish I were."

"Is that the reason you're marrying Kipwick? Because you're comfortable with him?"

He wanted to bite his tongue. Her reason for marrying the earl had no bearing on the matter, and yet it seemed significant to know that she hadn't given her heart to the man.

"I love him. I have since I was a little girl."

There was no passion in her words, no conviction. "A girl's love is not the same as a woman's."

"Is that the voice of experience talking?" she asked curtly as they reached the lobby. "Have you had a girl's love and a woman's in order to compare the two?"

"I have known girls and I have known women. Their passions are very different. A girl may desire a doll or a puppy. A woman's desires have more consequences, are more passionate, more . . . let's just say they're likely to keep her tossing and turning through the night." He escorted her into the ballroom, took satisfaction in her surprised gasp.

Mirrors ran up one of the walls, while red and gold brocade wallpaper lined the other two. At the far end, windows and glass doors gave a view of the outside. While gaslights illuminated the intricate gardens, he would like for her to see them in full daylight. They were small but intimate, not designed for lengthy strolls but for taking tea in the afternoon or relaxing with a book, a book that might very well be purchased in Fancy's shop.

In a gilded balcony, an orchestra played. Tittlefitz had outdone himself, ensuring flowers and plants lined the edges of the floor, but allowing enough room for small sitting areas here and there. Footmen walked the outskirts, offering food and beverages.

"It's gorgeous," she said.

Not as gorgeous as you hung on the tip of his tongue, but he couldn't bring himself to voice the words, no matter how sincerely he felt them. A time would come when she might view his words from the perspective of betrayal, and she'd think he'd lied. Yet seeing the delight mirrored on her face made him want to do all in his power to bring enchantment her way. "I hired a man with an eye toward creating beauty."

"I might have to get his name from you when I begin setting up my own household."

For the residence where she would live with Kipwick, where he would come to her bed. Would she quiver in his arms, whisper naughty things in his ear? The jealousy that surged through him took him off guard. "Your betrothed doesn't seem to have left the card room yet. Would you honor me with a dance?"

Her eyes nearly popped out of her head at the question. Anger riffled through him because she would think him too crass, too beneath her for so much as a waltz.

"Since your brothers don't dance, I assumed you didn't, either."

His anger dissipated like fog before sunlight. Perhaps he was too sensitive about his origins. "It would be dangerous to assume anything about me."

She gave him an impish grin, her smile hitching up slightly higher on one side. Another imperfection that made her the most intriguing woman he'd ever met. "Are you trying to frighten me away?"

"I'm trying to be honest with you." Probably more honest than he'd been since he met her. Suddenly he wanted true honesty between them, wanted to leave all the falsehoods behind, wanted to tell her everything. Have her judge him, whether well or poorly. No, he wanted more time, an opportunity to present the best of himself before he revealed the less than favorable aspects.

"Does honesty not come naturally to you, then? You have to work at it?"

"I suspect there is a bit of the dishonest in all of us."

She blushed at that, and he wondered what deceits she might have engaged in. Nothing too nefarious. Possibly plucking a flower from the garden when it was forbidden. She haughtily angled that tipped-up nose of hers, and those lush lips he wanted to taste curled up on one side. Then she issued her bold challenge. "All right, then. Prove to me you can dance."

CHAPTER 9

She should have declined. Any respectfully affianced lady would have. Not that a betrothed woman wasn't allowed to dance with a man who wasn't her intended, but she certainly shouldn't be so near to a man whose hands, although properly placed — one on her back and the other providing a haven for her fingers — caused her to long for them to be improperly placed, caressing the nape of her neck, stroking her bared shoulders, cradling her face as he leaned in —

Oh, dear Lord. She wanted that deliciously wicked mouth of his doing all the things she dreamed of his hands doing. It was wrong, so wrong.

And he was incorrect. She did experience passion where Kip was concerned, and it was more than the childish desires of small things like a butterfly landing on her outstretched hand or a day without lessons.

She had womanly passions. How often had she thought about Kip kissing her? A thousand at least, although not nearly as often as she'd envisioned Mick kissing her during the short time she'd known him.

Mick. She couldn't call him that to his face. It was far too intimate, but in the hidden recesses of her mind where she held on to dreams that would never see reality, she could be less formal. *Mick.*

"Is it short for Michael?" she asked.

He arched a dark brow. "Pardon?"

"Your name. Is it short for Michael? Is that the name that was registered at your birth?"

"My birth wasn't registered. My mum just called me Mick."

She'd never given any thought to the fact that there were those for whom records were not kept. Her ancestry as well as Kip's were charted back generations, their births heralded, applauded, blessed. While Mick's had come about in secret and in disgrace. Suddenly it seemed wrong that any child should be looked upon with shame, as though it were responsible for its existence. "It's a strong name."

"I think it was Ettie Trewlove's husband's."

"She's a widow, then."

179

"She is."

"I'm sorry. It's sad for a woman to lose her man."

He nodded. "She didn't marry him for property, title, position or wealth, as he possessed none of those things. But he did possess her heart."

She was touched by his words. She'd not expected such sentiments from him. "You're a romantic, deep down."

"No. A realist."

"A realist who waltzes like a dream." She couldn't have spoken truer words. As he swept her over the floor, his movements were smooth, confident, poised. Never before had she been treated to such exceptional dancing. She had no fear he would step on her slippered feet. "Where did you learn?"

"From my first lover."

A bubble of self-conscious laughter burst forth. She could scarcely believe he'd tossed out the words so matter-of-factly, as though discussing one's paramours was not scandalous in the extreme. "Ah, I suppose I should appreciate the honesty." Even if she didn't want to think about him in the arms of another woman. "She liked to waltz, did she?"

"Not particularly. She was the widow of a

duke, liked a bit of the rough, and I suited her purposes. The first time we came together, afterward, she offered me a quid, like I was a bloody whore."

She fought not to look appalled, and yet she was. Not so much by his crude words, although no one had ever spoken to her so bluntly before, but that his actions had been viewed as a service by a lady of the nobility. She was equally appalled a lady of high standing would seek such services. Men had carnal needs. That was understood, accepted. But ladies were above all that. Or so she'd always thought. Perhaps her latest wanton musings were not without merit. "It must have hurt your pride."

The words seem trite and stupid when voiced aloud. "I mean —"

"Don't make a fuss over it. I told you, a woman's passions are different from a child's. She was a young widow with a great deal of pent-up appetites. She wanted things from me in the bed. I wanted things from her out of it. So we struck a deal. She taught me how to dress for the position I wanted in the world — not the one I held. How to address my betters —"

She couldn't quite envision him thinking anyone was his better.

"— drink tea in a nobleman's parlor, dine

with a queen, waltz. In essence how to be a gentleman. I've yet to drink tea in a nobleman's parlor or dine with the queen, but perhaps an opportunity will yet present itself. Just as tonight, this moment is the first time I've put her dancing tutelage into practice."

He made her feel special in ways she hadn't since her own introduction to the queen. "I'm honored. Why wait so long?"

"Because there was no one with whom I wished to dance."

She nearly stumbled, might have, but his hold on her tightened fractionally, his gaze never wavering from hers. "A proper gentleman doesn't say something like that to a lady who is betrothed," she chastised.

"But I am not a proper gentleman."

"Yet you claim to want to be one, and that involves more than tea, dining and dancing. It involves knowing what is proper to say to a lady and what is not."

He bowed his head slightly. "I've made you uncomfortable. That was not my intent. It seems my lessons are lacking to some extent."

She suspected he knew precisely what he was about, what was acceptable conversation and what was not. Still, with no wish to insult him, she shook her head. "I may have overreacted. I'm not accustomed to harmless flirtation. From the moment I had my coming out, gentlemen knew I was spoken for, even if it wasn't formally announced yet. When they danced with me, we usually discussed the weather."

"They were idiots."

"They were behaving as gentlemen. Did your lady friend not teach you the acceptable topics of conversations?"

"I could make you blush if I shared with you the topics we discussed."

She should cease the discussion, yet she found herself intrigued by it. Kip never spoke to her about unsuitable subjects; he never spoke with her passionately, never made her blush with little more than an intense look, a smile, an innuendo. "I do hope you won't try. I don't blush prettily."

"You're blushing right now, and I've never been so mesmerized."

"Mr. Trewlove —"

"Mick."

"Mick."

"I like the way my name sounds on your lips."

"Please don't do this."

"Don't do what precisely, Lady Aslyn?"

Make me wish I wasn't yet betrothed, make me question the passion I feel for Kip — or the lack of it. They were friends. They'd always been friends. How often had the duchess told her that a fortunate woman married her dearest friend? That a deep and binding love might not be there in the beginning but it would arrive with time. "We're moving into inappropriate waters."

"If you were offended, you'd move out of my arms."

"I was taught not to bring embarrassment to my host."

"Is that the only reason?"

"No. I'm indebted to the widowed duchess. You are a marvelous partner. You make me feel as though I'm waltzing on clouds."

His eyes darkened with his pleasure, even as their intensity increased. She had the fleeting thought that if the music never ceased its playing, she wouldn't object. And yet it did end, the final strains of the melody drifting away.

Releasing his hand, stepping back, she fought not to have a sense of loss as the distance between them grew. "Thank you for the dance." She said it as kindly, yet as dismissively as she could. For her own sake and as a reminder to herself regarding where her loyalties resided.

"It was my pleasure."

"I daresay I really have kept you too long

from your other guests. I'm certain there are numerous ladies who will seek you out for a dance now that they've witnessed the grace with which you command the dance floor."

"Then they will face disappointment."

She didn't know how to respond. He said things she longed for Kip to utter. What a beastly fiancée she was, to compare her betrothed with a man she barely knew and certainly could never marry. After giving him a small smile, she made her way off the dance floor, grateful he didn't attempt to accompany or follow her.

She needed to find Kip. Where the devil was he? He'd been gone far too long, and she suspected he'd gotten up to some mischief. She was grateful when she spied Fancy talking with a slender man who possessed the most vibrant red hair she'd ever seen.

The girl's face brightened. "Lady Aslyn, allow me to introduce Mr. Tittlefitz."

"It's a pleasure," she said.

His cheeks flushed so deep a red that his freckles nearly disappeared. "My lady."

"Are you enjoying yourself?" Fancy asked.

"I am indeed, but I seem to have lost my escort. I wondered if you'd seen him about."

"Not since he wandered off to the card

room with my brothers. Although I have seen them here and there, as cards never seem to hold their interest for very long. I suspect because they probably lose their hard-earned coins too rapidly. I daresay if Lord Kipwick is still playing, he must be frightfully skilled at winning."

"Would you mind directing me to the card room, then?" If Kip was still there, perhaps she could convince him to set aside the cards in favor of a dance with her.

"I'll escort you," Mr. Tittlefitz said.

"Thank you."

Unlike Mick, he didn't offer his arm or stand so near to her that she could inhale his fragrance. "I'm to understand you're Mr. Trewlove's secretary."

"Yes, m'lady."

"That must involve an inordinate amount of work."

"I'd do anything the man asked of me without complaint. I'm alive only because of him."

His words stopped her in her tracks. "How so?"

"People think because my father wouldn't marry my mother that I must have inherited his low morals. Or hers, for being bedded by a man to whom she was not wed. The only work I could find was on the docks."

186

He looked down on himself. "And as you can see, I'm not built for hauling cargo. I usually got let go before I got paid. I was fourteen, thinking of doing something I ought not, something that would prove I was indeed cut from the same cloth as the man who sired me, something that, if I were caught, would see me on the gallows. Mr. Trewlove heard of my plight somehow. Dunno. Maybe my mum told his mum. We lived in the same squalid area. Anyway, he offered to hire a tutor for me and told me if I could learn everything I needed to learn within a year, I'd never go hungry. He provided for my mum so we had a roof over our head and food in our bellies. Not a lot but enough. I learned everything I needed to learn. Became his secretary. I wanted to pay him back, too. Every penny that it had cost him during that year when he took a chance on me. He instructed me to use my money to help some other lad. If you owe Mick Trewlove, you pay him back by helping someone else. And here I am blathering on and on when I'm supposed to be taking you to the card room."

"You admire him."

"No better man as far as I'm concerned." He ducked his head slightly as though embarrassed by his vehement support of his employer. "Card room's just up here."

As impressed as she was with the hotel, she was more impressed with what she'd just learned about Mick Trewlove. A man who had gained so much yet continued to reach back to pull others up after him. In comparison, the frocks no longer in style or with which she'd grown bored that she donated to charity seemed a rather paltry effort at improving the state of the world.

She followed Mr. Tittlefitz down the corridor and into a room that wasn't nearly as well-lit as the ballroom. A smoky haze burned her eyes. There were several circular tables around which men and women sat while cards were tossed in front of them.

"Can I help you with anything else?" Mr. Tittlefitz asked.

"No, thank you. I should be able to make my way from here." If Kip was within these walls, she'd find him, and if he wasn't, well, she wasn't certain what she'd do then, except perhaps have the carriage brought around and see herself home. She didn't believe he'd leave without her, but at that moment she didn't know what to think, except to feel a measure of frustration with him for abandoning her completely for so long.

She wandered around the tables. Coins

and paper currency were heaped in the center of some. Footmen hurried about, not carrying trays, but carrying bottles, continually filling glasses as they were emptied. Some men puffed on cigars while others smoked a pipe. She saw two ladies — although *ladies* might have been a generous identifier — holding very thin cheroots between their lips. Amid harsh curses, raucous laughter filled the air, along with the thickening smoke as she journeyed farther into the bowels of lessening refinement.

Earlier, when Mick had told her about those he'd invited to his affair, she'd admired the fact that he didn't divide people into social classifications, that he welcomed the less well-to-do as equals to the affluent. It seemed an open-minded approach, far different from the narrow one under which she'd been raised. She'd thought him progressive, but now she felt remarkably uneasy and out of place in these environs. She didn't belong here. Not because these people were beneath her — they weren't. But they were more worldly, more experienced, more daring. They took risks. The ladies especially, not caring that they remain above reproach. They had freedom while she'd never felt more confined. She needed to leave, was desperate to do so, but she couldn't desert Kip. She had to find him, which meant moving forward, aware of the stares landing on her, the whispers. Holding her head high, she fought not to give the impression she was uncomfortable here, didn't want anyone to take offense, to think she considered herself better.

Then she spied Kip at a corner table, looking vastly different from the stylish gentleman who had walked through the front door with her. His disheveled hair stuck up on the ends as though he'd plowed his fingers through it repeatedly. His eyes were red and held a desperation she'd never seen. He lifted his gaze from the table, caught sight of her, and relief washed over his features, giving him the appearance of a much younger man, the teasing, playful one she'd come to love. Shoving back his chair, he stood and waved her over. She couldn't deny the gladness that swept through her at his enthusiasm for having her near.

When she was close enough, he snaked his arm around her waist, drew her against his side and whispered in her ear, "I need your pearls."

"I beg your pardon?"

"I have an incredible hand. I know no one can best me, but the blighter who is playing me has raised the stakes, well aware I no longer have the means to cover it. If I can't match his wager, I'll lose by default. Your pearls will ensure I don't."

She slapped her hand to the necklace at her throat. "These belonged to my mother and her mother before her."

"You're not going to lose the necklace. I just need it as a sign of good faith to cover my wager. You don't even have to take it off. Please, Aslyn. It's a small thing to ask, and the rewards will be beyond compare."

She assumed the rewards would be the money piled in the center of the table. There were five other gents sitting around it, but only one was still holding cards.

"I have a plan," he said. "I promise you will walk out of here wearing them."

She hesitated. *The best laid plans . . .*

"If you love me . . ." he said, his voice low.

"You know I do."

"Splendid." He retook his seat, met the gaze of the man sitting opposite him, the one wearing an ill-fitting brown jacket and tapping his cards on the table. "Her pearls should cover it."

The man opened his mouth, ran his tongue over his teeth, one of them very nearly all black. She fought not to shudder

191

at the sight. "They real?"

"Of course they are," Kip said. "What use would she have for fake ones?"

The man lifted his burly shoulders until they nearly touched extremely large ears that reminded her of an elephant's. "All right, then. Since you called —"

"Actually, now that it's settled we're even, I'm going to raise you — her hair comb. Pearls and diamonds."

"Kip —" she began.

He held up a hand to silence her objection. "Not to worry. I have the situation well in hand."

"What's it worth?" Brown Coat asked.

"A hundred quid."

Brown Coat laughed, a mocking sound that grated on Aslyn's nerves. She didn't know this game, didn't understand quite what was happening. Would Kip win if the man didn't pay that amount? Was that his plan? To reverse the tables and win by default?

"All right, mate. In for a penny, in for a pound." He picked up a handful of coins and tossed them negligently into the pile as though they were worth nothing. "Let's see what ye got."

Aslyn held her breath even though she had no idea what a winning hand might look like. Kip set down three cards and announced, "Three aces."

"Not bad," Brown Coat said.

He laid down the rest of his cards. "And two threes."

Brown Coat's eyes widened and he grinned. "Not bad at all."

Did that mean Kip had won? His theatrics at displaying his cards made her think he did indeed have a very good hand.

"I can see why you was willing to risk so much," Brown Coat said. "Unfortunately, for the lady, I'm holding . . ." He flipped his cards one at a time onto the table. "Four eights."

Kip didn't laugh or shout with joy. Instead he seemed to shrink before her, his shoulders rounding.

"Kip?"

With a shaking hand, he reached for his glass and tossed back the amber contents.

"Spud, take me winnin's from the lady."

Spud was much thinner than his friend, and she wondered if his motley face had anything to do with his name. While he looked regretful approaching her, she still didn't want him touching her. "I'll do it," she announced, and, without hesitation, reached back and unlatched her necklace. Carefully she pulled the comb from her

193

hair. With the reverence they deserved, she placed them gently on the table.

Kip twisted his head up. "Have you anything else on you?"

He could not be serious. And yet he appeared to be deadly so. "No. I believe it's time we went home."

He shook his head. "Aslyn, all I need is one more chance. I was so close. All I need is one more hand."

Was this the future he was planning for them? What about the investors he'd been so keen to meet? This creature to whom she'd handed over her pearls and comb could not be a successful businessman. He'd never be allowed in the duke's parlor to discuss investments.

"It's time for you to leave, my friend," Mick said, as he wrapped his hand around Kip's arm. Although the words may have come across as a suggestion, there was a steeliness in his tone that indicated they were a command. She wondered how long he'd been standing there, if he'd witnessed her humiliation. If so, he gave no indication, seemed merely intent on the task at hand, getting Kip to his feet.

Kip didn't object, but he did stagger back once he was standing. "I lost to a bloody bricklayer. He probably can't even read."

There was a slurring to his words she hadn't noticed before. "You're foxed."

"No, but the room is spinning. What an odd thing to put in a hotel. A spinning room."

"Your betrothed is correct, my lord," Mick said. "It's time you were away."

It became clear rather quickly, when Kip rammed into a table, that he couldn't walk a straight line without assistance. Mick provided it once again.

"Lead the way," he instructed her.

She nodded. Much better to march forward than to follow behind, while Kip stumbled, in spite of the support the hotel owner provided him. Avoiding eye contact with anyone, she charged straight ahead, grateful when she finally burst through into the hallway where there was less smoke and she could at last breathe again, and her eyes weren't smarting. She blinked back the tears and they didn't return. She would not think about what she had lost. She would not.

If her parents' deaths had taught her anything, it was that nothing was to be gained in mourning what could not be changed, in railing against it. Anger, tears, fists did not alter an outcome once it was realized.

When they reached the lobby, she spied

Fancy near the stairs where she'd first seen Mick and spun around, obviously catching him by surprise because he nearly rammed into her, in spite of his sagging burden. "If you'll give me a moment, I wish to say goodbye to your sister."

He nodded. "I'll take him outside, send someone to fetch your carriage."

"Thank you." She strolled toward the stairs.

Fancy left the group of people to whom she was speaking and gazed toward the door. "Is his lordship all right?"

"He's imbibed a bit too much."

"I don't understand why men do that. It's such a silly thing."

"Yes, well, we're leaving now, and I just wanted to say that it was a pleasure to see you again."

"I do hope you'll come to my bookshop when it opens."

"I look forward to it. Good night, Fancy."

"Safe journey home, Aslyn. And sleep well."

She doubted she was going to do that. When she got outside, she was grateful to see the carriage was already there. Mick Trewlove stood there empty-handed. She assumed he'd already stuffed Kip inside.

"Thank you for inviting us. You have an

extraordinary hotel here, Mr. Trewlove. We wish you great success with it and all your future endeavors."

"That sounds like a forever sort of goodbye, Lady Aslyn."

"I think it unlikely our paths will cross much in the future."

"One never knows what the future might hold." He held out his hand. She placed hers in it. Such strength there, such warmth, such surety. He handed her up into the carriage, and she settled on the squabs opposite Kip, who was slumped into a corner.

"He's going to have a devil of a headache in the morning," Mick said.

"Good."

He grinned. "You have a vindictive nature, Lady Aslyn."

"Until this moment, I'd have not thought so. I hope it's only temporary, as it's not a very pleasant trait."

"Sometimes life calls for unpleasantries. Good night." He closed the door, yelled up to the driver and the carriage took off.

She refrained from looking out the window, looking back to see if he was still watching her. For some unfathomable reason, she didn't want him to dismiss her and merely go on his merry way. But neither did she want him to know she was indeed vindictive. She kicked Kip in the shin.

"Damnation!" he blurted, stirred, straightened a tad and glared at her through one eye.

"You lost my mother's pearls and comb."

"I'll purchase replacements."

"They won't be the same. I treasured them not because of what they were but where they came from. I have so little of her, hardly any memories at all."

"I'm sorry, Aslyn. I thought I would win. Instead I lost everything I had on me."

"How much?"

"A thousand pounds."

She stared disbelievingly at him. "What were you doing with that much money on you?"

"I thought to go to the club afterward. The money is inconsequential."

"I don't think so."

"I lost my pocket watch."

"The one your father gave you when you reached your majority?"

"Don't tell him," he whined, and snuggled deeper into the corner.

A timepiece that had been passed down through at least three generations. "I don't understand how you could gamble everything away."

"Because you don't know what it feels like."

"To lose?"

"To win." Shoving himself away from his little hovel, he leaned earnestly toward her. "You can't imagine it. Your heart pounds so hard you can hear the blood rushing through your ears. There is an elation in your mind that makes it seem the entire universe is expanding. Your nerve endings tingle and become incredibly sensitive. Every sensation, every emotion is heightened. It's like nothing else. It's like being alive."

Only she'd felt devastated, dead, handing over her pearls. "You must stop. You can't continue doing this after we're married."

Slowly he blinked, as though having a difficult time processing her words. They should probably wait until liquor wasn't sloshing through his veins, but the anger and disappointment were roiling through her now, and she was having a difficult time containing them.

"Are you forbidding me?" he asked incredulously.

"Yes, I believe I am."

"Wives do not forbid."

"Husbands honor their wives' requests if they want accord in their marriage."

199

"Not when they're unreasonable."

"You lost your father's watch. You lost a thousand quid. You lost my pearls, my comb — all in a single night. I'll not have the money in my trust frittered away after we're married."

"I'm not going to give up my life. I'm not going to become my father, always doting on my mother to the exclusion of all else, including his own son. You can't expect it of me, and if you do, you're going to be sadly disappointed."

"No, I don't think I shall be disappointed, as I very much doubt I'm going to marry you if you're not willing to forgo this incessant gambling." The words came out unbidden, tightening her stomach into a knot, and yet she could not deny the truth of them. She knew beyond any doubt that she would not find happiness with the man — drunk, disheveled and demanding — who was currently sitting across from her.

"You're being absurd," he stated. "Overreacting. I enjoy gambling. It's harmless. It's not as though I'm going to be beating you."

The conversation was deteriorating quickly, upsetting her even more. Not once had she considered him capable of this unflattering demeanor. "I never thought you would, but you hurt me tonight. And embarrassed me, as well as yourself. You made a spectacle of us both."

"To a bunch of commoners whose opinions have no merit. They're nothing — oh, dear God." Bracing his hand on her seat, he lowered his head.

"What? What's wrong?"

"I'm going to cast up my accounts."

"Stop! Stop!" she shouted as she banged on the ceiling.

The carriage came to a halt. Kip flung open the door and staggered out. She heard him retching, felt rather ill herself. The man traveling with her was not one she could admire. She couldn't even claim to like him, to enjoy his company.

She feared she may have become betrothed to a man she didn't really know. More, she feared the man she'd witnessed tonight was the true Kip — and that man she could not marry.

Some hours later, after everyone had left, all the lights had been doused and silence wove itself through all the rooms, Mick stood at the window in his library and gazed out on the night, slowly pulling the pearls on a serpentine path through his fingers. He could well imagine he felt the warmth from her neck still pulsating through the white.

He'd never had much respect for the aristocracy. Bloody toffs who were given so much, didn't appreciate it and tended to lose it with such ease, as though it were of no consequence and more was to be found with the snap of fingers. In his desk drawer were half a dozen markers attesting to that attitude. Also in that desk drawer now rested a gold pocket watch that bore an intricate engraving of a stag, similar to the one that occupied a corner of the Hedley crest. Perhaps one day he would attach the chain that accompanied it to a button of his waistcoat and tuck the watch into the small pocket where he could easily reach it, gaze down on it and mark the time.

Tonight his focus was on the pearls. He knew the moment she realized they were lost to her. She'd been devastated. He'd seen the shattering in her eyes, then gone, with little more than a blink. If he hadn't been watching so closely, he'd have missed it. But he had been watching, studying her all night, searching for weaknesses — and all he'd found were strengths.

He'd wanted to applaud when she reached up and unlatched the pearls from about her neck. Spud didn't realize how lucky he was that she'd taken the initiative. If he'd touched her, Mick would have broken his fingers or at the very least punched the man. He wouldn't have been deserving of either treatment. Spud had been following the bricklayer's orders to gather the winnings, but Mick recognized that where Lady Aslyn was concerned, he seemed to lack the ability to think with any rationality.

When she had walked from the room with her head held high, her shoulders back, her spine straight — in spite of the mortification that the drunkard Mick had been dragging along had caused her — he thought he'd never seen anyone with more regal bearing. And the lady — a true lady, if ever there was one — despite everything, had taken the time to say a few words of farewell to his sister.

Kipwick was undeserving of her. He wondered if she might realize it before it was too late. Or if it would be left to him to prove it to her.

He'd once thought her crucial to his scheme of bringing about Hedley's downfall. Now he feared that she might very well lead to his.

CHAPTER 10

Aslyn awoke to sunshine pouring in through her bedchamber window. She hadn't expected that. With such a heavy heart, she should be greeted with rain, an abundance of it gushing down in sheets that hampered visibility. Heaving a deep sigh, she shoved herself up and settled against the pillows. Last night, she'd instructed Nan to bring her breakfast. She couldn't face the duke across the dining table.

Fortunately neither he nor the duchess had been waiting for her when she returned home, so they'd been spared wondering why their son didn't escort her inside. After his bout of retching, he'd clambered back into the carriage, curled up on the seat and begun to snore loudly as though her threat of calling things off mattered little. For all of a heartbeat, she'd considered waking him so they could finish their conversation and come to some sort of terms or an understanding, but she'd been unable to rely on any rational discourse in his current state. She'd have to wait for him to sober up.

Upon arriving at the residence, she'd made a hasty retreat from the carriage, leaving him to see his own self home, where she assumed his servants would either assist in getting him inside or simply leave him to sleep it off in his conveyance. She rather hoped for the latter. He'd betrayed her trust, proved himself unworthy of her affections.

Where he was concerned, how could she have been such a fool? While she'd been brought up to expect marriage, to see becoming a wife and mother as her duty, presently she wasn't convinced she wanted it. Never before had Kip shown such blatant disregard for her feelings.

With a deep sigh, she scrubbed her hands over her face. Melancholy didn't suit her. She was weary of being so passive, of waiting for life to happen to her. She was as dependent on Kip for her happiness as he was on his damned cards and wagering for his own. When he had described what it was to win, all she'd been able to think was that the same things happened to her when she was near Mick Trewlove. She wasn't exactly sure precisely what that meant. The man confused her in ways she'd never even known existed.

And with whom could she discuss all these confounding feelings, the ones about Kip whom she'd once admired and whose actions she now detested, Mick whom Society insisted she shun because of his birth, and yet she'd grown to admire?

She couldn't seek advice from the duchess, couldn't tell her about her son's abhorrent behavior nor could she reveal what a gentleman she found Mick Trewlove to be. So who was there for her to talk to? She'd been raised in near isolation at the ducal estate until it was time to have a Season. She'd met other ladies, but she hadn't become close to them; they didn't share intimacies, only gossip. Kip was the one to whom she'd always spoken before, had shared her doubts and fears, her hopes and dreams. She felt as though he'd squashed them, torn them up, cast them aside and in so doing had cast her aside as well, with little thought, and anger, and words that could never be unheard.

Tossing back the covers, she scrambled out of bed, unable to abide this moping about. She was going to join the duke for breakfast. She was going to find a purpose to her life that didn't involve marriage. She was going to determine how best to help Kip realize he needed to leave the gambling tables before they destroyed him. She wouldn't abandon him, but neither could she embrace him, not as he'd been last night, not as he may have been many nights before.

A soft rap sounded on her door just before Nan opened it and walked inside carrying a tray. "I thought you wanted breakfast in bed."

Oh dear. She couldn't very well not eat in her room after putting her servant to such bother. "I'll have it in the sitting area."

Nan set it on the low table before turning to face her, looking rather guilty as she did. "Another package arrived for you — same as before. Well, not quite. It wasn't the same gent who delivered it but a scruffy little lad who was told to give it only to me and I was to give it only to you." She held out a leather box, similar in shape to the other, but larger.

Aslyn took it, opened it. On a small card was written: *A lady should never be separated from her pearls.*

She lifted out the note. Beneath it rested her necklace and comb. There was a pain in the center of her chest, a tight knot as though her heart were being squeezed tighter and tighter. Her eyes burned more than they had when she'd walked into the smoke-hazed card room. More than they had when she'd realized Kip had not kept his promise to her, that he had in fact lost the wager.

Mick Trewlove was showing her a kindness that her own betrothed had failed to do. A second man was stepping into her life while the first was stepping out of it. Confusion rocked her. She felt as though she were perched on the deck of a ship in the midst of a tempest. She had no business whatsoever thinking about Mick, but the horrible realization struck her that she had no desire to think about Kip.

Still, two hours later she found herself standing in the foyer of Kip's town house.

"I'm sorry, m'lady," his butler said, true sorrow reflected in his tone, "but his lordship is quite under the weather today."

Glancing up the stairs, she wondered if she looked hard enough if she might see him suffering. She needed to speak with him; they needed to get things sorted out. Too much had been said, too much left unsaid. "Let him know I came by, and that I expect him to call on me as soon as he is able."

"Yes, m'lady."

She turned to go, stopped, swung back around. "Is he often under the weather?"

Clearing his throat, the butler looked down as though needing to check the polish on his shoes. His silence revealed his loyalty as well as providing the answer.

"My apologies. I've put you on the spot. I'll be certain to let him know you hold his trust."

"Thank you, m'lady."

She walked out with her two maids following. All her life she'd listened and adhered to the duchess's admonishments that dangers loomed afield, and she must never stray far from the familiar. Yet it was the familiar causing her heartache. She needed to help Kip, but she didn't know how. Although she thought she might have a good idea regarding where to begin.

She waited on tenterhooks until the residence was completely quiet and absolutely still. Eerily so. She ignored Nan's warnings and declined her maid's offer to accompany her. If something went awry, she didn't want her loyal servant to be faulted. Besides, there was a thrill to walking out of the residence unaccompanied. Until the precise moment when the door closed behind her and she found herself standing alone on the

209

stoop, she didn't realize she'd never ventured forth without a cadre of servants waiting for her or following in her wake, or Kip offering his arm.

But tonight it was only she. Well, she and the hansom driver waiting at the end of the long drive that now echoed her hurried footsteps. She'd made the arrangements earlier in the afternoon when she'd supposedly gone shopping. Instead she'd been scouting out her options for making a clandestine escape.

An unfortunate word that, but there were numerous ways to be caged and not all of them came with steel bars or locked doors.

The driver tipped his hat and opened the door as she approached. "Miss."

"Thank you, sir, for meeting me."

"Not often I get paid double in advance of the journey."

Her earlier outing had included a visit to the bank in which she had an account where a small bit of money from a trust her father had set up for her was deposited each month — so she had some spending money. Most of the monthly allotment went to the duke so he could oversee her needs without causing a burden to his own family. When she married, it would go to her husband. If she were unmarried at twenty-five, it would all begin coming to her. Until last night she'd never contemplated the final option. But now it loomed clear and welcome.

As she placed her hand in the one the driver extended to her, a quiver of foreboding shimmied through her. If she was going to change her mind, now was the time to do it. Instead, she took a deep breath, climbed up and settled onto the seat. The door closed with a rather loud snap that gave her a little start.

"Where to, miss?"

She gave him the address.

"I'll have you there in a thrice." The driver climbed up. The horse took off.

She pulled the hood of her pelisse up over her head, not that she thought where she was going anyone would recognize her, but it seemed the sort of thing a lady traveling alone should do: hide her identity as much as possible. A lady going about without a chaperone was no lady at all.

A chill hung in the air, or perhaps it was simply fear making her bones cold. All the responsibility rested with her, weighed on her. What if she'd judged Mick incorrectly, what if he was exactly the sort of rapscallion the duchess had warned her about, a man who would take advantage of a woman alone? With two sisters, how could he be?

How could he look them in the eye if he treated another woman poorly?

It was nearing eleven. Few people were out but more than she expected wandered about. She'd often returned from a ball late at night but never given any heed to what was going on around her. Now she wondered who these people were. Why were they not abed? What entertainments did they find?

She saw the hotel long before they reached it. It stood out like a talisman. The carriage came to a halt, and she realized she had one more chance to change her mind, to instruct him to carry on, to take her home. Instead, when he opened the door, she allowed him to hand her down.

"I'll wait till yer safely inside."

She wasn't quite sure she was going to be any safer inside than out here, but appreciated the sentiment. Marching up the steps, she saw the red-clad porter who was standing outside the double glass doors straighten his spine and touch his finger to his top hat. "Miss."

As long as she could remember, she'd been addressed as "my lady." No doubt the term had followed her into the crib. It was odd to have two gentlemen not refer to her as such, but then proper young ladies weren't expected to be skulking about at all hours of the night.

"I'm here to see Mr. Trewlove." It suddenly occurred to her that it was very likely he wasn't in residence. In which case it would turn out to be a good thing the hansom driver had remained.

"Top floor, miss." He pulled open one of the doors.

"He's in?" An inane thing to ask at that moment since he certainly wouldn't have provided entry if the person she was seeking wasn't about.

"Aye."

Giving a nod, she glanced back at the hansom and the driver waiting patiently. "Will you wait twenty minutes? I'll pay you for your time." Her visit shouldn't take any longer than that.

"My pleasure, miss. And don't you be worrying about the additional fee. You've more than covered my time already."

"Thank you!" With a little wave, she turned back and strolled inside.

A man stood behind the desk where guests received the keys to their rooms. "Evening, miss."

"I'm here to see Mr. Trewlove." At this rate, all of London was going to know she was here and who she'd come to visit. She really hadn't given this part of her plan adequate thought. Obviously organizing clandestine meetings wasn't her forte.

She started up the sweeping staircase and climbed, climbed, climbed until there were no more red-carpeted steps, only a long hallway with several closed wooden doors and one glass one. Etched in the glass was *Trewlove.* As it was nearest to her, and she could see a light shining from within the depths beyond, she decided to start there.

The door silently opened into a sitting area with a large desk where she suspected Mr. Tittlefitz worked while people waited to have an audience with Mick. She assumed that was the owner's office farther inside. The door was open. She crept toward it —

He sat behind a desk of dark wood, almost ebony in color, twice the size of Tittlefitz's. He wore no jacket or waistcoat or cravat. The buttons at his throat were undone, the sleeves of his white shirt rolled up past his elbows as though he were in the thick of laboring. His hair curled in disarray. Little bits of shadow just above and below his beard hinted he had not shaved recently. He seemed rough, dangerous, a product of his origins. Her mind betrayed her with the thought that she'd never seen anyone look so marvelously masculine and alluring.

He was reading from a stack of papers, occasionally scratching a pen over the parchment. The sight of him did funny things to her insides, as though a thousand butterflies were fluttering around. He went to dip his pen into the inkwell, paused, lifted his head, pierced her with his blue gaze, and it was like the one time she'd dared to climb a tree, fallen from her perch and hit the ground hard. She struggled to draw in breath, thought it would forever be denied to her — and then it swooshed back in with a sweet, delicious ache.

Slowly, so slowly that his movements were almost imperceptible, he set down his pen and came to his feet. "Lady Aslyn."

His voice was raw, as though he'd not had anything to drink in a century, although there was a glass of amber liquid on his desk, near the edge of the papers, within easy reach. Perhaps whatever he'd been sipping had burned his throat.

"Mr. Trewlove."

He darted a glance toward the windows as though to confirm it was still night beyond these walls. His gaze came back to her. "How might I be of service?"

Gathering her resolve, she marched forward and set the leather box in the center of his desk. "A lady cannot accept such a precious gift from a gentleman with whom she is merely an acquaintance."

Slowly his deep blue gaze traveled over her, seeming to halt a fraction of a second at each button, each ribbon, each clasp. "The last time you returned a gift to me, you had a solicitor handle the matter."

She noticed a small leather box on the corner of his desk. Was it the cameo? Did he keep it visible as a reminder that she'd rejected his overture? But if he were bothered by it, surely he wouldn't have given her a tour or danced with her. "At the time, I didn't know where to find you."

He dropped his gaze to the box containing the pearls and comb, then looked at her through lowered lids. "It's not a gift but simply the return of something that belongs to you."

"I'm certain you had to pay to obtain it."

He gave a little shrug as if it were of no consequence. "Purchase it from me, then."

A hundred pounds alone for the comb. The pearls had probably been valued the same or perhaps more. She was quite certain it wasn't going to be an even swap, but she did long to have them. "How much?"

"A quid."

"I'm certain he charged you more. I have a thousand —"

"Have you taken leave of your senses?" he bellowed, the blue of his eyes reminding her of the hottest flames dancing in a fire. "You're walking about London at night with a thousand pounds on you?"

"No, I traveled in a hansom."

"And what if some bloke decided to stop that hansom and rob it? Rob you? Take that money off your pretty little person?"

Did he think she was pretty? He was angry with her, and yet she couldn't seem to be frightened by his belligerence. Rather it warmed her that he seemed to care about her safety, even though she felt she'd taken adequate precautions to ensure it. "Why would someone think I was worth robbing?"

"Because you're dressed in finery like a lady who might be silly enough to walk around London with a thousand quid stuffed in her —" He waved his hand at her as though he thought she might have stashed it in an unmentionable area.

"My reticule."

"Well, he'd have not stopped with the taking of it. He'd have given you a thorough search —"

She didn't care to hear where he might have searched. "As I said, I did not walk. Well, except up your steps, and then there was your man to look out for me."

The fury seemed to deflate out of him. "There are men around here who would kill for a thousand quid."

"I suspect there are some who would cheat for it, as well. Did your bricklayer cheat while playing cards with Kipwick?"

"No. My people know I don't tolerate cheating. I'd have let him go. A man who cheats at cards might cheat elsewhere, including in the work he gives me. Besides, my brothers were watching. The problem, Lady Aslyn, is that your fiancé bends his elbow as much as he holds the cards. Guzzling too much drink hampers a man's judgment, his ability to calculate the odds of winning."

She feared drinking wasn't the only problem Kip had. "Since he lost fair and square then, and you've offered to sell the items to me, tell me how much I owe you."

"I told you. A pound."

"I don't believe you."

He arched a dark brow over one of those beautiful blue eyes. "Are you calling me a liar?"

She angled up her chin. "Yes. I quite believe I am."

His laughter, deep and masculine, circled around her, sent the calming butterflies back into flight. "No one has ever dared call me a liar — at least not to my face."

"I just find it very difficult to believe the gent last night would be willing to settle for so little when he obviously knew the pieces were of value."

"He had no idea of their value. He based their worth on what he could tell about the lady who was wearing them. He knows quality when he sees it."

"What did he insist you pay in order to hand them over to you?"

"He owes me his livelihood. As a favor, he traded them to me for a quid."

She shook her head. "I can't give you only a quid. It doesn't seem right."

"I gave a crown to the lad who delivered them to Hedley Hall. You can reimburse me for that as well."

Stubborn man. If he really paid a quid, she'd eat the hood of her pelisse. Opening her reticule, she scrounged through it until she located the two coins she needed. She placed them on the desk, took the leather box and dropped it into her bag.

He left the coins where they were, tipped his head toward the corner of his desk, grinned. "You can purchase the cameo for a shilling."

She wasn't half tempted. "You paid a good deal more for it than that. I, too, recognize quality. And don't tell me the jeweler owes you his livelihood so he sold it to you on the cheap. It is frightfully pretty, though."

"My mum always longed to have a cameo, thought it was something posh ladies wore."

"You should give it to her, then."

"I've given her a dozen by now. Anytime I see one that's a little bit different, I pick it up for her. Makes it special that I was thinking of her when I bought it. I wasn't thinking of her when I purchased this one."

She felt her cheeks warm. He'd been thinking of her. It wasn't as though she hadn't known that fact. Still, having it voiced made it seem all the more scandalous, especially because she found herself wondering exactly what visions of her might have been prancing through his head at that time. "I can't accept it."

"Not even as a betrothal gift?"

Her cheeks warmed further, and she was surprised they didn't ignite. "That would be entirely inappropriate."

"Pity."

She glanced around the room, at the bookcase of ledgers, the one of books, a piece of wooden furniture that was naught but nooks, crannies and drawers in an assortment of sizes. In addition to the chair behind his desk, there were two in front of it. Black leather, thickly padded. Those who carried on business with him would be comfortable while doing it. The room was dimly lit, the only light coming from the lamp on his desk. She wondered why she hadn't noticed before. He had seemed to loom within her vision, to absorb her entire focus. "You have a very nice office." A corner one at that, with windows behind him and on the wall off to the side.

She wandered over to a side window and glanced out. It faced the street where the hansom had stopped. The driver was still waiting, even though she suspected twenty minutes had passed. Although he made not a sound, she was acutely aware of Mick coming to stand just behind her left shoulder. The room shrank with his nearness.

"That building across the street, on the corner, is that the one your sister wants for her bookshop?" Based on the windows, it was three stories in height and had a quaint appearance to it.

"It is."

"Are you going to let her have it?"

"If she truly desires it." His voice had gone lower, raspier, as though he were answering a different question entirely. His mouth was hovering extremely closely to the nape of her neck. She could feel his breath stirring loose tendrils of her hair.

Her mouth was suddenly dry. She couldn't have swallowed if her life depended on it.

"Why are you truly here, Aslyn?"

No formality. His use of only her name created an intimacy that was thick with promise. She shouldn't be here, and yet she seemed incapable of forcing herself to leave. Was this how Kip had felt at the table last night, when he'd been desperate for her pearls?

"You've been spending time with Kipwick."

"On a couple of occasions, yes. He had an interest in the questionable parts of London."

"I want you to dissuade him from traveling these paths that will lead him to ruin."

Although she gazed out on the street, and he was behind her, she was very much aware of him going very still. "I cannot prevent a man from seeking what he desires, but I can see he comes to no harm in his pursuits."

"You wield that much power within the darker realms of London?"

"They shaped me into what I am. Unlike Kipwick, I neither worship nor bow before them."

"Yet you make use of them."

"When it suits my purposes or the purposes of those who come to me seeking something that lies beyond their reach but is within my grasp to grant. Tell me, Aslyn, what do you desire?"

His low, mesmerizing voice shrouded her in a veil of trust. All the naughty images, the improper thoughts that plagued her when she let down her ladylike guard came rushing to the foreground. Images that inappropriately filled her mind when he was near. "Things to which I can give no voice."

"The darker pleasures, then."

His mouth, hot and moist, landed where her neck curved into her shoulder. Her eyes slid closed. His tongue lapped at her skin. Of its own accord, her head dropped back as heat sluiced through her, pooled in her belly, swirled lower to settle between her thighs.

His lips trailed along her throat. His hand cupped her cheek, turned her head slightly, tilted it up. His mouth retreated. Opening her eyes, she found herself staring into the blue depths of his.

"So many sins from which to choose," he rasped, just before lowering his mouth to hers.

With a gentle nudging of his tongue, he urged her to part her lips. She complied, and her world spun upside down as he explored the hidden depths with a fervor that matched her own. Here, here was the heat she'd expected of a kiss. The demand for more, the yearning for all.

His mouth was delicious and wicked and skilled. She didn't want to contemplate all the practicing it had taken to hone such remarkable talent. There was nothing cool, nothing proper, nothing distant in his actions. He was fully involved, devouring her mouth as though she alone provided sustenance, as though only through her could he be sated.

Her heart pounded with such ferocity that she was certain he had to feel it when he pulled her in closer, flattening her breasts against his broad chest. The blood rushed through her ears. Her nerve endings tingled, dampness formed between her thighs. There was a throbbing, a pulsing at her feminine core that urged her to press herself nearer. He growled, his vibrating chest sending ripples of pleasure coursing through her. She needed to put a name to what she was feeling, to the sensations bursting through her. An insane thought flashed through her mind.

The kiss felt like winning.

Kissing her was the best decision he'd ever

made in his life. Kissing her was the worst decision he'd ever made in his life.

He'd been intimate with women, but none had ever kissed him like this, as though their very existence relied on their mouths staying latched together, their tongues swirling, one part velvet, one part silk. Her moans and sighs urged him to take the kiss deeper, even as the soft sounds tightened his bollocks, hardened his shaft. Christ, he was in danger of spilling his seed without even feeling the dampness between her thighs that he was certain was waiting for him, hot and glistening with need.

From the moment he'd looked up from the contracts he'd been studying and seen her standing there, he'd wanted his mouth on hers, his hands on her back, her buttocks, her breasts. He had yet to move beyond the small of her back, to go further. He didn't want to frighten her with his needs, his longing to possess her.

Especially as his own yearnings scared the hell out of him.

She was no longer the means to an end, but had become the end itself. He was supposed to be cool and dispassionate in taking her. His purpose was to draw her in while keeping himself at a distance. Instead, she'd managed to entice him into a maelstrom of emotions and sensations, needs and desires, that were foreign to him.

He was a man accustomed to controlling his world, his fate, his destiny — yet where she was concerned, he'd lost his bearings. He felt as though she possessed a sledge-hammer and was knocking away his wall of indifference, brick by brick. How would he protect himself when they were all gone? He didn't know if he could find the resilience to stack the bricks back up.

She smelled so bloody good, like flowers after a rain. Her fragrance was probably taken from a single blossom, but he knew little of plant names. Flowers were pretty to look at, but he had no time for learning the details about them. Yet at that moment he had an insane need to smell every bloom he came across until he found the one that matched her scent.

Sliding his hands beneath her pelisse, he cradled her sides, her back. So narrow, so delicate, so fragile. He suddenly realized he would hate the man who took her innocence from her — even if it was he.

Drawing back, he was surprised to discover his breathing was labored and harsh. Hers might have been the same, but he hardly noticed. Instead, he was arrested by the sight of her swollen, damp lips and the intense heat in her eyes. He saw the cooling, the arrival of confusion, quickly followed by horror.

Staggering back, she slammed her shoulder against the edge of the window casing, grimaced, shuffled away, her hand coming up to cover the mouth he was desperate to once again plunder. Then she spun on her heel and ran.

CHAPTER 11

Dear God in heaven! What had she done? What had she allowed him to do? Allowed? She'd wanted, encouraged, taunted and. teased him into doing it.

She dashed down the stairs. So many blasted stairs. Why did he have to build a hotel with five floors? Were there really that many people in need of lodgings for a single night?

She hated that she had enjoyed the kiss so much, that it had stirred things within her that Kip's hadn't. She could barely remember Kip's. It had been as nothing while Mick's had been as everything. Her body had responded as though he held the key to unlocking her soul. Never before had she been so terrified, confused . . . shamed, because every inch of her demanded she return to him and let him finish what he'd begun. To lay her out for his pleasure, to touch her in ways she yearned for even though she didn't know precisely what they were. But he knew. He knew how to lure, entice, deliver.

So many sins from which to choose.

She found herself wanting to experience the gravest of all: giving herself to a man without benefit of marriage.

Love was supposed to center a person. No, this wasn't love. Far from it. It was passion and desire; it was animalistic instincts. Humans mated. Men had barbaric cravings that women were charged with keeping in check. It was the reason men sowed wild oats while women embroidered samplers. They had different needs, different purposes. Men were weak when it came to the flesh, women strong.

So why had she nearly melted into a puddle at his feet?

Finally, she reached the lobby.

"Is everything all right, miss?" the gent behind the desk asked, but she ignored him, drew up the hood on her pelisse.

The porter who stood beyond the glass doors must have heard her coming, because he looked back and opened the door for her. She rushed through, hurried down the steps and stopped short. The hansom was gone. Of course it was. The driver had stayed longer than twenty minutes, but he couldn't wait here all night. He was needed elsewhere. Especially as a light mist had begun falling.

Wandering beyond sight of the door, she leaned against the front of the building past the steps, below the eaves. She wondered how long before a hansom might pass by. Ages, she suspected. There was no theater to draw crowds. It was late. Who would think to come here to look for a woman in need of rescue?

Moving away from the wall and peering around the corner, she called up to the porter, "Where might I find a hansom?"

"I don't rightly know, miss." The door opened, and he hopped aside as Mick charged through it — properly done up with a knotted neck cloth, waistcoat and jacket — and started down the steps. "Would you like me to go search for one for you?"

"No need, Jones," Mick called back to the servant. "I'll see the lady home."

She retreated three steps as he neared. "That's not necessary. I can see myself home. I just need to locate a hansom."

"My carriage will be here in a thrice. I've already sent for it."

"I don't think that's wise, considering." The thought of being in a cramped conveyance with him where she could smell his marvelously masculine scent was unnerving.

Seemingly oblivious to the mist drifting down from the heavens, he leaned a shoulder against the wall. "I'm fairly certain you wish me to apologize, but an apology would imply I was sorry. I'm not. I've wanted to kiss you from the moment I met you."

She felt as though he'd slammed his mouth back against hers. Warmth infused her, her lungs deserted her, and her ability to respond had gone on holiday.

"It's the reason I made the wager with Kipwick in order to have you attend my affair," he continued.

The words were a jolt, knocking her out of her stunned state even as they carried her further into it. "What wager?"

"He didn't tell you?"

He did not. Her anger with Kip continued to grow. She was going to smack him the next time she saw him — for so many reasons. "He said you invited us to your affair."

His shoulder lifted, dropped. "I suppose those words contain some truth."

But not the entire truth. She heard it in his tone. "What is the whole truth, Mr. Trewlove?"

"I do wish you'd call me Mick, especially

after the intimacy we shared, the scorching kiss you delivered."

"I delivered?"

"I can still taste you."

Was it because of his lowborn status that he spoke of things that shouldn't be voiced aloud? "You shouldn't say such things."

"They embarrass you."

"Of course they do. They're improper."

"Not between two people with feelings for each other."

Jerking her head to the side, she gazed down the dark street. Lamps had yet to be installed. There was naught but construction, and she couldn't make out any of the details. She wanted to deny she had feelings for him, but she couldn't when she felt something, yet couldn't identify exactly what it was she was experiencing. The kiss had made her aware of things she'd never before felt, had made her want to follow wherever it might have led — even as she had a very strong understanding that it might have led to a bedchamber. She'd never felt that way with Kip, had never envisioned tangled bodies among tangled sheets, but then he'd never kissed her as though his life depended on tasting every aspect of her.

Her thoughts were brought back to the

problem at hand as a carriage pulled by four horses came around the corner and drew to a halt in front of the hotel. Mick shoved himself away from the wall. "Let me take you home."

"No, I'll find a hansom."

He sighed. "I won't touch you. I give you my word."

As though that was her worry. Her concern was that she might not be able to resist touching him. He was sin and danger and desire, liberating urges within her that had never known freedom, urges she feared wouldn't be content to be locked away without experiencing fully what he'd offered. "You shouldn't have to go to all that bother."

"It's no bother. I have some appointments I need to keep." A corner of his mouth hitched up. "Dark pleasures and all that. They're best seen to at night."

Was he headed to a brothel or a mistress after delivering that blistering kiss to her? What did it matter? He was not for her, nor was she for him. Not when all was said and done. "No, thank you. I'll find a hansom. There has to be one around here somewhere."

Another sigh, this one riffed with impatience, maybe a bit of disappointment.

"Take the carriage, then. I won't go with you."

"No, I won't inconvenience you, keep you from your appointments." Even as she loathed the thought that they very likely did involve another woman.

"You're a stubborn wench."

She'd never considered herself as such. It was odd, the various previously hidden aspects he brought out in her. "I suppose I can be when the situation warrants."

Another deep sigh, this one fraught with defeat. She'd have thought him a man to never surrender. "I'll send my man to find a hansom. It may take a while. At least come inside while you wait, where it's dry and warm. There's a parlor off the lobby. Imagine a fire blazing."

Although the rain wasn't hitting her directly, she'd grown chilled standing there with the mist circling about. "Yes, all right. Thank you."

He raised a hand and with two fingers, signaled someone over. The porter, carrying an umbrella. She supposed he kept one handy to assist those who arrived at the hotel in the rain. "He'll escort you inside. I'll join you in a minute."

Holding the umbrella over her head, not bothering to shield himself, the porter offered his arm. Gripping it to ensure she remained steady as they traversed the slick brick path that led to the steps, she glanced over to see Mick talking to his coachman. She hadn't meant to be such an inconvenience, should probably have accepted his offer of the carriage, but it seemed wrong in light of what had happened in his office.

The porter guided her along the path, up the steps, the rain pattering the umbrella, a bit harder than she'd expected. Its strength was increasing. She'd have been drenched if she'd tried to make it back inside on her own. So many things she didn't consider because they were automatically done for her. She didn't like realizing she was so incredibly pampered, protected, shielded.

They'd barely gotten inside when Mick joined them. "Go on into the parlor, make yourself comfortable."

She left them there, with him giving instructions to the porter — Jones, he'd called him earlier. For some reason it seemed important to remember that. She hadn't viewed the parlor the other night; it hadn't been part of her private tour. Dark wood paneling and dark red velvet chairs with fringe dangling from the seats made the room seem at once both masculine and feminine. She chose a chair near the fireplace where no fire burned. A chill swept through her. She'd been silly to insist on a hansom when a perfectly good carriage waited outside. But she wasn't going to delay his seeing to his business, wasn't going to be any more beholden to him than she already was.

The tread of heavy footsteps had her glancing over to watch Mick stride into the room, so gracefully, with such strength, such command. This was his domain, his lair. He was lord here, and she had the sudden thought she might have been better off walking home, even as she found herself mesmerized by his movements.

Without a word, he crouched before the hearth and began the task of lighting the fire. He wore no gloves. Those strong, capable hands adjusted the placement of the logs, did other things, the purpose of which she hadn't a clue.

"Don't you have servants to do that?" she asked. The duke, bless him, called in a footman if the fire was in need of stirring.

"I'm not going to wake them for this. I've been building fires since I was seven, Lady Aslyn."

She didn't like that he'd added the title back to her name, wanted the earlier intimacy when she shouldn't. The fire caught, the wood crackled, the warmth began to spread beyond him.

He unfolded that tall, marvelously sculpted body of his, turned, stepped forward and took a blanket draped over the desk clerk's arm. She hadn't heard the man arrive. Not unusual. Staff learned to walk on silent feet. Still, she was surprised by his presence. Holding two snifters, he set one on the small table beside her chair, the other on a table beside a chair opposite hers, then quickly made his exit.

"I thought you had appointments," she said to Mick.

He shook out the blanket, bent at the waist, draped the covering over her lap, tucking it in against her sides. He leaned in nearer, his eyes holding hers. "They can wait. They're not nearly as important as you."

It wasn't fair when he spoke words she'd longed for Kip to say. "I was being considerate, trying to save you some bother." Her voice came out low, raspy. Nothing about her seemed to stay as it was whenever this man was near.

"No bother. I enjoy seeing after you." Words a suitor might utter, but Kipwick never had. But then he hadn't had to court her; their eventual arrangement had always been understood. She should have made him work for it. Maybe then he'd appreciate what he had — or had once had. From her viewpoint, their understanding was no longer what it had been.

Mick moved away, dropped into the vacant chair and lifted the snifter. "This will warm you better than a blanket or a fire."

"Brandy?"

"Cognac to be precise." He waited until she'd retrieved her glass, raised his slightly higher, bent his head just a tad in a very inviting manner. "Cheers."

She sipped. The liquid was velvet on the tongue, smooth as it seared its way along her throat. She couldn't recall tasting anything as rich or flavorful. She imagined it had cost him a pretty penny. "It's delicious."

"I'm glad you enjoy it."

Taking another sip, allowing the warmth to seep through her, to give her a sense of lethargy, she was half tempted to curl up and go to sleep. "So tell me the details of the wager."

"Hmm." He shifted his gaze to the fire, which was blazing now, creating a comforting atmosphere, one that required a book or a dog in the lap. "We were at the Cerberus Club, Aiden's gaming establishment. The game was poker. I'd only just sat down to play. Kipwick had been at it a while. Our first hand, I knew I could outbid him so I offered him an exchange." His eyes returned to her, level, honest, bold. She always felt he studied her with every fiber of his being, that he marked her breaths, the beat of her heart. That not even a blink escaped his scrutiny. "If I won, he'd bring you to the ball. If he won, he'd not only gain the pot but all the chips that remained to me. With what I'd wagered and what remained, he'd have taken in more than a thousand pounds."

She was immediately struck with two realizations: that Mick would risk so much to have her here and Kipwick would risk *her* for monetary gain. Flattery and disgust battled within her. "And you won."

He gave a long, slow nod.

"You both used me as an object." Her voice was tart, reflected her anger.

"I wanted your company, your presence here that night. I didn't care what anyone else I invited thought of the place, but I valued your opinion. I was willing to engage in a questionable tactic. I'd already asked him to bring you and he'd refused, fearing for your reputation."

"And you didn't care about my reputation."

He gave her a pointed look. "It was a ball. I didn't see that your reputation would be in any danger. You hadn't struck me as someone who lorded her position in Society over others."

A spark of shame skipped through her. "I didn't mean to imply that associating with your guests was beneath me."

"Nor did I mean to imply I saw you as an object to be bartered. I see you as anything but. You intrigue me, Lady Aslyn, but I can't call on you for two reasons — you are already betrothed, and I sincerely doubt your guardians would welcome me into their home."

They wouldn't. The duchess had made clear her opinion on the illegitimate. But to look at him, no one would know. She saw him as a businessman, a success, a man who went after what he wanted. And he'd wanted her company. Kip had abandoned her for cards, and Mick had only left her side when she'd insisted. He might not be courting her, but he certainly had a way of making her feel treasured.

"Besides, I hoped you might enjoy the evening."

"I did," she admitted softly. "Until the end."

"Rather unfortunate that."

With a nod, she sipped the cognac and turned her attention to the fire. "Shouldn't your man have returned with a hansom by now?"

Out of the corner of her eye, she watched as he stretched out his legs as though settling in for a long wait. "Not a lot of need for cabbies this time of night in this section of London. Someday there will be. Just not yet."

She peered over at him. With his elbow resting on the arm of the chair, he held the stem of his snifter nestled between two fingers, his palm cradling the bowl, no doubt warming its contents. The pose shouldn't have made him look so enticingly masculine, but she suspected he could be decked out in petticoats and still give the impression nothing about him ever had been or ever would be feminine. "I suppose I should have taken you up on the offer of your carriage."

"It's not too late, although now that we are further into the night, if you're in my carriage, I'd have a responsibility to accompany you."

To sit in the dark confines across from her, their knees possibly in danger of touching. His mouth not so far from hers. She felt as though he'd branded her, in ways Kip never had, had never even tried. Better to wait for the hansom than to risk discovering she was weak where Mick was concerned. "Regarding Kipwick, as you've admitted to spending time with him, answer me this. Was last night an aberration?"

He sighed. "You should ask him."

"You don't gossip or tell tales out of turn."

"When you grow up as the object of gossip, you learn to loathe it."

She couldn't imagine a child being gossiped about, but her experience with children was limited. She'd been tutored at the estate. Growing up, she hadn't run around with anyone other than Kip, and then only when he made time for her. He'd gone off to school. She'd always expected she would, as well. She'd had a short stint at a ladies' finishing school, but other than that, until her first Season, her life had been rather confining. "Was it the circumstances of your birth that caused the gossip?"

A corner of his mouth quirked up. "Some questioned the absence of a father. Some knew Ettie Trewlove took in bastards. People tended to avoid us as though we might infect them with our illegitimacy. I grew up angry, quick to lash out."

"You're still angry." She could see it in the tautness of his jaw.

"I am, but now my anger is directed at only one — the man who spilled his seed into a woman and created me."

His words surprised her. "Do you know who your father is?"

"I do."

"Does he acknowledge you?"

"Not yet, but he will. Eventually."

She didn't understand people not acknowledging their children, regardless of the circumstances of their birth. "How can you be so certain?"

A muscle in his jaw tightened, jumped. At the audacity of her question, or the means he intended to employ to ensure his father complied with his wishes? She didn't believe he'd use physical force, but he was a man with wealth, power and friends who flourished in the shadows. He studied her, and she suddenly wished a more concrete trust existed between them. "I apologize. How you deal with family is not my business."

"He's not family. He's blood. Family has naught to do with blood."

She understood that sentiment. "Very true. I've been with the duke and duchess for so long that they are more parents than guardians. They've always treated me as though I were their true daughter."

"You love them." It was a statement, but

one edged with surprise.

"Of course. They've been very good to me, but it's more than that. They're the ones who comfort me when I'm melancholy, who made me feel safe when I awoke frightened in the dark of night. The duchess taught me how to be a lady, to walk throughout the manor with a book balanced on top of my head. The duke taught me how to waltz." She laughed lightly. "I would stand on his feet, and he would circle the room until I grew dizzy."

"He's a man of patience, then."

She didn't know why he sounded so disgruntled by the notion. "And one prone to indulging the ladies in his life. I've never heard him have a harsh or unkind word for his duchess. Whatever she wishes, he accommodates."

"Is that what you want? A man who never challenges you?"

With her mouth open and no words pouring forth, she stared at him like she was a carp tossed onto shore.

"I believe you'd grow bored with him after a time," he continued.

Goodness gracious, it hit her as though she'd been struck by lightning: she did find Kip boring — at least when compared against Mick Trewlove. She shouldn't be comparing them, and she realized she had been doing exactly that from the moment she spied Mick sauntering toward them at Cremorne as though he owned the night and everything within it. "Where is the damned hansom?"

A corner of his mouth kicked up. "The lady uses profanity. I'd have not thought."

"It's late and the lady is tired."

"I can let you a room for the night." A room to which he no doubt had a key. "There should be more cabbies about in the morning. At the very least it'll be safer to walk about searching for one."

She shook her head. "I'll wait. It can't be much longer, and I'd hate for your man to go to all that bother and then have to send the hansom on its way." She went to take another sip of the cognac, discovered her glass empty. How had that happened?

"Would you care for more?"

"No."

Apparently he didn't believe her as he took her glass, replaced it with his. She didn't want to consider that it tasted richer because his mouth had been against the rim.

"You've never been kissed before."

Indignation raced through her. "I most certainly have."

"He didn't do a very good job of it, then."

245

He hadn't. She hated that Mick knew it, that he probably guessed correctly who'd kissed her. "You didn't seem repulsed by my efforts."

"On the contrary, you're remarkable. Yet in the beginning you hesitated to part your lips, seemed surprised by my . . . urgings."

"I will admit to being taken off guard by your unusual method of kissing."

He chuckled darkly. "Unusual? Sweetheart, any man who is kissing you properly is going to want his tongue in your mouth, your tongue in his."

The sensations slammed into her as though his mouth was once again claiming hers with a ferocity that bordered on barbaric. "Must we analyze what transpired in your office?"

She had no idea what he might have said because Jones chose that moment to hurry into the room. Thank goodness. She started to rise —

"I'm sorry, sir, but I can't find a hackney anywhere."

She sank back down. Blast it all. How had she come to be in this awkward position?

"Thank you, Jones. I know you did your best."

"Aye, sir." The man strode out as though

he couldn't leave fast enough.

"A room or the carriage?" Mick asked.

CHAPTER 12

As his carriage traveled swiftly through the nearly vacated streets, he fought not to be disappointed that she'd chosen the carriage over a bed in his hotel. He had an irrational urge for her to christen every single one of them. He'd known eventually they'd end up in the carriage together because he'd instructed Jones to stay beyond sight for an hour and then return with the news no hansom was to be found. Although she didn't want him kissing her, didn't want him touching her, he'd insisted on traveling with her.

He couldn't explain this irrational need he had just to be with her, to give her something Kipwick hadn't. Or the jealousy that had coursed through him when she'd confirmed the earl had kissed her. While she hadn't given him a name, he knew her betrothed was the only man to whom she would have given that privilege. Her kissing

Mick had been an aberration. Although his ego took a measure of satisfaction in knowing she might have found the earl's kiss lacking in passion, another part of him didn't like learning that Kipwick might not be giving her his all. She deserved everything a man had to offer.

That thought he shoved back into the corner of his mind where it couldn't prick his conscience. She deserved far better than what he was going to eventually offer.

"What is the fragrance you wear?" he asked. It would linger in his carriage, always reminding him that she'd once been a passenger, had sat mere inches from him. It would mock him, reminding him he hadn't crossed over and taken her in his arms, captured her mouth in order to ensure her passionate noises also resided within the confines of the vehicle.

"Gardenia. It was my mother's favorite. When I first apply it, I'm always swamped with memories of her hugging me before she would go to a ball."

"You have a lot of memories of your parents." He wasn't certain if it was a statement or a question.

"Not so very many actually. Most revolve around my mother. My father was rather intimidating. So tall that I'd get a pain in my neck looking up at him. He seemed a giant at the time. In truth, I doubt he was even as tall as you. Our perspective changes as we grow older, grow taller. I would have liked to have had the opportunity to become less wary of him."

He had no memories of the woman who'd given birth to him, didn't even know what she looked like. As for his father, his height wasn't going to intimidate him.

"What of your mother, what does she smell like?" she asked.

He'd never given it much thought. "Bread, fresh from the oven, vanilla, recently brewed tea."

"She sounds warm and homey."

"She's always quick with a hug, was equally quick with a slap if we didn't behave."

"I suspect she fairly bruised her hand with you about."

He grinned. "Even when I grew tall enough to tower over her, she was never daunted. Earlier you spoke fondly of your guardians. What sort of punishment would they mete out?"

"I never exhibited any behavior that required punishment. I was always quick to obey, wanting to please. Although if I'm honest, they are rather overprotective. Do you know, before tonight, I had never walked out of the residence unaccompanied? And I certainly never traveled in a carriage with a gentleman I barely know. I'm probably being exceedingly careless to do so now, yet I feel remarkably safe. I don't believe you'd take advantage."

"You are rather foolish to believe that."

"No. If you were going to do something untoward, you'd have done it in your office, your lair where you rule."

"You don't consider the kiss overstepping the bounds?"

"Of course I do. It shouldn't have happened." She glanced out the window, presenting him with her profile, limned by the occasional streetlamp. Odd, how even with the shadows, he could discern the upward slant of her nose. He should have kissed it while he had the chance. He'd certainly do so the next time an occasion presented itself. Her nose, her brow, her cheeks, the top of her head. Damnation, he was reacting like a besotted schoolboy, wanting to kiss every quarter inch of her.

She turned her attention back to him. "As I mentioned, I've been protected. Sometimes I feel as though I will suffocate. I was curious as to whether all kisses were the same, so I welcomed the opportunity to discover the truth of it."

"Are they . . . all the same?" For him it was a rhetorical question. He knew the answer, but he was curious as to whether she'd admit to or accept the reality of it.

She looked back out the window. "No, they're not."

She sounded somewhat disappointed, which should have pleased him. It didn't. He didn't like the notion of her being disenchanted with anything, even as he knew a time would come when he'd disappoint her most of all. The irritating besotted fool who apparently was considering taking up residence within him wanted to ask if she preferred his kiss. Based on the way she'd run, he might have thought she didn't, but he also contemplated the alternative: that she enjoyed it far too much. A lady betrothed to another man might feel a need to run from the realization she'd chosen poorly.

"Kip and I have an understanding," she said softly, as though reading his thoughts. "Although at the moment it's on shaky ground."

Her words pleased him far too much, made him want to cross over the narrow expanse separating them and kiss her — hard, thoroughly, to distraction. He didn't push her, didn't question her further because he didn't want to expose his hand, to make her suspicious, to think he had too much interest in her relationship with the earl.

"The rain has stopped," she said quietly.

"So it has."

They settled into silence. He was surprised by how much he enjoyed merely being in her company, inhaling her fragrance — he might have Tittlefitz fetch him some gardenias for the offices, for the lobby. He wouldn't mind being greeted by her scent when he strode into the hotel.

He didn't spend a great deal of time in the presence of others, unless it was required for business or a family obligation. He preferred keeping his own counsel, his own company. He'd never been one for light, trivial banter. But with her, even the most trivial seemed important. He liked learning things about her. Not because he could use them to manipulate her, but because every aspect of her fascinated him.

The carriage came to a halt. He opened the door, leaped out and reached back for her, taking incredible pleasure from her placing her hand in his without hesitation. He wished they wore no gloves, no clothes at all for that matter.

"Very wise to have your driver park on the street," she said.

"Our arrival will be less conspicuous, especially if someone is wandering about the hallways."

"They were all abed when I left."

"You assume once abed, people stay abed. I assure you, my lady, they do not." He offered his arm.

"You don't need to accompany me."

"I'm not going to leave you on the street."

"And if you are seen, my reputation will be ruined."

Eventually it would be, but not tonight. He wasn't yet weary of the chase. "We'll keep to the shadows."

He didn't much like the relief that washed through him when her hand alighted near the crook of his elbow nor his desire to flex his muscles in order to remind her of his strength. He'd never before felt the need to puff out his chest or demonstrate physical domination, preferring instead the mental prowess needed for negotiating. He wanted her sitting in his office, watching as he conferred with solicitors and investors in order to ensure the deal favored him. She'd no doubt be bored to tears. Or perhaps not.

They strolled along the edge of the drive, keeping their distance from the lighted path.

"You're welcome to use my hotel parlor anytime you feel the need to escape the restraints here."

She peered over at him, her crooked smile soft, intriguing. He wanted to taste it once more. "I'll keep that in mind."

They reached the wide steps.

"Thank —"

"I'll escort you to the door, see you safely inside."

He had the sense she wanted to argue, then decided she'd gain nothing from it but a delay in being rid of him. At the door, he held out his hand. "Your key."

She scowled at him. "It's not locked."

Only when he tried the latch, he discovered it was. "I fear it is, my lady."

Her eyes widened. "It can't be." Brushing aside his hand, she gave it a try.

"I know how to open a door," he said laconically.

"I don't understand. It wasn't locked when I left."

"Obviously the butler made his rounds, locking things up, after you left."

She sagged against the door. "I hadn't considered he did that. To be honest, I'd never given any thought to those rituals. Someone is always waiting for my return, no matter the hour. Of course, they'd always

255

known I'd left."

Tonight they'd assumed she was abed. She looked devastated. All her plans ruined for want of a key.

She moved away from the door, stretched her neck, looking one way and then the other. "Perhaps I can find a tree to climb, a window that's open."

"And risk breaking your neck?"

"Better than having to explain to the duke and duchess what I'm doing out here this time of night."

With you was left unsaid, but she telegraphed it clearly enough. He shouldn't have been hurt by the implication she was ashamed to be seen with him. His entire life had involved facing the fact he was a shameful secret, and his rational self understood that no lady could effectively explain away being alone with a man, any man, in the dead of night. He always managed to master his emotions, but she somehow succeeded in leading them into rebellion. "I'll get you inside with none being the wiser."

Ceasing her survey of trees and windows, she swung around to face him. "How?"

"I'm a man of many talents." He held out his arm. "Come on. We'll go 'round to the back."

When she placed her hand on his arm, he

noted a small tremble. She was far more upset than she was letting on, and he recognized that she had every right to be. The future she'd planned could come crashing around her with the discovery of the night's adventures. He escorted her around the side of the house and into the back gardens, then along the path that led to the servants' entrance. Once there, he knocked briskly on the door.

"You're going to awaken people."

"Only one if we keep very quiet."

A young lad of about twelve, no doubt the duke's boot boy, opened the door and squinted out. His eyes widened. "Lady Aslyn! What are you doing out here?"

Mick held up a coin. "If you ask no questions, seek no answers and forget that you were awakened tonight by a knock on the door, I've a sovereign for you."

The boy grinned. "I can forget. Easy as pie."

Mick flipped the coin toward him, and the lad caught it handily. He turned to Aslyn. "In with you."

"Thank you, Mr. —"

"No names."

"Right. Thank you for seeing me safely home."

"It was my pleasure."

She seemed to hesitate as though there was more she wanted to say. Finally, she gave a little nod. "Good night, then."

"Sleep well, Lady Aslyn." Generous sentiment on his part when he hoped she slept not at all, preferring she toss and turn with thoughts of him.

She skirted past the lad holding the door, and Mick watched her rush toward the darkness, watched as it swallowed her up and she disappeared completely. Everything within him wanted to go after her, wanted to save her from the heartache that was to come. But he'd waited so long, schemed so carefully. He couldn't allow a mere slip of a girl with a tipped-up nose and a crooked smile to thwart him. Shoving back his doubts and ignoring the possibility of regrets, he tossed another sovereign to the boy. "That's so if I ever call upon you to remember this night, you do so in extreme detail."

"I can remember it all."

"Smart lad. There will be four more of those for you if you recount those details to the persons I indicate." He leaned down. "And just so all the details are clear, I go by the name of Mick Trewlove."

"Yes, sir."

"And you, lad, should I need to find you,

who do I ask for?" Since Aslyn hadn't called the boy by name, he doubted she even knew who he was.

"Toby. Toby Williams. I'm His Grace's boot boy."

"Remember, Toby Williams, His Grace's boot boy, not a word to anyone without my permission." Turning on his heel, he headed back up the path, already arguing with himself, already knowing he'd just wasted a sovereign. He'd never call on Toby Williams to tell a soul what he knew.

CHAPTER 13

She hardly slept at all.

Sitting at a table in the gardens, reflecting on the tossing and turning and tangled mess of her sheets when she'd finally arisen from her bed, all she could surmise was that her body had been in need of . . . fulfillment was the word that came to mind. It was as though spending so much time in the company of Mick Trewlove had wound up her feminine yearnings until they'd felt a need to explode like a host of fireworks.

Guilt surged through her because she couldn't seem to stop thinking about him. She shouldn't have gone to see him, shouldn't have allowed him to get so close, and most certainly should not have succumbed to the temptation of his kiss. How was it that he managed to elicit all these urges when Kip didn't? Quite possibly because he kissed her with far more enthusiasm than the earl, that he gazed upon her as though she encompassed his entire world. Kip never looked at her with intense heat burning in his eyes, with desire and longing and . . . *want*. It was the last that unsettled her the most.

Because there was a secretive part of her that yearned for more than casual touches, a gentle press of lips and polite conversation. There was a part that longed for the wickedness.

And Mick provided it. He was a . . .

She didn't know how to describe him: a scoundrel, a rake, a rogue. A man. A man who made her very much aware she was a woman. Even now memories of his touch, his mouth playing over hers, were enough to make her feel as though the sun had dropped from the sky and fallen into her lap.

"Not making any calls today?"

Startled, she looked up to see the duchess standing there. "No, I thought . . . I thought to just enjoy the gardens, some tea . . ." *My own company for fear a stray thought of Mick Trewlove might cause me to blush unbecomingly at inappropriate times.* "Would you care to join me?"

"You seem lost in thought. I wouldn't want to intrude."

"You could never intrude. Please." She

began pouring tea into an extra teacup that had been on the tray when the servant brought it to her, as though she couldn't envision her ladyship not being joined by someone. "I've grown quite bored with my own company already."

The duchess sat, elegantly and delicately, as she always did. A good strong wind would no doubt blow her away. "What were you thinking of? Your wedding?"

"In a manner. Did anyone other than the duke ever take your fancy?"

She smiled softly, as though in remembrance. "I had a swarm of beaux, but they were all pleasant, like a warm summer afternoon. Then I met Hedley, and he ignited a storm within me. With him, I felt alive." She shook her head. "It's difficult to explain." Her gaze zeroed in on Aslyn. "Are you having doubts?"

Aslyn took hold of her teacup as though it could provide her with some sort of stability, when the bone china was likely to crumble if she held on too tightly. "I do love Kip. I just don't know if it's the sort of love a woman should have for a man she's to marry. I suppose of late, I've been giving a lot of thought to the intimacy of marriage" — she released a self-conscious laugh — "and I'm just having a difficult time envisioning it." *With Kip.*

"The experience can be quite lovely. I'm certain Kip will lead you into it gently." Averting her gaze, she sipped her tea, a blush creeping along her cheeks. Aslyn realized she probably was not at all comfortable contemplating her son in bed with her ward. Not that she blamed her.

"Do you think the duke cared for anyone before you?"

The duchess sighed. "It's quite possible. I didn't ask. I didn't want to know, but ladies adored him. He was so handsome and charming. I could hardly fault them." She set her cup down and held Aslyn's gaze. "Yes, I suspect there was someone before me. But whoever she was, she couldn't hold on to him. And since we've married, he's never strayed and that's what matters." Reaching across the table, she placed her hand over Aslyn's. "Love grows with time and deepens over the years. You'll have struggles and challenges, but you'll lean on each other and your relationship will grow stronger."

Aslyn worried that the trials they might face would not be ones they could easily overcome — not when they were the result of one person's actions, actions that could be controlled, altered, changed if he so chose, which he apparently did not.

"I've always thought of Kip as a dear friend, as my . . . destiny." She laughed lightly, embarrassed by the absurd remark. "I've never looked at anyone else, never considered anyone else, never doubted Kip's devotion to me or mine to him."

"Are you doubting now? Has he done something to warrant your qualms?"

How could she tell his mother about the lost pearls and comb? "I'm certain the reservations rest with me, with my recent worry that I've not experienced enough of life to know for certain I'm making the correct decision. I've never spent any considerable time in the company of another gentleman."

The duchess jerked her head back as though she'd been punched. "Well, proper ladies don't, of course."

"Proper ladies have an assortment of gentlemen call on them and sit in the parlor enjoying each other's company. I've never welcomed another's suit." Another harsh laugh. "Although to be honest, no one ever asked to call on me. Everyone always assumed Kip was it for me. I fear I've missed out on courting rituals that are designed to help a lady choose."

"You've grown up with Kip. I daresay

there is little about him you don't know."

Only there were some things, some horrific things if she were honest. The night before last, she'd seen an unflattering side to him. "How do we ever learn everything there is to know about a person?" Without question she didn't know a good many things about Mick Trewlove.

"I doubt we ever do. Not really." The final words were said softly as the duchess turned her attention back to the gardens. "That's not a bad thing, necessarily. We all have our secrets."

But shouldn't she know everything about the person she was going to marry?

The duchess reached for her tea, turned her head slightly and smiled. "Well, speak of the devil."

Glancing over her shoulder, Aslyn saw Kip walking toward them. He looked considerably better than he had the last time she'd seen him. She was glad his expression reflected a bit of contriteness.

"Mother," he said, leaning down and bussing a quick kiss over the duchess's cheek. Finally, he looked at her. "Aslyn. I hope you're well today."

"I am. Quite." A lie. She was tired, grumpy and confused. Two men were responsible for all three. She was rather put out with both.

"Mother, would you give me a moment alone with my betrothed?" he asked.

"Of course," she said, smiling brightly at Aslyn as though to say that everything was all right, that all would be well, that her life with Kip would be extraordinary. "It's nearly two. Time for your father and I to take our daily stroll through the gardens."

Elegant and graceful, she wandered off to inspect the roses, providing them with privacy.

Kip took the chair his mother had vacated, sitting across from Aslyn. "I know you're put out with me."

"I am rather, yes."

"I'm certain things were said that were not meant."

"Not by me."

He didn't appear too pleased by her answer. Glancing off to the side, she watched as the duke joined his duchess and escorted her farther into the gardens. While Aslyn found the duke's attentiveness to his wife touching, she realized now she couldn't rely on Kip to show her the same consideration.

"I have something for you," he said, bringing her attention back to him.

She watched as he reached into his jacket and brought out a small leather box. He set it on the table, then with two fingers pushed it toward her. "Open it."

Doing so, she stared at the string of pearls. "I couldn't find a comb —" He scoffed. "I don't remember what the comb looked like, to be honest, but if you could draw it for me, perhaps I could have one made for you."

She lifted her gaze to his. "As I mentioned, they can't be replaced."

"Of course they can be. I realize they won't be your mother's —"

"But that's what made them special."

"So these will be special because I gave them to you."

She supposed he had a point, and yet the reason he was giving them to her soured any sentimentality that might have accompanied them. "It doesn't matter, Kip. Mick Trewlove returned to me what you lost."

His jaw tautened. "He did, did he? And when were you going to mention that?"

"When an opportunity presented itself as it just did."

"When did he return them?"

"Yesterday."

"I spent all morning at a jeweler's."

267

She very much doubted he'd spent *all* morning there. "I'd have told you yesterday, but you weren't receiving when I went to your residence."

He had the good graces to look abashed. "I was a bit under the weather."

"I can well imagine." Only she couldn't, as she'd never imbibed to that extent. An occasional glass of brandy — and the cognac with Mick — was all she could claim.

Earnestly he leaned forward. "Did you say anything to my parents?"

"No." A measure of loyalty to him had caused her to hold her tongue, but she'd also not wanted to explain doing something of which they'd heartily disapprove. "However, in exchange for my silence, I expect you to take me with you the next time you go gambling."

He sat back. "Don't be ridiculous."

"I don't think I am. The other night I saw a side of you I'd never known before, that I didn't even know existed. I need to understand what I observed, Kip."

"There is nothing to understand. I enjoy gambling. Granted, I usually have better luck, but that's not something one can control — which is what makes it so thrilling."

"You're going to continue with it after

we're married?"

"Naturally."

"Then I need to experience it with you so I can comprehend all the ramifications."

"It has nothing to do with you."

"When you lose my valuables, it has everything to do with me." Balling her hands into fists, she planted them on the table and leaned forward. "Do you not understand how much it frightened me to see you as you were the other night? You were a man I did not know, did not recognize."

"What does it matter what sort of man I am at the gambling table when I behave as you expect at the dinner table?"

"Because how am I to know when that vile creature from the other night will suddenly make an appearance in my parlor . . . or worse, in my bed."

"Vile?"

She swallowed hard, striving to stop the sudden pounding of her heart. "It was awful. I fear I'm on the verge of marrying a man I truly do not know, that what I know of you doesn't go below the surface. That I do not know your true depths. That's the reason I want to go with you, to see if the other night was an aberration or merely another side of the man I might wed."

"Might wed? In the carriage you mentioned not marrying me, but I assumed you were being overly dramatic."

She glanced down at her hands. Her knuckles had turned white. "I must admit to having doubts regarding our suitability as a husband and wife."

"You're making much ado about nothing. We get along."

Lifting her gaze to his, she hated all the doubts swirling through her. "Ah, yes. We are quite compatible when dining."

He scoffed. "Aslyn —"

"I'm not striving to be difficult, Kip, but I fear we've fallen into a trap of doing what is expected of us rather than being prompted by any sort of desire."

Crossing his arms over his chest, he leaned back. "We've announced our betrothal. You can't cry off."

Where were the words of love, of want, of need? Why was he not leaning earnestly across the table, taking her hand and declaring he could not live without her? "Making an announcement is hardly a reason to go through with something we've begun to doubt."

"I don't doubt it."

"Why? Why do you want to marry me?"

"My God, Aslyn. I've known you forever —"

"Is that reason to marry? I need to get to know you better. That's all I'm asking. To go out with you tonight."

"I don't understand your obsession with intruding upon this portion of my life."

She stared at him. "Intruding upon? I'm asking to share it."

"But it doesn't involve you. A man needs time that is his and his alone."

"Then I shall grant you all the time you require. Consider our betrothal on hiatus." Shoving back her chair, she rose.

He came to his feet. "You don't mean that."

"Indeed I do. I cannot — will not — exchange vows with a man who has a life of which he wishes me to take no part and considers me an intrusion."

"You're being unreasonable."

In silence she held his gaze, watching as frustration washed over his features.

"Don't say anything about this to my parents as you'll merely upset them when there is no need, because this decision of yours will not stand. Send word when you've regained your senses." He stormed away toward the farthest reaches of the gardens where his parents were studying the

271

carnations. He no doubt didn't want them questioning his leaving without having a word with them.

She may have just had the shortest betrothal in history, but she couldn't help feeling that her senses had not deserted her. In fact, they were more keen than ever.

She'd come to the park earlier than usual, in need of fresh air, sunshine, a cool breeze, the scent of flowers, greenery, evidence of life because she'd felt so damned dead inside after her row with Kip. She could not — would not — marry him. How was it that she'd ever wanted to? How was it possible she knew so very little about him?

She couldn't imagine Mick excluding her from a portion of his life.

It wasn't fair to compare the two, and yet she felt as though she was better acquainted with Mick than with Kip. From the beginning she'd sensed some sort of connection with the hotel owner, been drawn to him, had found him inappropriately waltzing about in her mind with his slow smiles and his intense gaze and his scratchy voice and his workman's hands.

Sitting on a blanket beneath the shade of a nearby tree, she looked down at her sketch pad, surprised and relieved to discover she hadn't drawn those hands when she'd been envisioning them in such exquisite detail. Last night they'd held her, spanned the expanse of her ribs, had urged her closer, and she'd welcomed the urging.

Ridiculous to give the man any thought at all when there could never be anything between them. If she married a man of questionable, immoral origins, she'd find herself cast out, her children not accepted by Society. Even the duke and duchess would turn their backs on her. She would see the disapproval in the duchess's eyes, know she'd disappointed her, and in so doing disappointed her parents. Even from the grave they had influence.

She would not marry Kip, but neither could she turn her affections toward Mick Trewlove — although she did fear it might be too late for that.

"You're quite the artist."

With a little screech at the deep voice, she jerked her head around to find Mick crouched beside her, on the grass, the toes of his polished boots a fraction of an inch from the blanket as though he was well aware he was beyond her reach, that he wasn't allowed to occupy the same space as she. Why should the circumstances of his birth label him, brand him? Why wasn't he judged only on his merits, what he'd made of himself, his accomplishments? He was a man who had begun life with nothing and now possessed much to be admired. And she did admire him, more than she admired any lord of her acquaintance, including Hedley.

Looking a bit farther behind him, she could see the two maids and two footmen standing about, watchful, but not interfering. But then why would they think she wouldn't welcome Mick's nearness when she'd walked with him through the park before?

"It's our kissing couple," she said, self-conscious that he'd seen her work. She only ever shared it with Kip who had declared it, "Not bad." Discreetly she pointed to the couple standing a short distance away, near the pond, watching as children placed toy sailboats on the water.

"She's not carrying a parasol," he said.

It pleased her that he'd noticed, made her feel as though they were sharing an intimate secret. "I think their relationship has developed to the point that she can say whatever she wants, that he welcomes her speaking her mind, that she need not use frivolous objects to communicate with him."

"Do you know them?"

"No. They're obviously well off. Their dress and bearing tells me that, but I don't think they're nobility. If they are, I've never seen them at a ball or any other affair. I wonder about their story, though."

"What do you imagine it is?"

She peered askance at him. "What makes you think I've given it any thought?"

"Because you drew them, and I suspect you were weaving their tale as you did. There's a bit of the romantic in you."

A good deal more than a bit. "I think the world has judged their love illicit, that it won't let them be together, but here within the park, they can shut out the world. None of it matters."

Silence stretched between them until finally he murmured, "Hmm."

"What?"

His eyes held a sparkling, a teasing. "I'd have thought you'd give them a happier ending."

She turned her gaze back to the couple. "She's afraid. Marrying him will take her away from everything she knows."

Even without looking, she knew he was studying her intently, that his eyes were no longer sparkling. She laughed self-consciously. "They're probably married, have a dozen children and come to the park for a bit of peace."

"If that were the case, she'd have not had to use her parasol the other day to lure him into a kiss."

They were talking nonsense, and yet it was a balm to her aching heart. "What do you think their story is?"

He sat on the grass, apparently not giving a whit that his trousers might become stained. Draping a wrist over a raised knee, he was a model of masculinity, strength and power. A man comfortable in his own skin. "They met as children. She grew up in wealth and privilege. Her father's a banker, I think. He grew up with nothing, the son of a fishmonger. But he loved her, so he went off and made his fortune. Now he's returned . . . but she's making him work to prove his affections. Eventually they'll marry and have a dozen children and come to the park for peace."

She smiled softly. "I'd have not thought you'd give them a happy ending."

"It does seem out of character, but I wanted to make you smile. I enjoy your smiles."

After her afternoon, she was in danger of bursting into tears at his kindness. "In truth, I don't think our tales are better than her reality. She strikes me as being content.

Happy."

She dropped her gaze to the couple etched out on her pad. Their faces were merely shaded in ovals as she had no talent for drawing features. Still their nearness to each other, the way his hand rested on the small of her back — in a protective way Kip's had never rested on hers — brought her the realization that she had somehow inadvertently missed capturing something she wanted. "Kip and I had a row earlier."

"About your visit to me last night?" His voice was even, and yet she heard a sliver of danger slithering through it, and she was left with the impression he'd be her champion if one were needed.

She laughed caustically. "No, I didn't tell him about that. I wouldn't." She couldn't. She couldn't tell anyone. If found out, there would be consequences for her and him and whatever future each of them might have envisioned for themselves. "I insisted he cease with his gambling. I told him I couldn't honor our understanding otherwise." Another laugh, this one sad, with a hint of embarrassment. "I don't know why I'm telling you this."

"I think you do."

She did. Awful girl that she was, she wanted him to know she had doubts regarding her future. With a nod, she looked back toward the couple who were now walking away, to find their happiness she hoped, when she was beginning to doubt hers was on the horizon.

"What was his reaction?"

"Anger. He instructed me not to say anything to his parents when it would only upset them and I was certain to regain my senses in time."

"It seems to me you've already come to your senses."

And there it was, the reason she'd told him. He was familiar with Kip's behavior, understood her struggles. "But he's correct. I can't tell them, because I would have to explain his behavior and it will break their hearts. I don't know how he's managed to keep it from them all these years."

"You don't have to say anything. It'll come out eventually. It always does." He sounded so certain.

"He needs help," she said quietly, feeling impotent with her lack of knowledge.

"I'll see to it."

"You shouldn't have to. He's not your responsibility."

"But he's traipsing about in my world now, and I know how to set matters to rights. You needn't worry. No harm will

278

come to him."

And she believed him. With all her heart and soul. "How fortunate I am that you happened upon me and have brought me some cheer."

"It wasn't happenstance. I was looking for you." Because he knew about her daily afternoon visits to the park. "Fancy is taking a group of orphans to the seaside tomorrow. I thought you might like to join her. I know it would please her to have your company."

"Are they taking your carriage? It'll make for a long day."

"No, we'll be traveling by railway."

Her heart gave a little lurch at the mode of transportation and the fact that it wasn't only his sister who would be on the journey, that he was doing more than asking her to join Fancy. He was asking her to join him. "I've told you — I fear trains. They're too dangerous. There were more than a half dozen accidents last year alone."

"We can't live our life based on what scares us. If we did, we'd spend our days curled up into little balls, whimpering."

"I can't imagine you being afraid or whimpering." She didn't want to think of him as a child, frightened and crying, his young life fraught with challenges.

279

"Everyone has fears. The secret is not to let them take hold."

And she'd done that with trains, allowed them to sink their claws into her, terrorize her with their noise, their speed, their ability to destroy lives in mere seconds.

He leaned toward her, still not touching the blanket, still revealing his respect for their boundaries, acknowledging she had not moved into his world. Yet she suddenly found she longed to. "Conquer your fear of trains," he urged quietly, almost desperately. "When you subdue your anxieties, nothing, no one, will have the power to hold you back."

She had the sense he was referring to something else entirely, something that would lead to her standing before a rippling pond with a man's arm around her. She nodded, thought better of it. "The servants would be tagging along."

"They're welcome to. I'm certain Fancy can use the extra help with the orphans."

His words confirmed that this wasn't an opportunity for him to get her alone, even if she halfway wished it was. "I look forward to it."

Lounging in his mother's parlor while she prepared dinner, Mick contemplated his visit with Aslyn earlier. He was not one for creating fairy tales, for waxing on poetically about love or happily-ever-afters, so he had no inkling where his fantastical story about the parasol-less couple had come from or what had spurred him to spout such drivel when he was a man dedicated to accepting the harshness of reality. Yet sitting there on the grassy knoll with her had apparently served to seize his common sense.

Hence the sickening spouting.

Then she had smiled, sweetly, softly and a bit crookedly, and he'd been glad for the trite tale he'd woven for her, had wished his imagination were such that he could have woven another. Instead, he'd come up with fanciful plans for the morrow to explain his reason for seeking her out at the park — when his true reason had been that he'd simply needed to see her again, inhale her fragrance of gardenia.

The fact that he'd considered it a loss when his own bath had removed her scent from his skin irritated him. He'd very nearly gone into mourning when he'd realized her fragrance had not lingered in his carriage as he'd assumed it would. He'd come close to dismissing his coachman for opening the door in order to air out the conveyance. It hadn't needed airing out. It had carried the fragrance of gardenias, a flower that Tittle-fitz was having a devil of a time finding.

"How many orphans were you thinking?" Fancy asked him now, studying him as though he'd asked her to fly to the moon.

He shrugged. "Half a dozen or so. Young enough that they won't be rebellious, striking out on their own. We want them sticking close. I have no plans to go chasing after any of them as I did the last time we took some to the seaside." He'd be otherwise occupied this time.

"The difficulty will be deciding who to bring on such short notice. Rather bad planning that."

"Surely there are some who should be rewarded for good behavior."

"I suppose. I'll talk with the matron."

"Good." He started to rise —

"And Lady Aslyn is joining us." Unnecessarily repeating words he'd used only a few minutes earlier, she informed him with her tone that she was stepping onto a path of inquiry.

He settled back down. "Yes. However, should she ask, it was your idea to invite her."

"Odd how I keep finding my way into your little scheme." She gave him a pointed look.

"Consider your involvement an induce-
ment toward my giving you a damned bookshop."

Releasing the tiniest of squeals, she
clapped. "So it is going to happen?"

He shrugged. "I don't see the harm in it."

Earnestly she leaned forward, whispering
low, so their mum would not hear, "Have
you lured Lady Aslyn away from her earl?"

He had. Partially if not completely. Tempo-
rarily if not permanently. It was what he'd
wanted, and yet he took no satisfaction in
it. Odd that. He should have felt triumphant. Instead, he felt as though her sadness had traveled like wispy smoke from her
to him and settled beneath his skin, taking
up residence near his beating heart. He
didn't want her sad. He simply wanted her.

Not because of how possessing her would
destroy Kipwick or Hedley. But how it
would serve to make him whole. Until he'd
kissed her, he hadn't realized something in
him was missing. It unnerved him, but he
wanted a day with her, a day without shadows, with sunlight and salt air. He wanted
time with her when he wasn't thinking of
retribution and she wasn't thinking of her
future with Kipwick.

But he wasn't going to explain all that to
his sister. For some reason, telling her

anything at all about what he'd learned at the park seemed a betrayal to Aslyn. She'd trusted him, shared a burden she carried that he didn't think she'd confessed to anyone else. "Don't bring him up tomorrow."

She nodded. "I suppose the children and I are just a prop to give an innocence to the foray to the seaside just as I was a prop that night at Cremorne. I probably shouldn't agree to this."

"There is nothing sinister in the outing. She needs a distraction. I'm providing it."

"I think you've come to truly care for her."

Another thing he wouldn't admit as it would make him vulnerable. "Put your romantic notions aside. All I want is a pleasant day." And to ensure one for Aslyn. He wanted her to have no regrets when she completely broke off ties with Kipwick. The man was destined for ruin, and Mick intended to ensure the earl didn't ruin her, destroy her innocence, in the process.

Odd to realize that he was now striving to protect her from what he'd intended for her in the beginning. Finding himself even more desperate for Hedley's acknowledgment, for it was his only hope to have any sort of lasting relationship with Aslyn.

CHAPTER 14

As Aslyn stood on the Brighton Railway platform, she could hardly breathe as the behemoth of a train loomed before her. Smoke billowed, burning coal scented the air. People scurried about, and she would soon join them in the scurrying, but for now she stood as near to the edge of the platform as she could without falling off, so she could make a hasty retreat if she changed her mind.

Mick had told her where to wait, had assured her he would come for her. She halfway wished he wouldn't keep that promise, prayed that he would. She wanted to be the brave sort he believed her to be.

She'd lied to the duchess and the duke, and sworn the servants who accompanied her to secrecy. She'd done it all with a straight face and an air of confidence. Her guardians didn't question that she was spending the day with Ladies Katharine and

Catherine — the Cats, she'd teasingly told them, was how she referred to the dear friends — touring museums when she had no dear friends Katharine or Catherine or Cats. Much easier to keep the truth of a lie if there was no one to accidentally dispute it. Although ladies did call on Aslyn, the duchess seldom intruded on the visits because she had no interest in the gossip since she didn't involve herself much in Society and never entertained.

If her guardians were more open-minded, if she hadn't been able to envision a row where they forbade her to spend time in the company of Mick Trewlove because of his unfortunate and unfair start in life, she'd have told them the truth. The one thing she'd not needed to lie about was her excitement about the adventure — not the riding the railway part, which still terrified her, but the opportunity to spend more time in the company of a man who actually carried on conversations with her. Who asked questions of her, listened to her answers. She doubted Kip even knew she was terrified of trains. He certainly didn't know how she moaned when a man's mouth urged hers to open or his hands spanned her waist and his fingers dug into her hips, holding her near.

And he was certainly unaware that gladness swept through her and warmed her cheeks whenever she caught sight of Mick Trewlove striding toward her. He cut a swath through the bustling crowd that bumped and jostled mere mortals, but then he always gave the impression that he existed on a separate plane from everyone else. Silly of her to give him powers he certainly didn't possess — powers she'd convinced herself would allow him to keep the train safe.

As he neared, she saw the pleasure in his eyes that her presence brought him. She had no plans to spend the day comparing Kip to him, but the earl had never gazed on her as though she were the only thing that mattered in his life. Mick's regard was at once humbling and terrifying in its intensity.

"Lady Aslyn," he said politely, a perfect gentleman.

"Mr. Trewlove. My servants, Nan and Mary, Thomas and John."

Slipping a hand into a pocket inside his jacket, Mick slid his gaze past her to the brigade forming a protective half circle behind her. She feared they might be most troublesome and ruin her day. "Gents." He held up a small packet, extended it to Thomas. "You have the day to do as you will. There's enough blunt in there to see that you both, along with the coachman and tiger, can go exploring the pubs or do anything else you care to — just don't return to Hedley Hall. Be here at seven for her ladyship."

"We can't leave her in your company," Thomas said loyally.

"Her maids will be adequate chaperones as will the dozen urchins we're taking to the seaside."

"Dozen?" John repeated.

"Aye. Oldest is six, youngest four, I believe. Quite the handful, the lot of them. We certainly welcome you helping us care for them —"

"I'd rather have a pint," John interrupted.

"I thought you might."

"My lady?" Thomas began.

"You should take the day to enjoy yourselves," she assured him. "I'll be perfectly fine with Nan and Mary to see after my needs."

"Very good."

The footmen wandered away, and she breathed a little easier, not certain why she was relieved to have fewer witnesses to her day's adventures. Perhaps because she feared she might embarrass herself with her cowardice once she was actually aboard the train and rattling along the tracks.

"If you'll come with me, ladies," Mick said.

He didn't offer her his arm, and she realized that in public, away from his hotel, he was as aware of the social divide between them as she was. It was possible, but very unlikely, she'd run into someone she knew at this terminus. If those with whom she associated were going to the seaside for the day, they'd no doubt take a coach. "We've yet to purchase passage."

"It's been taken care of," he told her. "I see you brought your parasol."

"I might wish to communicate with you."

"You have merely to voice what you want, and it shall be granted." His sensual smile indicated she could ask for anything at all.

"Right, then."

She walked beside him, with her maids trailing, toward the rear of the train, to a car where small faces peered out through the glass window. She recognized the smartly dressed servant opening the door. It seemed his duties extended beyond that of porter at the hotel. "Good morning, Mr. Jones."

With a smile of pleasure, he tipped his head. "It's simply Jones, miss."

Forcing herself to stride in as though she'd

traveled in this manner a dozen times before, she was surprised to discover it appeared to be a private car. Small sofas sat before the windows on either side of the car. A much larger one, which she didn't want to consider could also serve as a place to sleep — or make love — dominated the center of the room.

"Lady Aslyn!" Fancy said, holding a little girl sucking her thumb in her lap. "I'm so glad you could join us on our outing. Children, say hello to Lady Aslyn."

A chorus of "Hello, Lady Aslyn!" rose from the dozen claimed urchins who actually numbered half that amount.

"You seem to be missing some children," she said to Mick, as he followed her maids inside.

He didn't even have the good graces to appear abashed. "Counting never was my strong suit."

A lie if she'd ever heard one. To have the success he did, he no doubt excelled at counting.

"It will help to keep the little ones calm if your maids will each see to two of them," he said. "You and I can sit over here." With a bow of his head, he indicated a sofa at an opposite window.

While giving instructions to her servants

to assist Miss Trewlove, she considered helping out as well, but she didn't think it would calm any of the children to become aware of her trembling. Sitting on the small settee he'd indicated, she clutched her hands together and gazed out, giving a little start when the whistle blew.

"That's a signal we'll be leaving shortly," Mick said, as he dropped down beside her.

The door opened and Jones strode in, immediately scooping down and lifting a towheaded boy into his arms.

"Are these outings to the seaside a common occurrence?" she asked Mick.

She nearly protested when he went to work unknotting her fingers. "They are. We have a home for society's discards."

"They're not legitimate," she whispered.

He didn't take his gaze off the task of removing her glove. "No."

"How do you find them?"

He scoffed. "There are thousands of them, tens of thousands, in London alone. Parliament enacted legislation that made women ultimately responsible for their children born out of wedlock, thinking it would give them incentive to keep their legs crossed, but when there's an itch" — he did look up then, holding her gaze — "one hardly thinks of the future, merely the need to scratch."

Before meeting him, she hadn't known those itches existed. She certainly knew now, realized if she were smart, she would exit the conveyance. But her curiosity kept her pinned to the spot. "You said *we.* 'We have a home.' "

"People still bring the unwanted to Ettie Trewlove's door. My siblings and I lease a residence and hire a staff to see to their needs. Our mum spends a lot of time there, caring for the small ones, but they are no longer her responsibility."

Slowly he tugged off her glove, intertwined their fingers, securely, comfortingly. The back of the sofa prevented the servants or anyone else from seeing what he'd done, to see her hand closing more tightly around his. The train lurched. She squeezed her eyes shut, but still she could feel the rocking. "Keep talking."

"Open your eyes, sweetheart." His voice was gentle but firm, tinged with a bit of sadness, the endearment making his urging all the more profound. She considered chastising him for the intimacy, but convinced herself he meant nothing by it. For him, it was no doubt simply a word. Besides, she liked the comfort it brought her, wondered if he could sense the pounding of her heart. Even if the train didn't wreck, she might die

— with his large, warm, roughened hand cradling hers.

Licking her lips, gathering her resolve, she opened her eyes, met his.

"There's not going to be a wreck, we're not going to die."

All the duchess's warnings about the need to be careful, the necessity of never taking a risk, bombarded her. "You don't know that."

"I know there's no benefit to expecting the worst." He nodded toward the side. "Look what you're missing."

She glanced to the window where the scenery formed a changing panorama of buildings and trees and people and roads. "It's like being in a carriage."

"Except there are no horses to grow weary."

Glancing down, she saw that her knuckles had gone white. Little wonder her hand was beginning to ache. "I must be hurting you."

"I'm not so delicate as all that."

He wasn't delicate at all. He was all strength, determination and courage. "Do you fear nothing?"

"We all fear something."

His words made her feel slightly better, not quite as timid. "We're traveling at a good clip."

"We'll be at the seaside before you know it."

The journey had been at once satisfying and torturous. Because she was so near, because he could not have her. Because he had to give the impression that he wasn't aware of every breath she drew, that he didn't think a thousand times about leaning in and taking possession of her sweet mouth, that helping her relax into the motion of the train didn't make him want to see her settling into the motion of lovemaking. That her gardenia scent surrounding him didn't give him hope that when all was said and done, she wouldn't hate him.

She overwhelmed him in ways he'd never been, so he'd nearly burst out of the compartment when the train finally reached its destination. The children weren't his responsibility. He was going to pay her maids for assisting Fancy with caring for them. They walked ahead now, along the sandy shore, two urchins each, while he and Aslyn followed leisurely behind, her hand nestled in the crook of his elbow.

They were unlikely to run into anyone she knew; they weren't limited to the shadows or the night. If he were not a realist, he would consider that they could have a future of walking in the sunshine, but the practical side of him knew that future was unlikely.

"Was the outing with the orphans an excuse to spend time with me?" she asked.

"Yes."

She jerked her head around to look at him. Her parasol rested on her right shoulder. He wanted it closed with the handle against her lips. He arched a brow. "You didn't expect me to answer honestly?"

Her laughter rose above the cries of the squawking gulls and the roar of the sea in constant motion. "I suppose I didn't."

He almost told her that he wasn't Kipwick; he wouldn't hide things from her. Only he was keeping secrets, and he certainly didn't want her attention turning back toward the earl. "You're not completely comfortable when I approach you in the park. You're always looking to see who might have spotted me with you. I thought here you might let your guard down a bit."

She gave a little nod. He wasn't certain if she was acknowledging his cleverness or the fact that she was more relaxed here. "The hotel we passed reminds me very much of yours."

"The Bedford. I modeled mine after it and a few others. Mine is a combination of the things I favored in the hotels I visited. When

I was a lad, I used to steal rides on the train to get to the seaside. It always smelled so much cleaner here, seemed so much cleaner. A person had room to breathe."

"You traveled alone."

He shrugged. "Sometimes my brothers would travel with me. Sometimes not."

"You never feared the railway, never at all?"

"For me, it represented freedom. It allowed me to dream that where I was, was not where I needed to stay." He shook his head. "Sounds silly said out loud."

She squeezed his arm reassuringly. "No, it's a beautiful sentiment. I'm impressed you realized it so young when I'm only just beginning to feel the confines, to question them, to want to step beyond them."

She averted her gaze as though embarrassed by her words, and he wondered if she would permanently step away from Kipwick. He didn't want to push her, didn't want to give her cause to doubt his intentions, but decided it would be to his advantage to leave her thinking on what she'd said. Glancing back, he signaled to his man. "Jones, let's set up over here. Fancy!"

His sister looked over her shoulder.

"Over there!" he shouted and pointed.

"Jolly good!"

They spread out blankets. He helped Aslyn lower herself to one of them, then joined her there. Fancy opened a basket that Jones had been carrying and brought out an abundance of food their mum had packed for them. Several meat pastries, blocks of cheese, even a bottle of wine, which he poured for the adults and passed around.

"This is quite impressive," Aslyn said.

"Mum worries about people being hungry," Fancy said, leaning over to wipe a little girl's dirty chin. "It's a wonder we're not all fat. She's always feeding us too much."

"Because there was a time when she didn't have anything at all to feed us," Mick said.

Fancy stilled. "Of course. I don't remember it. It was before I came along, I think."

"By the time you joined our merry band, we were old enough to start working. That helped."

"It must have been difficult, though," Aslyn said. Sitting on a blanket on the sand, she was still regal in her bearing. No one could mistake her for being anything other than an aristocrat. She was so beautiful, so prim, so bloody clean. He couldn't help but think she would have the power to wash the dirt off him, to make him all shiny, perhaps more so than Hedley's acknowledgment would. "What was it like?"

How to explain it to someone who'd never gone hungry? He didn't resent that she hadn't. He was glad of it, wished no one ever experienced a gnawing in the gut, but how to describe it so he didn't come across as a victim? He'd never considered himself one. He shrugged. "Some nights you had a full belly, some you went to bed with a hollow belly. You didn't cry about it. It's just the way it was." And the reason those who took in bastards didn't spend much effort keeping them alive. It was costly to feed them.

"It's so unfair."

"Life isn't fair. You can either rail against it or do what you must to make it fairer."

Aslyn smiled, the teasing of it wreathing her face. "I think I'd have done both."

He held her gaze, which reflected the sky above her, and admitted, "Sometimes I did."

She glanced over at the children. "I don't suppose those little ones go hungry."

"Never."

"If Mick discovers one of the staff punishes a child by denying him his supper, he lets that person go," Fancy said. "The children must be well cared for above all else."

"Where do you find the time?" Aslyn asked.

"You find time for what's important to you. The home is important to my mum, so it's important to me."

Aslyn couldn't help but think that being important to Mick Trewlove would be one of the finest experiences of someone's life. He was so passionate about anyone or anything he cared for: his mother, his buildings, his family, the plight of the unloved children.

Staring out to sea, with her legs drawn up, arms wrapped around them, her chin on her knees, she sat alone on the blanket with her various musings. Mick and Jones had gone to secure ices for everyone. Fancy, Nan and Mary had taken the children to play at the edge of the water. They'd discussed the possibility of using a bathing coach, but as none of them had brought bathing attire, the water's edge seemed adequate. She'd considered removing her shoes and joining them, letting her toes sink into the sand as the water swirled around her ankles, but without a button hook, it would be a challenge to get them off. Bad planning that. Next time —

Would there even be a next time? She

wanted there to be. Another ride on the train, another day at the seaside, more time with Mick. Even knowing she shouldn't want the latter, she couldn't seem not to yearn for it. From the moment the train had begun rolling along the tracks, she'd given no thought to Kip, all her attention focused on Mick. She knew in the future, if she were with Kip, she'd be thinking of Mick. Yet even as she considered him, she knew her guardians would never approve of her taking up with a commoner, no matter how successful he might be. It was one thing for a lord to marry an American heiress — that was accepted. But for a British heiress to become involved with a commoner . . . it was inconceivable. Especially when that commoner couldn't even claim legitimacy as part of his heritage. It wasn't fair, but there it was. While with hard work he'd managed to improve his circumstances, there was little he could do, save an act of Parliament, to make himself legitimate.

With a start, she noticed the dark head bobbing, the arms flailing in the water and realized her thoughts had drifted off to such an extent her gaze had lost its focus, but now it came in sharp and frightening. It was one of the children, one of the little boys. How had he gotten so far out?

Shoving herself to her feet, she began running toward the shoreline, casting a quick glance over her surroundings, searching for help. Nan and Fancy had wandered down a bit, were distracted with the other children. Mary stood at the water's edge, just watching, a satisfied smirk on her face. Aslyn would think on that later. For now, she started screaming for help, while she began wading into the sea, the sand sucking at her feet, the waves pushing against her.

The water was nearly to her hips when she reached the lad, grabbed his arm, even as another pair of hands — large and scarred — snatched the child up. His dark eyes were round and huge as he began retching.

"It's all right," Mick said. "It's all right."

She didn't know if he was talking to her or the boy, but it didn't matter. The words were soothing, filling her with relief, as he cradled the boy in one arm and wrapped the other protectively around her shoulders, drawing her in against his side. "I thought he was going to drown." She heard the tears in her voice, only then realizing they were also streaming down her cheeks.

"He would have," Mick said, as they began trudging back to shore, "if you hadn't yelled and gotten to him."

The weight of her drenched skirts threatened to drag her down, might have if Mick hadn't held her so securely. He wasn't going to let the sea have her, she knew that, drew comfort from it. Waiting at the shore, Jones draped a blanket around the weeping child, took him from Mick, while Fancy offered her a blanket, but Aslyn ignored it, instead working her way free of Mick's hold and marching ungainly toward Mary.

"Why didn't you scream? Why didn't you yell for help?" she asked the servant.

"He's a bastard. They're all bastards. What does it matter if he drowns? It's one less ill-conceived —"

The flat of Aslyn's hand struck quick and hard, its meeting with the woman's cheek echoing around them, the jolt of pain going up her arm, the sting of her palm taking her by surprise. She'd never before hit anyone. It took everything within her not to strike again. "You're let go. I don't care how you make it back to London, but you'll not be traveling with us."

"The duke and duchess —"

"Are not going to hear a single word about this day. You will pack up your things and leave quietly and thank God that I don't have charges for attempted murder brought against you."

"He's worth nothing. No one cares about him."

"I care! And who do you think a jury is going to believe? You or the daughter of an earl?"

"Don't forget the fate of Charlotte Winsor," Mick said quietly. The maid's eyes widened slightly. "Aye, you remember her, don't you? They hanged her for killing a by-blow."

"My lady —" She held out a hand imploringly.

"Off with you now, Mary," Aslyn said. "Before I change my mind and seek out a constable."

As the maid shuffled away, weeping, Aslyn wandered over to where Nan sat on a blanket, rocking the boy who had fallen asleep. She lowered herself to the wool, spread out her skirts and held out her arms. "Give him to me."

As she gathered him up, he barely stirred, weighed hardly anything at all, couldn't have been any older than four or five, was all long limbs. He'd be a tall fellow when he grew up. The fact that someone thought he might not be worthy of growing up broke her heart.

"We need to get you dry, my lady, before you catch your death," Nan said.

"The sun is warm enough to dry me in no time at all." Still she welcomed the blanket Mick draped over her. "Nan, go help Fancy with the other children."

Her maid left her, heading toward the young ones, gathered in a circle around Fancy, with Jones keeping watch, enjoying ices. Mick dropped down beside her, facing her, partway on the blanket — they weren't in her world any longer; they were without boundaries — his thigh lightly touching hers.

"She was watching him," she said, hating the words even as she spoke them, "watching him struggling in the water and doing nothing. How could she just stand there and do nothing?"

"Some people believe those born in sin have no right to life." Gently, with his thumb, he slowly swiped the tears from her cheeks. "Don't cry, Aslyn. The boy's alive thanks to you. Although your parasol is broken."

"My parasol?" It seemed an odd thing to think about at that moment.

He held up the mangled object. "Apparently you stepped on it in your rush to get to him."

The tears started up anew, stinging. "I was afraid I wouldn't get to him in time."

Tenderly, he cradled her cheek. "But you did, sweetheart."

The endearment again, used so casually. She should have objected, but it brought such comfort. For the longest moment, he merely held her gaze and she found herself becoming lost in the blue of his eyes, thought he might lean in and kiss her. For a moment, she thought she wanted him to. No, she didn't think, she *knew*. As a reaffirmation of life. Only he didn't. Perhaps because there were people around, strangers they didn't know, his sister, Nan, Jones, the children. Or perhaps he feared she'd rebuff the overture.

"Who was Charlotte Winsor?" she asked.

With a sigh, he dropped his hand, looked past her to the others, and she rather wished she'd kept quiet, missing so much his touch. How could she long with such yearning for something she'd barely had, probably shouldn't have had at all? "She advertised that, for a modest fee, she was willing to take in babes born out of wedlock. Then she would strangle them, wrap them in newspaper and leave them on the side of the road, to be carried off by wild animals, I suppose."

"My God."

His gaze came back to her. "Someone saw

her disposing of a child, authorities were notified. They have no idea how many she murdered. It was about four years ago, I think, when her trial brought to light the darker aspects of the baby farming trade."

She couldn't recall reading about it, but she'd have been sixteen at the time and her focus had been on preparing for her first Season that would take place a year later.

A corner of his mouth hitched up, and he said dryly, "Well, today certainly didn't turn out to be the sunny, pleasant day I'd planned for you."

"I'm sorry for what this little one had to go through, but today has given me a clearer understanding of things. The circumstances under which children are brought into the world is not their fault. They shouldn't carry the stigma."

"Yet, they do."

Even as adults they carried it, which she suspected was the reason he hadn't leaned in to kiss her earlier. There was a barrier between them, even if it wasn't visible. In the shadows of the night, sin could take hold. But not at a sun-bright seaside.

He watched her sleep on the large sofa in the center of his car, the urchin curled against her lap, her chest, where Mick longed to be. She'd relinquished claim to the lad only long enough for Mick to carry him from the sand to the railway station and into the car. Then she'd settled on the sofa like a queen and signaled for the boy to be handed over. He'd have handed over anything she asked.

He'd been carrying some of the damned ices when he'd heard her cry for help, had seen her rushing headlong into the waves, not seeming to realize that the water would soak her dress, could suck her under, could carry her out to sea. His heart had rioted, threatened to burst through his chest as though his legs were not churning fast enough for it and it could reach her more quickly if not encumbered by ribs holding it in place. He'd never moved with such speed or ferocity in his life — not when chased by a constable for nicking an orange when he was seven, not when he'd needed to fetch a physician because his mum was writhing in pain striving to give birth to a child she'd eventually name Fancy, not when word had come to him that one of his brothers was in danger of dying. But for her, he'd damned near taken flight. To get to her, to save her, to ensure the world didn't continue on without her.

Even if she wasn't part of his world, she

should be part of another's. Just not Kipwick's. She deserved so much better than a
man easily ruled by his vices. She deserved
better than a man consumed with gaining
what another didn't wish to grant him.

Inwardly, he cursed Hedley to hell and
beyond, grateful he had a scapegrace for a
legitimate son. Not so grateful that Aslyn
might reconsider her hiatus and marry the
scourge.

Sitting in a chair that gave him the perfect
view of her, he sipped his whiskey, a tiny
girl with the courage to approach him coiled
in his lap, sucking her thumb, the fingers of
her free hand toying with the buttons on his
waistcoat as though they fascinated her. No
doubt by the end of the journey, the threads
would be loosened to such an extent he'd
have to hand the clothing over to his tailor
to set to rights. He should be irritated by
the prospect. Instead, he thought of his own
not-yet-born daughter nestled there, one
with blond hair and blue eyes and a crooked
smile.

He wasn't supposed to fall for the woman.
His plan was to use her, then lose her. But
how could he not come to care for Aslyn
when she had a hidden courage she wasn't
even aware she possessed? On the surface,
she gave the appearance of being timid,

afraid of trains, for God's sake, but he'd seen her pride and courage not falter when she'd had to hand over her jewels and witnessed her bravery today. And more than that: her willingness to stand up for injustice. She hadn't hesitated to let the servant go, had even threatened her with an arrest, possible prison. She'd been magnificent in her fury and just as glorious in her compassion. Her tears hadn't been for herself and that had made them all the more profound.

"I loike 'er," a tiny voice whispered.

He glanced down at the mischievous lass. "Hmm?"

With the finger attached to the thumb in her mouth, she pointed toward the sofa. "I loike 'er."

Leaning down, he whispered, "As do I."

Far more than he'd expected, far more than he wanted.

CHAPTER 15

She wasn't surprised to see the footmen waiting for her at the station. She suspected everyone, even those not employed by him, obeyed Mick Trewlove's orders. After giving each of the children a hug, an extra-long one to the lad she'd rescued, she smiled at Fancy. "Thank you for thinking to invite me. It was a wonderful outing."

"I'm glad you could join us." She looked at her brother, gave him a wicked grin. "I'll have to think of something else we can do together."

"I'd like that." The words were true even as she wondered how many lies a person was allowed to tell before getting caught. Perhaps she'd misjudged how the duchess would react.

Without thought, she slipped her hand in the crook of Mick's elbow as he began escorting her to her carriage. He seemed at once startled and pleased.

"I can't believe I slept on the train," she said.

"I'd say you've overcome your fear of it."

"Yes, I rather think I have."

"Think of all the places you can go now."

She could have gone to them before in a carriage, but she suddenly felt a sense of freedom and expansion of possibilities she hadn't before. Fear did have a tendency to narrow one's world. When next she traveled on a train, she would think of him, and every time after.

"Your dress and shoes are ruined," he said. "How will you explain it?"

"I'll go in through the servants' entrance and up the back stairs. Nan will see that I'm not spotted. I'll change and go down to dinner with no one the wiser."

"If there is any trouble —"

"There won't be." And if there was, she'd handle it. For some reason, today's outing had liberated her in ways she didn't even realize she needed liberating.

Stopping near the carriage where a footman held the door ajar, he held her gaze. "Thank you for coming."

"Tell me true. Was the outing Fancy's idea?"

"No."

He didn't hesitate, never hesitated with

the truth. She liked that about him, was beginning to think their relationship was the most honest one in her life. If she hadn't centered her marriage hopes on Kip ever since she was a little girl, would she have been equally intrigued by another gent? Or was it just him? Would it always be only Mick?

"Would you send me the address of the orphanage? I'd like to visit on the morrow, make certain Will has recovered fully from his ordeal." Not that she had any idea what she would do if he hadn't, but she did care about the lad, cared even more for the pleasure that made Mick's eyes sparkle like sapphires.

"I will."

"I suppose I should be off."

"I suppose you should."

Only she didn't want to leave. She wanted another few minutes with him, another few hours. Longer.

But he took charge of the matter, moved up to the coach, totally ignoring the footman, and held out his hand to her. Neither were wearing gloves. The salt water had ruined hers. She placed her hand in his, welcomed the closing of his fingers around it, wondering why it was that the merest of touches from him could send sensations rioting throughout her.

Holding her gaze, he brought her fingers to his lips, pressed his mouth against the middle two, allowed it to linger, hot and moist. Then his tongue gave the tiniest of licks across the narrowest expanse of her skin, and her knees nearly buckled, pleasure tightened her belly, and it was as though his tongue had dared to touch the most intimate part of her. The intimacy of the moment, the action, made her profoundly regret there could be no more between them than friendship, that he could not call upon her, that his courtship would be met with fierce resistance. Her birth determined her destiny to marry a titled gentleman. His decided that no matter how high he rose, he would always fall short of being considered good enough for the daughter of an earl. No matter how that daughter felt.

She was barely aware of his mouth leaving her fingers, of his handing her up into the carriage.

"Safe journey home, Lady Aslyn," he said. Then he released his hold on her and was striding away, although she felt that he hadn't let go at all, that he'd somehow managed to anchor her more securely to him.

While she managed to get to her bedchamber and change into dinner attire without her guardians any wiser concerning her day, she lost some of her joy when she strolled into the parlor and discovered Kip waiting with his parents.

He approached, bussed a quick kiss over her cheek. "Aslyn."

Where was the warmth from him, from her? Why did she feel naught but cold?

"How was your day at the museums?" the duchess asked.

Museums? Ah, yes, her lie. "Lovely."

Kip wrinkled his brow. "Mother mentioned you were spending the day with *the Cats*?"

"Ladies Katharine and Catherine. Just a silly moniker I gave them."

"Do I know them?"

"Probably not. They debuted this Season, were snatched up rather quickly."

"By whom?"

"I'm not quite sure." She needed to stop spinning before she toppled into discovery. "I am sure, however, that I'm quite famished. Shall we go into dinner?"

In hindsight, she should have claimed a sudden megrim and returned to her bedchamber. She'd never known such awkwardness at the dining table.

"Have you two decided when the wedding

314

is to take place?" the duchess asked.

Kip looked at her, studied her, but she kept her face impassive, unwilling to give her thoughts away, willing to let him squirm until he told his parents the truth of their situation. "We're still discussing it," he finally said.

"After all this time, I'd have thought you'd be rushing to the altar," the duchess said.

"As you say," Aslyn began, "it's been a long time. I see no need to rush."

"But —"

"Darling, let them move at their own speed," the duke said. "They'll have years together."

Aslyn very much doubted it. "I shall be going to an orphanage tomorrow." She held Kip's gaze. "Perhaps you'd care to join me."

His brow furrowed. "What interest have I in an orphanage?"

"I thought you might have an interest in the orphans."

He looked at his parents, looked back at her. "No, I haven't."

Because he had no interest in anyone other than himself. How had she not noticed it before?

"And I'm quite busy these days handling a goodly number of the affairs of our estates. I don't have time to take off during the day for play."

But he had time to lie about being sick from too much drink.

"Aslyn," the duchess said tentatively, "you don't want to visit an orphanage, dear."

"I do actually. I thought to take them some toys — tops, dolls and tin soldiers."

The duchess stared at Aslyn as though she'd admitted to wanting to dash down the street without a stitch of clothing. "No," she finally said. "We don't involve ourselves in the dregs of society."

"Dregs? They're children. With no parents, no advantages. I want to do what I can to help."

"You have a wedding to plan and then a household to oversee. You'll not have time for such nonsense."

"I don't see that helping the unfortunate is nonsense."

"They will not appreciate your efforts. They will not be glad of your presence. They will resent anything you do for them. They are the dregs of society for a reason, my dear. You cannot lift them up. You must not even try. You will gain naught but heartache. You have been bred, trained, educated in your role as a future duchess. You must not abandon your charge for those who couldn't care less about you."

"I want to be useful."

"You are useful by seeing to your duty." With near desperation, she leaned toward Aslyn and placed her frail hand over hers. "Promise me you will not do this, that you will not go out among the poor, the disadvantaged. That you will not place yourself in harm's way."

"I will take servants with me."

The duchess looked to her husband. "Hedley, forbid her to go."

Aslyn wasn't certain she'd ever seen the duke look so sad. "She's no longer a child, Bella. We can't clip her wings if she's ready to fly."

"She doesn't understand the dangers."

"I'll send extra footmen. They'll stay close. She'll travel in the coach. All will be well."

"It's not as though she's headed into the rookeries, Mother."

The duchess gave her attention back to Aslyn. "Simply send them the toys. You don't have to take them yourself."

"I will be perfectly safe. No harm will come to me. I know it."

"That is when you are at your most vulnerable, when you believe no one would wish you ill. You cannot see the dangers."

"They are children in need of love. They will not hurt me."

"But others would."

"Bella, my love, I promise to see that she is protected."

"Do not give me a promise you cannot keep."

The duke appeared devastated by the words, leaving Aslyn to wonder what promise he may not have honored.

The duchess set her napkin beside her plate. "I am done here. I must abed."

She scooted back her chair. The duke shot to his feet and helped his wife rise. "Carry on without us," he ordered before escorting the duchess from the room.

Kip settled back in his chair, called for more wine. "That was rather odd."

She hadn't wanted to upset the duchess, but she was also weary of feeling like a canary trapped in a cage, with freedom always in view, but never obtainable. "Sometimes I feel as though I'm suffocating here."

"Let's go for a turn about the gardens, then, shall we? I think we could both use some fresh air."

She nodded. He rose, drew back her chair. Standing, she ignored his proffered arm — suddenly tired of any and all assistance as though she wasn't fully capable of taking care of herself — and walked through the manor and into the gardens.

He fell into step beside her and held his silence until they were well beyond the house. "I thought we might enjoy a game or two of cribbage this evening," he said.

"I'm quite weary from the day's activities. I'll be retiring as soon as we've finished our stroll."

"You're still put out with me."

"I am." Although she had appreciated his defense of her going to the orphanage. Tension stretched between them, taut and brittle. He sighed, clucked his teeth. She suspected he was clenching them, as well.

"I owe you an apology," he said quietly, "for my behavior yesterday as well as the night before that. I was troubled by my losses and embarrassed that you saw me lose."

"Telling me you owe me an apology is not apologizing," she stated succinctly.

"Aslyn." He stepped in front of her, halted her steps. "I'm certain this evening my parents noticed there is a bit of a strain between us. It might have even led to my mother's upset or whatever it was."

"Which is the reason we should tell them how things are between us."

"And how is that precisely?"

"That we've ended our arrangement."

"But we haven't. It's merely on hiatus

319

while we . . . couples have rows all the time. They work things out. I'm trying to make it right."

"You can't."

Squeezing his eyes shut, he released a deep breath. "I apologize." He opened his eyes. "I'm sorry. Tell me what more I can say."

"There is nothing you can say, only things you can do, and even then, you are unlikely to change my opinion regarding our suitability."

"Why are you being so blasted stubborn about this? Men gamble, drink, go to clubs. It's what we do."

"The man I marry will not." Edging around him, she began walking toward the rose trellis. He quickly caught up to her.

"Do you want me to go to the damned orphanage with you? Will that make you forgive me?"

"No, actually, I don't want you along. You don't want to be there, and the orphans would sense it. I would sense it. You'd mope about, and it would ruin my outing."

"What has gotten into you? Where is the biddable woman I asked to marry me?"

She swung around to face him. "You broke her heart, and all the love she held for you spilled out. You can't gather it back up." She shook her head. "That's not entirely true. I was hurt, and I saw a side to you I cannot embrace. But I've come to realize I've always viewed you more as a brother, that my feelings for you are not such that we would make good lovers."

"Lovers," he repeated softly, his tone one of someone testing a newly discovered word. He blinked, stared at her as though he'd not considered that once they married they would indeed become lovers. He shook his head, obviously in need of clearing it. "This is not at all like you. Why cast me aside because of one error in judgment? What has brought this on?" His eyes narrowed as he studied her, but she couldn't tell him the truth, couldn't tell him that another man intrigued her, caused her heart to pound, her fears to dissipate —

"Good God, it's Trewlove, isn't it? That's why he insisted I bring you to his affair." He laughed, the sound ugly and horrid. "He's using you just as he's using me."

"To what purpose?"

"Because it elevates him. To be seen with those of noble blood when his blood is tainted beyond redemption."

"You're wrong. He doesn't need us to elevate him. He's risen to great heights on his own volition. With his businesses and his buildings and the kindness he shows others."

"You must know my father would never let you marry him."

She did know. "If he knew him —"

"Never." He looked to the rose trellises. "You will come back around to the notion of marrying me."

"Never," she said, repeating his word.

He swung his gaze back to her, and she saw a humbleness in his features that she'd never before seen. "I remember when I first saw you. You were lying in your bassinet. I was all of eight. My mother was holding my hand. She leaned down and said, 'You will marry her someday.' We are fated, you and I, whether we like it or not."

She liked it not one whit, and if she'd learned anything from meeting Mick Trew-love, it was that destinies could be changed.

Sitting behind the desk in his office, Mick stared at the deed that had been given to his brother, who now lounged in a nearby chair with a smirk of satisfaction. He was familiar with the small estate of Candlewick, but then he'd made himself familiar with all of the duke's holdings — the entailed and the non.

"He just handed it over to you?" Mick asked.

Aiden studied the nails of his right hand as though trying to determine if they were in need of another buffing. Mick didn't know anyone who was so fastidious about his hands. "I told him I couldn't continue to loan him money without some sort of collateral — as he's yet to pay back a penny owed. Apparently his father has signed all the nonentailed properties over to him. He was quite boastful about it."

Things were happening, coming together, much more quickly than Mick had anticipated. "Although I knew he had a gambling habit, I didn't realize he was so remarkably reckless with it."

"He's reckless with everything."

Including Aslyn. The man was not aware of the treasure he held, was in danger of losing. May have already lost. He was so unworthy of her. Leaning back in his chair, Mick tapped his fingers on his desk. "Loudon Green is the one I want. Everything falls apart without it."

"For you or for them?"

Both. "For them. It accounts for the majority of their income. They can't support the other estates without it."

"I find it difficult to believe you sprang

from the loins of a man with no business acumen whatsoever. What possessed him to give his scapegrace son such a valuable property?"

"Because he's his legitimate son. Takes no more than that for the duke to trust him with his valuables — his name, his titles, his legacy."

"But surely he must know the trouble his heir is heading toward."

Mick doubted it. The man never seemed to take much interest in anything beyond his wife. On the one hand, he wanted to admire the duke for his devotion to his duchess, but he suspected that devotion had resulted in him being handed over to Ettie Trewlove. God forbid the duchess discover her duke had sired a by-blow.

His actions wouldn't gain him legitimacy, but they would prove he didn't belong in the gutter. He might be a bastard, but he came from nobility — and that would make him worthy of Aslyn.

CHAPTER 16

"Another package delivered secretly."

Nan didn't sound too pleased, possibly because the package was larger than the others, not easily hidden within the folds of her skirt.

Aslyn rolled out from beneath the covers, walked over and took the long, slender box from her maid. She carried it back to the bed, opened it. Nestled inside was a beautiful white lace parasol, the note accompanying it lengthier than any of the ones that had come before. *Someone I hold in high regard once told me white goes with anything.*

He held her in high regard, remembered her words. Clutching the note to her breast, she knew she shouldn't be so pleased by the knowledge, and yet she was. Kip was wrong. Mick wasn't using her; he had a care for her. She imagined how lovely it would be to begin each day with sentiments expressed by him.

Taking out the parasol, she held it aloft. "Where the devil does he do his late-night shopping?" she wondered aloud.

"My lady, all of this is very improper. He's improper, not the sort with whom you should have secret trysts."

Not the sort with whom she should have public trysts, either. Then she saw the second note, one that had been hidden by the lacy contents of the box. *The Trewlove Home,* he'd written, along with an address. Her heart very nearly stopped, as her first thought had been that he was inviting her to tea at his mother's. Quite suddenly, she realized he was referring to the orphanage, not his mother's home. Silly girl, to be so disappointed.

"We need to dress for going to an orphanage today," she told Nan. "We're to be subtle in our leaving, as I don't wish to upset the duchess."

"Yes, m'lady."

"And we shall need to stop at a toy shop on the way."

She brought a hoard of toys with her, and the orphans gathered around her like she was the Pied Piper. Lowering herself to the floor, giving no thought to the dirt that would infect her lilac skirts, she hugged each and every child who approached. Her laughter floated on the air, a wispy trill that rivaled that of the nightingale in beauty. Her smile wreathed her face, and Mick thought of the joy she'd show to her own children, the love she would shower over them. How fortunate those children would be.

Standing with his back to the wall and his arms crossed over his chest, he took her in as though he were a parched flower and she was both rain and sun offering life. It was obvious she saved her longest, tightest, warmest hug for Will. He found himself envious of a scrawny little urchin.

Finally, she lifted her gaze to him and gifted him with a lopsided, almost shy smile. It was a hard blow to the gut, a kick to the groin, a punch to the chest. No other woman affected him as she did. He should avoid her at all costs, but convincing himself to do that would be no easier than convincing the sun not to show itself at dawn. If she were near, he would always look for an excuse to close the distance between them.

"All right now, that's enough," he shouted, shoving himself away from the wall. "Thank Lady Aslyn and be off with you. No sense in suffocating her for her kindness."

All the children scattered except for the thumb-sucking lass who now clutched a rag doll and stared up at him. He glowered in return. "Off you go, Amy girl. I'll give you a ride on my back later."

Fortunately, it was enough to appease her and send her scampering away. Approaching Aslyn, he held out his hand. She placed hers in it and he drew her to her feet, fought the urge to draw her into his arms. Her ever vigilant maid was standing watch.

"They adore you," Aslyn said. "How often do you come?"

"Every couple of weeks or so. We all rotate checking in, making sure it's all as it should be."

"It's a magnificent residence. You pay a pretty penny for it."

"We wanted to give the children something as close to a home as we could."

"Because you grew up without one."

"We didn't grow up in anything fancy, but our mum's love made it a home."

"Of course it did. I didn't mean to imply otherwise."

He almost offered to show her where he grew up, but she didn't need to see or understand the exact harshness of his life. He'd moved beyond it. All that mattered was where he stood now.

"Mr. Trewlove?"

He glanced over at the matron. "Yes,

328

Nancy."

"The tea is set up on the terrace as you asked."

"Thank you." He turned back to Aslyn. "Would you care for some tea?"

That smile again, the one that would haunt him if his actions caused it to fade away. "Practicing for the day you're invited into a nobleman's parlor?"

It pleased him that she remembered. "No, simply an excuse to spend more time in your company."

Her cheeks flushed pink, and he wondered if he could make other areas of her turn pink with strategically placed kisses.

"Tea would be grand," she said.

All the guilt she'd felt at coming here against the duchess's wishes dissipated the moment she'd walked through the door and seen him waiting for her. His eyes had warmed with pleasure, his mouth had tipped up slightly at the corners. Joy had surged through her, and she'd known that she would willingly go against any of the duchess's wishes in order to spend more time in his company.

Here was further proof that Mick had no interest in using her to elevate himself, because there was no one of any consequence to see them together. He was ever mindful of her reputation, carefully guarding it by keeping his distance when he should. The one time he'd overstepped the bounds they'd been alone, with no witnesses, and while the kiss may have been inappropriate, her reputation had remained intact. Sitting here with him on the terrace, sipping tea, she wished it was night, all the children abed, and they were alone to indulge their desires.

And she did desire him, but what future was there for them? Last night the duchess had once again made her position clear regarding those she saw as beneath her. But in five years, Aslyn's trust would be handed over to her in full. She would move out of Hedley Hall, into her own residence. She would be on the shelf, no longer a woman men sought for marriage. She would have complete and full independence, absolute say in all the decisions affecting her life. Would Mick Trewlove wait five years for her?

She nearly laughed aloud at the absurd thought. He'd made no claims on her, professed no love, although he did offer sweet endearments. Still, it was likely he wouldn't wait so long as a week for her, that she was to him what she had carried in her arms into the orphanage: merely a toy to be played with until broken or grown weary of, forgotten. He had once played with a duke's widow. Why not an earl's daughter?

"I'm not certain I like where those thoughts are taking you," he said quietly, sending her morose musings scattering.

She focused her attention on him, his hand resting near a china teacup it would dwarf when he picked it up. "I'm sorry. My thoughts were drifting."

"Not toward happy places if that tiny dent that formed between your eyebrows was any indication."

She was flattered by how closely he watched her, how much attention he paid to her. "Are you ever invited to balls?"

"Hosted by the lords and ladies of London? No."

"The duchess never hosts balls. If she did, I would invite you."

"I would weather the censure and cuts for you."

"Perhaps there would be none."

"We exist in real life, Aslyn. Not in a fairy tale. There are no happily-ever-afters between a lady and a bastard."

Then what am I doing here?

"Did Kipwick ever take you to Cremorne during the later hours when proper people aren't about?"

His change in topic startled her, yet she welcomed it, not favoring the direction the conversation had been going.

"What makes you think I wanted to go during that time of night?"

His gaze demanded the truth, and she realized he was the sort of man with whom lies did not sit well. She suspected no one uttered falsehoods in his presence.

"The way you asked to stay the night I met you. I suspect if Fancy and I hadn't been there, you'd have argued with him in hopes of convincing him to stay later."

She shrugged. "I have a mild curiosity."

"I have business there tonight. Care to join me?"

The duchess would definitely not approve of this. "I would have to sneak out —"

"You seemed to handle that well enough the other night. I'll have my carriage at the end of the drive at midnight. Just remember to bring a key."

She met him. He'd known she would. She possessed an adventuresome spirit they couldn't tame, and he was grateful for it. In his carriage, she'd sat opposite him, fairly bouncing on the squabs with her excitement. Now they'd disembarked and were preparing to walk into the gardens.

"What if I see some lords I know?" she asked.

"There will be some fancy swells about, but it's unlikely they'll recognize you. This time of night they're not studying faces, they're concentrating on bosoms." There wasn't enough light to see if she was blushing although he suspected she was.

"You like to shock me — or at the very least try to do so."

"Did I succeed?"

"I wouldn't admit if you did."

"Good girl. Keep the hood of your pelisse up and your hand on my arm. No one will bother you." *Except for me, possibly.*

"Except for you, possibly," she said as though she'd read his mind.

"I will be on my best behavior."

But he recognized that even his best wasn't good enough for her. She deserved a man of pedigree. Not one who'd been conceived in error, deemed unworthy of life, and was unwanted.

She couldn't say why she was willing to risk so much to see Cremorne at its darkest. Rumors abounded that activities had become so disgraceful late at night, the area drawing such incorrigibles, that the gardens' very existence was in jeopardy. Some were calling for it to be shut down. Perhaps a chance to see a bit of history before it was gone was what drew her.

Whose leg was she striving to pull? While she wanted to see the wickedness people got up to, she welcomed any opportunity to spend time with Mick.

As they wandered into the gardens, she felt remarkably safe in his company. No one was going to bother him. He swaggered with a confidence and a predatory air that signaled he was not one to be challenged, wasn't accustomed to losing.

She spotted two lords she recognized, one an earl, the other a viscount. While they were dressed in fine attire, they walked as though the earth had suddenly tilted on its axis and they couldn't find their footing. Raised to understand that one's carriage spoke volumes regarding one's place in the world, she was suddenly intrigued to see how very true the axiom was. Neither man possessed the bearing of someone who would sit in the House of Lords. Several second, third, fourth sons wandered by. Having never even danced with them, she wasn't concerned they might find her familiar.

All of the men and the few women who paraded by were loud and boisterous, laughing gaily.

"Let's have something to drink," Mick said.

She wasn't at all thirsty, rather more curious about what she might find deeper into the gardens, but he hardly gave her a choice as he led her into a tavern-like structure and ordered up two pints of ale. Immediately she was intrigued, having never tasted it before. With her first sip, of its own accord, her face skewed up. He laughed.

"It tastes better once you get to the bottom of the tankard."

"Why would they put the best at the bottom?" And how had they managed it? What a trick that must be.

"They don't, but by the time you get to it, everything tastes better, every aspect of life seems vastly improved." He lifted the tankard to his lips and, mesmerized, she watched his throat muscles work. He must have drained half the contents when he finally moved it away from his mouth. She didn't want to contemplate that she was actually jealous of the pewter because his lips had closed over it. "We'll take it with us," he said, leading her back outside.

She took another sip and another, striving to find the portion that would finally be tasty. The odd thing was that it made her body feel warm and snuggly, and eventually she didn't care about the taste. She liked the way she felt after a sip.

Kipwick never would have offered her ale, never would have even thought to let her sample it. Ladies might drink a glass of wine or champagne, a spot of brandy perhaps, but they certainly didn't indulge in something as crass as beer or ale.

"Don't judge ale as a whole too harshly," he said. "My sister has better offerings."

The tavern owner. "What is the name of her tavern?"

"The Mermaid and Unicorn. Gillie's always had a whimsical bent."

"I'd like to meet her sometime."

He studied her, his gaze intense. "I could arrange that."

It would be another excuse to be in his company. How many was she willing to make? A thousand perhaps. Every aspect of him fascinated her. "I'd like that."

Her guardians wouldn't. It would no doubt involve sneaking out again. But she didn't want to have another clandestine meeting with him. She wanted him to call on her properly.

"We'll discuss it later," he said.

With a nod, she turned her attention to her surroundings. It didn't look that much different from when she'd been here before, at least at first glance. Yet the atmosphere was very distinctive. The ladies — and she was being kind and generous to call them such — wore revealing frocks. If one were to sneeze, her breasts would no doubt pop out from behind the cloth. Yet they seemed perfectly comfortable with being so exposed, and the men, based upon their ogles that made her skin crawl, seemed to enjoy the view immensely. She wouldn't want them to look at her in the same leering manner.

On the stage where before a soprano had filled the night with love songs, now a gent sang a ribald tune with crude words that referred to mating. It didn't sound romantic at all. As a matter of fact, she wondered why any woman would want to engage in such sport when it was made to appear so animalistic, so barbaric, so tawdry.

She saw a man and woman, deep within the shadows, her back against a tree, the man's hips cavorting —

Swinging around, she found her cheek pressed against Mick's chest; his arms came around her in a protective embrace. "They are not doing what I think they're doing."

"Depends what you think they're doing."

When he set his mind to it, the man could be quite irritating. "I thought it happened in a bed."

"It can happen anywhere — a bed, a chair, the floor."

"Horizontal. I thought it a horizontal endeavor." Having never discussed so intimate an act with anyone, she couldn't believe she said that to him.

"Horizontal, vertical, sitting, standing, kneeling . . . the positions are limited only by the imagination."

And she suspected he'd imagined and engaged in them all. She didn't want to think about that, didn't want to contemplate him taking a woman against a tree like a barbarian.

"What did you think to find here, Aslyn?" he asked quietly.

"I don't know." She lifted her gaze to his. "Drunkenness mostly."

"Well, there is certainly that. Sip your ale."

He took a long swallow of his. It was such a masculine endeavor. It fascinated her to watch him. His hand fairly dwarfed the mug, would dwarf intimate portions of her if he were to ever touch them. Not that he would, not that she would allow him to take such liberties. She sipped her brew. He was correct. It did taste better the more one drank. Or perhaps it had killed her ability to taste, and nothing would ever taste right again.

She began to wonder what she'd do if Kip crossed paths with her here, for surely he would recognize her. "What if we run into Kipwick?"

"We won't."

His certainty surprised her. "Do you know where he is?"

"There are a few places where he might be."

"Because they provide gambling?"

"Exactly."

"Will you show them to me?"

"Absolutely not."

He sounded so blasted final about it. The matter wasn't even open for discussion. "Why not?"

"They aren't gentlemen's clubs. Men might get the wrong idea about why you are there, so I'd end up with bruised knuckles, and a few men would find themselves missing their teeth."

The happiness that swept through her at an image of such violence was uncalled for. Obviously, ale changed one's perspective, caused one to act out of character. A more horrifying thought occurred to her — that it made one act in character. "You would defend my honor?"

He looked down on her, gave her a wolf-ish smile. "As long as you are on my arm."

Which she'd known if she were honest with herself. It was the reason she'd accepted his offer to come here. For all his humorlessness and questionable origins, he was a gentleman at heart. But also a rogue and a scoundrel. Strange how the latter appealed to her when it absolutely should not. Perhaps she was not truly the lady she'd always assumed herself to be.

A man staggered toward them. Mick's arm came around her back, his hand clamping on her waist, and he fairly lifted her out of the way and to the side as though she weighed as much as a billowy cloud. The gentleman stumbled to the ground, grunted and promptly began to snore. Three laughing men came over to haul him up. His chums, she supposed.

"Why do men overindulge?" she asked.

"It makes their cares go away."

What cares did Kip have that he didn't want? "Do you often get foxed?"

"Never. When you're sober again, the troubles are still there and you have to face them with a blinding headache."

"You're a practical man." He didn't answer; he didn't have to. He wouldn't have dragged himself out of the gutter if he didn't accept reality.

His reality had been harsh, while hers had given her a false sense of the world. She'd been sheltered from all this. Men took swings at each other, cast up their accounts and stumbled around. Bawdily dressed women were kissed, touched in places they shouldn't be, walked off snuggled against a man's side. Children ran around, unaccompanied, thieves, she assumed, when she saw one being chased by a gentleman yelling, "Stop, thief!" She was glad when Mick led her back to the carriage.

Having finished off her ale and a second, she was feeling warm and lethargic. Settling in across from her, he somehow seemed larger. "What was your business here?"

He shrugged as the carriage bolted into the street. "He didn't show."

"Why would you meet someone there and not in your office?"

"Many reasons. Mostly to keep our meeting a secret."

"Who was it?"

"If I tell you, then it's no longer a secret."

She found herself wondering if there had ever been anyone or if he'd made up the excuse in order to give himself a reason to bring her here. She wished the night would never end.

At Cremorne, there had been no one for him to meet, no business to attend to, but he'd feared she'd reject his offer if she knew that all he wanted was more time with her. He couldn't bring her during the proper hours because they would be spotted by people she knew, word would get back to Hedley, and he had no doubt she would be forbidden from associating with him. Even meeting her at the park too often could cause gossip.

He shouldn't enjoy her company so much, should ignore her, at least until his plan came to fruition. Then he could call on her properly, like a gentleman. But where she was concerned, he seemed to have little ability to deny himself. His entire life he'd put yearnings and desires on hiatus in favor of a greater goal, but he was not willing to sacrifice time spent with her. In the end, it could very well cost him everything, and yet he couldn't seem to regret it.

She was unaccustomed to spirits. The ale had hit her hard. She now wore a whimsical smile, as usual one side of her mouth crooked, going up a little higher than the other. He wanted to kiss that higher corner, then the lower one, then her full mouth. He wanted to thrust his tongue between her lips; he wanted to thrust his cock into her heated core. He had no doubt she was a virgin, so she would be tight and he would stretch her —

"She didn't appear to be enjoying it," she said quietly, a thread of sadness woven through her voice.

He blinked, abruptly brought from his fantasy back into reality. He stared at her. He'd been in need of distraction, but he hadn't expected her to provide it with such a nonsensical statement, but then he realized she was referring to the dove against the tree.

"She wasn't being paid to enjoy it."

Her eyes widened slightly. Perhaps it was the bluntness of his words. "She was a strumpet, then."

He shrugged. "That's as good a term as any."

She looked out one window, then the other. Glanced up at the ceiling. Released a long, slow breath. "Is it not enjoyable for women?" She slapped her hand over her mouth. "I can't believe I asked that of you."

"It's the ale. It tends to loosen one's tongue." He grinned. "I like it when your tongue is loosened."

343

"Oh." Her gaze was focused so intently on him that he thought she might be boring into his soul. "Is your tongue loosened enough to provide the answer?"

Maybe hers was a bit too loosened. "I could demonstrate."

"The remainder of my body would have to be loosened for that to happen. Is that why you gave me ale, hoping I would lose all my inhibitions and my moral compass so that you might take advantage?"

"Not exactly. I wouldn't bed you if you were foxed. There would be no enjoyment for either of us in a situation such as that."

"So women can enjoy bedding?"

"If the gentleman is the considerate sort."

"Are you?" Again her hand covered her mouth, her eyes widened. "The words seem to come out before I even realize what they're going to be."

The conversation could become very interesting if he handled it just right. "I am given to believe women find pleasure in my bed."

"Will you go see someone after you deliver me home?"

He needed to. His body was aching with need, and yet he knew any encounter would be unsatisfactory. "No."

She glanced down at her hands, knotted

in her lap. "I'm feeling a bit light-headed."

He stiffened, straightened. "Are you going to be ill?"

"No. I just have all these thoughts that don't want to stay where they belong."

"You can tell them to me. I won't tell a soul." *Tell me something about Kipwick that I can use, that will speed things along.*

"It's a confession of sorts."

Even better. His gut tightened at the thought of her revealing her fantasies.

"I wanted to touch your beard, that first night, when we met."

He almost laughed aloud. He'd been envisioning sins worthy of an afterlife spent burning in hell.

"I didn't even think to do it while we were kissing the other night," she said. "I was so absorbed by the kiss."

"Surely you felt it around your mouth."

She finally looked up at him. "I did a little. It was softer than I thought, but I was focused on other things. I wanted my fingers to touch it."

Leaning forward, he pried her hands apart, took one of them in his. "I propose a trade. You can touch my beard, and I'll kiss the tip of your nose."

"My nose? You can't be serious."

"I adore it. And if I ever meet that obnoxious cousin of yours, I'm going to flatten his nose against his face."

She laughed. "Well, then, I do hope you cross paths with the Earl of Eames someday."

So did he. "Are you agreeable to the terms of the trade I proposed?"

Even in the shadows, he saw her nod. "Don't do anything," he ordered as he gently returned her hand to her lap. Quickly, he yanked off his gloves before loosening the buttons on hers and slowly tugging it off. In spite of his best intentions, he couldn't stop himself from tracing a figure eight over the back of her hand. So smooth, like polished marble — only warm, not cold. Warm and fetching. Turning her hand over, he glided three fingers along her palm. The same smoothness greeted him. He wanted that luxurious silkiness against more than his fingers, more than his beard. He wanted it everywhere.

With the back of her hand nestled in the palm of his, he slowly carried her hand to his jaw where her fingers flexed before combing through the coarse strands. The gentle touch nearly undid him. Keeping his hand over hers, he leaned in farther, filling his lungs with her fragrance as his lips landed lightly against the adorable, imperfect tip of her nose.

She sighed. Whether from his touch of her or hers of him, he didn't know, he didn't care. There was bliss in the sound, joy and contentment, and he couldn't remember the last time he'd experienced any of those sensations.

Because he was so near to other things he wanted, he tipped her face down slightly and planted a kiss on her brow, her temple near the corner of her eye, her cheek —

"You're taking liberties," she whispered, cupping his jaw with her palm, stroking his skin with her fingers. Against his hand the delicate muscles and tendons of hers worked slowly, gently.

Drawing back, he held her gaze. "I am indeed. It seems where you are concerned, I'm not very disciplined."

In the darkness, he heard her swallow. "The ale wants you to kiss me again."

"Well, I would not wish to disappoint the ale." He lowered his mouth to hers.

As their lips merged and their tongues were reintroduced, she was vaguely aware of his crossing over to her bench without staggering or falling in spite of the moving carriage. Her hand remained on his jaw while his continued to cover it as his free arm snaked around her back, drew her in nearer, nestling her partially against his side, partially against his sturdy chest. She wished the waistcoat and jacket were absent, as they'd been that night in his office, so the heat from his body had less fabric through which to travel. It still reached her, seeped through her clothes into her skin, but it wasn't nearly as pleasant.

The kiss, however, was more than it had been before. Perhaps it was because she now knew what to expect of him, or perhaps it was because the ale had chased away all her inhibitions, doubts and guilt, but when he angled his head to take the kiss deeper, she adjusted hers so she could welcome him fully. His deep growl served as both reward and encouragement. He tightened his hold, and she wondered if it were possible for them to be absorbed into each other.

She had intended to remain strong, to resist his allure, but the gentleness with which he'd rained kisses over her face had been her undoing. Bringing her free hand up, she cradled his bearded face between both hands. His whiskers fascinated her. They were at once silky yet coarse. She longed to watch him trim his beard, shave around it. It should have made him look scruffy and common. Instead, it made him appear forceful, dangerous. A man to be reckoned with.

All the dire warnings the duchess had given her were for naught. A woman could be alone with a man without sacrificing her reputation and self-respect. A woman could ask for a kiss without being made to feel as though she deserved nothing better than wandering the streets.

Being in his arms elevated her. It was wrong, on so many levels, in so many ways, and yet she couldn't seem to regret it.

He dragged his mouth from hers, took it on a slow journey along her chin, her jaw, her throat. "Dear God, Aslyn, I would have you here in the coach if you but whisper yes."

"A kiss. Only a kiss." Her response came from a seemingly great distance, and she wasn't altogether certain it was the answer the ale desired, but the lady groomed inside her would let no other pass between her lips.

"Then I shall be content with that."

Disappointment warred with relief. His mouth returned to hers, hungrily, eagerly, and this time the kiss seemed to reach all the way down to her toes. They curled within her boots. She wanted to kick off the heavy leather coverings and run her stockinged feet along his calves, wanted his bare hand to close around the arch of her foot, squeeze it.

Instead, he took the kiss deeper until it obliterated all thought, ignited a blaze of frenzied yearnings that fairly consumed her. How could the mere press of lips, the waltzing of tongues, create a myriad of sensations in every part of her body? Heat swirled, nerve endings tingled, limbs went lethargic even as they seemed energized. She wound her arms around his neck, scraped her fingers up into his hair, relished the silken strands curling around them.

Moving aside her pelisse, he cupped his hand around her waist, glided it up her side, held it there for three heartbeats before moving it along her ribs —

Up. To cradle her breast, squeeze lightly.

She should have been appalled, should have shoved him away. Instead, with a moan, she continued to explore his mouth as though on the morrow she would have to recount every exquisite detail. He brushed his thumb across her nipple, and it responded with a sweet, painful tightening, straining for another stroke.

When it came, she nearly wept. When his mouth left hers, she nearly cried out.

She was disoriented, so it took her a moment to realize they were no longer moving.

Breathing heavily, she stared at him, the glow from the nearby streetlamp chasing away enough of the shadows that she could see him relatively clearly. Not the precise details, not the colors, but the hunger. His desire for her was evident in his expression, as though he suffered greatly.

"I fear I've worked you up into a lather. I suppose you'll go to a brothel now." She hated the notion of another woman touching him, of another being able to touch him in ways that a lady of her station could not, must not, would not.

"No." His voice was raw as though he'd had to drag the word up from the depths of his soul.

"I lied. It wasn't the ale that wanted you to kiss me."

He flashed a grin. "I know."

Sobering, he cradled her face, stroked his thumb over her high cheekbone. "Never in my life have I longed to be legitimate more so than I do at this very moment."

His words devastated her. Leaning in, she took his mouth, sweetly, tenderly. "The circumstances of your birth shouldn't matter."

"Yet they do. I can't take tea with you in a nobleman's parlor nor waltz with you in his ballroom. I can't escort you to the theater or be seen walking you through the park too often." He shook his head. "Even once more and tongues will wag. But I want to see you again. Have dinner with me tomorrow night at the hotel. Currently the few guests we have are not nobility. They are simply people passing through. Even if they see you they won't know who you are. Your presence there will never be found out. There's something I want to share with you."

She could think of many things she'd like him to share with her: his mouth, his hands, his broad chest, the hollow at his shoulder where she was relatively certain her head would fit perfectly. Before her thoughts could careen to portions of his body located below his waist, she cut them off and focused on what he was asking, implying, suggesting: a tryst at his hotel. Another illicit evening spent with him. She knew what her answer should be: *No. Absolutely not. It simply isn't done.*

But where he was concerned, she'd already done a great deal that simply wasn't done. She'd lied, sneaked about, spent time in his company without benefit of a chaperone.

So her answer was not what it should have been, but clearly was what she wanted it to be. "I'll find a way to sneak out."

He stroked his fingers along the edge of her face, along her hairline. "Splendid. I'll send my carriage —"

"No. I'll see to the arrangements. After our outing to sea, I trust my servants to hold my secrets close."

"They'll answer to me if they don't."

She smiled. "Until tomorrow then."

"I shall count the minutes."

As would she. Each and every one until she was again in his arms.

CHAPTER 17

"I'm sorry, m'lady, but he is not at home."

Aslyn gave Kip's butler a stern look. "*Literally* not at home?"

"Literally, m'lady. He has yet to return from last night's" — he cleared his throat — "adventures."

Gambling and drinking and God knew what else he was up to, what other indulgences might be occupying his time. Blast it all! She spun on her heel and strode out of the town house, her entourage of servants in her wake. They needed to talk, to reach an understanding regarding their betrothal: it was over. She could not — would not — marry him when she harbored such intense adoration for another man, when she drifted off to sleep with visions of Mick Trewlove prancing through her head. Although he hadn't truly been prancing. In truth, he'd been barely moving at all, simply holding her gaze and slowly trailing his finger along her throat, over her collarbone, across the swells of her breasts —

Her errant thoughts centering around Mick were more intense, more detailed, more consuming than any she'd ever envisioned with Kip. Mick had the right of it. Where Kip was concerned, her passions had been those of a child, a sister toward a brother, a friend toward a friend. Mick brought forth her womanly passions with little more than a look, a smile, a touch, a word, passions that were very far removed from anything resembling what a sister might feel toward a brother.

The duke and duchess needed to be informed that she was crying off, that she would not marry their son, but she wanted Kip there with her, wanted it understood no hard feelings existed between them — they were simply not suited for each other, not when it came to marriage.

A footman handed her up into the carriage, and she settled back against the squabs. It was an odd thing to realize she had floated through most of her life, never questioning the direction she traveled, the decisions made for her. If Fancy Trewlove hadn't accidentally bumped into Kip that night at Cremorne, she'd have a very different life unfolding before her. She would have continued on her path of merely existing. Being with Mick made her feel alive.

She pondered the way the duchess had described falling in love. The description very much applied to her. She was falling, and she had no doubt Mick would be there to catch her.

She was beautiful, gorgeous, as he handed her down from her carriage. He'd been standing on the front steps of his hotel, staring down the street, like some lovesick loon waiting for her arrival because he was anxious to see her again, to touch her, to inhale her fragrance, to bask in the gentle smile she bestowed upon him.

"I thought you'd never get here."

"For a lady to make a proper entrance, she must arrive somewhat tardily."

The little chit had tormented him on purpose, and he couldn't find it within him to take her to task. She was here now, and that was all that mattered.

With her hand nestled in the crook of his elbow, he began leading her up the steps. "Are your servants going to wait for you?"

"I think it best. I've sworn them to secrecy. My maid isn't too happy about my being here. She wanted to accompany me inside, serve as chaperone."

"But you don't want a chaperone."

That crooked smile again, the one that made his chest expand even as it tightened into a painful knot. "No. She'll wait in the coach."

They reached the doors, and he jerked his head back. "Jones, let them know you'll watch the carriage if they want to enjoy dinner in the dining room and relax in the parlor with some port until they're needed."

"Yes, sir." He pulled open the door. "I'll see to it immediately."

"Are you striving to spoil my servants, Mr. Trewlove?" she asked teasingly as they strolled over the threshold.

"Trying to ensure their silence and reward their devotion to you. Whatever is necessary to safeguard your visit here."

"Having a pristine reputation is such a bother."

"I wouldn't know."

Her tinkling laughter echoed through the lobby. She was at home here, comfortable, and it occurred to him he'd built this place for her before he'd even known she existed.

As they glided through the lobby, the gas-lit chandeliers revealed her in all her glory. She wore a gown that was neither blue nor green, but the manner in which the light caught it made it appear to be both. It reminded him of the sea, seen in the distance, reminded him of their day at Brighton.

At her throat were the pearls he'd returned to her. In her upswept hair was the comb. If she were his, he would gift her with all the jewels in England and beyond. But he had the promise of her for only tonight, for only as long as his secret held, for only as long as she didn't know the truth.

He considered telling her, telling her everything, but it would test her loyalties, and he wasn't confident hers would remain with him. She'd known him such a short amount of time and known them forever. They were family and he . . . he couldn't be certain he was more than a curiosity. She was learning to spread her wings, preparing to take flight, and he had no guarantee she would fly to him. He began leading her up the stairs.

"I thought we were going to have dinner," she said, looking back toward the dining room.

"I want to show you something first." Something he'd not shared with anyone else, something he'd not wanted to share. Until now. Until her.

She didn't object as he continued up the stairs, floor by floor. He had her trust. It humbled him. She humbled him.

"You should know I'm ending things with Kipwick."

He very nearly tumbled back down the stairs with her quiet pronouncement. "Does he know?"

"Only that I've been considering it. I was going to confirm it for him today, but when I went to his residence, he wasn't in."

"He'll be disappointed."

"But not heartbroken. I don't think he truly loves me, and what I feel for him is the love of a girl for a boy. I do not think it would stand the test of years spent in each other's company."

And what of years spent with me? But he didn't ask. It was possible even Hedley's acknowledgment wouldn't be enough to cleave her to him for any great length of time.

"I'm glad." Remarkably so. He nearly went mad anytime he thought of Kipwick kissing her, touching her, having her. Visions of bursting into the church and claiming her there in front of God and everyone had begun visiting his dreams. "I'm glad you're free of him."

"Almost free of him. Our separation is not complete until he also acknowledges that our betrothal is at an end, but it is a bit of a relief to have made the decision."

"He'll try to change your mind." *He needs your dowry.*

"I shall stand firm, because I've no doubt it's the correct decision, and he'll come to understand that as well, in time."

After witnessing her with the servant at the seaside, he didn't doubt her strength of conviction. But he questioned Kipwick's willingness to give up easily, knowing he would never find anyone as beautiful, as courageous, as dignified, as elegant.

When they reached the top floor, he walked her past his office to a solid door that gave nothing away regarding what was inside.

"Your rooms?" she asked.

"Yes. You'll be as safe in here as you were in my office."

Her look was pointed. "You kissed me in your office."

"True. And I'll probably kiss you in here, as well. Would that be so awful?"

Her cheeks flushed. "Carry on."

With a measure of victory, he swung open the door. His butler stepped forward.

"Shall I take the lady's wrap?" he asked.

"In a bit. She might yet have need of it."

She gave him an odd look. "Have you no fireplaces?"

"Not where we're going."

"So mysterious."

"You'll love it, I promise."

Aslyn heard the utter confidence in his tone, and she wondered if the man ever doubted anything in his life. His entryway branched off into a huge parlor and two hallways, one on either side. She assumed the one down which he did not take her led to bedchambers. The one they traversed ended in an enormous library with a wall of windows and three of shelves with enough books to fill a small bookshop. But it was the spiral staircase leading into the ceiling that captured her attention.

"Where does that go?"

"To heaven."

He took her hand, entwining their fingers, holding her firmly as though fearing he could easily lose her on the trek up. The stairs were narrow, they couldn't walk beside each other, and she found herself in a position where she could study his back, his buttocks, his thighs without his being able to see where her eyes wandered, and they wandered over the entire length of him. She did wish he'd dispensed with his jacket, perhaps even his waistcoat —

Heat swarmed through her as she realized she'd very much like to see him trudging up those steps with no clothing at all. She wanted to see his muscles bunching with his movements, wanted to see the strength and firmness. She wanted to see the flawlessness of his flesh.

Never before had she thought in such detail about any man's person, and yet she found herself constantly considering every aspect of his, yearned to see it all revealed, wondered if it would be as magnificent as she imagined.

When the steps came to an end, she found herself enclosed in a small pantry-like room. He shoved open a door and stepped out, pulling her along with him.

Onto the roof.

Into the night. A rare clear one that nearly took her breath.

"We're perfectly safe. There's a wall around the edge." Tightening his hold on her hand, he escorted her across the flat expanse to the short brick barrier that came to her waist. On top of it was what appeared to be a wrought-iron railing, although the dimness of the light prevented her from knowing for certain. In the distance she could see balls of light, the illumination from streetlamps, she assumed.

No moon hovered. The sky was adorned with so many stars she doubted any astronomer would ever be able to count them all.

"It's beautiful," she whispered in awe.

"When all the shops and houses are built, I'll be able to come up here and see the lights glowing in windows and know that inside people are content, happy, hopefully well-fed and warm. I'll have a sense of accomplishment. People can have good lives because of what we're doing here."

People who might have been impoverished otherwise. He might have amassed a fortune, but he hadn't been doing it all for himself. She could hardly see his features in the darkness. "You're remarkable."

"Hardly. In lifting others, we lift ourselves."

He was a man of such confidence, it had never occurred to her he'd be modest as well.

"Can you imagine it?" he asked. "With all the lights?"

"It'll be incredible."

"There are other lights." He drew her in close, her back to his chest, and closed his arms around her. "Watch the sky," he whispered near her ear, his breath wafting over her cheek.

His tongue outlined the shell of her ear, and she sank against him. She should have handed her pelisse over to the butler, as

Mick was making her exceedingly warm. His mouth dropped lower, to the nape of her neck, then moved slowly, provocatively, leaving little nips along the way, to her jawline. The sensations were so exquisite, velvet lapping at silk. Was she the only woman to not know that such sweet surrender existed?

Closing her eyes, she began falling into the bliss.

"Keep your eyes open," he rasped. "Don't look away from the sky in the distance."

The vast expanse before her. The stars tossed across the inky blackness like diamonds on velvet. Her breath caught. The fireworks.

Far, far away, but there all the same, filling the darkness with color, rivaling the stars for attention.

"I'm going to unleash the fireworks inside you," Mick vowed, his voice deep, low, nearly feral in its intensity.

"Mick —"

"Shh. Just keep your eyes on the distance." He suckled at the underside of her jaw, dragged his mouth — open and hot — along the column of her throat.

Yes, she wished the pelisse was gone and the frock, and all the lace and linen beneath it. What a wanton she was. The cool breeze wafted over her, but it did little to dissipate the heat scouring through her.

He unclasped her pelisse and it was gone, falling quickly to the rooftop as though fearing it was in danger of being scorched, as well. His hand glided with assurance and purpose over her ribs, her waist, her hips. Lower still, somehow grabbing her thigh, lifting her leg —

"Open for me," he ordered as though he were Ali Baba intent on stealing treasure.

— and placed her foot on the low brick wall where it met wrought iron. His fingers slipped beneath the hem, wrapped around her ankle, began moving up, deliciously slowly in little circles.

"People will see us."

"There's no light up here. We're one with the night. If they see anything at all, it will be only shadows. They won't be able to discern what those shadows are doing."

She almost asked what the shadows were doing, but she knew. She'd witnessed it the night before, in secretive places between buildings, behind trees, wherever the shadows were the thickest. She hadn't understood why people would risk so much, risk being caught. She understood now, because now she had the itch. The itch for sensations she'd never before known, the pleasure spiraling through her, the promise of it filling her with bursts of color: red, green, white — not only what she saw in the deepening sky but every color and shade that existed in the universe, hues she wasn't even aware were possible.

He cupped her knee, his long fingers toying with the back of it, a place where she'd never realized the skin was so sensitive. "Tell me to stop and I will."

Lethargically she shook her head. "I'm on the train now, I can't disembark."

Her reward for her words was a low chuckle just before he nibbled on her earlobe. How was it that such a small action could create such an enormous tide of sensations? His fingernails scraped along the inside of her thigh, deliciously wicked, scandalously so.

This was what she had craved and yearned for without even realizing what it was she longed to feel. A woman's passion, one that was not satisfied with the landing of a butterfly on a palm, but one that required a man's touch, a man's hands, a man's desire to please.

It was a chore to keep her eyes open as the sensations rioted through her, as her mewling escaped into the emptiness and filled it to bursting. She gasped as his fingers grazed over her curls, as his mouth journeyed over her shoulder, creating an outline of dew where cloth met skin. Separating her folds, he homed in on the tiny little bud at her intimate core. He dragged one finger over it, and she moaned in torment, sweet, exquisite torment. Another stroke, a longer one, a circling.

Her knees threatened to buckle. If not for his arm at her waist holding her against him, she'd have melted into a molten pool at his feet. His thumb replaced his finger, working earnestly to elicit more cries from her, and they were accompanied with gasps and shudders. Slowly, provocatively, his finger entered her and she cried out.

"Not quite yet," he ordered.

Lost in a myriad of sensations, she didn't know what he meant. She couldn't control the tingles, the pleasure dancing along her nerve endings, as another finger joined the first, moving in and out.

"Christ, but you're tight." He seemed pleased by the discovery.

Reaching back with one hand, she grabbed his thigh, dug her fingers into his muscles, searching for purchase, as the fireworks grew larger and larger, filling the sky, filling her, reaching for the heavens —

She cried out as an explosion of ecstasy ripped through her, claiming her, destroying her, rebuilding. Then his mouth was on hers, capturing the cries, devouring, his tongue thrusting with the same urgency that his fingers had only a few seconds before. Her foot was no longer on the brickwork, but was back on the ground, his arms cradling her body against his as his mouth continued to plunder, as though he could share everything she'd just experienced, make it his own, but it was already his as much as it was hers.

He'd given her something no one else had, and at that moment she couldn't imagine anyone else gifting her with it. Tearing his mouth from hers, he cradled the back of her head with his large hand, pressed her cheek against his chest where she heard the rapid thudding of his heart beating in tandem with hers.

"Did you enjoy the fireworks?"

A quick burst of laughter escaped from her. She nodded, taking satisfaction in his low, dark chuckle. "I think I would stand here every night watching them," she said on a soft sigh.

"The rooftop is yours whenever you want it."

But she only wanted it if he was there to share it with her.

■ ■ ■ ■

He sat against the arm of the sofa with one leg stretched out on the cushions, the other foot on the floor, and her nestled between his thighs, her back to his chest, sipping her wine. He'd never known such satisfaction as he had the moment she'd come apart in his arms. Nothing he'd ever purchased or acquired in his business dealings had brought him such pleasure. With her cheeks still flushed, he knew the only thing he'd ever enjoy more would be taking her to his bed and possessing her completely.

"Did you choose this location because you could see the fireworks of Cremorne?" she asked.

A low fire burned on the hearth. It wasn't really needed for heat, but he liked the atmosphere it created. One perfect for seduction, although this night it seemed he was finding himself the seduced rather than the seducer. "No, it was a lovely surprise I discovered much later. I wanted access to the roof so I could look out over everything I'd accomplished, take a measure of pride in it." Reaching for a small chunk of cheese on a platter on the nearby low table, he carried it to her mouth, fought not to grow hard as her lips closed around it, grazing his fingers.

"I thought we'd be dining downstairs in your hotel dining room."

He heard no chastisement or disappointment in her voice. "That's what I'd planned, but then I decided I wanted you all to myself."

Watching the blush creep up her neck, he pressed a kiss to her nape. Her willingness to accept pleasure at his hands had taken him by surprise. Other than the desperate duke's widow, no other lady of quality had ever given him leave to put his roughened fingers on her, in her. Tonight, for Aslyn, he wished they'd been as smooth as silk, had never grown callused lifting tin pails, had never grown rough hauling bricks.

"I should think your wife will have a jolly good time furnishing all the rooms," she said, no doubt an attempt to keep the conversation bland rather than naughty.

He'd taken her on a tour of the flat. Other than the rooms for which he had an immediate use — the front parlor, the library, his bedchamber — he'd done very little in the way of readying the place for visitors. His brothers and Gillie generally joined him in the library where they could pour from decanters to their hearts' content. Fancy and his mum took tea here in the parlor. "What would you do with the rooms?"

"Brighten them up a little bit, I think. You have enough dark in the hotel. After a while I think too much of it could become oppressive."

"I wouldn't want the pink of your bedchamber."

Twisting around, with her elbow digging into his stomach, she caused him to grunt. Her brow was furrowed. "How do you know the color of my room?"

"It was a guess. All the pink I've seen you wear."

"I'm not wearing pink tonight."

"No, tonight you're dressed like the sea." He skimmed his finger along the low neckline, tempted to slip his hand beneath the cloth and cradle her breast, show her how every aspect of her body was created for pleasure. "I like it. Although I'd rather have you with nothing on at all."

Her eyes widened as she swung back around and settled against him. "The things you say."

He pressed his open mouth on the curve where neck met shoulder. "You'd be disappointed if there wasn't some gutter in me."

She sat up, faced him, and he wished he'd kept his mouth shut. "What you said isn't something that came from the gutter. If you're drawn to someone, shouldn't you want to see them without their clothes? I constantly think of you going about without a stitch of clothing."

He arched a brow. "Do you?"

"Well, not constantly. Often."

"I didn't think ladies of quality had such thoughts."

"I didn't." She knotted her fingers together, studied them. "Until you."

Shoving himself up, he cradled her cheek with one hand. "I'm glad."

"It's one of the reasons I know Kipwick and I aren't suited. I could never —"

She lifted her gaze to the ceiling, and he knew she was seeing beyond it to the roof.

"There's more, much more. What I did on the roof . . . I can do it all with my mouth."

The blush that took over her face was the reddest hue he'd ever seen. He loved her innocence, loved how she wanted so desperately to be sophisticated, to act as though carnal desires weren't new to her. But they were, and he wanted to introduce every aspect of them to her. He wanted to take her on a sojourn of pleasure that would leave her too exhausted and sated to ever leave his bed.

"You're wicked. You know saying that is going to make me think about it."

He grinned. "Which means you'll be thinking about me."

"I would anyway." She skimmed her fingers over his beard before cupping his chin in her palm. "Sometimes I wonder what you would look like without it."

"I'm curious myself."

Her eyes glinted. "Have you always had it, then?"

"From the day I noticed whiskers."

She scraped her fingers along his jaw. "You have a strong jaw." Toward his chin.

He swooped down, captured two of her fingers with his mouth. She released a tiny squeal of surprise. When she would have pulled them free, he wrapped a hand around her wrist, licked the tips that tasted of a strawberry she'd eaten earlier.

"Oh my," she whispered on a sigh.

Slowly he began moving her fingers in and out of his mouth, like the waves rolling onto shore, like his cock wanted to thrust in and out of her. The delicate tendons at her throat worked as she swallowed, her eyes focused on the erotic play, the blue of her irises deepening.

He stroked his tongue along the seam between the two fingers, suckled gently.

Without averting her gaze, she closed her hand around his that rested on his thigh and carried his hand up.

Her lips parted slightly, her tongue slipped out to coat them in heavenly dew before her mouth closed around the middle two fingers of his hand and the velvety heat consumed him as though she'd taken in his entire body. He grew so hard he ached for the want of her. As he continued to stroke her fingers, he watched mesmerized as she pushed his into the sweet confines of her mouth, suckled briefly, only to withdraw them, dragging them over the velvety roughness of her tongue. In. Out. In. A swirling of her tongue. A suck. Out.

She mimicked his actions, and he didn't know if he'd ever experienced anything so erotic. If anything had ever made him grow so hard, so fast, so near to bursting.

He'd thought only to stop her exploration of his chin, and now he wanted nothing more than for her to explore every inch of him.

Her eyes were filled with heat and desire. He suspected his were, as well. Christ. Even the duke's widow hadn't done this to him, hadn't taught him the pleasures to be gained in going slowly, in taking one's time, in merely tasting.

He pulled her fingers out of his mouth, pulled his out of hers, cupped the back of her head and brought her down to him so their tongues could experience what their fingers had. Leisurely, yet deeply. Stroking and thrusting, suckling and soothing.

His groan was low, nearly feral, perhaps because he knew she would give him no more than this tonight, that he would ask for no more, even as his body was tense with need, with a hunger for her that would terrify him if he thought about it later when she wasn't in his arms. But as long as she was curled against him, he would face the hell of not possessing her completely, if only for this. For now this was enough, this was everything.

This was a promise of more.

He was offering more. She knew that as she explored the sultry confines of his mouth laced with the dark, rich wine he'd been drinking. He was offering everything even as he had to know that she would not take it, that she was not yet ready to cast aside all the morality she'd been taught.

But oh how she was tempted.

Draped over his chest, his belly, between his thighs, she could feel the hard length of him pressed against her. It had startled her at first, when she'd taken his fingers into her mouth, and she'd become aware of his body changing. Startled her but not frightened her. Instinctually she'd understood what was happening, that he was preparing for the taking of her —

But as he'd initiated no advances toward that completion, she realized he quite possibly had no control over that aspect of the mating ritual, and that pleased her even more. That she could have such influence over him, that she could drive him to such distraction. He wanted her, he desired her, and she'd never felt more powerful in her life.

This was a man who controlled everything around him, and yet she could control him.

She wondered if she took him upon the roof if she could show *him* fireworks. Some night she might, but for now she was content to be where she was, with his broad hands running over her back, her buttocks, squeezing, lingering, moving on.

The sensations he elicited from her were what she'd hoped being with a man would be like. All heat and hunger and need. The need to be touched, stroked, kissed. The need to be held as though it was the only way to stay anchored, the only way to fly together.

Here was the itch about which he'd spoken. Now she understood why a woman would risk so much for a moment's pleasure. Because it extended beyond the moment, because she would carry it with her into tomorrow and the day after. Because it elevated her, gave her confidence, made her feel loved.

Loved as she'd never felt before.

Cupping her face between his hands, he drew back, held her at a short distance, his gaze searching, and she wondered if her lips were as swollen as his. They felt as though they were when she ran her tongue over them, taking delight in the way his eyes tracked her movement, the way they darkened.

"Damn, but you are temptation and sin," he rasped. "I should see you home while I still have the will to resist."

"Am I so hard to resist?"

"Nearly impossible."

She grinned, delighted by his words.

"You little witch. You're happy about that."

"I am. I feared I wasn't."

His thumbs stroked her cheeks. "You are the most tempting creature I've ever known."

She ducked her head into the curve of his neck. "You humble me."

377

"My God, Aslyn, I am the one humbled. You're the daughter of an earl, and I'm but a bastard."

Her head came up. "You're a successful businessman."

"With no lineage to speak of."

She shrugged. "You'll be the first of your line. Every great dynasty must have a start somewhere."

He chuckled low. "You see me with a dynasty?"

"I see you being — doing — anything you want." She pushed herself up until she was sitting on the sofa. "It's not all fun and games, being part of the nobility, you know. There are expectations, duties and responsibilities. We're not allowed to scratch itches until we're wed."

He shoved himself up until both his feet were on the floor and he was sitting beside her. "You're not allowed to lose your virginity until you're wed." Leaning in, he kissed the side of her neck. "I think you learned tonight there are other ways to scratch itches."

"I suppose you know them all?"

"I know a good many. I take great care not to have any by-blows."

He would, of course. He had a keen understanding of the price paid by the illegitimate while until recently she'd only had a vague notion that they existed.

Standing, he held out his hand to her. "Let's see you home."

Shortly thereafter, they located Nan and the coachman in the parlor, sipping brandy before the fire, talking low. When they spotted Aslyn, they both jumped to their feet as though caught doing something they shouldn't.

"Did you enjoy your relaxing evening?" Aslyn asked.

Nan bobbed her head. "It was a lovely dinner. Thank you, Mr. Trewlove."

"You can thank me by keeping where you came tonight to yourself."

Nan tilted up her chin. "After dinner, my lady went to bed with a megrim. We never left the residence."

He grinned with approval. "I hope she feels better on the morrow."

"I'm certain she will, sir."

"We should be on our way, then," Aslyn said.

As they neared the coach, Mick asked, "Nan, have you ever ridden atop a coach?"

"I most certainly have not." Her tone indicated she was offended by the question.

"Then you're in for an adventure."

Her maid came to an abrupt halt. "My lady?"

Aslyn looked at Mick. "My maid doesn't travel outside of the carriage."

"Tonight she does. I'm seeing you home."

"That's not necessary."

"I insist. I'm not sending you through the London streets without escort."

"I travel in this manner, with only Nan, the driver and the footman, all the time."

"Not tonight, not anytime after you've been with me."

The man was so stubborn. "Then they'll have to bring you back."

"I'll walk or find a hansom." In front of her servants — thank goodness they were the only ones about at the moment, except for Jones at the door — he cupped her face, tilted it up and held her gaze. "You are too precious for me to risk that something might go awry on your way to Hedley Hall. It's late. Ruffians are likely to be about."

Her heart warmed with his words that she was precious to him, but she also saw no need for his protection. "So we'll both be at risk."

His grin was wicked and dangerous, as though he were spoiling for a fight. "I can hold my own against them."

She had no doubt of that, and she did appreciate that he worried for her. "All right. But Nan does not ride atop."

"There's a hundred pounds in it for her if she does."

"You can't buy —"

"I've always wanted to ride atop a carriage," Nan suddenly announced. "I think it'll be jolly good fun."

Mick's smile was one of victory that made her want to kiss him. "Fine," Aslyn said. "Let's be on our way."

Like a gentleman, he took the seat opposite her. He had the sense she wasn't quite pleased with his high-handedness, that she wasn't happy he'd been unwilling to let her travel without his escort. The odds were she'd get home safely. But even a one in a hundred chance she wouldn't was too high as far as he was concerned. And he did know how to handle ruffians. He and his brothers had been dealing with them their entire lives.

Once the carriage bolted forward, he crossed over to her, took her in his arms and claimed her mouth with his own. He would make her grateful he was there.

It took very little. An urging of her lips to part, a thrusting of his tongue, and with the sweetest of moans, she sank against him, into him, her slender arms coming around his neck, her hands clasping the back of his head, holding him in place as though she feared he'd only tease her, then withdraw.

But teasing her teased him as well, and he'd had enough of it for tonight. She was no doubt blissfully unaware of how tightly strung he was, how her hand below his waist, at the fall of his trousers, would have him embarrassing himself. He'd never before been so near the brink of release without being buried in a woman.

She unmanned him.

It took so little on her part to have him raging with need. A dozen times since he'd met her, he'd considered seeking surcease in the arms of another, and yet he wanted no other, understood wholeheartedly that no other would satisfy. Even taking himself in hand did little to assuage his desire, his need, his want for her. He couldn't even claim the release to be temporary because it brought no satisfaction whatsoever, no dulling of his yearning for her.

But the yearning went beyond the tasting of her haven between her thighs, the ecstasy of her muscles closing around his cock, his thrust taking him deeper to the heart of her — the yearning encompassed what he'd always considered mundane: her smiles, her laughter, her fragrance, the lilt of her voice. Her mere presence.

Whether she sat across from him or was nestled against him, she satisfied something deep within him that had never before been touched. Now it was awakened and would not settle back into slumber.

He dragged his mouth over her chin, along her jaw to the sensitive area just below her ear and nibbled as if it were the finest delicacy. To him it was. "When can I see you again?"

"I have to settle things with Kipwick first," she said distractedly, as though being awakened from a pleasant dream.

"Speaking with him might be difficult."

She drew back. "Why do you say that?"

"He's spending a good deal of his time at Aiden's club. He's taken a room there, to be honest." Not a room exactly. A bed, a pallet, to catch a few winks before asking for another loan and returning to the tables. Not that he was going to tell her all of that.

"I must speak with him."

"Not there."

Shoving away from him, she gazed out the window. He wished he'd kept his tongue in her mouth instead of giving it freedom to speak. "I'll get word to him that you need to see him."

"He told me that winning was a thrill."

"It is. The problem with thrills is that after a while they become mundane when they are the same one over and over, so one must look for ways to make them bigger. A larger wager, more at stake. To lose is a harder kick in the gut, but to win is an elation like no other. However, it, too, becomes the same. Habitual gamblers are always in want of a more intense thrill."

"It's an addiction of sorts, isn't it?"

"For him, yes."

She turned to him, a sadness in her eyes. "Can you help him? Can you have your brother close his doors to him?"

"Yes." *As soon as I've acquired what I want.* But studying her, he wondered if it was worth it, if there was another way to gain the acknowledgment he wanted — needed — more than ever. Recognizing his bloodline — even if his blood wasn't pure — would gain him admittance into Hedley Hall, would allow him to be seen with her in public.

He wanted her on his arm, proud to accompany him, into a fancy ballroom filled with those of noble birth.

"I'll speak with him," he added, as though Kipwick would listen to anything he had to say. Although when Mick presented him with all his markers and deeds, the man would pay a great deal of attention to his words.

As the carriage turned onto the drive, she smiled. "I have faith in you."

Her words devastated him. He should confess everything, but in the confessing he'd lose her. However, if he plowed ahead, he would make things right. She would see that everything had been necessary to ensure they could step out of the shadows.

Chapter 18

The one place and time the duke and duchess could be counted upon to be together, without fail, was the gardens at two every afternoon, and so it was there that Aslyn sought them out.

Watching as they slowly strolled from one trellis of roses to another, smiling at each other, talking softly, the duchess reaching up to touch her husband's jaw, he bending his head to kiss her brow, Aslyn realized that what they had, the love they shared, was what she had always longed for. She'd have not had it with Kip.

She'd have it with Mick. She had it with him now. His protectiveness, his gentleness, his yearning for her, his refusal to push her beyond what she was ready to give.

She loved him. It was that simple, that complex.

Their road would not be an easy one, but all the same she wanted to travel it.

"I daresay, the gardener has outdone himself this year," she announced, approaching the couple.

The duchess turned, smiled softly at her. "I was just saying the same thing to Hedley. I'm particularly fond of the pink ones."

"They're quite lovely."

"I suppose you've come to tell us you're going to make another visit to that awful orphanage."

"It wasn't —" She bit back her retort. This was not the direction she wanted this conversation to go in. "No, actually. I wanted to get your permission to invite someone to dinner."

"Kipwick, perhaps? I don't know where he's been of late, but he certainly doesn't require an invitation."

"He's been at his clubs."

The duke furrowed his brow. "Every night?"

"As I understand it, yes."

"He attributed his recent absence to business dealings concerning the estates."

"You've spoken with him?"

"A couple of days ago."

"Perhaps I have the wrong of it, then." Although she very much doubted it. "But no, I wasn't considering inviting him. As you say, he requires no invitation." Although things were likely to go more smoothly if he wasn't present. "I was hoping you'd be open to inviting Mick Trewlove."

"No."

The duke's response came so fast, so stern and with such thunder that Aslyn was taken aback, wasn't quite certain what to say.

With her eyes blinking and her delicate brow creased, the duchess looked from him to her. "He's the bastard Kip was telling us about, isn't he?"

She hated having that particular moniker associated with him when he was so much more. "He's a successful businessman."

"He's not welcome here," the duke said.

"But —"

"No discussion. That is the end of it. Bella?" He held out his hand to his duchess.

"He's quite right, my dear. We don't associate with that sort."

"With a man who works hard, who has risen from nothing, who helps others? A man who —"

"That's enough!" the duke bellowed. "You are not to speak his name, and you most certainly are to have nothing to do with him."

"Do you know him, Hedley?" the duchess asked.

"No. I only know of him, and none of it good."

"If you believe that," Aslyn said, "then you don't know him at all."

"How is that you do?" he asked, his gaze boring into her.

Swallowing, she clasped her hands before her. "Kip and I met him at Cremorne. He was quite fascinating —" She couldn't tell them that she'd met him on several occasions since. The awful realization struck her that the duke might actually lock her in her chambers. She'd never seen him so angry, so forceful. "I thought we all might enjoy the opportunity to get to know him better."

"No."

Again the single word delivered like a death knell.

"You're being unreasonable, to not even give the man a chance to prove himself."

"But, my dear," the duchess whispered conspiratorially, "low morals and all that."

"His parents most certainly, but not him."

"Associating with him, no matter how innocent, will lead you along the path to ruin."

She bloody well didn't care.

"You will not be seeing him again," the duke commanded, and she wondered if he suspected Cremorne wasn't the only occasion she had spoken with him. "Bella." Once more he held out his hand to his wife. She thought she saw it shake before the duchess slipped hers into it.

"I'll send word to Kip that he's expected for dinner tonight," the duchess said.

Then they strolled away as though they weren't the most unreasonable, close-minded couple she'd ever known.

Darkness had only recently fallen as Mick sat at his desk in his office and studied the markers, vouchers and deeds in his possession. He still didn't have the one he craved, but wondered if these would be enough to convince Hedley to acknowledge him. He was growing impatient —

Impatient to publicly claim Aslyn, weary of keeping the truth of his paternity from her, feeling guilty that he'd introduced Kipwick to the Cerberus Club, knowing his weakness.

She'd never asked anything of him before, but she asked this: that he have the doors to the club closed to the earl. And it was within his power to grant her wish. How could he deny her this one small request?

Bloody damned hell.

He'd argued with himself all day about going to have a word with Kipwick, but he'd known a word wouldn't be enough. It was

Aiden he'd have to talk with. No more markers for the earl, no more accepting property as collateral. Then Mick would have to spread the word to every lowly club that existed throughout London that the Earl of Kipwick was not to be welcomed.

For her, he'd cut off his means for acquiring what he longed for.

Hearing the echoing footsteps, he glanced up to see her marching toward him. Opening the top drawer in his desk, he surreptitiously slid the documents inside, closed it up tight and came to his feet just as she barged into the room.

"They won't have you to dinner."

He stared at her, unable to make sense of her pronouncement. "I beg your pardon?"

"The duke and duchess. I asked them to invite you to dinner and they refused. Because you're a by-blow."

Of course they had. Or at least the duke would have. Mick doubted the man had ever told his wife that not ten months into their marriage he'd sired a son by another woman. If the duchess did know of her husband's transgressions, she'd have not wanted evidence of his unfaithfulness at her table. "Why would you —"

"Because I'm tired of us being in the shadows." She began pacing. "Because I

391

wanted them to meet you, to know what a remarkable, wonderful man you are, to understand why I can't marry their son."

"You told them you weren't marrying Kipwick?"

"No, not yet, but when I do I want the reasons to be perfectly clear."

He'd never been so humbled, so touched. He had *hoped,* but to know that she was willing to acknowledge him publicly —

"You're the daughter of an earl and I —"

"Am a bastard. Yes, I know. But if you didn't tell anyone, who would know? It's not as though it's branded on your forehead." She charged forward. "You're someone's son. What does it matter that your parents weren't married? I don't care how you came into the world. I only care that you're here. I only care that when I'm with you I'm happier than I've ever been in my entire life."

She was magnificent in her fury on his behalf. He thought he could never love her more than he did at that particular moment. For her courage, her determination, her willingness to fight for him.

"You don't keep me in a cage." She cradled his cheek. "You pushed me to travel on the railway. You don't strive to keep me innocent. You take me to Cremorne when it's naughty, you create fireworks within me. But more than that, you're a good man. I know about Tittlefitz, what you did for him. I think the night I heard that story is when I might have begun falling a little bit in love with you. I told Kipwick I couldn't marry him because of his gambling. But I lied. You're the reason. I can't marry him, because I want to marry you."

He jerked her to him, claimed her mouth. All his life he'd been searching for acceptance, and here it was in the form of a woman with a tilted-up nose and crooked smile.

Drawing back, he gazed into her eyes. When she looked at him as she did, he could almost believe when he touched her, he wouldn't leave grime in his wake. "Your guardians would not approve of my marrying you. Society would not approve."

"I don't care. When I am with you, I feel as though, for the first time in my life, I am real, I am seen. It's difficult to explain, but I want to experience everything with you that a woman can experience. Would you make love to me?" she asked softly, and yet his body reacted, growing hard and tense, as though she'd licked the words over his skin.

"If I touch you, Aslyn, I'm not going to

stop touching you until I've touched every aspect of you."

"I don't want you to stop."

"You will leave here ruined."

"You won't ruin me."

"I will take your virginity."

"You can't take something if it's given to you."

He was not worthy of her, yet even knowing that, he couldn't stop himself from lifting her into his arms and carrying her to his chambers.

Cradled in his arms as he trudged down a hallway, she'd never been more sure of anything than she was of him and her. It was imperative he understand what he meant to her, that she cared for him in spite of his origins.

She was not like the duke and duchess; she did not judge people based on aspects of their life over which they had no control.

He burst into the bedchamber, a huge four-poster taking up a good bit of the room. She had no doubt it had been made especially for him. He came to a stop near it, lowered her feet to the floor.

"You haven't a tree in here. I suppose we'll have to make use of the bed."

He laughed, deeply and richly. "What a

tart you've become."

"Only for you." She began working on the buttons of his shirt.

"Be sure, sweetheart," he said solemnly, causing her to recognize the gravity of what they were doing, how it would affect her life. She was opening one door, but closing all others.

"I am sure, more so than I've ever been."

When half the buttons were undone, with a growl, he dragged the shirt over his head and tossed it aside before turning his attention to her. With a swiftness she'd not expected, he had all her clothes in a heap on the floor and she found herself standing before him without a stitch of clothing. She thought she should have been embarrassed. Instead, she felt free.

"My God, but you're beautiful," he said reverently "Perfect. Every inch."

"Hardly."

"To me you are."

He claimed her mouth so sweetly, so tenderly, that she nearly wept. She wanted this man as she'd never wanted anything else. She ran her hands over his bare chest, while his traveled over her bare back, and she sensed that he was striving to go slowly for her, only she was weary of being pampered. She was the one who broke off the kiss, who stepped beyond his reach. "The boots need to go."

He dropped into a nearby chair. "Onto the bed with you," he ordered while tugging off a boot.

She clambered onto the mattress, resting back on her elbows, watching him. When he was down to his trousers, he placed a knee on the bed. She held up a hand. "No, no, no. The trousers go."

"Later."

"Now."

He held her gaze. "You've never seen a man when he's aroused. Let me ease you into it."

"No."

"Aslyn —"

"We're going to come to this bed as equals."

He gave a brusque nod. "As you wish."

He shed his trousers. She stared at his swollen, jutting cock. Obviously, she had a misconception regarding what took place during mating because she'd always assumed a man entered a woman, but he was not going to be able to put that inside her. Still, she was mesmerized by it, by how proudly it stood at attention. "I want to touch."

With a groan, he climbed onto the bed,

stretched out beside her. "Oh, you will, my lovely. But first —"

Cradling her cheek, he took her mouth with urgency. She opened to him, loving the heat, the parrying of their tongues, the thrusting, the suckling. The light coating of hair on his chest tickled the side of her breast, while his hand closed around the other, kneading it gently. His thigh came between her legs, his knee nudging them apart.

It was marvelous, so marvelous to have so much of him touching her. She scraped her fingers through his hair, over his shoulders and back. Such strength there. She loved the play of his muscles, bunching and flexing, as he moved various parts of his body to have easier access to hers. His member was hard and warm against her thigh. She could feel a bit of dampness at the tip. She wanted to touch it with her tongue, but that would mean ending the kiss, and she wasn't quite ready to do that yet.

She loved the sounds he made, the growls and groans. The curse when his lips abandoned hers to trail over her throat before returning to her mouth. She found herself writhing as her body strained against his.

His mouth moved away from hers. The absence of a curse alerted her that he wasn't going to be returning immediately for another kiss. Instead he nipped at her collarbone with his teeth, gently, before soothing it with his tongue.

"There it is," he said.

"What?"

"The freckle. I knew you'd have one."

He lowered his head to her breasts, pressed a kiss to an inside swell.

"I don't know that it's a freckle. It's just a blemish of some sort."

"It's perfection."

He peppered kisses all over her breast as though it were home to a constellation of freckles, when there was only the one. Then his tongue circled her nipple before his mouth closed over it and he suckled.

She nearly came off the bed. She might have if his body wasn't half covering hers. Such sweet torment. Her sighs floated around them, seemed to encourage him to become even more diligent in his efforts. She skimmed her hands over every aspect of him that she could reach. He was such a fine specimen, with a well-toned body. She suspected every now and then he hauled carpentry materials or assisted with the building. It was impossible to imagine him not occasionally getting involved, lending a hand, taking part in what he was building.

For all his sitting at his desk and looking at papers, she suspected there was a part of him that grew bored with it, that yearned for the physical activity. He'd never go to fat. She suspected when his hair turned white, he'd be as fit as he was now.

She wanted to see his hair turn white, kiss the wrinkles that would appear on his face.

She wanted the past not to matter to him. Only the future.

He eased down, planting kisses on each rib as he went. His tongue circled her navel as he scooted farther down. He lapped at the juncture where thigh met hip. Sitting up, she scraped her fingers along the length of his back.

He released a low moan. His hand came up, plastered over her chest and pushed her back down.

"I want to touch you," she told him.

"Later."

Nibbling at the inside of her thigh, he spread her legs, positioning her knees so they were raised. Vulnerable, she was vulnerable to him, and yet she'd never felt more sure of herself.

He blew on her curls. She laughed. "That tickles."

He lifted his gaze to hers, and in the blue depths, she saw with startling clarity that what was to come next was not going to tickle, was not going to make her laugh. Lowering his head, he stroked his tongue over the most intimate bit of her.

"Oh my word." She pressed her head back against the pillow. Her hands clutched the sheets as his mouth worked an incredible magic, licking and sucking. She felt his finger slide inside her.

"So tight. So wet. So hot."

"Is it a problem that you're larger than your finger?"

"No, sweetheart. You'll be glad of it when we're done."

His mouth returned to its endeavors, and sensations gathered at her core. Her cries sounded almost desperate. Her hands ached with their hold on the sheets. Her thighs squeezed against his shoulders. There was no relief from the increasing pleasure. It hovered, it hovered.

And then it was as though he struck a match to a box of fireworks and set each one off within her. She cried out, her back arching, her hands clasping his head as ecstasy shot through her with bursts of sensations, colors and emotions she couldn't describe, that thrilled, excited and terrified her.

Slowly he moved up her body, reminding

her of a wolf that had scented its prey.

"Dear God, but you're beautiful when lost in rapture," he rasped.

She smiled, laughed. "I'm a wanton."

"A gorgeous one." Resting on his elbows, he kept much of his weight off her as he lowered his head and took her mouth.

She could taste herself on his lips, his tongue. Scandalous to allow him such intimate liberties, certainly not something she'd ever imagined a man might do with a woman, and yet why shouldn't he when she wanted to kiss him everywhere, as well?

He shifted his hips, and she was aware of his nudging the damp area where he'd just feasted. Instinctually she lifted her hips to him, felt him poised at the opening.

"Stop me if it hurts," he whispered near her ear before taking her lobe between his teeth.

Only she didn't. She couldn't. She wouldn't. He stretched her, filled her. His sigh was low, dark, drawn out. She gloried in the sound.

"Christ, you feel so good," he ground out. "Velvet. Hot, molten velvet."

"You feel good, too." She buried her face against his chest.

He laughed, but there was warmth in it, joy, happiness. She reveled in this moment when he seemed without cares, wanted more of them shared with him, a lifetime's worth.

He began to withdraw.

She dug her fingers into his buttocks. "Don't leave me."

Looking down on her, he grinned. "I'll come back."

And he did, over and over, his hips pistoning, hers rising to meet him. He kissed her deeply, thoroughly, all the while thrusting, thrusting . . .

Her body tightened, the sensations began to build again. As he rode her, she held him close, with her arms, her thighs, her feet. Their movements became frantic, fevered, fierce.

"Come for me again," he urged. "Aslyn . . . Aslyn . . . come with me."

And she did. Her cries mingled with his groans as he tossed his head back and pumped into her so deeply that she thought he might have reached her soul.

Panting hard, he buried his face against her neck, breathed in deeply. They lay for the longest time, not moving, slick with sweat, catching their breath. She loved the weight of him resting lightly on her, raised slightly on his elbows. He kissed just below her ear.

Then he stiffened, growled. "Damnation!"

Panic surged through her. "What's happened? What's wrong?"

He lifted his head, held her gaze. "I've never done that before, never not been sheathed or not withdrawn before spilling my seed."

"Oh."

"You felt remarkably good. I lost my senses."

He'd grown flaccid, but he was still there. She squeezed. He groaned from the pleasure of it, shook his head.

"I want no bastards, Aslyn."

"Oh." It seemed the only word that remained in her vocabulary as the significance of what he was saying hit her. He might have done more than spill his seed. He might have planted it. In her womb. "It only takes once?"

"It can."

He didn't sound particularly happy about it. She had mentioned her desire to marry him, but he hadn't proposed. "Well, that would certainly create scandal for me, wouldn't it?"

He rolled off her. For all of a heartbeat she felt forlorn at the loss of his nearness, before his arm came around her and he drew her up against his side. "So would marrying me."

She trailed her fingers over the springy hair on his chest. "I don't care what others think." Lowering her head, she pressed a kiss to his nipple.

He groaned. "Don't start something you can't finish. I suspect you're too sore for another go."

"I shall prove you wrong."

She did just that, straddling him and teasing his cock until it shut down his brain and had its way with her. He'd never known anyone like her, bold and shy, a lady and a tart.

She shouldn't be here, in his bed, in his arms, her head nestled in the crook of his shoulder, her breath stirring the hairs on his chest. He'd never known such contentment, and it scared the bloody hell out of him. The woman snuggled against him made him wish for more. No, she did more than that. She made him believe more was possible.

"Why do you suppose this is considered a sin?" she asked quietly.

Grazing his fingertips up and down her arm, he inhaled her sweeter scent: gardenia intertwined with the musky fragrance of sex. "Because it's so pleasurable, I suppose."

"That doesn't make any sense."

"You're asking me to make sense of something that I've never understood, either."

She lifted her head, dug her chin into his chest, making it easier to hold his gaze. "It's a sin for women, not for men."

"It's a sin for men. We just don't care."

"Because you don't get caught. Women do."

She could get caught. He'd been reckless, careless. She was the most precious thing in his life, and he'd taken the least care with her. He should grant Hedley leave to flay his back. She had said she wanted to marry him, but did she truly understand what it entailed, what she would be giving up? Her family, her friends, her place in Society. Was she really willing to sacrifice —

"Mick!"

Groaning at Aiden's voice echoing through the rooms, he rolled away from the warm woman nestled against him. Aslyn released a tiny peep, clutched the covers and brought them up to her neck.

"Mick! Good news, brother! I've got it!"

Releasing a harsh curse, he tossed back the covers and scrambled out of the bed. "Stay as you are."

"What's he doing here?"

He began dragging on his trousers. "My brothers are always barging in. As I never bring women here, they know they aren't going to disturb me."

"I'm the first?" She seemed pleased.

"You are." Fastening his buttons, he headed for the door, stopped, looked back at her, disheveled in his bed where he wanted to see her every morning of every day for the remainder of his life. "I'm going to —"

"Mick!"

"— send him on his way. Don't leave this room." He didn't wait for an answer, just slipped out, closing the door in his wake and heading down the hallway. He entered the foyer just as Aiden exited the corridor that led to the library.

His brother grinned like an idiot. "There you are! Where the bloody hell were you?"

"Abed. Come back tomorrow."

"Abed? This early in the night? It's not like you to retire before things get interesting."

He was in no mood to discuss his sleeping habits. "Off with you, I'm tired."

"This is going to perk you right up." He gave off a whoop, held up a folded sheet of paper and shook it like it was a tambourine. "I've got it. Finally. The last piece you needed. Loudon Green. Kipwick clung to it until the last."

He was barely aware of moving forward, taking it from Aiden, unfolding it and staring at the words he'd longed to read for ages. Soon would follow a letter in the *Times* written by the Duke of Hedley proclaiming to the world that he'd sired a bastard and declaring Mick as his. Many shied away from admitting their illegitimacy, but Mick had always worn his like a badge of honor.

He imagined the reverence that would be given to him when he strolled into a ballroom. The dinners to which he'd be invited. The soirees he would attend.

He considered the pride with which Aslyn would walk beside him, knowing from whence he'd sprung and knowing how far he'd had to climb.

He might even discover who had given birth to him. He wanted to know about the woman who had brought him into the world and then allowed Hedley to cart him away. Had she been a longtime mistress? A lover for only a single night? Was she some servant he'd taken advantage of? Was she still alive? Did she ever think about him?

"The man was a wreck," Aiden said, interrupting his satisfying musings, "sobbing like a babe in need of a tit, when he realized his wager hadn't paid off and he wasn't getting that property back."

"He wagered it?"

"He was desperate to win that final hand at all costs. I had to do some negotiating with the fellow who did. You owe me five hundred quid."

Five hundred? This property's annual income was worth ten times that. He'd hoped for it but never truly believed Kipwick would be desperate enough or stupid enough to give it up.

"This is the last piece," Aiden said. "You can destroy Hedley now if he doesn't acknowledge you."

"Why would Hedley acknowledge you?"

At the soft voice, the voice that only minutes ago had been screaming out his name in rapture, Mick squeezed his eyes shut. Damnation. Spinning around he faced her. She stood in the opening to the hallway, as beautiful as always, his dressing gown drawn protectively about her.

"Why?" she repeated insistently. "Why would he acknowledge you and as what precisely?"

He hadn't meant for her to find out like this, had wanted to prepare her gently, once he had the promise of the duke's acknowledgment.

"I'm his bastard."

CHAPTER 19

It couldn't be true. It couldn't.

The words spun through her mind like a child's wooden top, only she would be the one to topple over when everything came to a stop.

Mick was the duke's bastard? Certainly she'd had a passing thought there was some resemblance, but dark hair and blue eyes were not all that uncommon. The ramifications that the duke had been unfaithful to the duchess sickened her, caused her stomach to roil, but not nearly as much as the realization that she knew as little about the man with whom she'd fallen in love as she'd known about Kip when she'd accepted his offer of marriage. Had she learned nothing from that disastrous affair?

"Why didn't you tell me?" she demanded. During all the moments when they were together, surely there had been one when he could have told her who he was.

"Because I couldn't be certain you'd choose me over him."

She slid her gaze over to the brother, the one who had burst in so jolly pleased that he now held the deed to Loudon Green. Kip's heritage. It wasn't part of the entailed properties, but the beautiful estate in Yorkshire had been in the family for at least two generations. She'd always preferred it to the ducal seat, had even imagined she would eventually make her home there when she'd thought she'd marry Kip. She cut her gaze back to Mick. "You took him to your brother's club."

"Yes."

"Knew he gambled to distraction."

"Yes. I needed him far into debt. I needed the properties. I need the threat of ruining him to convince Hedley to acknowledge me as his son."

"Meeting at Cremorne wasn't happenstance."

"No."

At least he was admitting —

Her thoughts slammed to a halt; her stomach was on the verge of heaving. "Am I part of your revenge or whatever the deuce it is you think you're doing here?"

He didn't look away from her, but she saw the guilt wash over his features. "In the beginning . . ." he said slowly, quietly.

Covering her mouth with her hand, she spun around, presenting her back to him. Dear God, her chest hurt. Her heart hurt. "All the random times our paths crossed . . . they weren't random at all, were they?" Every encounter played itself over through her mind. She twirled around. The brother was gone, thank goodness. She didn't need an audience to witness her humiliation, far worse than what she'd experienced when Kip had gambled away her jewels. "The urchin who nicked my bracelet . . . tell me he didn't do it on your behest. Tell me it was not a ploy to speak with me, to appear to be heroic."

He said nothing, and in the silence she heard his answer so loudly she thought she might go deaf. She slammed her eyes closed as every warning the Duchess of Hedley had ever given her mocked her. "I was such a fool."

"What was I to do, Aslyn, in order to spend time in your company? I wasn't invited to balls, soirees or dinners."

"You could have called on me like any other gentleman."

He laughed harshly. "Hedley would have kicked me out the moment he saw me. Do you think he would have been pleased to know his bastard had an interest in his ward, a woman he intended to marry off to his heir?"

If that were true, the duke's acknowledgment wasn't going to change anything, wasn't going to allow them to be together. "If I wasn't his ward, if the gossip rags weren't speculating that Kip and I would marry, if White's wasn't wagering on my receiving his proposal by the end of the Season, would you have even given me a glance?" Into the silence, she cursed and fought back the tears. She would not give him the satisfaction of seeing her weep. "This scheme of yours — why not just ask him for the acknowledgment?"

"I did. Half a dozen times. He ignored every missive I sent except for the first. 'I have no bastard.' That was all he wrote. You think I look like him now? You should see me without the beard. I have his damned dimpled chin."

"And if he will not acknowledge you?"

"Then I will see his heir ruined."

"You can't ask Kip to pay for the sins of his father."

"Why not? I've paid for them my entire life. I'm the duke's bastard, Aslyn. His *bastard.*" He fairly spat the word. She flinched at the disgust she heard in his tone.

"But you've risen above it."

"You never rise above it. Always it's there. Do you know there are foundling homes that won't take in bastards? Neither will workhouses. Because we are born in sin, of sin. We are the devil's work."

"But Kip's done nothing to you."

"He's lived within the shadow of the man who sired me then cast me aside."

"Then punish the father not the son."

"I am punishing the father. He will see his legitimate son ruined and his bastard succeed. He will know he is leaving his titles and estates to someone unworthy of them, while the worthy one can't have them."

"If you do this, you're not worthy of anything. You shall be the lowest of the low, not even worthy of a gutter in which to lie."

"He wanted me killed!" He charged away from her. "He gave me to a woman knowing she would kill me." He spun around and glared at her. "No. Worse. He paid her to starve me. That is how bastards are dealt with when they are not considered deserving of life."

Her stomach roiled. "I don't believe the duke would condone such a horrible practice, would partake in it."

"My mum took out an advert in the *Daily Telegraph,* saying she would take on a sickly child for a fee. There were code words in the advert, in the way it was written, alerting potential customers to the fact she would dispose of the child. He brought me to her in the dead of night, naked except for the blanket in which I was wrapped. 'I don't want it to suffer,' he told her. *It.* To him, I was not even human. But she couldn't bring herself to kill me. Two others had been brought to her. She'd kept them tranquil with laudanum until they eventually died. Then her own three children died of typhus, and she thought God was punishing her for the deaths she'd brought to innocents. So I was spared. She raised me as her own. But it did not change the fact that my father — and I suppose my mother, whoever the hell she was — wanted me dead. I often wonder if he continued to fuck her, if his other bastards were put to death without any more thought than one might give the killing of a fly."

She didn't know what to say. She knew the Duke of Hedley, had grown up in his residences, had taken breakfast with him nearly every morning since she was nine years old. "The man who raised me would not have done that."

"A hundred and fifty quid. That's what my death was worth to him."

He seemed so sure, yet it was inconceivable to her that Hedley would condone murder. It was also inconceivable that this man would seek to destroy those she loved. "Being wronged does not justify hurting others."

"Tell that to your precious duke. All I want is for him to publicly recognize me as his son. To admit to me what he did — he does not have to do that publicly. But he does have to acknowledge me, invite me to their affairs —"

"They don't have affairs. They never entertain."

"Then he can take me to his clubs, introduce me as his son, assist me in gaining the respect I deserve."

"But you've done that on your own, with your business —"

"I can't get into his bloody clubs!"

That was what was important to him? Membership in gentlemen's clubs? Disappointment slammed into her. When it came to men, apparently she was a terrible judge of character. "All the wooing. Was your goal to ruin me or to wed me?"

"One way or the other I will be accepted by the nobility. I will move about in their circles."

"Even if it costs you whatever affection I

might hold for you?"

"You don't love me, Aslyn. I'm a commoner to play with for a bit, to come to when you're looking for some scandalous adventure, a bit of the rough. When your life is too clean and you want to play in the dirt for a while. Then you can scrub it all off and forget you'd ever dallied with the likes of me."

"You're wrong."

She arrived at Hedley Hall in a hansom that she had walked miles to find. Past the area where Mick's buildings loomed, she'd marched with dogged determination. He'd offered use of his carriage, but she wanted nothing from him. He'd used her, she'd been part of his scheme. Even with her disgust of him radiating from her, he'd walked along behind her, serving as her silent protector until she'd finally located a hansom.

The front door was locked, but she used the key she'd procured. The silence that greeted her wasn't surprising. If things were locked up, everyone was abed.

Gathering what little strength remained to her, she dragged herself up the stairs. All she wanted was to take a bath, to wash him off. Every touch, every caress, every kiss, every lick. The things he'd done to her, she'd done to him. The cries, the raw need, the way her body had sung to his tune only added to her humiliation, to her anger, to her fury.

Opening the door to her bedchamber, she came up short at the sight of the solitary lamp illuminating the figure sitting in a chair in the corner.

"Where have you been?" Kip asked.

"None of your concern." Closing the door quietly behind her, she wandered nearer to him. He looked awful, worse than she'd ever seen him, with his hair greasy and unkempt, his jacket wrinkled, his waistcoat unbuttoned, his neck cloth unknotted. He'd not shaved in days, in nights. His eyes were bloodshot, the lids swollen and red-rimmed. His cheeks were hollowed out, his skin sallow. She could clearly envision him as Aiden had described him: desperate to win that final hand at all costs.

He'd paid the price with his heritage, his pride, his manhood.

"What are you doing here?"

"I'm in trouble, Aslyn." Leaning forward, he braced his elbows on his thighs, bent his head as though it weighed too much to hold upright. Finally he lifted it, met her gaze. "I've lost everything. Everything."

She'd known that, of course. Knew what he'd lost, the circumstances that had led to the loss. He'd played so easily into Mick's hands. At that moment she despised them both.

Shakily he shoved himself to his feet, held out a trembling hand toward her. "I need you." How she had once longed for words spoken so passionately from him. "If we marry quickly, soon, I will be given access to your trust and can put everything back to rights before Father finds out what I've done. Else I am ruined."

How was it that she managed to circle herself with men who wanted her only for their own gain? She was bloody well tired of it. She angled up her chin, faced him squarely. "What's in it for me?"

He seemed taken aback, whether from the bluntness of her question or her demanding tone, she didn't know. "You will become a countess, one day you will be a duchess."

She shook her head. "I don't want to be a duchess. I want only to be loved." As she'd believed Mick loved her. Moments filled with smiles, laughter and believing that happily-ever-afters existed.

"I love you. Of course I do."

"Not as much as you love your gambling."

"I'll do as you ask. I'll give it up."

"I can't marry you." She didn't trust him to keep his word. Nor had she fallen in love with him as she'd fallen in love with another. Now that she knew what it was to want, to desire, to yearn for — how could she ever settle for less? Even as her heart ached with Mick's betrayal, she wouldn't marry a man who couldn't stir passion within her breast, who didn't make her more than she'd thought herself capable of being.

"We have an understanding."

"We don't. I've been trying for days to meet with you so we could officially call off our betrothal, so I could stop making excuses to your mother for not discussing the details of the wedding. Kip, I love you as a brother, not as a man to warm my bed."

"Are you going to marry *him*? Trewlove?"

"No." He'd betrayed her, used her, schemed to destroy those she loved — all for want of an acknowledgment that would gain him nothing he didn't already possess. "He's your brother."

He blinked, looked as though he might be more ill. "I beg your pardon?"

"He's your father's by-blow."

"Did Trewlove tell you that?"

She nodded, sank into a chair. "But once he told me, I could see it. I don't know why I didn't see it sooner."

"You care for him."

She had. What she felt now was a maelstrom of conflicting emotions. She wanted to never see him again, wanted him to comfort her. She wanted him to have been honest from the beginning, yearned to know if he'd ever meant anything he'd ever said to her or if it had all just been posturing, to put himself in a position to destroy the duke. She hated him with every fiber of her being.

Unfortunately she loved him just as deeply — which was the reason that the truth of him hurt so damned much.

CHAPTER 20

I have managed to obtain the deeds to the properties you lost as well as your markers from various gaming hells. Bring the duke to my office at eleven so we might discuss the terms upon which they will be returned to you. No duke, no meeting. No meeting, and I shall see you ruined.

— Mick Trewlove

Mick had the missive delivered to Kipwick first thing that morning.

Now as his valet brushed shaving lather over his thick beard, he studied his reflection in the mirror. When he'd discovered the bones in Ettie Trewlove's garden, he'd also uncovered his own past. She'd given him the tattered remains of the blanket in which he'd been wrapped, and she'd told him the tale of the gent, in the fancy carriage, who'd brought Mick to her door. The man had never given his name, and it was possible the blanket had been nicked, but the first time Mick had caught sight of Hedley, he'd known the truth: his father was a bloody duke.

He'd seen himself in the tall, slender man with the black hair and the vivid blue eyes. He'd seen himself in the pronounced dimpled chin. The same chin that the Earl of Kipwick sported.

He'd been fifteen at the time, hauling the dustbin out of the iron trench near the servants' entrance where it was kept. The duke — striding toward the stables, no doubt about to enjoy his morning ride — hadn't even bothered to give the laborers who disposed of his rubbish a passing glance. Not a tip of his hat nor a "Good day to you."

They were beneath him, not even worthy of being noticed.

He'd damned well notice Mick today or tomorrow or the day after. Whenever it was that he decided the reputation of his legitimate son was worth saving. He had no guarantee the man would heed his summons for a meeting today, but eventually he would come.

As the valet carefully scraped the razor over his jaw, Mick felt the cool air touch upon skin that he'd not seen in years. As soon as he'd begun to sprout facial hair, he'd set about hiding beneath dark whiskers what he considered a mark of his heritage. The duke hadn't wanted him when he was born. He'd determined he'd gain nothing by approaching the man directly, since the scapegrace didn't believe his own flesh and blood deserved to breathe London's air and all but one of his missives for a meeting had gone unanswered.

Mick was fairly certain he wouldn't want him now, but his plans would remove the duke's wishes on the matter. He would be publicly acknowledged before the week was out. Then he would call upon Aslyn as a gentleman would and convince her that what had been done had been necessary if they were to have any future together.

As the dent in his square chin was revealed, he shifted his gaze to the bed, visible behind his reflection. It was still scented with gardenias mingled with the musky fragrance of sex. After he'd followed the marching Aslyn until she'd located a hansom — dear God, even when her fury was directed at him, she was magnificent — he'd returned here, stretched out on the bed and relived every moment he'd been in her company, from that first night in Cremorne to her standing in the hallway clad in his silk dressing gown. It had clung to her curves and thighs as though worshipping the flesh it had the honor of touching. He tormented himself by recalling every smile, every laugh, every tease, every look of want, every kiss. She'd claimed to hold affection for him, then she'd walked out on him.

Having experienced the wrath of her guardians not wanting to allow him entry into their residence, having seen their disgust at the thought of a bastard crossing their threshold, did she not understand that he would do anything, everything necessary to have his existence acknowledged?

She was angry now, hurt, but she would see that he was paving a future for them. That the price paid now would be worth the rewards. That it would all be worth it.

"As I understand it, he's your bastard."

"I have no bastard."

Kipwick stood before his father's desk as he had a thousand times in his life, fearful of disappointing him. "He seems to be under the illusion you do."

The duke tapped his forefinger on the desk, all the while his gaze never leaving Kipwick. "Why approach you to arrange this meeting?"

He'd so hoped to avoid his father learning

the truth, but there was no hope for it now. "I've gotten myself into a bit of a bother."

His father arched one dark brow over startling blue eyes — a shade that so matched Mick Trewlove's, Kipwick realized in retrospect. Perhaps one of his father's brothers had sired the man. Or he had nothing at all to do with anyone in the family. It wasn't as though blue eyes were uncommon. He swallowed hard, clasped his hands behind his back until they ached. "I've been gambling of late. Ran into a spate of bad luck."

"How bad?" It would be easier if his father would raise his voice, but he kept his tone flat.

"I lost all the properties and the funds you'd allotted for their upkeep."

His father's eyes slid closed.

He took a step nearer, even though his sire couldn't see him. "He will see me ruined. If word gets out that I have lost all this, who will lend us money when it is needed? Who will find me trustworthy? Who will allow his daughter to marry me?"

The duke's eyes sprung open. "You are betrothed to Aslyn."

"He has turned her against me."

"How the devil did he come to be in her company so he could influence her at all?"

425

"It's a rather lengthy story."

"Then I suggest you immediately get started on the telling of it."

He had investments to analyze, a new business venture in need of partners and recently constructed buildings to walk through to ensure they met his standards. Yet he seemed incapable of focusing on what needed to be done, and instead continually stared at the contents of the box that had been waiting on his desk when he arrived: a pearl necklace, a comb, a parasol.

No note but the message was clear. She was done with him. As though she hadn't made that obvious last night. She'd been in a bit of temper, but he'd thought once she'd had time to truly consider it, to sleep on it, she'd come around and understand how very important the duke's acknowledgment of him was, how it would open doors to him, to *them.* Apparently, sleeping on it had made her only more determined to be rid of him.

Fine. He'd been tossed aside by a noblewoman before. With Hedley's acknowledgment and influence, he would be invited into dukes' ballrooms and earls' dining rooms. He could court every lord's daughter who caught his fancy. He didn't need Aslyn.

The whole world was about to open up for him, and he could do with it as he willed.

The quiet rap on his door snapped him back to the present. "Enter."

His secretary opened the door, stepped inside and closed it behind him. "The Duke of Hedley and the Earl of Kipwick are here to see you."

Rising, he tugged on his waistcoat, retrieved the golden watch from his waistcoat pocket and glanced at the time. They were prompt. He'd give them that. "Send them in."

Looking concerned, or perhaps a bit discombobulated, Tittlefitz blinked, nodded, blinked again, all the while studying Mick as though striving to decipher a puzzle. "Yes, sir."

He went out, held the door open and invited the two gents into the room. Then he quietly closed the door with a hushed *snick,* leaving the gents and an awkward silence filling space.

It had been years since Mick had seen Hedley and never from such a short distance. The resemblance was uncanny. Little wonder Tittlefitz had seemed uncomfortable. The man wasn't an idiot. He was no doubt figuring things out.

Mick took a great deal of satisfaction in

the blood draining from Hedley's face and the way Kipwick stared at him. Now that his beard was gone, he knew both men would see the truth regarding Mick's parentage. Hedley recovered quickly enough, his expression showing no reaction when confronted by the reality that his bastard didn't reside in Ettie Trewlove's garden.

"Gentlemen." Mick didn't bother to soften the hard edge of his voice.

"I understand you have some deeds we wish to reclaim and some markers that are causing my son some annoyance. I'm here to pay them off."

Not exactly the homecoming Mick had expected or wanted. "They're not for sale."

"Then our business here is done." The duke turned —

"I am willing to trade." Mick hated the desperation he heard in his voice, hoped the duke and his son were unaware of it.

Hedley faced him. "The terms?"

He'd considered them all morning, as he'd walked over land he'd purchased, wended his way among the buildings that were nearly complete, stood on the rooftop and looked toward the sky where he knew come nightfall fireworks would light it up with color. "Give me leave to call on Lady Aslyn, and I'll hand them over."

"No." The single word echoed through the room like the retort of a rifle.

The rage slithered through him. "Because I'm your bastard, you think me not worthy of her?" He hated the doubts that plagued him, that whispered perhaps the man was correct.

The duke's face remained a mask of no emotion as he shook his head. "You are not my bastard."

Scoffing harshly, his anger intensifying, Mick came around his desk, advancing until he was mere inches away from the duke. He would deny him both Aslyn and the truth of his paternity? "We share the same hair, eyes and damned dimple in our chin. Do you need me to have a mirror brought in here so you can see us standing side by side? Looking at you is like looking at my own reflection. And I have this." He pulled the frayed crest from his pocket. "It is all that remains of the blanket in which I was wrapped when you handed me over to a baby farmer."

The duke did blanch then, averted his gaze for half a heartbeat before meeting Mick's stare with hard-edged resolve. "To have you in our lives will see my wife destroyed."

"To not grant me what I want will see

your heir destroyed."

"He can survive the loss of a few properties."

"Loudon Green provides the most income of all your holdings. Without it your estates cannot be maintained."

"You've done your research, I see." He almost thought he heard a measure of respect in the duke's voice. "But we will find a way to manage."

The man's calm resolve was fueling Mick's anger and resentment. He understood only too well the merits of giving away nothing, often used the tactic himself. Apparently he'd inherited more from his sire than physical attributes. He possessed his cunning and calm resolve. "I shall see you and your son ruined. No one will lend you money. I have that much influence over bankers. What you have will dwindle away. Rumors regarding your solvency will be spread about. You will lose respect, influence, position. Your heir will be left with nothing of worth to inherit."

"I've no doubt. You seem quite intent on your purpose."

"Then give me leave to call on Aslyn, to at least give her a choice as to whether she will accept or rebuff me."

"Mr. Trewlove," the duke began quietly,

"as long as my wife lives, I will not — I *cannot* — give you what you desire. You will never be welcomed into our home or into our lives. But consider this — if you are correct in your assessment regarding your paternity, the man you are seeking to destroy here is your brother."

He began marching toward the door. It took Kipwick a second to realize the meeting was at an end. He rushed after his father.

"At least tell me about my mother," Mick demanded.

Coming to a halt, the duke glanced back over his shoulder. "She was the most beautiful woman I'd ever seen, the gentlest, kindest woman I've ever known. I fell in love with her on the spot. I'm ashamed to admit it, but I miss her terribly."

"Was she as anxious to be rid of me as you were? Or did she beg to be allowed to keep me? Did you tear me from her arms or did she willingly hand me over?"

"Nothing is to be gained, Mr. Trewlove, by going into the past."

Then he turned on his heel and walked out.

Mick Trewlove *was* his son. When he strode into that office, the realization had nearly dropped him to his knees. It had taken every ounce of strength and resolve within him to give nothing away, to show no recognition, no acknowledgment of the truth. Even now he fought desperately to maintain a cool facade. If he lost it, he feared he'd never regain it. For Bella's sake, he ignored the crushing sensation in his chest and stared out the window as the coach rattled along.

"I can only guess at his age. I put him a few years older than I. Were you married to my mother when he was born?"

"Pardon?" He swung his gaze over to the son who had brought them to this moment with his recklessness. He'd never gotten over the guilt he'd felt at taking the babe to the Widow Trewlove, and so he'd indulged Kip when he should have taken a much firmer hand with him.

"Were you unfaithful to my mother?" Kip asked, disgust evident in his voice. How could he blame him? It seemed he was destined to betray his sons.

"I will not discuss this with you any more than I'll discuss it with him. The past is the past. We must move beyond it."

"Where is the harm in allowing him to call on Aslyn? She fancies him."

"He is not for her."

"But he will see me destroyed."

"We have the weight of my title and the

influence of our name. We will not fall easily."

"But why risk falling at all?"

"I'll not be extorted. Nor will I allow Aslyn to be used in so crass a manner, for another man's purposes."

He turned his attention back to the window, more determined than ever to protect Bella from the truth.

"Is that your doll?"

Aslyn looked up from where she sat on the grass in a secluded corner of the gardens, holding the rag doll Charles Beckwith had given her when he'd brought news to the house of her parents' death. "Mind your own affairs."

Kip sat beside her. "I always thought it the most hideous thing in your possession. Gave me nightmares."

"Brings me comfort." When she was in sore need of some. She'd spent the morning bouncing from raging anger to profound sadness. She'd thought she'd found something special with Mick. Someone who understood her. Someone who loved her for herself, not gain.

"I haven't done that much of late, have I?"

"No."

"I mucked things up."

"Yes, you did."

"I can always count on you to be forth-right." He sighed. "We're not going to make a go of it, you and I, are we?"

"No."

"Even without Trewlove in the picture?"

Plucking at some stray threads on the doll's dress, she shook her head.

"We met with him, Father and I."

Of course they had. It was what Mick Trewlove had planned. A confrontation, a flexing of his muscles, an opportunity to gain what he desired most.

"You are correct. He is Father's bastard, even though Father claimed he wasn't, as though Trewlove would believe that rubbish. He's the spitting image of the old man. Shaved his beard, by the way."

She didn't care, and yet she wondered how different he might look. "Is the duke not going to acknowledge him, then?"

"Odd thing that. I, too, assumed Father acknowledging him was what he wanted."

"He *told* me it was what he wanted or he'd see you ruined."

"It's not what he asked for. He wanted permission to call on you."

Clutching the doll, she swung around and stared at him. "I beg your pardon?"

434

Kip shrugged. "He wants to call on you. Father said no."

"Jolly good for him, as I have no desire for Mick Trewlove to call on me." It was too late. A tug on another string.

Reaching over, he covered her hand with his, stopping her from pulling any more threads free. "Do you love him so very much?"

"Not anymore."

"You can stop loving him that easily?"

She shook her head. "None of it was real, Kip. The times we were together, the things he said . . . it was all a deception, a ploy. It meant nothing. I meant nothing."

"I can't quite believe that. He must have fallen for you a little."

Releasing a slow breath, she pressed her head against his shoulder. "If he did, it wasn't enough."

He let out a long-suffering sigh. "Then he shall see me ruined."

"Your father is a powerful and influential man. I think Mick Trewlove will discover he has met his match."

"Don't be so sure. If there is anyone in this household who is his match, I suspect it is you."

CHAPTER 21

The table in the back corner at the Mermaid and Unicorn was dark and shadowy, which reflected Mick's mood and suited him as he poured more whiskey into his glass. He'd told Gillie to leave him the bottle. She didn't argue. Whatever his face reflected, she wanted none of it.

"I can't get used to the beard being gone," Aiden said.

It wasn't long after he'd arrived that all three of his brothers joined him. He suspected Gillie had sent word to them that he appeared to be in a foul mood. If his mother and Fancy made an appearance, his mood was going to darken further.

"I suppose you wanted to make a point when you met with Hedley," Finn said. "Is he going to give you what you want?"

Shaking his head, Mick went to rub his beard, hit his bristly chin instead. He wasn't used to the damn whiskers being gone, either. His brothers all thought he'd asked Hedley to acknowledge him. He couldn't quite bring himself to admit what he'd asked for. They wouldn't understand. He wasn't quite certain he did.

"He's willing to let you ruin his son?" Beast asked.

"You sound surprised. He was willing to kill one son. Why would he care about the other?"

"Kipwick is his heir."

"Apparently he doesn't give a bloody damn." He downed his scotch, poured more.

"You have the girl," Finn said. "Surely he cares about her reputation being ruined."

He didn't have the girl. He'd had her. He'd lost her. Whatever feelings she might have had for him had died when she'd learned about his scheme. That much was obvious, but if he could see her again, if he could call upon her like a gentleman, as he should have in the first place —

She would probably give him the same answer Hedley had. No.

"I can vouch for your compromising of her," Aiden said. "Threaten to ruin her reputation, and Hedley is bound to come around."

Mick glared at him. "Say that again, out

loud or to another soul, and I'll beat you to a bloody pulp."

Aiden's eyes widened, then narrowed. "I thought bedding her and not wedding her was part of your plan to bring Hedley to heel, to threaten him with scandals involving his heir and his ward if he didn't acknowledge you."

"But then he went and fell in love," Beast said, and Mick had a strong urge to warn him off as he had Aiden, only he'd never been able to best Beast when it came to fisticuffs.

"What makes you say that?" Finn asked.

Beast shrugged. "You had only to look at him the night he introduced her to us to see he was well on his way to falling."

Aiden gave a quick bark of laughter. "To be quite honest, I was too busy ogling her —"

Mick's fist struck Aiden's jaw hard and quick, nearly toppling his brother out of his chair.

Aiden righted himself, rubbed his jaw and grinned. "Bloody hell, Beast has the right of it. You're in love. You're not going to use her to force Hedley into acknowledging you."

He would never use her. No matter how much she enraged him with the accusations she tossed at him — rightfully deserved. No matter that she'd walked out. No matter that she'd continued walking without speaking a word to him until she'd located a damned hansom. No matter that when just before she'd climbed into the cab she had looked at him with such sadness and disappointment that he'd felt for the first time in his life that he did indeed belong in the gutter. "I don't want the bloody acknowledgment. I want her."

"She's nobility," Finn said quietly. "You're a bastard."

Only that difference hadn't mattered to Aslyn. It hadn't existed when they kissed. In his bed, they'd been equals in standing. No, never equals. In his eyes, she would always be elevated, a goddess. When he was with her, talking with her, when she smiled at him, he was more than the circumstances of his birth. With her he was more whole, more complete than he'd ever been in the entirety of his life.

And he'd been willing to throw it away for something that, in the end, meant nothing at all.

The following afternoon, Hedley stared at the calling card his butler had handed him. "What the devil is he doing here?"

"Who, Father?" Kipwick asked. They'd

been discussing how best to handle this mess with Trewlove.

"I can't say, Your Grace. Mr. Trewlove said only that he required an audience with Lady Aslyn, but I thought you should know," Worsted said with a sniff and an upturning of his nose. "I'm not certain he's the proper sort for her."

Hedley jerked his gaze up to the man who had served him loyally for more than a quarter of a century. "Where is he?"

"I left him to wait in the foyer."

Panic gushed through him, his heart slammed against his ribs as the clock on the mantel struck the hour of two, the hour when every afternoon he and Bella took a stroll through the gardens. "No."

He surged to his feet.

"Father?" Kipwick asked.

"He can't be here now. Not now." Then he was dashing from the room, his heir close on his heels.

Mick stood in the foyer, hat in hand, staring at the various black veins that ran through the mostly white marble floor. He refused to look at the portraits covering the walls, portraits of those to whom — despite Hedley's words — he was certain he was related.

He'd always envisioned walking into this

residence, taking in its grandeur and being filled with the wonder of knowing he had come from a lineage that had managed, through the centuries, to build something to be envied, something of such magnificence that it was admired throughout Great Britain. From the moment he'd discovered the bones in the garden and the truth about himself, it all seemed to matter so much. Knowing that a part of him was associated with all this had meant everything.

Now the only thing that mattered was Aslyn. He'd had thirty-seven hours, thirty-three — he checked his watch — thirty-five minutes without her in his life, and he'd never known such desperation. She was like the fresh air he'd breathed when, as a small lad, he exited a chimney, the blue cloudless sky when he emerged from the darkness.

He knew there was a good chance she would send him packing, would refuse to see him — but he was not going to give up easily. He'd wooed her before, and while she may have thought there was no truth or honesty in any of it, from the moment he'd gazed into her eyes at Cremorne, he'd never lied to her. He may have used some questionable tactics to ensure they crossed paths, but he'd never once not been candid with her regarding his feelings for her. If it took him the remainder of his life, he would convince her that every moment with her had been a true, sincere and authentic one.

And if she would not see him today, he would return tomorrow. If Hedley had him forcefully removed, he would return tomorrow. If Kipwick beat him to within an inch of his life, he would return tomorrow. As long as he had breath in him —

"Hello."

Only then was he aware of the light footsteps. He lifted his gaze. The woman who approached was so slight he wondered how she managed to carry herself with such elegance. She reminded him of a fledging bird he'd once found that had fallen from the nest. Carefully he'd climbed the tree and placed it back inside with its siblings, only to descend to the ground and watch as the mother bird — or perhaps the father, he really didn't know — had worked to shove it back out of the nest. He'd taken it home, nursed it with drops of milk, wrapped it in a handkerchief, sought to keep it warm, but it had eventually succumbed to death, no doubt its heart broken with the abandonment of its parents.

His mum assured him the tiny bird had already been ill, too weak. Probably the reason it had been tossed from the nest.

He'd wondered if he'd been ill as well when he was born. If that was the reason he'd been unwanted. He'd always been searching for a reason until he finally accepted *he* was the reason, he and the circumstances of his birth.

And this woman smiling softly at him, this woman whose husband didn't want her to know of his unfaithfulness. He had never met, never seen, the Duchess of Hedley, but he'd wager every penny in his possession he was looking at her now.

The woman had refused Aslyn's request to invite him to dinner, the woman who no doubt was partially responsible for Hedley not granting him permission to call on Aslyn. He was determined she would not see garbage when she looked at him. He held himself a bit straighter, met her curious gaze with an unwavering one of his own.

"Are you here to see someone?" she asked, her voice lyrical and soft, and he could imagine her singing lullabies to her son.

"I'm here to call on Lady Aslyn, Your Grace."

She stopped walking, studied him as though he were an enigma to be deciphered. "And you are?"

"Mick Trewlove."

Her smile withered. She paled as though

she'd seen a ghost. "The bastard."

Her pronouncement grated, as though he were no more than the sum of that word. Perhaps once he had been, perhaps once it had defined him. But when he looked at himself through Aslyn's eyes, he realized he was so much more. "I'm the man who loves Lady Aslyn Hastings with all his heart. I'm the man who will wed her if she will have him."

He heard the gasp, looked to the side and saw Aslyn standing at the foot of the stairs, her hand covering her mouth. Reaching into his jacket pocket, he pulled out a packet of papers and took a step toward her. "The deeds, the markers, they're yours, no strings attached. Return them to Kipwick, burn them. I don't care. I won't ruin him. I don't need an acknowledgment. All I need is you."

Slowly, suspiciously, as though she had years to do so, she reached out and took the packet from him.

"I want you to know —"

"You're the bastard," the duchess interrupted as though he were not in the process of laying his heart bare.

With a deep sigh, he turned back to her. "Yes, madam. I'm a bastard."

She shook her head. "Not a bastard. *The* bastard."

As though there were only one in the entirety of Britain. "If you wish."

"My God. You're *his* son."

With a single affirmation he could bring Hedley to his knees, could destroy his relationship with his duchess. A month ago he'd have done it without hesitation. A month ago he hadn't been the man he was at that moment, one who understood a man put the welfare and well-being of the woman he loved above all else. He would not shove this little bird from the nest. The circumstances surrounding his birth no longer mattered. All that mattered was Aslyn. "No, madam, you're mistaken."

Tears welling in her eyes, she shook her head. "I have gazed into those blue eyes for thirty-three years." Reaching up, she touched his chin with trembling fingers. "I have kissed that dimple a thousand times. More."

"I assure you, madam, I am not his son."

"Bella!" the duke shouted as he ran into the large foyer, panic clearly written on his face, horror reflected in blue eyes that so mirrored Mick's in shade.

With a hand covering her mouth, she turned to him. "The bastard is your son."

"No, my love."

"For God's sake, don't lie to her," Kipwick stated emphatically as he staggered to a stop behind the duke. "Not when the proof stands right there. She's not daft, and she has a right to know you were unfaithful, that you sired a by-blow."

Shaking his head, slowly the duke crept toward her, as though she were a skittish filly that would dash off, his outstretched hand imploring. "Bella —"

"It *is* him, isn't it? The one you took away."

"Darling." The answer was there in his eyes, in his shaking hand.

She released a heart-wrenching sob. "My God, Hedley, I was wrong. All those years ago I gave birth to *your* son."

Chapter 22

Mick was so stunned by the duchess's revelation he very nearly missed the fact that she was sinking to the floor in a faint. Dropping his hat, he swept her up into his arms. She was as light as a willow branch.

"Give her to me," the duke ordered.

Only Mick couldn't seem to make himself obey the command, couldn't force his arms to relinquish the precious bundle they carried. Only now did he realize the duke had never once denied he was his son. He'd only ever denied he was his bastard.

Christ! The woman he held — the duke's wife — was his mother? Why had they taken him, a legitimate son, to Ettie Trewlove? Had he indeed been like the fledgling bird, too sickly — what the deuce did it matter now?

"I have her," he said somberly. "She's safe with me. Where shall I take her?"

"This way," Aslyn said, her hand coming

447

to rest lightly on his arm. "We'll take her to her bedchamber." She guided him toward the stairs.

"Worsted, send for Dr. Graves," Hedley shouted.

Mick could only assume Worsted was some damned servant. He couldn't seem to focus on his surroundings, on what was going on around him. He had the fleeting thought he might be on the verge of swooning himself, but there was no way in hell he was going to do anything that caused him to drop the woman he carried.

He was vaguely aware of Hedley and Kipwick following. At the landing, Aslyn led him along a hallway, stopping partway down to open a door. "In here."

The large chamber, decorated in pale blues, reminded him of summer skies. He crossed over to the four-poster and gingerly laid the duchess onto the thick robin's-egg blue duvet. She didn't stir.

"I'll get her smelling salts," Aslyn said.

"No," the duke said, working his way past Mick to sit on the edge of the bed and take his wife's hand. "Let her sleep for a bit. It'll be less confusing for her if she wakes up naturally."

Mick didn't see how any of this could be less confusing. "I don't understand," he said, feeling like an intruder in an intimate moment.

The duke merely nodded. "Kip, take him to the library. Pour him some scotch. Pour us all some scotch."

"Yes, sir." The earl sounded as lost as Mick felt.

"I'll stay with her," Aslyn said softly.

The duke again nodded, but he didn't move from his place.

She looked at Mick. "I need to stay with them."

He wanted to draw her to him, hold her close, have her hold him, but through the turmoil he'd created with his actions he feared he'd lost the right to ask for any comfort from her. When he'd decided to come here, it hadn't occurred to him that he would cross paths with the duchess. In a residence this large, how could everyone know who came and went?

"Come with me," Kipwick said, his voice brooking no disobedience. For the first time Mick experienced a spark of respect for the man.

While he was loath to leave until he knew the duchess was going to be all right, he followed the earl into the hallway. They were at the landing when he heard the patter of heels and glanced back over his shoulder to see Aslyn.

Leap into my arms. Hug me. Forgive me.

She staggered to a stop feet from him, but near enough that he could smell gardenia. With tears glistening in her eyes, she took a step nearer and placed her palm against his freshly shaven cheek. "How could I have not seen it? You look just like him."

"I should have told you, from the beginning. I should have —" There was too much to say, too many amends to make. Now was not the time, not when they were all still reeling from the implications of the duchess's pronouncement.

Closing his eyes, he laid his hand over hers, turned his head slightly and pressed a kiss to the heart of her palm. He would be content to stand here, just like this, for the remainder of his life. And if this was the last time she would ever touch him, he would find a way to be content with that, as well.

"I hardly know where to begin."

The duke's words echoed throughout the library. Entering only a few moments earlier, he'd assured Kipwick, who'd dropped into a chair by the fireplace after pouring Mick a glass of scotch, that the duchess had been examined by the physician, was resting comfortably and would recover from the shock with no ill effects in due time with proper rest. Aslyn was watching over her. He'd adroitly avoided looking at Mick as he quietly prepared a scotch for himself before taking up a post near the fireplace, near his son, his back to the wall as though he needed it for support.

Standing beside the window, Mick was strung as tightly as a bow pulled taut on the verge of letting loose an arrow. He and Kipwick hadn't exchanged a single word since leaving the duchess, which had left Mick with nothing to distract himself from all the afternoon's revelations and their ramifications. He wasn't a bastard, had never been.

"I don't understand how any of this can be as it seems, so simply start at the beginning," Kipwick offered quietly.

The duke gave a brusque nod. "There was a time when Bella was bold and uncompromising in her belief we had a duty to see after the poor. She would visit the rookeries and do what she could to better lives, especially those of children. She delivered clothing and food, blankets, dolls and wooden tops. I worried over her, sent footmen with her, but she was always sending them off on one errand or another. Why would anyone harm someone who was offering naught but kindness?"

He stared at the floor, and Mick suspected he saw the past swirling around the dark grains of wood. "One afternoon, late, as darkness was settling in, she was accosted by a brute, dragged into an alley . . . where he had his way with her."

Mick's stomach knotted, roiled as he thought of the frail, slender woman he'd held being abused in any manner at all, but to have been denigrated in the vilest way possible had rage seething through him. His right hand balled into a tightened fist as though already preparing to deliver the blow the villain deserved.

The duke tossed back his scotch, no doubt seeking fortification for what came next, although Mick couldn't imagine it being any worse. "She knew — or at least believed — she was not with child before the attack. For some time afterward, she could hardly bear for me to hold her, wanted no more intimacy from me than that. So when she realized she was with child, she assumed — rightfully so — that it was not mine." Finally he looked at Mick. The sadness and regret in the duke's expression very nearly knocked him back on his heels. "Had you been a girl, I might have been able to convince her to keep you. But she was sickened by the thought that vile creature's spawn might inherit my title and estates. So I tried to make it right . . . for her. But she was never as vibrant, as unafraid as she'd been before."

A part of him understood their actions, a part of him rebelled against them. "Were you aware how baby farmers cared for the infants placed in their care?"

The duke shook his head. "Not at the time. A friend of mine told me he farmed out his bastards. It's a common practice. Not until a few years ago when people began advocating for change, for licensing baby farming, when so many graves were found . . ." His voice trailed off.

Articles had appeared in the newspapers. Reading them, Mick had assumed the duke had known what his fate would be. "You didn't revisit Ettie Trewlove to try to find out if I was alive?"

"What did it matter by then? You were either dead or a grown man. I'd given her extra coins to see you had an easier start in life than the small payment she'd asked for would have given you. While it brings me shame to say it, I felt I owed another man's bastard no more than I'd already given.

"When I saw you yesterday, I knew the truth, knew you were my son. I was devastated to realize we had made such a grave error, but how could I tell Bella? She begged me to give you up all those years ago. She would never forgive herself, *will* never forgive herself. Her heart breaks anew. How many times can a heart break without crumbling completely?"

"So he's truly your legitimate heir? And I'm the *spare*?" Kipwick scoffed. "I don't bloody well believe this. You told him to his face he wasn't your son. You told me that you —"

"Had no bastard," the duke finished for him, a terseness in his voice as though he were disappointed that the earl was so concerned with his title. "I have no bastard, but it has become apparent I do have two sons." He returned his attention to Mick. "You are my son. Our son. Mine and Bella's."

"Do you know who attacked her?"

Hedley jerked his head back as though he'd been punched. Obviously he'd expected Mick to crow about the fact he was heir to a dukedom. "What difference does it make?"

"I shall see him put to death."

"So your mother — who has only just learned your true identity — can watch you swing from the gallows?"

"The dark underbelly of London is my playground. His body will never be found."

He watched the duke struggle with emotions he could no longer hold in check. He didn't know whether to be impressed or appalled by what his firstborn had just revealed and the actions he was willing to take. "He was seen to, long ago. You are not the only one with connection and means."

Mick's respect for the duke went up a notch.

"So what do we bloody well do now?" Kipwick asked. "You can't just magically produce another son out of thin air."

The duke held Mick's gaze. "We shall work out a story. We shall see your birthright restored."

Sweet Christ! He was about to become a bloody future duke.

CHAPTER 23

Aslyn desperately wanted to be there when the duke entered the library and Mick confronted him, but she couldn't bring herself to leave the duchess's side. She'd awoken shortly before the physician arrived and immediately burst into tears, asking Hedley for forgiveness while he held and rocked her. It had broken Aslyn's heart to see her tormented so. After giving her a sleeping draught, Dr. Graves had asked Aslyn to stay until the duchess drifted off.

But sleep eluded the poor woman while her gaze continually fluttered around the room as though she searched for something lost. Finally, she settled into stillness, her focus on the window where late-afternoon sunlight filtered in, capturing dust motes in their slow descent.

"We'd been married only a month," she said flatly, quietly, and Aslyn wasn't certain she was speaking to her, was truly aware of her presence. "I bled. Not much, but still I assumed it was my monthly. I thought the lightness of my bleeding was a result of losing my virginity. I bled after the attack, naturally. How can a woman not when she is treated so roughly? But afterward I had no more menses. Hedley hadn't touched me — I couldn't stand for him to touch me after that ruffian . . ." She swallowed, tears misted in her eyes.

Aslyn squeezed her hand. "You don't have to talk about it."

Slowly the duchess turned her head until she held Aslyn's gaze. "We hadn't been intimate you see. After what I thought was the monthly bleeding, after the attack. I didn't see how the babe could be his. A boy. An heir who might not carry his blood." Desperately she clutched Aslyn's hand. "Do you understand? I had no way of knowing for sure. During all those long months, still I prayed it was Hedley's. I knew when we'd last been intimate. I counted the weeks. I knew when the babe should be born if he was my love's, but the day came and the day went and the babe stayed within me. I convinced myself, it couldn't be his. Two weeks later, when it finally arrived, the timing indicated it had been sired by that monster. Now I know he was merely tardy."

"So you told people the child died."

She shook her head. "No, no one knew. When I realized I was increasing, we moved to an obscure estate where Hedley's father had kept his mistress. They were both dead. They didn't need it. We isolated ourselves. Only a handful of servants. We waited. Day after torturous day. I thought I would go mad." She gave Aslyn a sad smile. "I think I did a bit." She looked back out the window.

"It's understandable," Aslyn said gently. "The horror you endured, survived . . ." Now she understood all of the duchess's precautions, worries. "I'm certain Mick holds you no ill will."

"He loves you." She pierced Aslyn with sad, brown eyes. "I do not think we kept watch over you as closely as I thought we had."

"I was not as obedient a ward as I should have been."

She smiled knowingly. "Women never are when they're in love."

"I suppose not."

"Poor Kip. To discover he has a brother. And my poor Hedley. The guilt he has suffered all these years for taking the boy away. He did it for me. Perhaps if I had looked at the babe, held him, I might have discerned the truth." Once more, the window drew her attention. "But all I wanted was to forget."

He wasn't a bastard. He'd been born to be a duke. Not a street urchin, not a dustbin boy. Those thoughts kept running through his mind, as he stood in the library, Hedley's vow to see his birthright restored still echoing between the walls. He should have felt empowered. Instead, for some unfathomable reason, he felt less, unmoored, a ship lost at sea in the midst of a tempest. His entire life, every action he'd ever taken, had been fueled by the anger over the circumstances of his birth. The anger was still there, but now it was directed at Fate and its cruelty.

He imagined the duchess as a young woman, younger than Aslyn, as young as Fancy, being forced upon and the man who loved her striving to lessen her anguish. And all the while a child growing within her to serve as a reminder — at least in her mind — of the horror that had transpired.

Infanticide was not uncommon. Even legitimate children were often unwanted, snuffed out. Society was finally beginning to take notice. Parliament was enacting laws to protect infants and bastards. But thirty years ago, bastards died and no one wept.

He'd been spared because Ettie Trewlove had lost her own children to typhus and had thought it a punishment from God. He'd forgiven her for her past. How could he not forgive the duke and duchess?

The duke tossed back what remained of his scotch, cleared his throat, met and held Mick's gaze. "You are my legitimate heir, and now that we are aware of that truth, we must determine how best to proceed in order to make things right. I can compose a letter to be printed in the *Times,* speak with my peers —"

"And tell them what?"

"I shall declare you as my legitimate heir."

"How will you explain my sudden appearance, or more importantly my disappearance years ago? I assume you announced then that I'd not survived my birth."

"We never let it be known she was with child. Only Bella, I and a few trusted servants knew of the situation."

"So you must also explain a child no one knew was expected, and you can't do that without revealing the truth and the shame that goes along with it, for you and your wife. She was raped. It is not something about which people speak. And they certainly don't announce it in the *Times.* If you do so, it will merely make her and you relive what you have struggled for years to forget."

"Your rightful place —"

"Is exactly where I am. I didn't want you to acknowledge me because I wanted your titles, lands, or properties. I wanted you to recognize me and explain why you cast me aside. You have done that. To be honest, in similar circumstances, to protect the woman I loved, I might have done the same."

"And *there* stands the man with whom I fell in love."

Turning slowly, he faced the door where Aslyn waited. In her eyes he could see that there also stood the man who had broken her heart. If he could do it over again, he'd have stopped his quest the moment he met her. "Can you spare me a few minutes in the gardens?"

She looked to the duke, to Kipwick, back to him. "A few."

He followed her into the hallway, down a long corridor, through a door and into the dimming sunlight. Most of the day had passed, and yet it seemed like he'd been here years already. They stepped onto a path filled with an abundance of flowers. He wondered if he took the time to sniff each bloom if he would find a gardenia.

He didn't offer his arm; he doubted she

461

would take it. Like Hedley earlier, he hardly knew where to begin.

She wasn't only physically separated from him but mentally, as well. There was a wall between them that hadn't existed before, and he hadn't a clue how best to knock it down. Not reassuring for a man who had made a good deal of his fortune tearing down walls.

"She wants to see you," Aslyn said quietly.

She. The duchess. The woman whose body had nurtured him, brought him into the world. He shook his head. "I am but a reminder of a past best forgotten, unfortunate decisions made."

"She never forgot you. You were always there. For the duke, as well."

"Everything I always thought I knew about myself has been shattered. I spent years imagining what my mother might have been like. Not once did I imagine her a duchess. I concocted a slew of reasons for why I was delivered into Ettie Trewlove's arms. Not once did I ever consider what I learned today."

"Why would you? I grew up in their household, and the duchess never revealed by word or deed that she'd been violated. It is not something about which people speak. I knew only that she was wary of the world beyond Hedley Hall and overly protective where I was concerned. Now I know the reasons. Neither of us can alter the past, but we can ensure it doesn't influence the future."

"It always influences the future. I was intent on destroying them, Aslyn."

"And me."

Stepping in front of her, he stopped walking. "No, never you."

"Never?"

He squeezed his eyes shut. "Originally, yes." He opened his eyes, longed to cradle her face between his hands, draw her in and just hold her. "But then I came to know you, and you sent all my plans for you to hell. You don't realize how courageous you are, and that makes you braver still. You gave no thought at all to the dangers when you saved Will. You didn't hesitate to let Mary go. You're curious about the lives of those who live outside the aristocracy, yet you don't judge. At Cremorne, you accept that sometimes people are forced to do things Society frowns upon in order to survive. At my affair, you walked among bankers, bakers" — he lifted a corner of his mouth — "and candlestick makers, men with rough hands, and women with rough lives, and you never looked down on them. You never looked down on me. That first night, you spoke with Fancy as though you'd be equals in a ballroom."

She scoffed lightly. "You give me too much credit."

"I did not give you enough. You let me touch you when I believed myself marred with filth."

"And here you are. Now you could have a dukedom."

He hadn't been raised to oversee a dukedom, to sit in Parliament, to be addressed as "Your Grace." But he was intelligent enough to learn, to adjust, to adapt. He had no doubts there. But what place would his mum, his brothers, his sisters have in that world? He would make a place for them, see them accepted —

But how to explain them and his absence all these years? The secrets behind his existence were certain to come out, to create undeserved pain for all involved.

"We can't erase thirty years, pretend they didn't happen. I can't step into a role that another has been groomed to hold."

"It happens all the time. An heir dies, upending the life of the next in line."

"I don't need a dukedom. I think Kipwick does. Who is he without it? Who am I with it?" He lifted his shoulders, dropped them back down. "I am the same man either way. I didn't realize it until you. For so long, I believed if people knew I had blue blood coursing through my veins, I would be accepted by all. I wanted that acceptance, I craved it with as strong a ferocity as Kipwick craves his next win at the tables. It was an addiction, an obsession. Until I found something I wanted more — you."

Tears welled in her eyes. "You broke my heart. I trusted you with every aspect of me."

"I know, and I didn't deserve your trust, your affections. I came here today with the intention of winning you back." He shook his head. "Not in one go. I didn't expect you to forgive me from the start. I wouldn't ask you to. But I thought if I could convince you to give me a chance, to perhaps start anew, that I could convince you slowly, over time, that I was worthy of you. I was willing to take as long as it took."

She said nothing, merely studied him as though searching for the truth and fearing what it might be. He'd done that to her. The duchess had given her years of admonishments regarding the dangers in the world, but it had taken him to prove that trust couldn't be easily given. She was so beautiful standing there in the waning light

465

that it hurt. It hurt to know he'd brought her pain and sadness. It hurt that he had disappointed her. It hurt to know that he had to walk away.

"I know you love the duke and duchess dearly." He looked to the darkening sky. "Kipwick as well in some manner." He returned his gaze, his attention, his focus to her. "I came here today because I love you, Aslyn. But I understand now that in trying to win you over, I would be forcing you to choose me over them, and I cannot ask that of you."

Her delicate brow furrowed. "I don't understand."

"They are your family."

"They're yours, as well. You're their son. They see that, they understand it."

"But it's not enough. In some ways, it's crueler that I am. I am not a product of what happened to the duchess, but I am a reminder of it. Even if we tell no one the truth, how do we explain my presence? I resemble Hedley too much for there not to be speculation, for there not to be the whisper of scandal. Their happiness and well-being — as well as yours — is best served by my absence."

"So you come here today, make me start falling a little bit in love with you all over again, and leave, never to return?"

"I can't be in their lives. I can't be in yours. Don't marry Kipwick. You will find someone else more deserving, more deserving than either he or I. You are worth so much, and somewhere there is a man who will realize it."

He didn't give her time to reply, to comment, to convince him he was wrong. He simply started striding out of the gardens, knowing if he stayed a minute longer, he was going to take her into his arms and never let go.

CHAPTER 24

When a knock sounded in the dead of night, Ettie Trewlove knew what it meant: someone was leaving a babe at her door.

But a knock during the day was another matter entirely. It wasn't one of her children. They always barged in, making themselves at home, because this *was* their home, even if they no longer lived here.

So she was a bit curious regarding her caller. Still, when she opened the door, she was taken by surprise at the sight of the man standing there. He hadn't aged particularly well, but then guilt tended to eat at a person, and she liked to believe that everyone who left their troubles with her suffered a little bit for it when they walked away. "Your Grace."

"Did you know from the beginning who I was?" he asked.

"Not until I saw the crest on the blanket."

He nodded. "You did an excellent job raising my son."

She gave him a pointed look. "He weren't yours. He became mine the second you placed him in my arms."

"You're right. Still I appreciate the life you gave him."

"He ain't done too bad for himself."

He grinned, and in it she saw Mick's smile. "No, he hasn't."

"So why are you here?"

"I need your help again."

He returned to her the necklace, comb and parasol. In the package, he also included the cameo. It brought him a measure of comfort that she didn't return it, that perhaps she kept it as a reminder of him and along with it, a few fond memories.

For three days in a row he received an invitation to dinner. The first came from the duke himself, the second from his duchess, the third from Aslyn. He didn't bother to respond. His absence would tell the tale. He was firm in his resolve that no good would come from his presence in their lives.

Instead, he buried himself in his work, searching for parcels of land to be had on the cheap, meetings with investors, negotiating contracts, looking over applications from those who wanted to lease his buildings.

When he wasn't out and about, he was in his office, reading through paperwork that would drive his brothers mad, but he'd always enjoyed it: the precise words, the turning of a phrase that could alter a meaning. The smallest of details, ignored, could lead a man to ruin. Acknowledged could lead a man to fortune.

The knock on his door scattered his concentration. "What is it?"

Tittlefitz peered into the office. "Jones, from the front desk, sent word up that a duke and duchess have taken a room. A duke and duchess! He let out the grand suite to them. Can you imagine the clientele we'll see if word gets around the nobility that we're a right proper place to stay?"

The muscles of his stomach clenched. "Who are they?"

Tittlefitz seemed surprised by the question. "Well, he didn't say."

"Find out." Even though he was willing to wager his entire fortune that he already knew.

His secretary looked considerably paler, on the verge of being ill, when he reappeared. "Hedley. The gent who visited you several days ago with his son. Why would he be here?"

Because he wouldn't go to them. Why

470

would they not leave him in peace? Why did they not understand the havoc his presence would cause? "Who the devil knows? Just see to it that they don't disturb me here."

"Yes, sir."

They didn't disturb him, but sometimes when he glanced out one of his windows, he'd see the duke strolling along the street, observing the construction taking place. He'd stop and speak with some of the workers, delaying them from finishing their jobs. The third afternoon, at precisely four o'clock, Mick received a missive.

The duchess and I would welcome the pleasure of your company as we enjoy our tea in the hotel gardens.

— Aslyn

So she was here as well, was she? Damn her. As with all the invitations to dinner, he ignored it. As well as the one that arrived the following afternoon. The one after that however —

Your mother, the duchess and I would welcome the pleasure of your company as we enjoy our tea in the hotel gardens.

— Aslyn

He came out from behind his desk so fast

471

he very nearly wrenched his back. He dashed out of his office.

"Is something amiss, sir?" Tittlefitz asked.

But Mick didn't stop. He carried on through, down the stairs, his heart pounding. He hit the lobby. Ignoring the few patrons standing about, he raced to the back doors that led into the gardens.

Several small white-cloth-covered round tables were set up, but only one was occupied. He slowed his step but lengthened his stride. The duchess was the first to smile at him.

"I'm so glad you could join us. Your mother was telling us about a fledgling bird you tried to save when you were a lad. The tragic outcome. I'm sorry it didn't go better."

"I remember your tears," his mum said.

"I didn't cry." She was wearing a plain navy blue dress, a recent purchase. No frays, no faded spots. Her hat hosted an assortment of colorful flowers, but then she'd always sought out colors in the drabness that was her life. He shifted his attention to Aslyn, as beautiful as ever, in pink. Her lips twisted into the familiar uneven smile that did not make her look at all innocent in this, and he wondered what part she might have played. A large part no doubt. She was

472

probably responsible for locating and getting word to his mum. Or maybe the duke had remembered where he'd delivered him that long ago night. Damnation, he should have made his mum move into better lodgings.

"I'm given to understand you prefer whiskey to tea," the duchess said, and only then did he notice the etched glass holding two fingers of amber liquid set in front of the empty chair that rested between his mum and Aslyn. Taking that seat would leave him facing the duchess.

"Do sit down, Mick," his mum said, her tone one of reprimand that he knew from experience would be quickly followed by a smack if he didn't obey.

"I see nothing to be gained by this." He gave his mum a hard stare. "You don't know what you risk." If they were to report her as being a baby farmer, the repercussions could see her imprisoned.

"They mean me no harm." She reached out for him. "It's like Pandora's box. You can't shove back inside everything that flew out. Besides, I rather like your mother."

"You're my mother."

"How fortunate you are to have two when there are some who have none."

He took her hand, squeezed it. He would

protect her unto death. Releasing his hold, he dragged out the chair and dropped into it. He glared at Aslyn. "What is the game being played here?"

"No game. The duchess was merely curious about your upbringing, your life."

"It was nothing at all like Kipwick's," he said tersely. "You don't want to know about it."

"It was hard and filthy — at least on the streets. I suspect your home was clean. It's obvious Mrs. Trewlove loves you dearly. I can't claim to hold that deep affection for you. I did not cradle you to my breast. I did not sing you lullabies. I wept when you were born, but the tears had nothing at all to do with joy."

"You don't have to tell me this."

"You have no idea what it cost me to come here. I shook the entire way. Do you know that except for when we travel to and from the ducal estate, I never venture far from Mayfair? I almost never leave Hedley Hall, to be honest. I have spent most of my life fearing my own shadow. But wanting to see what you have accomplished forced me out of my little hidey-hole."

He hardly knew what to say. He knew what Aslyn had told him about the duchess, but he assumed it was her frailty that kept her indoors.

"I am not your mother. I know this, but I look around and I see what you have built, what you are building, and I am impressed. I can take no credit for it. I did not influence you. But now that I know the truth of you, how can I not want to know everything?"

Her eyes delved into his, and he was very much aware of his mum holding her breath. She was the one who had raised him, who demonstrated kindness even though he didn't always embrace the lessons — especially where those of his past were concerned. And then there was Aslyn. For her, he wanted to be better than he was. He took a good healthy swallow of the whiskey.

"I have three brothers and two sisters."

"Four brothers," the duchess said.

He flashed a grin. "I doubt Kipwick is keen on acknowledging me as such."

"He's adjusting," Aslyn said.

He turned his attention to her. "Is he?"

"It's been a shock to him obviously, to all of us. I think he's struggling as much as you are with figuring out his place in the world now."

"I'm not struggling."

"You're denying the truth of your birth."

"No. I accept it, but it does not alter my

475

present or my future." He looked at the duchess. "I can't be part of your life without causing speculation, gossip and quite possibly scandal."

"I have a very simple solution for how you can be in their lives without anyone ever being the wiser," Aslyn said quietly.

He gave her a mocking smile. "Have you?"

"Yes. When you first arrived at Hedley Hall, you told the duchess you were the man who would wed me if I would have you. Well —" She gave him an impish grin. "I will have you."

Staring at her, he was vaguely aware of the duchess and his mum quietly leaving the table, like two old friends who communicated without words. He should have finished off his whiskey. Perhaps her words wouldn't have come as quite a shock to him then.

"Aslyn —"

"You're not going to cause an upheaval in their world by allowing them to declare you as their son. And I love you for it."

"Aslyn —"

"You're not turning your back on your adoptive family, and I love you for it."

"Aslyn —"

"You dashed out here to protect your

mum . . . and I think a good deal of your decisions are because of her, because you don't want her to feel as though you don't appreciate all she did for you. You are correct. There is no easy way to bring you back into their lives as their son, to resurrect you without weaving some tale that would be believable without causing harm. But to deny them the opportunity to get to know you — there's a certain sadness in that. You'll have children, their grandchildren. Would you deny the duke and duchess getting to know them? Would you deny your children time with their true grandparents? If you marry me, no one will find it odd that you and your family are embraced by my guardians, by the couple who have raised me since I was seven. It's the perfect solution."

"Marriage to me will not make you a duchess."

Her brow furrowed. "Do you think I care so much for a title?"

He shook his head. "No. I know you don't care at all. But I can't help but believe this will cause hardship for them, for you."

"It will be harder if you are not in our lives. I love you, Mick. You told me to find a man deserving of me, and I have. If you've changed your mind and don't want to marry me, at least spend time with them. Let them know the remarkable man they brought into the world."

He hardly felt remarkable, but he'd missed her, and he knew that with her by his side, he could be better than he was. Shoving back his chair, he stood, then dropped to one knee and took her hand. "I want a life with you, Aslyn. A dozen children and slipping off to the park for a bit of peace."

She smiled sweetly, crookedly. "A happily-ever-after."

"A happily-ever-after," he promised her before cradling her face and kissing her.

Chapter 25

Mick found the duke strolling the street, stopping occasionally to study a building. He seemed to be in no hurry, simply taking a leisurely meandering. He wondered if the man had known about the tea party in the gardens, had his answer when he came to a stop beside the duke.

"Did you enjoy your tea?" the older man asked.

"Fortunately whiskey was on hand. Didn't they invite you?"

Staring at the building that was nearly completed and would be a bakery, he shook his head. "Ladies will talk about things among themselves that they are reluctant to voice with a man about. My presence adds to Bella's guilt. She feels she denied me a son."

"Knowing what transpired, I don't hold the decision to be rid of me against her — or you."

"There should have been a better way."

"Aslyn mentioned that she might like to open a home that would welcome illegitimate children."

The duke glanced over, a corner of his mouth shifting up. "I am not surprised. We were too protective of her, I think. You will give her more freedom."

Mick's chest tightened. There was a part of him that wanted to lock her in a room and ensure no harm ever came to her, that wanted to guard her from all the ugliness in life. "Will you give us your blessing to marry, then?"

"Unequivocally. Although I would ask that you not keep her from us. She is like a daughter."

"She has already insisted I not. That we visit often. I am concerned that when people see you and I together, they may wonder —"

"If you are my by-blow?"

Mick nodded.

"I'm certain there will be some speculation. We can weather it. Some might think you're a distant relation. I would rather acknowledge you."

"There is no way to do that without causing pain — for you, the duchess, Kipwick. He has grown up expecting to inherit. It

480

will be hard enough that I am taking from him the woman he wished to marry. I will not take his titles, as well."

"He needs to change his ways."

"I can help him with that."

The duke nodded. "When I first saw you, when I realized who you were, I was torn between relief and despair. What I'd done all those years ago never stopped eating at me. I've tried to make amends with good works. But they hardly signify."

"There needs to be laws to protect infants. The practice of farming out babies cannot continue unchecked, and men cannot continue to be relieved of the burden of caring for the children they spawn."

"I shall work on that in Parliament. You could advise me, ensure reform does all it should."

"I shall make time in my schedule."

The duke glanced around. "Thirty years ago, this was the outskirts of London. It fell into disrepair, and you are reshaping it with your magnificent buildings. You are a man any father would be proud to call son."

Curled in a chair by the window in her room in the Trewlove Hotel, the low flame in the lamp barely illuminating the room, Aslyn heard the click of a key going into the lock, the snick of the latch, no opening of the door as the staff kept the hinges well oiled.

However, she saw it opening, the dim light from the hallway outlining the silhouette of a tall man with broad shoulders. He stood there unmoving, as though testing the waters, as though wondering if she would turn him away, wouldn't welcome this inappropriate clandestine meeting. But then when it came to Mick Trewlove, there was very little between them that was appropriate. Although that would soon be changing when he took her to wife.

He stepped into the room, closed the door behind him, and his soft footfalls barely echoed as he came nearer, stopping when he reached the bed, leaning against the poster, crossing his arms over that magnificent chest. "I see you're wearing the cameo."

On a ribbon about her neck. It was the only thing she was wearing. "I rather like knowing you were thinking of me when you purchased it."

"I'm always thinking of you."

"I was hoping you would come."

"Mum is staying in my suites tonight, and as I have only the one bedchamber furnished with a bed" — he lifted a shoulder — "I decided to go in search of another."

They'd had dinner earlier with the duke, the duchess and his mother. It hadn't been awkward, but neither had everyone been completely at ease. She had no doubt that would change over time. "How fortunate I am then that you happened upon this chamber."

"Is the bed available?"

She spread her mouth into what she hoped was a saucy smile. "I'll always make room for you."

"Ah, Christ." Stepping forward, he reached out and drew her into his arms, blanketing her mouth with his, the kiss deep, full of hunger and need. She scraped her fingers along his face up into his hair, holding him firm and near as he plundered and his broad hands stroked and caressed her bare back and buttocks. Up and down, over and around. Sensations building, heat consuming.

She'd missed this, yearned for it, longed for it. The way his passion engulfed her, swept her up into a rising tide of titillation.

"I thought I would go mad with the wanting of you," he said, dragging his sultry mouth along her throat.

"I miss the beard."

"I'll grow it back."

"Because I desire it?"

"Yes. I'll give you anything — everything — you desire."

"I desire you take off your clothes."

He broke away from her. She would have helped him, but he was too quick, a frenzy of action that found his clothes in a heap on the floor in no time and her back in his arms. She wondered if it would always be like this, the wanting, the desire, the passion. She rather suspected it would be for her, and when his head came up after he licked across her collarbone, and she gazed into his smoldering blue eyes, she suspected it would be for him, as well.

He lifted her up and tossed her onto the bed, capturing her screech with his mouth as he followed her down. "We're going to do this in every room in the damned hotel," he growled.

"How many rooms are there?"

"Not nearly enough."

She laughed, then went abruptly silent as he closed his lips around her nipple, suckled gently, then hard. She cried out, not with pain but with pleasure, wrapping her legs around his hips, holding him close, desperate for him to be even nearer, to be one with her, for them to be one.

"Now." The word was a breathy sigh. "Take me now."

"Not yet. I'm not done worshipping you." He slid down. His tongue circled her navel, leaving dew in its wake, creating dew farther down between her thighs.

Then his mouth was on that honeyed spot, feasting as though it was the most exquisite buffet he'd ever been served and he'd never have enough of it, would never have his fill. And she knew then that it would always be like this between them. The hunger would never be sated, not completely. It would always rise up and demand their attention, insist that they at least strive to tame it, but it would remain wild and feral, frightening in its intensity, satisfying in its power.

It was powerful as it rocked her to her core, had her screaming out his name until her lungs were empty of breath. His deep, smug chuckle echoed around them, and it pleased her that he took such pride in wringing pleasure from her, that her joy in the act was as important to him as his own.

Moving up, he slid into her in one long, smooth stroke. "So hot, so wet, so tight."

"So hard, so thick, so filling."

Resting on his elbows, he grinned down on her. "What a wanton I am going to have for a wife."

"Would you want any other kind?"

"I want you to be no different than you are. I love you, Aslyn. Every inch, inside and out." He began rocking his hips, slowly, provocatively, his eyes never leaving hers, his gaze challenging her to reach again for the fulfillment he was determined to deliver once more.

And she did reach, meeting his thrusts, skimming her hands over his back and shoulders, squeezing his backside, digging her fingers into undulating muscles. Their movements quickened, their breaths following suit. Faster, harder, until they were both crying out, until locked in a tight embrace, they found their way back to each other.

CHAPTER 26

"You're a bloody duke?" Aiden asked.

His family, along with Aslyn, were gathered in what served as his mum's parlor. His mum had insisted he tell his siblings the truth of his parentage. His secret would be safe with them, and she felt it important that they know.

"No. My father is a duke, which you knew. Legally I'm his heir, but as I explained, it's too complicated to see the matter righted."

"Do we have to bow to you, then?" Finn asked.

"Don't be daft."

"So you'll be marrying Lady Aslyn," Aiden said.

"You may just call me Aslyn," she said.

"But even if you marry him, you'll still be a lady, right?"

She nodded. "Yes, but not among family."

"The duke can't be too happy about gaining a family of bastards," Beast said. "There

487

will be scandal galore among the toffs."

"Could be fun," Finn said.

"You'll all behave," Mick admonished. "They'll be welcoming you into their home."

"How did Lord Kipwick take all this?" Fancy asked.

"As uneasily as the rest of us, but he's still the heir apparent."

"He hasn't been to my club," Aiden said. "Nor have I heard rumors of him getting into trouble elsewhere."

"He's promised not to do any wagering," Aslyn said. "He knows he's very lucky not to have lost everything."

"Promises can be broken," Aiden said, rubbing his thumb over his fingers. "When Lady Luck starts whispering in your ear . . ."

"How fortunate he will be, then, to have a brother-by-marriage with the experience to know when he's letting things get out of hand," Aslyn said sweetly.

"I'm not his keeper."

"But still you'll keep watch," Mick said pointedly.

Aiden shrugged, studied his nails. "I suppose no harm in doing so."

"It's going to be the grandest wedding," Fancy said. "I can't believe that during the wedding breakfast we're going to be in a grand salon overflowing with aristocrats."

"Not me," Gillie said. "Love you, Mick, and I like you well enough, Aslyn, but posh places aren't for me."

"Gillie!" Fancy lamented. "We'll get you a lovely gown and put flowers in your hair."

"Flowers in my hair? No, thank you! I'm not a bloody garden."

"Your language," his mum chided.

"Mum, I'm a tavern keeper. I've heard worse and I say worse when it's needed."

Ettie Trewlove released a long-suffering sigh. "Do you see what you're getting, Aslyn, when you marry into this family?"

His future wife smiled. "I could not be happier."

"I'm not truly the heir," Kip said quietly as he and Aslyn strolled through the gardens near twilight. "I feel like a bloody impostor."

"You have been the heir since the moment you were born. You have been raised to become a duke."

"As though that takes a great deal of learning. Trewlove could pick it up in a night." He sighed. "Father is transferring all the nonentailed properties over to him."

"And you'll have the entailed properties."

"At least I can't gamble them away."

"You probably shouldn't gamble at all."

He nodded, slowly, thoughtfully. "I lost my way there for a while, Aslyn, and in so doing I lost you."

With her arm wrapped around his, she pressed up against his side. "Before that, I'd begun to doubt we were well suited to each other."

His brow furrowing, he looked down on her. "Why?"

"It's difficult to explain. My doubts began when you kissed me."

"You didn't like it?"

"It was without passion."

"It was a gentleman's kiss."

"But it shouldn't have been." Stopping, she faced him. The blossoms were closing up for the night, but their fragrance still hung heavy on the air. "I love you, Kip, but I'm not in love with you."

"There's a difference?"

She smiled softly. "Yes, and one day I hope you will meet someone who will intrigue you in such a way that you'll fully comprehend the difference."

"So, you're in love with Trewlove." He said it matter-of-factly.

"Desperately."

"If you'd not discovered he was legitimate —"

"The circumstances of his birth matter not one whit to me. I'd already decided that I would have him."

"As a future duke, I do not have the liberty of following my heart wherever it might lead."

"If you truly love her, and are in love with her, you won't care, and there will be nothing strong enough to keep you from her."

By the time the wedding took place in August, Mick's beard was back, dark and full, evenly trimmed. While Aslyn missed seeing the little dent in his chin, she knew where to find it. Besides, it was his soulful eyes that had drawn her in from the beginning. The blue that called to her.

The blue that looked down on her now as they snuggled in their marriage bed.

"I can't believe you're mine," he said, skimming his fingers over her hair down to the ends that curled around her breast. "My wife."

"Not too many eyebrows were raised."

He grinned. "Oh, plenty were raised."

The church had been packed. They couldn't prevent people from entering the church, but the wedding breakfast at Hedley Hall had been a more intimate affair. Her heart had squeezed painfully and expanded at the same time when Mick had danced with his mum and then the duchess.

"I don't care what people think. You'll win them over. Most of the men already admire you, and the ladies are quite jealous that you settled on me."

"I didn't settle. If either of us settled, it was you."

"Well, I certainly didn't settle, so there."

Leaning down, he kissed the tip of her nose. "I love you, Aslyn. I want you to be happy."

"Then show me some fireworks, husband."

They were the brightest, most colorful, most glorious ones she'd ever experienced.

EPILOGUE

Two Years Later

Mick didn't know if he'd ever get used to the sight of his mum taking tea with the duchess in the hotel gardens. It had become a weekly ritual for them, and he often found an excuse to be in the gardens when they were about just so he could listen to their laughter. Today he was pushing a pram holding his infant daughter along the path while his wife strolled beside him, her hand tucked within the crook of his elbow.

"They're good for each other," she said. "The duchess is getting out so much more, and they are both so involved in the running of Safe Harbour that I'm hardly needed."

She'd opened a home for unwed mothers and their children to live without shame. Staff watched the youngsters while their mums worked, many of them in the shops Mick leased.

"I need you."

She smiled up at him. "I suppose I can be content with that."

"Mum is finally ready to live elsewhere. I think it's time we moved, as well." He glanced down at his wife's slightly rounding stomach.

"What did you have in mind?"

"I found some pretty land just outside London. I thought to build us a large manor on it, and then a small cottage for Mum so she isn't too far away."

"I like that idea."

"I'll purchase us a nice residence here in town as well, so it's convenient to visit the duke and duchess when they're in the city for the Season."

"A fine notion, because one of these days your daughter is going to need a Season."

"Not for a while yet."

"Probably sooner than you'll be ready for."

"You do know she's not getting married. There isn't a gent in all of England who will be good enough for her, to whom I'll give my blessing."

Some years later, he did give his blessing — to a duke. He gave his blessing to each of his daughters and to the gentlemen who loved them. Titled or not, legitimate or not. Mick cared naught about pedigree. He judged their suitability on how well they loved his daughters. As for the women who married his sons — his boys took after him and showed good judgment when falling in love.

With a dozen children, half of them adopted, he was kept quite busy giving his blessing to marriages, but still found time on sunny afternoons to slip away to the park with his wife for a bit of peace.

AUTHOR'S NOTE

I took a bit of literary license with this story. It's doubtful any babes would have been delivered to Ettie Trewlove's door. Baby farmers generally met their "clients" in alleyways, never advertised their names and seldom provided their addresses. Although the practice of baby farming was widely known and used, there was a clandestine aspect to it that allowed it to flourish in horrific ways.

Sometimes when an author is researching one thing, she discovers something else by happenstance that plants a seed and captures her imagination. Baby farming was a plot point in *The Viscount and the Vixen,* but still I couldn't let it go. Hence, Ettie Trewlove's bastards were born and survived.

As for the duchess mistaking whose baby she carried and the circumstances that led to her confusion — that, too, is based on a true account, although it occurred nearly a century later. DNA testing wasn't available when the child was born and placed for adoption, but many years later when it was, resulting tests indicated a DNA match for the birth mother's husband. This story too has haunted me.

Ettie Trewlove's bastards have more tales to tell, more sins to reveal. I hope you'll continue on the journey with them.

Warmly,
Lorraine

ABOUT THE AUTHOR

Lorraine Heath always dreamed of being a writer. After graduating from the University of Texas, she wrote training manuals, press releases, articles, and computer code, but something was always missing. When she read a romance novel, she not only became hooked on the genre, but quickly realized what her writing lacked: rebels, scoundrels, and rouges. She's been writing about them ever since. Her work has been recognized with numerous industry awards, including RWA's prestigious RITA®. Her novels have appeared on the *USA Today* and *New York Times* bestseller lists.